THE ROAR

EMMA CLAYTON

KU-477-588

Text © Emma Clayton 2008

First published in Great Britain in 2008
This edition published in 2014
The Chicken House
2 Palmer Street
Frome, Somerset, BA11 1DS
United Kingdom
www.doublecluck.com

Emma Clayton has asserted her right under the Copyright, Designs and Patents Act 1988
to be identified as the author of this work.

Cover and interior design by Steve Wells
Typeset by Dorchester Typesetting Group Ltd
Printed and bound in Great Britain by CPI Group (UK) Ltd, Croydon, CR0 4YY

The paper used in this Chicken House book is made from wood grown in sustainable forests.

1 3 5 7 9 10 8 6 4 2

British Library Cataloguing in Publication data available.

PB ISBN 978-1-910002-03-2
eISBN 978-1-910002-04-9

'All that glisters is not gold;
Often have you heard that told.
Many a man his life hath sold
But my outside to behold.
Gilded tombs do worms enfold.'

The Merchant of Venice – William Shakespeare

1

THE GULF OF SPACE

The sun was setting over the Atlantic and as it ran like molten gold into the waves, a girl in a Pod Fighter ripped through the scene, like graffiti sprayed across a landscape painting, and for a few startled moments, the sun and the sea trembled.

Ellie flew fast and low with her eyes fixed on the northern horizon. In the gunner's seat behind her was a capuchin monkey called Puck, whose brows fidgeted while he ate popcorn and admired the gun controls. Puck was glad to be out of his room with new things to look at. He didn't know they were running away or how much danger they were in. But there was no doubt in Ellie's mind; when Mal Gorman found out they were gone, he would want to slice them like Parma ham, then mince them to space dust.

'But I won't let him,' Ellie whispered. 'And anyhow, he's got to catch us first.'

As they flew north into darkness, leaving the warmth of the sun behind them, Ellie wondered whether her parents had kept her clothes. It was over a year since Mal Gorman had kidnapped her and she knew he'd told them she was dead.

No, she thought sadly, they've probably thrown them away.

For a moment she wondered whether they'd recognize her. Perhaps they'd be frightened to see her. Maybe she'd knock on the door and they'd look at her as if she was a stranger and tell her to go away. As Ellie considered this end to her journey, she felt panic rise like vomit in her throat and she accelerated until she was flying so fast she saw nothing but ribbons of half-light reflected on the water. The Pod Fighter ripped through the air, leaving sonic scars in its wake, and as she blinked away a tear, it dipped slightly to the left and a wing tip clipped the crest of a wave and reacted as if it had hit a rock – boom! For a split second, she thought she had lost it as the Pod Fighter threatened to spin off in horizontal cartwheels into a megaton wall of water.

'Frag!' she cursed, hot in the face as she struggled to correct her mistake. Another lapse of concentration like that one and she really was dead. She should know by now that crying didn't help; she'd cried a lake of tears since Mal Gorman kidnapped her that hadn't spirited her home, only cool logic and determination would do that.

She slowed down, exhaling her panic, and checked the co-ordinates in her visor. Then, with a roar that sliced chunks out of the waves, the Pod Fighter shot across the equator and into the turbulent sky of the northern hemisphere.

'We're going home,' said Ellie. 'And not even Mal Gorman can stop us.'

* * *

It was three o'clock in the morning in London when Mal Gorman was awoken by the news that Ellie had escaped. He was supposed to be on holiday; the first holiday he'd taken for over a year, but instead of having a relaxing time in his expensive hotel, he was pacing up and down with his slippers on the wrong feet and his temples throbbing. He felt too old to be chasing a twelve-year-old girl across the planet in a stolen Pod Fighter. The circular com over his right ear glowed while he talked to one of his men.

'What time did she go?'

'We don't know, sir,' the man replied sheepishly. 'Nobody seems to know *exactly* when she left.'

'Why not?' Mal Gorman bellowed, his pale grey eyes threatening to pop out of their bony sockets. 'What was going on up there? Were you all doing the can-can in the Officers' Mess? Having a slumber party?'

'No, sir,' the man replied. 'She just . . . slipped out without anyone noticing.'

'Slipped out of a locked room on a spaceship?'

'Yes, sir,' the man replied. 'We've been trying to figure out how she did it, but we don't even have any security footage because she destroyed it before she left. Somehow she managed to break into every Pod Fighter on the strip and plant a virus in their flight systems so we couldn't follow her.'

'Unbelievable,' Gorman snarled. 'You bunch of bumbling cretins! How could a twelve-year-old child escape from several hundred soldiers on a space station in orbit around Earth?'

'I don't know, sir,' mumbled the man. 'But we've got the programmers in the Pod Fighters and half are working again. We're ready if you need us. We can be there in ten minutes.' The man hesitated, then asked, 'Does she know The Secret?'

'Yes,' Gorman replied, heavily. 'But I don't think that's the reason she's run away. I told her recently her parents believe she's dead. I think that might have upset her. Did she take the monkey?'

'Yes, sir.'

'Oh no.' Gorman felt a pain in his chest as he considered the consequences of Ellie reaching home with a live black tufted capuchin monkey. He sat down heavily on the bed and fumbled around under the lamp for his Everlife pills. He was a hundred and eight years old; he needed them.

'What do you want us to do, sir?'

Mal Gorman thought for a moment, running his papery hand over the last strands of his brittle grey hair. He didn't want to kill Ellie; after all, he'd spent a year training her, and the other two children he'd kidnapped had died. And he liked her; she was sulky and difficult, but so bright, what a waste it would be to kill her now. But if they couldn't control her on an orbiting space station like the Queen of the North, they couldn't control her anywhere. Ellie knew The Secret and she was going home with a live animal. She was as dangerous as a nuclear bomb.

Gorman leaned over and pressed an icon over the hotel room bed so the curtains swung back to reveal a wall of glass and a five-star view over London. The new Golden Turrets, plucked from the pages of *The Arabian Nights*, glowed seductively around him, reminding him of all the sightseeing he'd planned for the following day. He huffed irritably and turned his back on the view.

'At least we know where she's going,' he said. 'She'll be heading for that hole of a town she comes from, Barford North, to see her family. Organize patrols across the south coast of England and get the police involved. Tell them she's got an animal with her. They'll be so scared of catching the Animal Plague they'll be fighting each other for the biggest guns. You must kill them *both* before they reach home and she talks to anyone.'

'Yes, sir.'

'I mean destroy them,' Gorman said. 'I want them pulped, puréed, minced, diced and buried somewhere under a ton of concrete. Do you understand?'

'Yes, sir.'

'And do it quickly. I'm supposed to be on holiday. Call me back when you've got a sighting of her.'

Gorman pulled the com from his ear and threw it on the bed. Then he shouted for his butler, Ralph, and ordered him to make tea. He had a feeling he was not going to be sleeping again that night, or spending the next day sightseeing.

'You silly girl, Ellie,' he said. 'You'll never make it.'

* * *

Ellie remembered every detail of the night Mal Gorman kidnapped her, and as she flew towards home the memories ran like poison through her blood. She remembered what they'd eaten for dinner and that her mother was wearing blue, that she'd yelled at her brother, Mika, because he messed up her hair, and that she didn't even say goodbye when she walked out of their fold-down apartment. She ran down the stairs because the lift was broken and never saw her family again.

It was the perfect night to kidnap a girl. The clouds rolled low over Barford North, smothering the light of the moon, and there was a ground-hugging Thames Valley mist, which made the hundreds of refugee towers look as if they were hovering off the ground like tombstones in a spooky, giant graveyard. There weren't many people out on the walkways that twisted around the towers like a tangle of concrete snakes, and eager to be with her friends, Ellie ran as fast as she could, half aware that something wasn't right, that there was something hiding in the shadows. But when Gorman's men melted out of them, dressed black as ninjas with slits for eyes, she had no time to realize what was happening. Of their hands upon her, the bright sting of a needle in her neck, she remembered nothing – one moment she was wondering if she had enough money for a strawberry Fabshake, the next her mind was sinking into a place like death.

When she awoke, her head was aching and she felt sick, but she didn't understand what had happened to her for several minutes. Everything around her was white and hard and smelled of toilet cleaner. It was like waking up in a horrible heaven when you can't remember dying. But it wasn't until she put her hand to her head and realized her hair had been cut that she began to feel fear. Her beautiful long, dark hair was gone. Shocked out of her stupor Ellie sat up with a jolt, her black eyes burning. She looked down at her body and saw that her clothes were different too; her new sneakers and jeans had been taken away and she was dressed in a white suit with these horrible shoes that looked like socks with rubbery pads on the bottom. She yanked them off and threw them at the wall, then stood up and staggered to the window and the shock of what she saw felt like boiling water on her skin. She could see Earth glowing in the distance and it looked no bigger than a tennis ball. She blinked and it was still there, small and insignificant. She rubbed her hands over her butchered hair. She turned round a couple of times wondering what to do. Then she exploded; wept and yelled and banged on the door, demanding that they let her out and give her back her clothes and let her go home. But nobody came. She banged until her hands were swollen and purple with bruising, then she curled up on the hard bed, stricken by horror and confusion.

Several hours later, an old man in a suit came in and sat on the end of the bed. He was so thin, Ellie could see his skull through the papery skin on his face and every brittle bone in his hands. His eyes were calm and grey and smiling a little as he told Ellie how special she was and that he'd chosen her from thousands, as if she was supposed to be pleased that he'd kidnapped her and cut off her hair. And when he realized she wasn't, because she threw a plate of food at his head, a darkness emanated from his eyes more hostile than the gulf of space separating her from her family, and when he told her that if she didn't behave herself, she would never see them again, she trembled with fear.

For a year she worked hard and tried to behave, motivated by the painful longing she felt to be with her family again, to be kissed by her mother, to feel her father's arms around her and to sleep in the tiny bedroom she shared with her twin brother, Mika. But the day Mal Gorman told her The Secret, Ellie knew he'd never intended to let her go home; she could never go home with a secret like that.

'I hate you, Mal Gorman,' she said, 'and I wish you'd kept your bony mouth shut.'

But some things he'd taught her were useful. At the very least he'd given her all the skills she needed to escape him and it had been much easier than she'd thought it would be. The Pod Fighter she flew was a sliver of curved black metal and glass, with hundreds of brightly lit icons covering every surface of the cockpit. She couldn't have flown that a year ago. A year ago she had problems finding her hairbrush.

At last, a thread of light appeared on the northern horizon, which quickly morphed into the salt-licked concrete of The Wall. For a moment her spirits soared. Behind The Wall was her family. Behind The Wall was the south coast of England and home. She was nearly home. But her happiness was quickly smothered by fear. Being so close to the people she loved made her long for them even more.

Shielded by darkness she hovered over the sea, which heaved beneath her like a black beast pitted by rain. Looking at the towering mass of concrete made her stomach tighten. The Wall had been built during the Animal Plague, long before Ellie was born, but she had grown up hearing its story until it was as familiar to her as the ones her mother read at bedtime. But this story wasn't half so much fun as *The Wind in the Willows* or *Winnie-the-Pooh*, because instead of friendly animals having happy adventures, it involved insane animals on a murderous rampage; animals that ripped the doors off cars to kill the people inside.

When Ellie was small, every time The Wall was mentioned, she burst into tears, not because she was frightened of animals but because she felt sorry for them.

'You're not supposed to feel sorry for the *animals*,' her mother corrected her. 'You're supposed to feel sorry for the *humans*.'

'Poor bears and tigers and birds and moles!' Ellie sobbed. 'They're all dead! We killed them all!'

'Of course we did,' her mother replied, exasperated. 'We had to kill them before they killed us. But now we live behind The Wall so we don't have to worry about those nasty animals any more. Now lie down and go to sleep.'

Ellie was good and lay down and went to sleep, but she never stopped feeling sorry for the animals.

The Wall was the largest man-made structure on the planet. It towered fifty metres above sea level and looped all around the top of the world, enclosing northern Europe, northern Russia and Canada. Where the sea licked it, the concrete was rippled like ice cream by salt, and above this it was streaked by rain. Where it protected the people on land, The Wall's foundations met bedrock so no burrowing animals could get under it. And on the top were three rows of electrified razor wire that would cut a rhino to ribbons. Every seventy-five metres were guard towers manned by Ghengis Borgs: three-metre battle borgs with the temperaments of wasps and laser guns powerful enough to blow a herd of elephants to biltong.

Through the windscreen, Ellie watched the closest Ghengis Borg swing its massive gun. In the darkness its eyes of red light looked like those of a demon. But Ellie wasn't scared of Ghengis Borgs; they would never consider the possibility that she had an animal in her Pod Fighter and that she was willing to take it over The Wall. What scared Ellie lay beyond The Wall. Gorman's men would be waiting for her on the other side, hovering over the hotels on the Brighton seafront, and they would have gunners in their Pod Fighters, not a monkey with a bag of popcorn. She breathed deeply.

You can do it. You know you can.

She had a pretty good chance, she thought, if she flew via London, because she'd be able to travel through the darkness of the first level, The Shadows. Then she'd follow the Thames Valley flood plain to her home town, Barford North, just south of Oxford. The new refugee towns were built on stilts to keep them above the floodwater, so she'd be able to fly under them and use them for cover. It would be very dangerous but not many of Gorman's men would dare to follow her.

She took off her headset and had a drink of water. Then, with difficulty, she undid her harness and twisted round to make sure Puck's harness was tight enough. Puck had been a birthday present from Mal Gorman.

Or a bribe, more like, she thought, to make me work harder. I bet he's regretting giving me an animal now.

'Everyone's going to be surprised to see *you*,' she whispered. 'And absolutely terrified.'

She bit her lip, imagining her mother's scream when she arrived home with a live capuchin monkey, and made a mental note to get in the apartment and close the door before she revealed him. Asha was even afraid of pictures of animals. Even forty-three years after The Wall was built, there was still a huge yellow plague siren on the tallest building in every town, just in case an animal got over. Puck was their worst nightmare, but Ellie couldn't have left him behind on the spaceship alone, no way. None of this was his fault.

She was relieved to see the monkey was sleeping. She smiled. He didn't look very dangerous. His bag of popcorn had spilled in his lap and his face was peaceful as if he too was dreaming of home. She took the bag, folded over the top and tucked it down the side of his seat.

'Sweet dreams,' she whispered, glad he didn't know what was happening. His fingers twitched and she touched them gently.

What a miracle he was. So beautiful. Every time she looked at him she felt her heart swell with wonder. His brown face was framed by a mist of golden fur. His arms and legs were black to the elbow as if he'd dipped them in a bucket of ink. Over his body his fur was longer and a darker shade of gold and he had a black Mohican – a strip of tufty black fur over the top of his head – that suited him perfectly. He was Puck by name and puckish by nature, the most dreadful pet imaginable. But Ellie didn't blame him. She knew Puck missed his family just as much as she did and the only way he could communicate his sadness was by being vicious and destructive. Poor Puck hadn't been allowed out of his tiny room for six months. She tightened his harness.

'They just didn't understand you,' she whispered. 'But I do.'

She prepared to fly again. Her body felt weak just from the

exertion of turning round in her seat and she realized how exhausted she was. She hadn't been able to eat or sleep during the days leading up to her escape.

I need to be careful not to lose concentration, she thought, but not long now, half an hour, maybe less, and I'll be home with my family.

She put her headset on and wriggled back in her seat so she was comfortable. She locked her harness, checked over the control panel and then fired up the engine, feeling waves of nervous energy ripple through her as it roared. The Pod Fighter rose vertically, and its power vibrated through her hands. The nearest Ghengis Borg turned and its red eyes watched as she flew over The Wall and crossed the strip of sea towards land. She reached Brighton in less than a minute, and like a swarm of black flies, Gorman's men fell out of the clouds.

'My welcome party,' she whispered sarcastically. 'How nice of you to meet me.'

She felt her stomach flip with fear, but she flew towards them with gritted teeth, and with a lightning quick twist and turn, shot sideways through a gap between two hotels with centimetres to spare.

'Beat that!' she yelled, as she came out the other side and banked quickly to avoid hitting a block of apartments.

She found herself in a narrow walkway behind the hotels on the seafront. It was lined with refuse containers and parked hover cars. There were two fighters waiting for her at the end, and above she could hear the rumble of a police freighter. She couldn't go up and she couldn't go forward, so she veered sharply to the left, narrowly missing the corner of a balcony as she shot into the lightless crack between another two buildings.

This is the only way, she thought, emerging in a shopping mall and immediately cutting between two stores to avoid the swarm of police pods coming towards her. She knew if she spent more than a second in an open space they would kill her. But she had played this game before in training, weaving through a lightless maze full of ravenous monsters in a flight simulator. The only difference being, when she played the maze game, she had three lives, but doing it for real she had only one.

* * *

'She's using the buildings for cover.'

'Well, of course she is,' Mal Gorman snapped, with a force that cracked his dry lips. 'She's not going to fly above them so you can all take turns at target practice! Which way is she heading?'

'Towards London.'

'She's going to fly through The Shadows,' Gorman predicted. 'Try to force her up on to the second level where there's more light. Get every man there, now!'

2

OR WE WILL DIE

By the time Ellie reached the outskirts of London, she wasn't thinking, only reacting to the maze of concrete and dozens of monsters coming after her. She and the Pod Fighter had become one, like an experienced rider on a well-trained horse, and although she was mentally and physically exhausted, she was flying better than she had ever done before and gradually she gained a strong lead. They simply weren't good enough to keep up with her.

London looked like a monstrous, two-tiered cake from a distance, the bottom layer dark and foreboding, and the top layer glittering with a frosting of gold and diamond light. She soon realized her path into The Shadows was blocked by a line of police freighters, so she banked up towards the second level. The Golden Turrets of the new city were a melt of organic curves and elegant spires with open spaces between them. She knew she would be very exposed among them and that the next few minutes as she tried to cross London would be the most dangerous.

* * *

'You might see her soon,' said the man. 'She's over level two, heading directly towards you.'

'Is she?' Gorman replied grimly.

He moved towards the glass wall of his hotel room and searched the sky over the city. It was almost four in the morning and the thousands of luxury apartments were dark, with only a few air cabs buzzing lazily around them.

Good thing, he thought, imagining the outcry if civilians were killed while his men were chasing Ellie.

The glass began to vibrate. He touched it with his bony fingertips and moments later a blistering roar ripped through the clouds above his head. He looked up and saw nothing but a few trails of agitated mist running in a line away from him.

'I just heard you over me,' Gorman said.

'Yep, that's us,' the man shouted. 'When she reached the outskirts of the city, she flew up into the cloud cover, but we're on to her, she's not getting away this time.'

The noise faded into the distance and Gorman stared up at the sky, wishing he could see more. Eventually, he heard them turn and come back again, and a second later a two-pronged spearhead of curved black metal and glass erupted from the clouds and flew straight at him at several hundred kilometres per hour. Instinctively he took a step back and watched the raindrops on the window perform panicky star jumps as Ellie banked sharply, metres from his face, up the front of the hotel. There were five fighters on her tail, and they split to the left and right rather than attempt to copy her. Gorman covered his ears with his hands as the scream of their engines pierced his head.

'Can you still see her?' he shouted, when the noise had subsided.

'Yes, sir, we're driving her down.'

'Good, get her into the Turrets and force her down to ground level.'

'Yes, sir.'

The Golden Turrets began to light up as residents awoken by the noise turned on their lights and opened their curtains to see what was happening outside.

'Looks like we have an audience,' Gorman said. 'Don't mess it up.'

'We won't, sir, I've a feeling we've got her this time. She won't stand a chance.'

Moments later, Gorman watched them drop out of the clouds, Ellie in front, with a whole squadron of fighters on her tail. He watched with his heart in his mouth as she flew a masterly corkscrew through the middle of the Turrets and then began a game of cat and mouse around them, giving a breathtaking display of acrobatic twists and turns as she threw off the pack on her heels. Gorman couldn't help but smile as he watched his men trying to catch her; time after time she slipped away, like a fish from their hands, to leave them flying off in the wrong direction or swerving to avoid the Turrets. They couldn't keep her in their sights long enough to fire a single shot. She flew so tight a loop around the golden dome at the top of one the Turrets, the cleaner borgs dropped off. Then a second later, she stopped dead and the men were taken by surprise and overshot her. Gorman saw it all before it happened and inhaled sharply as two fighters collided with another coming the other way, which spiralled out of control and crashed into a building. Then the first two exploded in a ball of flame so intense, it burned Gorman's retinas, while the force of the blast shattered the glass in front of him and hurled him back on the bed. His com fell off. Still in his pyjamas and slippers he groped around for it with a shaking hand and pushed it over his ear where it lit up again.

'Was that you?' he shouted, and his question was answered by silence. All he could hear was screaming from the streets below. He got off the bed and walked over the carpet of broken glass towards the gaping hole where the window had been. He knelt down and peered over the edge, feeling a swoon of vertigo as he looked at the street hundreds of metres below. The fighters had broken apart on impact and were scattered in burning heaps down the length of New Marble Arch. Every window he could see was shattered, people were pouring out of the buildings and the sky was filling with the sound of sirens.

He tried to contact another man, 'It's Mal Gorman, where is she?'

'We don't know, sir.'

'She'll be in The Shadows. Send half the men down there and the rest to wait at her home in Barford North. We may need to kill her family, so make sure the men are careful not to be seen.'

* * *

In the chaos of the explosion, Ellie fled, devastated by the shock of what had just happened. She realized she probably knew some of the men chasing her – they had given her sweets or those little cakes she liked with iced flowers on the top, or holopics of her favourite animals, or just kind words when she was doing well in training. And she'd just watched some of them go up in a ball of flames and crash into a turret full of sleeping people.

But they were trying to kill me! she cried inside. *They're not being nice now. If they hadn't died then it would have been us. And I don't want Puck to die like this and I don't want to kill people! I want to go home!*

She flew recklessly in her desperation to get away from them, and at the edge of the second level of London, she dipped sharply, turned and flew into the darkness of The Shadows.

She was six when they built the second level on London and she remembered sitting on the floor in her pyjamas with her twin brother, Mika, watching the pillars go up on television. She was eating strawberry Stir and Serve from a bowl with bears dancing around the rim, and Mika was eating toast and jam with the crusts cut off, close to each other, legs crossed, in a rare moment of companionable silence. The pillars grew before their eyes into the legs of giants with their feet in the city parks and their heads in the sky. They were hailed a marvel of modern engineering by lots of politicians.

'We considered all the options,' the Prime Minister said, 'and decided that building a second level on London is the only way to cope with the flooding and overcrowding. Since we've been living behind The Wall, there simply isn't enough space for everyone.'

'Mum! Dad! Look at this!' Ellie shouted, her eyes glowing with excitement. 'They're going to build a fairy palace on top of London!'

Her mother turned to the television and dropped her muffin on the floor.

'Oh my odd,' she said. 'What *are* they doing?'

'I told you,' Ellie insisted. 'They're building a fairy palace!'

'Not for everyone,' her mother muttered, forgetting the muffin and sitting down to watch a model of the new city rotate on the screen. 'It's only the rich who'll live on the second level in the fairy palace, Ellie. The poor people like us will be left in the darkness below.'

Ellie hadn't understood what her mother meant at the time, and had been upset that they were disagreeing again, like they did about animals, but as she flew through The Shadows and saw it with her own eyes, she was beset by gloom and realized her mother had been right. She wove around the giant pillars with the noise of her engine ricocheting like a cannonball off the metal ceiling overhead, and thought of the millions of people who lived in that slice of watery darkness with no sky, in over-crowded damp buildings, some of them ankle-deep in flood water, whilst overhead the rich were living in their golden-turreted fairy palace. She knew the poor people lived that way because they believed they had no choice, and she also knew they'd been told a lie, and that the world they lived in was not what they thought it was.

'I'm going to tell you the truth,' she said. 'And Mal Gorman is going to wish he was never born.'

She needed a break. She didn't want to stop in this nightmare place, but her hands were shaking so much she could barely control them and she was forced to land the Pod Fighter on top of a mouldy apartment block with hundreds of broken windows. She turned off the engine, yanked off her headset, and for a minute sat in silence, listening to babies crying in the damp apartments below her.

She turned to comfort Puck. He looked as if he'd been through the spin cycle in a washing machine and bared his teeth at her aggressively, his black Mohican extra tufty and his bright eyes full of fear.

'I'm sorry, Puck,' she said, remorsefully. She didn't try to pet him, knowing he wouldn't want to be touched; instead she searched for one of the bags of food. They'd broken open and scattered all over the floor of the Pod Fighter, popcorn and nuts, monkey chow and pieces of dried fruit. She scooped up a handful in the darkness and dropped it into his lap. She watched him pick through the monkey chow until he found a nut. 'Better now?' she asked as he inspected it with his quick brown eyes. He sniffed the nut suspiciously, but ate it. 'Good,' Ellie said. 'Not feeling too bad then.'

She was about to get out of the fighter so she could stretch her legs when she heard the roar of engines from the south. She hadn't expected them to find her so quickly and she was gripped by a fear that melted her into her seat. She didn't feel ready and for the first time since she'd escaped, panic overwhelmed her. She breathed deeply, trying to control her emotions, but tears ran down her face and her chin wobbled as she fumbled with her harness and jammed her headset over her sweaty hair.

You have to be ready, she told herself. Or we will die.

She fired up her engines and threw the Pod Fighter down towards the body of black water that used to be the river Thames, twisting west towards her home.

She began to realize that flying through The Shadows was a mistake; the buildings were much smaller, most of them built during the nineteenth and twentieth centuries when there weren't so many people. She had no cover apart from the monstrous pillars and the darkness and within seconds she had a squadron of fighters on her tail again and the air around her blistered and flared as bolts of laser fire narrowly missed her, blinding her so she could barely see where she was going. She could sense their grim determination now; their mood had changed since she'd killed their colleagues and they were baying for blood. She heard Puck shriek with fear as she ducked and twisted, throwing the fighter into impossible manoeuvres around the pillars. The faces of her family danced in her flare-blinded eyes as she tried to shut out the screams of the terrified monkey behind her. She fought for Puck in the last moments, but there were too many of them and she was too tired.

'No!' she screamed, as she felt the fighter take a direct hit. The control panel in front of her sputtered light, then died, and suddenly they were in total darkness, falling like a dead bird towards an undulating mass of cold, black water.

* * *

Since Ellie had disappeared, her twin brother, Mika, had slept in her bed. Their room was tiny; the two bunks hollowed out of the plastic moulding on one wall, with a narrow strip dividing them from the cupboards in which they stored their clothes and toys. They'd fought constantly over the small space since they were toddlers, especially over the bunks. Mika had insisted on sleeping at the top and this drove Ellie crazy.

'It's not fair!' she yelled in his face. 'You always sleep at the top!'

'That's because I want to more than you do,' he replied, turning his back on her.

'No you don't!'

'Stop yelling at me, Ellie. You're being a perp.'

Then Ellie would grab the edge of his cover and try to yank it off him in a frenzy of rage, and he would hold fast, still with his back to her, both of them determined not to give in.

'I hate you!' she'd scream.

'No you don't,' he'd reply quietly, which made her even angrier. 'You love me.'

'Don't flatter yourself! You stink!'

'And by the way, Ellie, I'm the oldest, so the bunk is mine by birthright.'

'Only by ten minutes, you selfish PIG!'

It was only the intervention of their parents that broke up their fights. If they hadn't been threatened with starvation, sleeping on the floor and never seeing the light of day again, Ellie and Mika would have argued from dawn to dusk because they were so similar. Both shared the same mix of Italian and Indian blood, both had the same dark eyes, intense with passion and intelligence. As they grew, they became long-limbed and languid, by turns stubborn and moody, sulking in bed, then spirited and funny and bouncing off the walls with energy. 'A right handful,' said their tutor, Mrs Fowler, with a withering look. 'I don't know how you cope.'

Ellie's disappearance had shaken Mika so badly that even a year later he was gripped by the desolation he'd felt the night it happened. But the worst aspect, as far as his parents were concerned, was his refusal to accept she was dead. Mika refused to attend the funeral, despite his parents' desperate pleas, and he stayed at home brooding in Ellie's bed. And from that day onwards, he became so angry when her death was mentioned that they didn't dare talk to him about it. He wouldn't let them wash her bedding because it smelled of her. She hung in the air like a ghost between them and they felt as if when Ellie died, so had a part of Mika, so they grieved for both of them. It was a terrible time, when it seemed like the sun had been plucked from their world and replaced by a black hole.

Mika was certain Ellie wasn't dead. The police had told them just after she disappeared that she must have fallen off the walkway and drowned in the floodwater. But he couldn't imagine Ellie 'falling' off the walkway – she wasn't that stupid. To accidentally 'fall', she would have had to climb over the barriers at the sides, and what's more, she was wearing brand new sneakers she'd just been given for Christmas. She was so proud of them she'd yelled at him for kicking one by mistake when they were on the floor in their bedroom. There was no way she would have been climbing over barriers wearing them, more likely avoiding the puddles so she didn't get them wet.

Mika knew she was far away because he felt the bond between them stretched like an invisible cord until it hurt. He felt angry with his parents for giving up on her, and distrustful of everyone who told them she was dead. The police, the coroner, his teachers, he hated them all, and he was existing in no man's land, in the place he had chosen to wait for her, and nobody else was allowed in.

As Ellie was fighting for her life around the Golden Turrets of London, Mika awoke, instantly alert with his heart banging in his chest. He sat up in the darkness wondering if he'd been dreaming about her, but he couldn't remember.

'Ellie?' he whispered, but he knew she wasn't close to him. He sensed something else though, something strange happening around him. He held his breath so he could listen to the quiet, night-time noises and heard his father turn in bed and mutter something in dream speak, but there were other sounds too which he knew were unusual for the time of night and he strained to hear them. Yes, muffled voices were coming through the wall. There were people in the hallway outside their apartment. He pressed his ear against the wall and listened for a while. He was unable to make out words, only that they were trying to talk quietly, and there were lots of them, mostly men. He felt anxious and swung round on the bed so his feet were on the floor and wondered if he should wake his parents and tell them.

No, he decided.

He looked at the clock blinking at the head of the bed. It was four in the morning. What was going on out there? There was a lot of traffic noise for the time of night, too. He stood up and walked quietly to the window, pulled up the blind and froze with shock. Hovering only an arm's length away was a police pod. The policemen inside were eating hot dogs and dribbling ketchup on their legs, and it was a few seconds before they noticed the naked boy staring at them with bold black eyes. For a moment, they too were frozen with shock, then their faces flooded with guilt and the pod zipped to the right, out of view. Mika pulled down the blind in a panic and groped around on the floor for his jeans with his heart pounding. Finding them, he yanked them on, cursing as he trod on something sharp, then he rushed into the living area where his parents were sleeping on a fold-down bed. 'Mum! Dad! Wake up!' he whispered, frantically. 'There's something weird going on!'

They stirred. His father leaned up on one elbow and rubbed his face with his hand.

'What?' he mumbled sleepily, his features crumpled as if he'd been lying face down in the pillows.

'There are men outside our apartment,' Mika whispered, fearfully. 'And policemen eating hot dogs outside my bedroom window.'

'Why do you think that?' his mother asked, pushing herself up on the pillows. 'Are you sure you haven't had one of those bad dreams again, Mika?'

'No!' he insisted. 'I saw them. I heard noises and I opened the blind. When they realized I was there, they disappeared. They looked guilty, as if they were up to something!'

His parents climbed reluctantly out of bed and pulled on their dressing gowns.

'Look out of the window, David,' his mother said, her eyes glittering in the darkness.

His father huffed impatiently as if he thought he was wasting his time. He opened the curtains and peered through a gap in the blind. He was quiet for a few moments and Mika stood beside him breathing hard and wondering why he felt so afraid.

'There's nothing out there, Mika,' he said, at last. 'Look for yourself.'

He raised the blind so Mika could see out. His mother put a comforting hand on his shoulder as they looked out at nothing but blackened concrete, rolling clouds and rain.

'Yeah, but I told you,' Mika insisted. 'When they saw me, they flew off. Look outside the door, I could hear them talking.' He shrugged off his mother's hand and felt a familiar wave of frustration and anger because his parents didn't believe him.

'OK,' his father said calmly, shooting his wife a meaningful look. He walked around the side of the bed towards the door.

'No, don't,' Mika said, changing his mind as he felt a surge of foreboding.

His father paused. 'Why are you so afraid?' he said. 'Even if there are people out there, I'm sure there's a perfectly normal explanation for it.'

'I don't know,' Mika replied, feeling confused. 'I just do.'

'Come on,' Asha said, comfortingly. 'Let's look and then you can go back to bed without worrying about it.'

The door slid open, flooding the tiny apartment with dim yellow light and cold air. His father shrugged and stepped out into the empty hallway. 'Come and see for yourself,' he said, and the three of them stood in the hallway, their bare feet cold on the dirty concrete floor, seeing nothing but a line of silent doors and mildew-stained walls. But only metres away from them, hiding in the stairwell and the lift, were the men Mal Gorman had sent to watch their apartment; thirty men with their fingers twitching on the triggers of their guns, waiting for the order to kill.

'Let's go back in,' Asha said, looking down the empty hallway with her teeth chattering. 'It's freezing out here and you've got to be up for school in three hours.'

Mika lay rigid in his bed as his mother attempted to tuck him in. He wished she'd stop fussing over him as if he was a child and he felt angry too; they'd made him feel like a fool because there was nobody in the hallway.

'Have you been eating noodles in bed?' his mother asked, eyeing the red splodges on Ellie's cover with distaste.

'Yes,' he replied hotly, turning his back on her and hugging the filthy cover.

'It's going to have to be washed, Mika.'

'No,' he said, adamantly.

'But it doesn't smell of her any more,' she replied, impatient with fatigue. 'It just smells of your feet and noodle juice.'

'Yes it does smell of Ellie,' he said, turning over again to glare at her. 'And I don't want it washed until she comes home.'

Asha was a beautiful woman for fifty. Her Indian blood had given her the fine bones and dark hair and eyes her children had inherited. But as she looked into Mika's face and felt the heat of his anger and pain, she felt herself wither like a tree receiving the first kiss of a forest fire.

'Stop it!' she said, sharply. 'Ellie has been dead for a year and the sooner you accept it, the sooner we can all move on! It's not fair, Mika!'

'No,' Mika said quietly, tears pressing in his eyes. 'It's you that's wrong. She's not dead. I can feel her.'

He felt her more than he knew. As Ellie's Pod Fighter was shot down and fell into the dark water of The Shadows, he felt as if he'd received a crushing blow to his chest. He tried to cry out but there was nothing to cry with, there was no air in his lungs and he couldn't breathe in. Blind with panic he managed to turn himself over in the bed, desperate for his mother's help, but although he wanted to move and to speak, he felt pressure pushing on him from above, a weight of cold darkness pressing him down. He lay paralysed listening to a terrible noise, unaware he was making it, a rasping as if his windpipe had been cut. He was falling into darkness, freezing cold.

'Mika!' Asha cried, leaning forward to grab his shoulders. 'What's wrong?' But he was unable to reply, only his black eyes pleaded with her to save him.

'David!' Asha screamed. 'Call an ambulance!'

3
YOU BELONG TO US NOW

Mal Gorman went down to The Shadows to see the proof that Ellie and Puck were dead with his own eyes. He wanted to watch as their bodies were pulled out of the river and sealed in coffins so he could be sure nobody would find out that he'd kidnapped a child or that an animal had crossed The Wall. He knew it was his fault; he'd given Ellie the monkey as a pet and underestimated her ability, and although he was confident he wouldn't lose his job, he didn't want to admit he'd made such bad mistakes. Mal Gorman wasn't used to making mistakes and they felt like bee stings on his brain. But how could he have known that a twelve-year-old child would be able to escape from a space station? Ellie was amazing; so powerful and strange, and although he was relieved the monkey was dead, he was annoyed the girl was. Now he would never know why she was so special and he wouldn't be able to use her. He felt as if he'd dropped a Ming vase and was looking at the pieces on the floor around his feet.

But there are more where she came from, he reminded himself, not many, but enough.

The hours before dawn in The Shadows were the same as midnight, sunset and early afternoon, the artificial darkness hardly touched by the yellow tinge of economy lighting. Only the temperature and the wind changed; in summer it was as hot and humid as a tin can of stagnant water and in winter it was bitterly cold. In all seasons damp crept up the buildings, covering everything in a mould that caused deadly lung disease.

Mal Gorman hated The Shadows, particularly at a quarter to five in the morning when he was supposed to be on holiday. He stood on the deck of a police boat, chugging up the old path of the River Thames, looking over the dismal landscape of damp buildings half-submerged in filthy water. The river had burst its banks long ago and spread across the low-lying areas of the city. He spotted the mouldy remains of the Tate Modern gallery and the Tower of London, but it wasn't the kind of sightseeing he enjoyed; these landmarks were lifeless and stripped of treasures.

Below him in the boat, the cabin staff were preparing breakfast and a small team of policemen were eating Fab egg and tank meat and drinking tea with their guns on the floor. Gorman felt too tired and stressed to eat.

But at least the worst is over, he thought. Soon I'll be able to forget about work and enjoy my holiday.

He shivered and pulled up the collar on his long coat to protect his neck from the bitter wind. His companion on deck was the Chief of River Police. An unsavoury character, Gorman thought, who spent his days hooking corpses out of the flood-water and his nights gorging himself in expensive restaurants in the Golden Turrets. His eyes were mean, his face was puffy, and his skin was spotty and sallow.

'I don't know how you can work down here,' Gorman said.

'Ah, you get used to it,' the Chief replied dismissively, his chins wobbling like a pile of undercooked pancakes. 'We shouldn't be here long. They know where she went down, and they've got plenty of experience – she'll be the twentieth corpse they've fished out tonight. Have to get them out otherwise they stink. Mmm, I can smell sausages.'

'Do you trust your men?' Gorman asked.

'Yes,' the Chief said, after a brief pause. 'They've brought plague suits and breathing equipment. They're so scared, they've been drawing lots to decide who has to deal with it. They won't tell anyone. Not even their wives and children will touch them if it gets out they've been near an *animal*.'

'Good,' Gorman replied. 'Because if they talk about what comes up in that Pod Fighter, I have the authority of the Northern Government to ruin your life. Do you understand?'

'Yes, sir,' the Chief replied, his chins wobbling pensively. He was quiet for a moment and picked the dirt from beneath his fingernails. There was something about Mal Gorman that chilled him more than the horrors in the dark water below.

Gorman looked over the side of the boat. Bobbing on the surface of the river was a carpet of rotting rubbish. He saw a child's doll float past, sightless and gruesome and covered in slime, fast food wrappers and a mouldy sneaker.

What a mess, he thought. Forty-three years of living behind The Wall had created hell on Earth. The entire population of the planet was now squashed into a third of the space to escape from the animals, and every acre of land had been built on. There were no fields any more, no woods or parks or gardens. There was no space for anything but concrete and people. Gorman had had a nice log cabin in Canada before the Animal Plague. He used to go *there* for his holidays, not London. But now his pretty cabin had a block of apartments built on top of it, and hundreds of people lived in the area that used to be his garden.

'Ah,' said the Chief of River Police, breaking Gorman's bitter reverie. He looked towards the dark silhouette of a boat in the distance near the old Houses of Parliament. 'We should be there just in time to watch the men bring them up. Then a hearty breakfast eh? To chase off the cold. In fact, I think I might have a couple of those sausages while I'm waiting.'

Gorman watched the Chief squeeze his huge body through the small door into the cabin, like a cushion into a mouse hole.

Disgusting man, he thought.

He was cold and tired and he wanted to sit down and rest his old knees. He cursed Ellie and paced across the deck of the boat, wishing it would hurry up so he could get back to his warm hotel on level two.

Good job her parents already think she's dead, he thought, imagining the uproar if they found out what had really happened to their daughter.

Gorman had lost his log cabin because of the Animal Plague, but in other ways what had ruined most people's lives had improved his dramatically; because of the plague, there were loads of good jobs available, so he'd been able to work his way up in the new Northern Government to become the Minister for Youth Development. He was part of the Cabinet. He had a fancy office in the new Houses of Parliament, and the Queen of the North, a whole space station, was under his command. He was now one of the richest and most powerful people in the north. So he was glad the Animal Plague had happened. He never would have done so well without it. And the other great thing about the disaster, as far as he was concerned, was that having babies had been banned for thirty years afterwards because there wasn't enough space for them. So not only did he have a much better job, he'd been able to spend his new money in restaurants without a child on the next table screaming its head off or rubbing chocolate pudding in its hair. He hated children and he didn't understand them. He remembered how rude Ellie had been. So ungrateful. In fact, all of them were; the three children he'd taken all came from poor refugee homes and they should have thanked him for the attention. He'd given them presents and sweets and kept them busy with activities, yet all they'd done was cry and complain about missing their families, and now they were all dead. He realized he would need to try a different tactic next time. Soon he would need thousands of children, not just three, and he had to be able to control them. It just wouldn't do if they were crying all the time and trying to run away. But before he could think about starting again, he had to clean up the mess his early mistakes had made.

The boat's engine cut as it approached the salvage boat and it drifted the last ten metres in silence. The salvage boat was much bigger than the police boat, low in the water with a wide deck. At the stern was a huge black crane, designed to haul heavy weights out of the water. Men threw ropes to bind the two crafts together and placed a wide plank to bridge the gap between them. Gorman watched the Chief of River Police shuffle across the plank, making it bow under his enormous bulk. Then he followed him on to the wide deck of the salvage boat. Afterwards, men dressed in plague suits and gloves carried two white coffins across – a large one for Ellie and a smaller one for Puck.

The boat was crewed by river police in black waterproofs and caps. The arm of the crane towered over the water and Gorman watched as a man operated the machine that reeled in the metal rope like a fishing line, creaking with the weight of Ellie's Pod Fighter below the surface.

'Nearly up,' the Chief said, taking a tank meat sausage out of his pocket and cramming it sideways into his mouth.

The divers were just coming out of the water. They seemed in a hurry and wrestled their masks off as they flopped like seals on to the deck.

'They're still alive!' one shouted, panic-stricken. 'What shall we do?'

Gorman and the Chief rushed to the bow of the boat and leaned over to look down into the murky water. The Pod Fighter was just below the surface and they could see Ellie thrashing around in the pocket of air inside it, her dark hair whipping around her pale face as she frantically banged around the edges of the windshield trying to force it open.

'Well I'll be blowed,' the Chief said. 'She's a little firecracker.'

'Stop the crank!' Gorman yelled. 'Get guns! I want six armed men here, now!'

The Chief of River Police stared, mesmerized, into the dark water, his heart racing as he caught a glimpse of the capuchin monkey in the submerged Pod Fighter. He hadn't seen a real animal since he was a child during the plague. He saw a blink of gold fur, a flash of sharp white teeth and a tiny black hand pressed against the inside of the windshield.

'Chrise,' he said, welling up with fear. 'I haven't got a plague suit. I think I'd better wait on the other boat.' He took a step back, and another, creeping towards the plank, but the men rushing the other way blocked his path and he was pushed forward again.

The policemen gazed in horror over the side of the boat into the submerged Pod Fighter and caught a brief glimpse of their worst nightmare.

'Kill them!' Mal Gorman ordered. 'Shoot them through the windshield!'

They hesitated. Puck disappeared for a moment and Ellie was looking up at them with her face wet with tears. She was just a child.

* * *

Ellie and Puck had been at the bottom of the river for over an hour. The weight of the dark water pressing on the windshield made it creak and groan and as Ellie's eyes adjusted to the darkness, she saw terrible shapes around her: wafting black weeds like evil spirits wanting to drag her and Puck out of their bubble of air and drown them. It was so cold and dark on the riverbed and what she felt was beyond terror, she was drowning in fear. She couldn't breathe for it. It tightened around her chest like iron bands and she choked. She undid Puck's harness, pulled him close and they clung to each other in the darkness waiting for the water to come in. They could hear it gushing into the engine, but by some miracle, the cockpit remained dry. Gorman would come for them.

Ellie knew that the evil old man would take no chances and would make sure that they were dead, and she wasn't sure whether to feel relieved or terrified. If he didn't come they would die of suffocation when the oxygen in the cockpit ran out; if he did, they would be shot. So she waited and tried to figure out how they could still survive and reach home. As the divers' lamps shone down through the water she saw the fear in Puck's eyes and this gave her strength. She would swim home through this filthy black water if necessary, with Puck clinging to her back.

The divers attached ropes to the Pod Fighter and Ellie felt it rock in the water as it was winched up. Her heart beat madly as she prepared for it to break the surface of the river and when she saw the men leaning over the side of the boat, she panicked for a moment and tried to push the jammed windshield open with her hands, then thought of a better idea.

'It's OK,' she whispered, with her mouth pressed to the monkey's head. 'We can do this. We just need to stay calm.'

She pulled Puck up so he was hanging off her neck, took a deep breath and focused her gaze on the windshield until it began to glow. Only Gorman realized what was about to happen. He saw Ellie's expression change and recognized the intense concentration in her dark eyes.

'Look out!' he yelled, lifting his hands to protect his face. But it was too late; a second later, every man on the boat was hit by a shower of filthy water as the windshield was blown clean off the Pod Fighter as if a bomb had exploded inside it. The next few moments were a blur of watery confusion. Some of the men dropped their guns on the deck and had to bend down and fumble around for them in the darkness. Others were blinded by the dirty water and had to wipe their eyes on the sleeves of their plague suits. By the time they had recovered, Ellie was gone, the Pod Fighter was filling up with water and the Chief of River Police was staggering around the boat with a monkey attached to his head.

'Help!' he screamed. 'Ahhhhhh!'

He lurched back and forth. Desperate to get away from him, the men forgot their guns and began running around as if they were playing musical chairs with no chairs left, and all this movement and noise made Puck even more afraid. Unable to see Ellie and wanting to stop the screaming and motion, the monkey bit the Chief's right ear, then raised his head, bared his blood-covered fangs and screeched at the men as if he was possessed by the devil. It was the most terrifying sight they had ever seen and as the Chief's blood bubbled in the monkey's mouth, they froze as if the game had changed and they were now playing musical statues.

'Don't just stand there like a row of cabbages!' Gorman yelled, frantically looking around for Ellie. 'Just shoot it, you fools! Where's the girl? Someone kill that monkey and find that FRAGGING GIRL!'

Ellie was clinging to the side of the boat in the darkness with the current tugging at her legs. The water was so cold she was already numb from the chest down and barely able to breathe. Choking and shuddering, she desperately tried to strengthen her grip against the deadly pull of the water.

Puck will never survive this, she thought desperately. The current is too strong, the water too cold.

Her jaw juddered and her left hand lost its grip for a moment and she only just managed to find another before she was swept away. She heard the Chief scream as Puck bit him, and Gorman yelling at his men, and spurred by a desperate urge to save her animal friend, she managed to clamber over the side of the boat and went and stood amongst them. They were spooked by the strangeness of her. In her wet white clothes, she looked like a child-sized angel, but her eyes were darker than the bottom of the river. She tucked her hair behind her ears and glanced at Puck, and he leaped powerfully from the Chief's shoulder to land in her arms, where he clung to her with his back to the men and his face pressed against her neck.

'Kill them!' Gorman rasped, so consumed by rage he sounded

as if he was trying to scream with lungs full of dry leaves. 'Quickly!'

They heard a heavy splash and looked round to see that the terrified Chief had jumped over the side of the boat into the river. They watched the darkness swallow his flailing arms, then raised their guns and pointed them at Ellie. There was no hesitation this time; the child had a plague animal hanging off her neck with the Chief's blood on its teeth, and by some witchery she had blown the windshield off a Pod Fighter. But stranger things were about to happen in the darkness, with the drifting, black water around them. They would remember meeting Ellie and Puck for a long, long time.

As they took aim and prepared to fire, Ellie's eyes began to burn like black coals and her pale skin glowed as if a white light had been turned on inside her. The men felt a strange sensation in their hands, a tingling sensation as if their veins were being invaded by her energy, then their guns moved, squirming and wriggling in their hands as if they had come alive and wanted to escape. The child didn't move, didn't blink or make a sound, she just watched them calmly. They couldn't shoot her. Their guns refused to point at her even when the men held them with both hands. And before they had a chance to figure out what she was doing, two of the guns were in Ellie's hands and the rest were in the river. The men looked at their empty palms as if they'd never seen them before, then at Ellie, with fear.

'Get away from us,' she said quietly, edging towards the plank leading to the other boat. 'Or I'll kill you all.'

The men began to move back, terrified, and a few looked over the side of the boat and considered following the Chief into the freezing river.

'Stay where you are!' Gorman yelled at the men. 'And you,' he sneered, glaring at Ellie. 'You take one more step and your brother, your mother and father *will die*. There are men outside your home in Barford North waiting for orders. You'll only have yourself to blame, Ellie. I have the power to kill them all.'

Ellie froze, her heart feeling as if Gorman had run it through with a sword.

'You know you can't go home, Ellie,' Gorman said, his eyes hard on her face. 'I need you.'

'I just want to tell them I'm not dead,' Ellie said quietly, her eyes brimming with tears. 'That's all. I won't tell them The Secret, I promise!'

'Well, you *can't*,' Gorman stated, coldly. 'You belong to us now.'

'Please!' she begged. 'Just let me see them! Just for a few minutes. I miss them so much!'

'No,' he said.

'Why?' she cried. 'Why won't you let me see them? What do you *want* from me?'

'You'll find out soon enough,' he said.

'Please tell me!' she cried. 'Why won't you tell me? You've taken me from my family but you won't even say why! *Please!*'

'No!' he said angrily. 'I'll tell you when I'm ready to tell you, not when *you* decide.'

She looked away from him, tears burning the back of her throat. It was impossible. How had she ever believed she could escape Mal Gorman? She felt her body slump with sadness and the guns fell from her hands to the deck.

'Get in that,' Gorman ordered, pointing at the larger coffin. 'And make Puck get in his before I decide to kill him for all the trouble you've caused me. You've ruined my holiday, Ellie.'

Ellie was shocked to see the coffins on the deck – the large one for her and the smaller one for Puck. Gorman grabbed her arm with his bony fingers. 'No!' she wept as he pushed her towards it. He was surprisingly strong for a walking skeleton. 'We won't be able to breathe in there! We'll suffocate!'

Gorman picked up one of the guns and shot a few holes in the lids.

'There you go,' he snapped. 'Air holes. Now get in.'

Her hands shook as she talked comforting words to Puck and

encouraged him to lie down in his coffin. It was awful, he was looking up at her with his bright eyes full of trust and she felt overwhelmed by guilt. Poor Puck. As she closed the lid she could hear him hooting with fear and confusion inside. She climbed into the other coffin with silent tears running down her face, feeling a new emotion: a murderous anger and hatred like she'd never felt before. She felt as if something was growing inside her, revving up, a heat, a noise like a stampede.

Gorman stood between the two coffins and looked down on her. He was also feeling a new emotion, or at least one he hadn't felt for a long time. He felt a bit warm inside, a bit glad. He had her back, alive, and all that effort and money hadn't been wasted after all – and, he realized, he'd learned through this experience how to control her. Perhaps this new job wasn't going to be so hard after all. All he'd have to do is threaten to kill the monkey and the people she loved and she'd do whatever she was told.

'Things will be better for you soon,' he said, almost kindly. 'In a few weeks you'll have some new friends to keep you company.'

'You're going to steal *more children*?' Ellie asked, glaring at him. 'Isn't killing two enough?'

Her chest felt hot and her head began to throb as her anger and hatred intensified, and the sound of the stampede become the roar of a single beast, a cloven rage beast in her mind.

'A *hundred* children wouldn't be enough,' Gorman said. 'One day you'll understand.'

'I hope not,' she replied, bitterly. 'Because if I did, it would mean I had become like *you*.'

'Your new friends will want to come,' Gorman continued. 'They'll be begging to work for me.'

Ellie glared at him, wishing he was dead, feeling all her hatred and anger coming out like black rods from her eyes. For a few seconds Gorman met her gaze confidently, he was even smiling a little, pleased with himself. She didn't mean to do it, she didn't even know she could do it, and when Gorman flinched and pulled his head back she made no link between her gaze and his

– 35 –

pain. He opened his mouth to gasp and his body turned rigid as if he was being electrocuted. His shoulders jabbed up and his hands began to shake as if he was a malfunctioning borg. Then a thin trickle of blood ran out of one of his dry nostrils and he closed his mouth again and made this awful creaking noise as his teeth ground together. Ellie became aware that her eyes felt like magnets locked to his head, and she tried to drag them away, suddenly understanding what she was doing to him. Gorman realized too. He could hear the roar, feel her anger and hatred like scalpels slicing his brain. It was the worst pain he had ever experienced.

'Shut the lid,' he rasped, falling against a policeman, who held out his arms to catch him. 'Shut it, quickly.'

The policeman kicked Ellie's coffin lid closed, and the last thing she saw for several weeks was the paleness of terror on Mal Gorman's face.

4

A VERY DISTURBED BOY

The Barford North Community Hospital was a hulk of rust-streaked concrete that looked like a prison. Unlike the private hospital in nearby Oxford, there were no plastic flowers in reception, no carpets on the floor, no relaxing music or smiling nurses in crisp white uniforms. In the Barford North hospital, the chairs in the waiting room were scratched and grey and screwed to the floor. There was no heating. The drinks machine coughed up watery coffee for two credits a cup and there was a drunken man asleep in the corner muttering something about kebab sauce.

Mika's parents sat in silence waiting for news, huddled in their coats against the early morning cold. Tears ran down Asha's face as she remembered how she'd shouted at him only moments before he'd started to choke – that she'd got angry with him, not only for waking them up in the middle of the night, but because he wouldn't accept Ellie was dead. And now he might die too and those angry words would be the last he heard. She felt terrible guilt and sorrow. She loved her children so much the pain was unbearable, and she felt as if she would rather die too than exist without them.

David took her hand and squeezed it. He did not find it easy to show his feelings in front of strangers, and to the passing hospital staff he looked calm, as if he was waiting for a train, but inside he felt cut to pieces by grief.

It was two hours after Mika's dramatic arrival in an ambulance pod that a doctor came to talk to them. David and Asha followed him along a dimly lit hallway and stopped outside Mika's ward. The doctor was a small, grey-faced man with serious eyes. He looked tired and anxious to get away.

'Well, you'll be pleased to know there's nothing wrong with him,' he said, looking at his watch. 'You can take him home.'

'What?' Asha cried, almost falling over backwards with shock. 'He was nearly dead two hours ago! What do you mean there's nothing wrong with him? That's impossible! He couldn't breathe! He was choking to death!'

'That wasn't the reaction I was expecting,' the doctor said. 'Parents are usually happy when I tell them their children are still alive.'

'Of course I'm happy,' Asha spluttered, her eyes filling with tears of confusion. 'I'm just amazed, that's all, he seemed so ill.'

'Well, not any more,' the doctor said, impatiently. 'He suddenly came round while we were examining him and sat up in bed looking disorientated. When we asked him if he knew what had happened to him he came out with some incoherent mumble about water in the engine and popcorn. And he says everything looks dark, but we've run full tests and he's perfectly healthy. His eyes are fine.'

'So what do *you* think happened to him?' David asked. 'A boy doesn't start choking to death for no reason.'

'I have absolutely no idea,' the doctor replied. 'Who knows

the workings of a prepubescent mind? Has he got any problems in school or at home?'

Asha and David looked at each other and their hearts sank horribly.

'Yes,' David said, his eyes dropping to the floor. He didn't want to tell the grey-faced doctor about Mika's obsession with Ellie, but felt he had no choice. 'His twin sister died a year ago and he refuses to believe she's dead.'

'Ah,' the doctor said. 'That could explain things. Twins have a strong bond – losing a twin brother or sister is like losing a part of yourself.'

'So you think this was all in his head?' Asha asked. 'That he made this choking thing up?'

'It's possible,' replied the doctor. 'I think he should talk to someone. He needs to see a counsellor and come to terms with his sister's death. He's obviously a very disturbed boy.'

They nodded in reluctant agreement.

'One more thing,' the doctor continued. 'I noticed Mika has webbed feet and yet he isn't registered as a mutant on his medical records. Why is that?'

'We didn't know he was a mutant until a day after he was born,' Asha replied. 'Ellie's mutation was more obvious – she was born with webbed fingers and they operated on her shortly after birth, but Mika's toes were overlooked because nobody noticed. Does it matter?'

'Legally he should be registered,' the doctor said.

'Why?' Asha asked. 'The mutation doesn't affect him in any way, and mutated kids get bullied and treated as if there's something wrong with them.'

'I know,' the doctor replied, shrugging. 'But you must do it, it's the law. You can register him in reception when you pay the bill.'

He turned and walked quickly away, leaving Mika's confused parents trying to feel pleased he was better whilst coming to terms with the fact that he was a very disturbed boy.

'Don't worry,' David said, hugging Asha. 'He'll be fine in a few months. We'll get him to talk to someone about Ellie, yeah? And we'll try not to get so angry with him. Perhaps we should encourage him to take up a sport or something so he doesn't spend so much time brooding in Ellie's bed. What do you think?'

'I don't know,' Asha sobbed. 'I just love him and I want him to be well again.'

* * *

A few weeks passed, and although Mika was sullen when he first started seeing his counsellor, Helen, he grew to like her very much. He went to her apartment every Wednesday after school. She was old and took ages to get to the door and she always ran out of milk and sugar sub or tea powder, so what Mika drank had an apology attached and something missing, but it didn't matter. Although being with her was sometimes boring, a bit like visiting a granny, her apartment, full of old paper books, plastic plants and curious ornaments, was the only place Mika felt he could relax, because Helen was the only person who even considered the possibility that Ellie was still alive.

'You know you're not supposed to believe me,' he said, sipping his tea. 'You're supposed to be curing my insanity, not making it worse.'

'I know,' she replied, giggling hoarsely. 'Do you want a biscuit?'

'I'll get them if you want,' Mika offered.

'No, you stay there, gorgeous, I can manage.'

Mika watched her get up from the sofa and shuffle towards the kitchen area. Rain hit the window like handfuls of grit, and the only other noises were the ticking of Helen's old clock and the sound of her breathing as she slowly bent down to get the biscuits out of the cupboard. She looked as delicate as the antique china she had on her shelves, as if she would shatter if she fell, yet he knew her appearance was deceptive, that it hid a bomb-proof interior; she looked like a witch, dressed like a bag lady and wasn't shocked by anything.

'I've been having nightmares again,' he said suddenly.

'Oh yes,' she replied, breathing heavily as she walked back to the sofa with the biscuits. 'Anything good?'

'Not good exactly,' Mika replied, smiling – he liked her sense of humour.

Helen settled herself comfortably on the sofa as if she was about to watch a movie and held out the biscuits. They were digestives, the same packet she'd got out the week before and he knew they were stale and probably went out of date a year ago but he took one anyway.

'Thanks,' he said, trying to eat it without grimacing.

'Well, are you going to tell me about your nightmares or was that just a trailer?' she asked.

'If you want me to.'

'Fire away,' she said enthusiastically, 'I like a good horror story.'

He finished his biscuit and she offered him another, he took it, but held it in his lap.

'Are the nightmares all the same, or different?' she asked.

'The same,' he said.

'How do they start?'

Mika pictured the beginning of his nightmare and wasn't sure whether he wanted to tell her. He could feel the sickening dread that was still with him the next morning – the dark cloud in his peripheral vision that accompanied him while he walked to school.

'Have you changed your mind about telling me?' Helen said, watching him fiddle with his biscuit. 'It doesn't matter. We could talk about something else if you want, or play poker.'

'No, I want to tell you,' he decided, turning to her. 'It's just horrible, that's all.'

'Come on, I'm intrigued.'

'OK,' said Mika. He took a deep breath. 'It starts with me lying on a bed and it's like the time when I went to hospital because I was choking. I wake up and there's a green curtain around me and I realize they've taken my clothes off and that I'm wearing one of those long white gowns that doesn't cover your bum.'

'Oh, I hate those,' Helen said. 'Most undignified – but appropriate wear for a nightmare. Sorry, this is good, carry on.'

'The curtain around me starts to move as if someone is about to open it, but not just in one place, all around me, the curtain's sort of shuddering and I can see the shapes of people pressing against it. Then all of a sudden it's gone, as if I'm in a theatre and the curtain's been lifted, and I find myself surrounded by these horrible people, crowding round the bed, pushing against each other and moving their heads from side to side so they can all see me.'

Helen nodded. 'What don't you like about them?' she asked.

'Their heads,' Mika replied, beginning to feel anxious. 'It's going to sound stupid.'

'Try me.'

'Well, instead of normal heads they have old television sets, the type that look like square boxes with a glass screen on the front, really big and heavy. They look too heavy for their shoulders.'

'I had one of those when I was kid,' Helen said. 'It was my bedroom telly. The picture was dreadful.'

'Chrise, you must be *really* old,' Mika said, then immediately regretted it. 'Sorry, I didn't mean that.'

She laughed. 'It's all right,' she said. 'I am *really* old. So, have these people got faces?'

'Yes,' Mika replied. 'They're on the television screens. They're gruesome. They scare me. They look like skeletons with eyes, their skin stretched and kind of papery and dry with hardly any hair like Egyptian mummies with their bandages taken off. They start talking, discussing how they want to eat me, as if I can't hear them, and they're arguing because some of them want roast beef and some of them want enchiladas. And at the end of the bed is the Knife Sharpener, he doesn't speak at all, he just scrapes his long knife on a stone and stares at me – and I'm really scared because I'm lying there, trying to move, but I can't. I'm paralysed. And suddenly it's dark around the bed and all I can see are their faces flickering on the screens. They stop talking and just stare at me, licking their dry lips with wrinkly tongues.'

'Do you recognize any of them?' Helen asked. 'Are they teachers from school or the policemen who came when Ellie disappeared?'

'No,' Mika replied, shuddering. 'They look as if they should be dead.'

'They sound like the type who take Everlife pills,' Helen said, in a disapproving manner. 'I wish those pills had never been invented. They do something strange to the people who take them. It's as if their bodies are clinging to life but their souls and all the goodness in them have given up and gone. Humans will try anything to escape death. Thousands of years ago, they tried magic and when that didn't work, they turned to God, that's why people still say, 'thank odd,' when something good happens in their lives. But when God didn't save them, they gave up on him and turned to science. But I can't be doing with this staying alive for ever business; paying a fortune for pills so you can walk around looking like a skeleton with eyes. All the worst people got the most important jobs in the Northern Government after the plague and now they never get replaced because they stay alive for so long. It's not natural and it's not worth it. I think people should die with dignity when their time comes. I wouldn't say that in public, mind you, it's not a popular point of view, so keep it to yourself.' She looked at him mischievously over the rim of her teacup.

'OK,' Mika said, smiling.

'What else can you tell me about the Telly Heads?' she asked.

'They're mostly men, though I remember two women. At the end of the dream the Knife Sharpener raises his knife and it glints in the light of their faces.'

'So how do you end up?' Helen asked. 'Roast beef or enchiladas?'

'I don't know. I wake up making this horrible groaning noise. It scares my mum.'

'I'm not surprised,' Helen said.

5

A NEW GAME

It wasn't easy living in a fold-down apartment in the new town, Barford North. The only green the refugees of the Animal Plague saw from their windows was the mould on their neighbours' curtains. Most had travelled thousands of miles, leaving the sun and their homes behind them, and it was as if all the people of the world had been mixed up in a big bowl and poured out again into concrete boxes. In Mika's tower lived people from every country; there was even a man from Mongolia who had grown up in a tent and a woman from Peru who was born on a llama farm. Now everyone lived in identical fold-down apartments four metres square, and living this way had taught them to be patient. There was no point having a tantrum in a fold-down apartment because they had to fold one thing away before they could use another, and if they did it in a hurry, it all went wrong and they'd end up with the washing line wrapped round their head instead of a sandwich in their hand. They had to fold the bed away to use the kitchen, then fold a bit of the kitchen away to use the shower. The shower creaked and sank when they got in it, the vacuumbot often ground to a halt with depressed wisps of smoke leaking out of its eyes, the handles fell off the kitchen cupboards if anyone sneezed and the walls were so thin they could hear their neighbours belch and fart. The only item of furniture they owned was the sofa in front of the television.

But there was no point complaining about how horrible their lives were, because nothing could be done. No one was going to wave a magic wand and make the world beautiful again. Nobody could bring back the forests and the fields that had been destroyed because of the Animal Plague, and as time went on, they got used to living behind The Wall in a concrete hell. And in some ways life was better; if they had an argument there was nowhere to go (unless you fancied standing in a gloomy hallway), so people made more of an effort to be nice to each other. Mika's family hadn't had a proper argument until the day he decided the school was trying to poison him.

Mika's school looked just like all the other buildings in the new towns that had been built following the Animal Plague. It was a square lump of concrete, rust-streaked, damp and cold, supported on four algae-stained legs that looked too skinny to hold up all those children above the floodwater. The playground was a slice of cold, dark air beneath the main building. The dimly lit hallways smelled of stale breath and the classrooms had unpainted walls and concrete floors. There were no real windows in Mika's classroom; on one wall there was a row of scratched screens showing views of a playing field that hadn't existed for forty-three years and on the other wall was a row of history posters, most showing holopics of animals with the plague, their eyes bloodshot and foam flecking their mouths. There were also two pictures of Earth, one showing it before the Animal Plague, with patches of green indicating the locations of rain forests and grassy plains, and one showing Earth after the plague, which was grey at the top above The Wall to represent all the concrete towers, and yellow at the bottom, below The Wall to show that everything was dead and covered in poisoned dust. There was nothing cheery to look at if you were born a refugee child. They didn't even have real teachers; they had cartoon teachers who taught them from the screens that slid up from the backs of their desks. Their tutor, Mrs Fowler, sat at the front, but the only thing she was paid to teach them was how to shut up and get on with their work.

In winter it was so cold in the classroom they wore their coats buttoned up to the necks, and Mrs Fowler put a blanket over her knees and wore fingerless mittens and a bobble hat. Heating was too expensive for a refugee school. You had to go to a private school for heating, teachers and windows. So Mika was extremely surprised when he entered his classroom one Monday morning to find balloons stuck to the grey walls and coloured streamers bobbing on the ceiling. The lurid colours burned his eyes and he stood in the doorway blinking for a few seconds, wondering if he'd walked into the wrong school by mistake. Then he saw Mrs Fowler at the front of the class, blowing up balloons. She had streamers tied to the buttons on her baggy old cardigan. Mika walked to his place along the front row and sat down. On his desk lay a cake on a small plastic plate and he looked at it suspiciously as he dumped his bag on the floor and unzipped his wet jacket. Around him his classmates were talking excitedly, awoken from their coma of boredom by the party decor.

'Don't eat your cakes yet!' Mrs Fowler shouted, sticking another balloon on the wall. 'Wait until everyone has arrived!'

Mika looked at his cake. It had the letters YDF written on it in blue icing. He pushed it away from him to the back of his desk and closed his eyes, fighting off the wave of depression he always felt when he arrived at school without Ellie. School had been the hardest thing since she had gone. For a few days after her disappearance, his classmates were kind and told him how sorry they were, but it soon became clear they thought she was dead. Ellie's friends went to the school memorial, cried like babies, then two weeks later were behaving as if she'd never existed.

Mrs Fowler was more considerate, although Mika found her attention embarrassing; she asked him all the time how he was feeling, and nodded like a priest at a funeral while he lied and said he was OK. He started avoiding her and in the end she gave up and left him alone, which suited Mika fine.

Then the mockery began. There was a boy in Mika's class called Ruben Snaith. He was a pale shrew of a boy who looked as if he had milk for blood and a nose sharp enough to peck holes through doors. Ruben was popular with the other kids, but only because it was better to be his friend than his enemy – he picked up and dumped people like a change of T-shirt, and he was cruel, always bullying the mutants.

When a body was found in the floodwater beneath the school and the police announced it was Ellie, instead of being sympathetic, Ruben taunted Mika. He gathered round with his friends, their eyes glittering, and tried to make Mika look stupid because he wouldn't accept the evidence that his sister was dead. To them it was just twisted entertainment, something to alleviate the boredom of the school day, but to Mika it was agony. The playground became a snake pit, the classroom, a lion's den, he couldn't concentrate on his work and he felt so unhappy, all he wanted to do was go home and sleep. But even in sleep there was no respite for Mika, because the moment he closed his eyes, he had the Telly Heads for company. He didn't think things could get any worse, but he was wrong, because a monster from his nightmares was about to join him in reality.

'Right, everyone!' Mrs Fowler said, her huge bosom heaving as if she'd been inflating that by mistake while she was blowing up the balloons. 'Quiet now! As you can probably tell, we've got some surprises in store for you today! A lady from the *Youth Development Foundation* is coming to talk to you in a few minutes about a wonderful new project to make you all . . . what was it, ah yes, it's written here, *Fit For Life*!' she read from the tablet in her hand. 'There are going to be *free* sandwiches at lunchtime and I think music too, yes, music at lunchtime while you eat your free sandwiches, and she's going to be telling you all about vitamins and exercise and a new *game* you can play after school. That sounds fun, doesn't it, everyone? You can eat your cake now while you wait for her to arrive!'

Mrs Fowler hurried out of the classroom looking flustered, the streamers tied to her cardigan buttons bouncing in her wake, and the class began to eat their YDF cakes and talk loudly.

Mika sat on Freak Row, where all the misfits, mutants and miscreants ended up, right in front of Mrs Fowler, so she could keep an eye on them. Other Freak Row residents included Roland, the Spelling Bee Champion, who used words like 'indicate' in normal conversation, Lara whose mutant teeth made her look like she had a mouthful of giant sweetcorn, and Carlos, who picked his nose and wiped it on his hair. Mika had been put at the front because his work was bad and it was supposed to be a punishment, but he preferred it to the place he'd sat before with Ellie's empty desk next to him. Now he sat next to the new boy, Kobi Nenko, who had moved to Barford North from The Shadows. Kobi looked like a bundle of rags dumped in his chair, and his long, straggly black hair completely covered his face. He scared the girls, but Mika liked him because he was quiet. The last thing he felt like doing was babysitting a new boy; his head was such a dark place he felt as if he burned holes in everything he looked at. But he was curious about Kobi. He felt drawn to him, aware that behind that tangled, black curtain of hair, a lot of thinking was going on. Thoughts that were about to break out from three weeks of silence.

'Why are they giving us cake?' Kobi muttered through his hair, and hearing the mysterious boy talk for the first time, Mika felt as if the sun had popped out of the clouds for a second.

'I don't know,' Mika replied, looking at his cake. 'They don't usually give us anything, except homework.'

'Don't you want yours?' the girl sitting behind Kobi asked

hopefully. She was so thin, her arms looked like twigs and her eyes too big for her face. Kobi passed her the plate and watched sympathetically through his hair as she stuffed the cake whole into her mouth, hardly chewing before she swallowed. Mika gave her his, too, and she did the same thing, gobbling it down with crumbs flying out of her mouth. Mika was glad the cake was gone. He felt as if he had disposed of something unpleasant.

There was a sudden hush at the back of the classroom as someone walked in. Her feet clip-clopped smartly on the concrete floor as she walked through the rows of desks to Mrs Fowler's at the front. She was wearing a white dress with a blue belt and smart black shoes, and her black hair was coiled neatly on the top of her head. She was carrying a large black bag and she put it on the desk. Mika was reminded of Mary Poppins – until she turned and he saw her face: her eyes were faded as if she took them out at night and soaked them in bleach; her skin was pulled tight over her skull like paper soaked in tea and her lips were dry and hard. She unpacked her bag and put a pile of cups on the desk and a name plate that said, 'Briony Slater – Fit For Life Nurse – Youth Development Foundation', and as Mika watched, he felt as if the lights in the classroom dimmed and he was on his own in a dreamlike place, a place with no walls but only a bed and darkness beyond. Her faded eyes, her bony lips flickered on the screen of an old-fashioned television set and by the time her bag was unpacked, he could see her leaning over him as he lay paralysed on the bed. His heart began to stampede in his chest. There was a Telly Head in his classroom. A Telly Head right here in front of him, while he was awake, during the day.

'Good morning, everyone!' she shouted, her smile stretching her papery face. 'My name is Briony Slater and I'm your Fit For Life Nurse!'

She was greeted by silence.

She smoothed down her dress with claw-like hands.

Stop being stupid, Mika thought. People in your nightmares don't exist – she can't be a Telly Head, it's not possible.

'You're probably wondering why I'm here!' the nurse cried, clasping her hands together and smiling as if she was about to perform magic tricks for their entertainment. 'I'm here on behalf of a new organization called the Youth Development Foundation. The Youth Development Foundation has been set up to make you all FIT FOR LIFE!'

'Lucky us,' someone muttered at the back of the class, followed by a flurry of sniggers.

She ignored the comment, and Mika watched her faded yellow eyes drift over them with disdain.

She doesn't like us, Mika thought, she thinks we're scum.

'We're going to be doing lots of exciting things today!' she enthused. 'At lunchtime you will all be given *free sandwiches*!'

'More free food?' Kobi whispered. 'Are we being fattened up for something?'

Mika looked at Kobi in alarm. With a Telly Head in the classroom, jokes about being fattened up were not funny. He felt frozen, unable to speak and he was barely able to control the waves of panic washing over him.

'The *Fit For Life* project will make you all fitter and cleverer!' the nurse continued, as if they should be weeping for joy at the prospect. 'And it's going to be lots of fun! Later on I'll be telling you about an exciting *new game*! But first, I'm going to tell you about Fit Mix.'

There was a pause while she rooted around in her bag and produced a small white sachet like a rabbit out of a hat. She held it above her head and moved from side to side so everyone could see it.

'This is Fit Mix,' she said. 'You will be drinking it every morning. When you arrive at school, you will find a plastic cup like this on your desk.' She held one up in her other hand just in case they didn't know what a plastic cup looked like. 'The cup will be half full of water. Next to the cup you will find a sachet of Fit Mix and a stirrer. You tear the top off the sachet like this . . . and you pour the contents of the sachet into the cup of water and mix it with the stirrer. Then you drink it.'

'Why?' someone asked.

'Fit Mix is a marvellous new formula developed to promote adolescent growth. You were the first children to be born for *thirty* years after the Animal Plague, and now you are approaching your teens, the Northern Government wants to take special care of you. We are concerned about your diet, particularly the amount of fake or 'Fab' foods you eat. Fab foods may taste nice, but they are not good for you. You might as well eat this,' she said, holding up her tablet pen. 'Or this.' She pointed to her shoe. Then she loaded pictures of real fruit, vegetables, bread and tank meat on to their desktop screens and they watched a slide show.

'You should be eating more of these,' she said.

There was an outburst of laughter.

'We can't eat real food! It's too expensive!' someone shouted. 'Only rich people eat real food!'

'I know,' the nurse said. 'Real food *is* expensive because it takes up valuable space to grow, so most people eat the cheaper Fab foods instead. That's why you're going to drink Fit Mix from now on. You could eat nothing but carpet and shoes and still grow big and strong.'

Mika looked at the nurse and all he could see was a Telly Head leaning over him, trying to decide whether to mince him for sausages or boil him like a ham. There was no way he was drinking anything she gave him.

'Excuse me,' he said, and her faded yellow eyes locked on his. 'Can you tell me what's in the Fit Mix?'

'Nutrients,' she replied, shortly.

'What kind of nutrients?'

'Special nutrients,' she replied, looking away. 'Vitamins and things.'

She thinks I'm stupid, Mika thought, bristling with anger.

'I want to see a list,' he demanded. 'If I'm expected to drink it, I want to know what's in it.'

'There's no point you seeing a list because you won't understand it,' she replied, without even looking at him. She began to pull the pile of cups apart and set them out on Mrs Fowler's desk.

'Why not?' he said defiantly. 'I'm not stupid.'

'I didn't say you were,' she said, turning briefly to give him an icy look. 'But you won't understand a list of chemicals' names, will you? Now, does anyone else have a question?'

Mika glared at her angrily as she continued to set out cups and answer questions.

There was silence in the classroom as everyone drank the Fit Mix. Mika watched Kobi. He hesitated as he picked up the sachet and stirrer and Mika knew he didn't want to drink it.

Don't do it Kobi, Mika thought.

It took Kobi a while to make up his mind, but eventually he shook the sachet into the cup and stirred it. Mika watched him drink the Fit Mix and felt pressure build up inside him. Kobi had drunk it. Everyone was drinking it. What were they doing? He couldn't believe they were drinking it without knowing what was in it. He began to consider the possibility that he *was* insane. After all, he'd just seen someone from his nightmares in his classroom. Maybe he was wrong about Ellie, maybe she was dead and all the people who had been trying to convince him of the fact for over a year were right; his parents, the police, the doctors, his classmates, maybe they were all right. A cocktail of bad emotions began to stir inside him; confusion, paranoia, despair, and he knew he had to get out of the classroom before he exploded. He stood up and grabbed his coat from the back of his chair. Kobi looked up at him and Mika saw a brief glimpse of intelligent blue eyes through his hair.

'Where are you going?' the nurse asked, sharply.

'I need the toilet,' he replied, stupidly.

She looked at the unopened sachet of Fit Mix on his desk.

'You've got to drink that first,' she said, pointing at it.

Mika shook his head, frozen like an animal trapped in a room with a butcher in the doorway. The whole class was staring, stifling their laughter. It was unbearable. He felt as if his skin was going to crack and a paranoid werewolf was about to jump out of it.

'Right,' the nurse said. 'I'm going to get your teacher.' She walked quickly out of the classroom with her arms rigid at her sides.

'You paranoid freak!' Ruben Snaith yelled from the back of the class. 'Do you think she's trying to poison you?'

'Get lost, Ruben,' Mika said. 'It's none of your business.'

'Mutant weirdo, you should be locked up,' Ruben sneered. 'By the way, how's Ellie these days? Back from her holidays yet?' Then he muttered something to the boy sitting next to him, who looked at Mika and laughed. He saw a girl playing with her hair and smiling.

They think this is funny, Mika thought. They all think I'm insane.

Burning with anger he pushed desperately through the desks, bouncing off the backs of chairs. But before he reached the door, the nurse returned with Mrs Fowler and the Headmaster, Mr Grey, and he was trapped.

Mr Grey looked as if he'd spent his life eating concrete and drinking floodwater. Even his collar, which came right up to his chin, looked as if was made of concrete. As he walked into the classroom the silence was so absolute, Mika could hear the hum of the processors sleeping in their desks. Everyone was scared of Mr Grey, even Mrs Fowler.

'Where are you going?' Mr Grey asked abruptly, his eyes rolling like stones.

Mika didn't reply.

'I hear you refuse to drink the Fit Mix.'

Still Mika was silent, worried that if he opened his mouth, he would say something he would regret.

'It's vitamins, Mika,' Mrs Fowler said, in a wheedling voice, as if she was talking to a baby. 'It's good for you. When was the last time you ate real food? Christmas? This is supposed to be a fun day, you'll be getting *free sandwiches* for lunch and you'll be hearing about a *new game ...*' She trailed off, fiddling with the streamers tied to her cardigan buttons.

How could he get out? He felt frantic now. The nurse and Mrs Fowler stood between him and the door while Mr Grey held a tablet in his hand and read Mika's student profile. Behind him, the whole class was staring and stifling their laughter.

'Mika Smith,' Mr Grey said, and his voice filled the classroom like train station air. He raised his eyes and looked at Mika calmly. Mika felt a cold chill penetrate his clothes.

'Why do you rebel against *everything*?' he said, quietly. 'I see from your profile that you are the most intelligent boy in this class, yet your marks are abominable and you are rude and disruptive. Have you become so paranoid that you believe that you, a twelve-year-old boy, know more than your government and school?'

Mika looked at his feet and shook his head. He didn't know what he thought about anything. He'd just seen a Telly Head in his classroom.

'Nurse!' Mr Grey barked. 'Get the Fit Mix.'

The nurse scuttled to Mika's desk and collected the cup, sachet and stirrer. Mika realized he was going to be forced to drink it and he ran forward and tried to escape round the side of Mrs Fowler, but just as he'd slipped past, Mr Grey grabbed his arm and dragged him back into the classroom.

'Oh no you don't,' he snarled, gripping Mika's arm so hard, he cut off the blood supply to his hand.

'You can't force me to drink it!' Mika said, trying to wrench his arm free of Mr Grey's grip.

'Yes I can,' Mr Grey said. 'Everybody else has. If you don't drink it, I'll give your parents a hundred credit fine.'

There were gasps from the class. A hundred credit fine was the maximum amount and Mika knew his parents would be mad as hell if he went home with that. The nurse held out the cup of Fit Mix with a brittle hand. It looked pink and slimy.

'Drink it,' Mr Grey said.

Mika took the cup, his heart thudding madly in his chest. Everyone was staring at him.

'Come on, you paranoid freak!' Ruben yelled. 'Get on with it!'

Mika wasn't quite sure how it happened. One moment he was staring into the cup of Fit Mix, willing himself to drink it; the next, the cup jerked up in his hand, and the contents flew out in a pink, slimy arc and hit Mr Grey full in the face. Everything froze for a moment as if someone had pressed pause during a movie, the Fit Mix, Mr Grey, Mika's heart, the nurse, teacher, classmates, everything, and there was a dreadful silence as everyone watched the Fit Mix begin to run down Mr Grey's face and on to his collar.

'*You ungrateful little—*' the nurse screeched at Mika, her pale eyes venomous. 'How *dare* you!' She stomped towards the front of the classroom, as if she'd had enough of it all, her shoes rapping like gunfire on the hard floor.

Mr Grey calmly took a handkerchief out of his pocket and began to mop his face. Mika felt his guts melt with fear. Ruben sniggered behind him.

'You!' Mr Grey roared, pointing at Ruben. 'Stand up! How dare you laugh! That's a fifty credit fine! Let's see how funny you find *that*!'

Then he turned his cold eyes on Mika, the pink slime still glistening on his grey lashes and brows. 'Come with me,' he hissed, and dragged Mika out of the classroom by the collar of his T-shirt.

6
DON'T BELIEVE THEM

After yelling at Mika for fifteen minutes, Mr Grey left him sitting on a chair in his office with instructions to 'think about what he had just done.' He left, Mika assumed, to go to the staff hygiene room and wash the Fit Mix off his eyebrows.

Mika had never been in Mr Grey's office before and he looked around miserably at the bare desk and three hard chairs – the sort that dig into your back when you sit on them. The walls were painted grey and the window looked out at the Fab Food Factory and an electricity pylon. Facing Mr Grey's desk was a bank of screens showing views from the security cameras – the dark playground underneath the school; dismal, deserted hallways; dripping urinals and classrooms of pupils doing their morning work. He stood up and searched for a view of his classroom. Finding it, he watched his classmates. The Telly Head nurse was handing out bags, walking through the rows of desks with a tight smile on her face and nodding abruptly as everyone said, 'Thank you'. He watched them snatch the bags hungrily and rummage, taking things out and putting them on their desks as if it was Christmas and they were opening Santa sacks. A baseball cap, a mug and lots of smaller things he couldn't see well enough to identify. The colourful balloons bobbed on the walls. They were enjoying themselves. He turned away and sat down again on the hard chair in front of Mr Grey's desk and put his head in his hands and tried to think about 'what he had just done'. He was as eager to know the reason for his behaviour as Mr Grey, but he had absolutely no idea. He felt confused, lonely and afraid.

I should apologize, Mika thought. Say that I'm really sorry and make up some excuse for what I've done. Make it all better so I can go back to class and be 'normal'.

But he didn't feel normal, so how could he act normal? How could he take a goody bag from a Telly Head and laugh and smile like everyone else? And the mayhem in his head had been getting worse since he left the classroom, not better. While Mr Grey was yelling at him, at the back of his mind was a whisper: 'They're trying to poison you, they're telling you lies. It's all lies. Don't believe them.'

Ellie's voice, he wondered. He'd thought he'd heard her speak to him many times since she'd disappeared. *Someone* was talking to him . . .

He rocked on the seat holding his head and the Telly Heads swarmed around him like umbra ghosts, knives raised, ready to chop him up and serve him as canapés.

I want Helen, Mika thought desperately. She'll make me feel better.

The office door hummed, startling him. He watched it slide open and Mr Grey and Mrs Fowler walked in. Mrs Fowler had taken the streamers off her cardigan. She looked anxious and hovered uncomfortably to the side of Mr Grey's desk. Mika sensed she felt uneasy about the way he was being treated, but he also knew she wouldn't do anything about it. Mr Grey was the boss.

Mr Grey looked smug now he was clean. He was holding his tablet in one hand and an object Mika recognized in the other – the detention collar. The last time Mika had seen the detention collar was on the neck of a boy called Detroit Pippin who'd tried to burn down the school when he was seven. The fire didn't take because the school was too damp, but by the time Detroit Pippin was eight, he was living in a prison complex off the north coast of Ireland.

'Your parents will be here soon,' Mr Grey said, placing the detention collar gently on his desk so the weight didn't dent it. 'We're going to have a nice little chat.'

Mika groaned inside. He was beginning to realize throwing Fit Mix in Mr Grey's face was a far worse crime than trying to burn down the school.

'Right!' Mr Grey continued in a businesslike manner, standing with his back straight and his feet together. 'Punishments!'

He delivered them as if he was reading a shopping list. 'A seven-day exclusion starting tomorrow,' he said, looking up briefly from his tablet to gauge Mika's reaction. Mika stared ahead and refused to give him one. 'The detention collar to make sure you don't go anywhere or have any fun during your exclusion; the sorting beads, ten thousand, six colours; and last but not least the *hundred-credit fine*. I'm sure your parents will be absolutely delighted.'

Mika glared at the detention collar and bit his tongue. He didn't care about the exclusion, the collar and the stupid sorting beads, but he did care about the hundred-credit fine – *he* deserved punishment but his *parents* didn't. It wasn't fair.

The collar was made of two pieces of hinged metal. Mika felt his body compress as its weight was fixed to his neck. Mr Grey turned the screws with alarming enthusiasm until Mika was fighting for breath and could feel his head swelling up like a tomato. He wondered whether he should say something, but remembered the fate of Detroit Pippin and stopped himself.

'I don't think he can breathe,' Mrs Fowler said, watching

nervously and biting her thumbnail.

'Really?' Mr Grey said, looking at Mika's face with a furrowed brow as if he hadn't noticed his eyes were popping out of his head.

'He does look a bit red in the face,' she added.

Mr Grey reluctantly loosened the collar.

It pressed into the skin on Mika's neck and cut into his shoulders. Mr Grey explained that the collar would give him an electric shock if he tried to leave his apartment.

'One foot outside your fold-down and you'll get a shock powerful enough to make you wee your pants,' he said, with a nasty smile. Then he went to one of his cupboards and took out a large container of sorting beads and dumped them in Mika's lap.

'Those should keep you busy,' he said.

Mika looked at the container blankly. The beads were so small they could only be picked up with a pair of tweezers, and Mika would have to separate the six colours into six smaller containers before he went back to school.

'Do you have anything to say?' Mr Grey asked, with an eyebrow raised.

Mika shook his head. Any thoughts about apologizing had vaporized.

'Fine,' Mr Grey said. 'Save it for your parents, eh? Right. I've got more important things to do. I'll see you in a week's time when you come to my office to tell me how sorry you are and drink the Fit Mix.'

Mika gritted his teeth.

You'll be lucky, he thought.

* * *

The Headmaster talked to Mika's parents in the hallway outside his office, and Mika sat waiting for them to finish, chewing his nails and imagining all the terrible things Mr Grey was saying about him. Mr Grey looked pleased when he re-entered the office, and Asha and David were speechless with anger; Asha's eyes were so hard and glittery, Mika couldn't look at her, and his father's face was pale and taut and his hands were clenched in bloodless fists. They turned and walked out of the office without saying a word, and Mika rose and followed, clutching the container of sorting beads, his heart feeling like a punchbag that was about to get a good pummelling.

He followed them out of the school gates feeling as dark as the clouds overhead. The walkway was dreary and deserted because everyone was at work or school and the wind blew gusts of drizzle in his face. His parents were still wearing their work uniforms, and Mika suddenly realized how much trouble they would be in for having to leave early. He watched their backs as they walked ahead of him, aware that he was in the eye of a storm and worse was yet to come. He listened to the roar of trains and hover cars on the traffic trunk into Oxford Central, the whine of the rich people's pods on the air roads above the clouds and the hollow clang of metal on metal in the Fab Food Factory and felt a wave of despair.

How, he thought, had the world become so horrible?

He looked around and all he could see were rain clouds, floodwater and concrete created by human beings. Even the plague had been a human invention; the animals had caught it from a mouse who'd escaped from a research laboratory, yet everyone blamed the animals. And because of the plague, humans had poisoned all the trees and plants so the animals didn't have anywhere to live or food to eat. Everything beautiful in the world had been killed. How had they ended up living like *this*? He yearned for what he had never seen. He ached for the grass he had never felt beneath his feet and the flowers he had never smelled. And he was angry that the world he had been born into was ruined. How could people have let this happen? It didn't make sense. His world didn't make sense and *he* didn't make sense. He felt as if he was staggering around with his arms outstretched and a blindfold on, trying to solve an impossible puzzle. But how could he, a twelve-year-old boy, find out anything? He wasn't even allowed to make the decision not to drink some stupid vitamins. And everyone laughed at me, he thought. They think I'm a freak. Even Kobi drank it.

They entered their fold-down apartment in silence. It was gloomy and cold, but Mika's parents didn't put the light on, they stopped by the sofa and turned to face him.

'Well?' Asha said, her face dark.

'I couldn't help it,' Mika muttered, feeling more afraid now than he was of Mr Grey.

'What do you mean you "couldn't help it"?' David asked, coldly. 'You couldn't help what?'

'Not wanting to drink the Fit Mix,' Mika muttered, shifting uncomfortably.

'So you decided to chuck it in the Headmaster's face?' Asha said. 'What a brilliant idea! Why didn't you kick him in the shins while you were at it!'

'What are you trying to do, Mika?' David said, rubbing his thinning hair with exasperation. 'Make us homeless? We can't afford to pay a hundred-credit fine! We haven't even finished paying your hospital bill yet!'

'I know, I'm sorry,' Mika said, earnestly. 'But Mr Grey was trying to force me to drink that stuff.'

'It was a party for *odd's sake*!' David shouted, unleashing his temper and beginning to frogmarch around the sofa. 'Do you think they were trying to poison you?'

'I don't know,' Mika said quietly. 'I got this bad feeling.'

'Oh Mika,' Asha said, feeling a surge of desperate sadness because he seemed so lost. 'Why would they poison you? You are the first children born for thirty years! They are trying to help you grow strong! The Fit Mix is extra *vitamins* and *nutrients* because all you eat is Fab food!'

Mika watched his father lean with both hands on the back of the sofa and for a moment he looked broken and Mika thought he was going to cry.

'Do you know what Fab food is?' Asha continued.

Mika shook his head.

'Mould!' she said, her eyes shining with tears. 'White fungus grown on walls in the Fab Food Factories! They scrape it off and mix it with colour and flavourings so it looks like food, but it isn't food! We only eat it because we have no choice! All it does is keep us alive! You should be *grateful* for the Fit Mix!'

His father seemed to pull himself together and stood up again.

'You've got to drink it,' he said, authoritatively. 'When you go back to school you're going to drink it.'

'I don't want to,' Mika pleaded.

'Well, I don't want to drive a stinking train every day!' David roared. 'Do you think I enjoy going to work? Every day I sit in a train and drive from Oxford to Glasgow forty-eight times! In fact I don't even *drive* the train! A *computer* does that! I just sit looking at a computer screen listening for warning beeps! Do you think that's fun? NO! I'm so bored I want to pull my hairs out one by one just so I can count them!'

David thumped the back of the sofa. Mika jumped with shock and so did the sorting beads in the container he was holding. He'd never seen his father do that before.

'Look at me!' David gestured to his blue train driver uniform with its tacky gold buttons and lapels, then glared at Mika. 'Look at your mother! How do you think she feels going to work dressed like *that* every day?'

Asha was wearing a cowgirl costume – a black and white cowskin-patterned Stetson hat with a white pearl-buttoned shirt, chaps and spurs. She worked as a waitress in a themed rich people's real food restaurant in Oxford. Every day when she left work, her bag was searched to make sure she hadn't stolen any half-chewed lumps of tank meat from the plates she scraped. Mika looked at her. He'd seen her dressed that way every day for the past seven years, so he was used to it, but for the first time he realized how ridiculous she looked – how incongruous the outfit appeared combined with her fine features and long hair.

'Sometimes you just have to do stuff whether you like it or not!' David shouted.

'NO!' Mika yelled and he ran into the bedroom and threw himself down on Ellie's bed. 'I'M NOT DRINKING IT!'

'Then you can stay in that bed until you CHANGE YOUR MIND!' David roared, yanking the door across.

'GOOD!' Mika yelled. 'I WILL!'

* * *

Mika stayed in Ellie's bed for the rest of the day, dozing on and off and staring at the low white ceiling of the bunk. The ceiling was usually decorated with holopics – most of Ellie that Mika had stuck up, grinning through her long dark hair or pulling stupid faces. The rest were pictures of animals Ellie had put up before she'd disappeared. Asha hated them. She couldn't understand why her children wanted to look at the reason their lives were so awful: otters playing in a river, a herd of zebra on an African plain and a pair of lovebirds sitting together in a tree, their emerald green breasts touching. Mika loved the pictures, but now he felt so upset, he couldn't bear to look at them. He took them down and held them in his hand under the cover, while his parents argued in whispers in the next room.

Later, he listened to them pull down their bed and settle for the night. He put Ellie's pictures under his pillow and turned on to his side hoping for sleep so he could escape his fractious thoughts. It was hard to get comfortable with the metal collar pressing into his neck. He drifted into sleep like a stone skimming over an endless stretch of ice, his eyes jerking open now and then as if he'd hit a tree or a rock. After a while his eyelids felt too heavy to lift, and in those brief moments of near-consciousness, he kept them closed and coaxed himself back into oblivion. He didn't know how long he'd lain in that state when he felt something cold and wet pressed against his left eye. He forced open his lids and started, pulling his head back on the pillow.

Close to his face was another face, with a wet black nose

shaped like a soft liquorice sweet. Two dark soulful eyes gazed into his and a pair of soft ears pulled back as he did, displaying the creature's alarm at his sudden movement. It was some kind of dog, Mika thought, but he wasn't sure; he'd never seen a real one, only plague dogs on television with their eyes full of blood, and this dog was particularly odd-looking – a big skinny dog, that looked more like a deer than a dog, and it seemed more afraid of Mika than Mika was afraid of it.

'Hello,' Mika whispered tentatively, trying to sound friendly because he didn't want to be bitten, and the dog responded by jutting its head forward to poke him in the eye again with its wet nose, then it slobbered all over his cheek with a smelly pink tongue. Mika could hear the dog's tail patting against the cover, and its breath was hot and excited. Reassured it didn't want to bite him, Mika pushed the dog gently on the side of its neck to stop it licking his face so he could get a better look at it. It was very heavy and felt warm and it was the colour of custard cream biscuits. Its nose, legs and tail were long and elegant, its fur short and silky; the softest thing Mika had ever felt. He ran his hand over the dog's head and down its neck, admiring the darkness of its eyes and nose, contrasting with its soft, creamy fur. He could feel the muscles beneath its skin, its warmth. Its expression was gentle and kind.

'You're beautiful,' he said. 'Why are you here?'

The dog sat down and gazed at him benevolently.

'What?' Mika asked.

The dog lifted one of its long front legs and pawed the cover, its claws pressing on Mika's arm beneath it. Mika heard a clink at its neck and saw the dog was wearing a collar with a round, metal tag. He pulled himself up in the bed and held the tag in his fingers, trying to read the inscription in the darkness.

'Awen,' he said and the dog's ears pricked up as he recognized his name. 'Awen, is that your name? Are you Awen?'

Awen panted cheerfully, his pink tongue hanging out of the side of his mouth.

'Hello, Awen, nice to meet you,' he said, stroking the dog's silky ears and filling up with wonder as he discovered the magic of boy and dog. He couldn't stop touching him – the feel of his silky fur and muscled body was addictive.

He likes me, Mika thought, and I like him.

The dog licked the fingers on his left hand, long slow licks like smelly caresses, and Mika felt his fingers tingle pleasurably. The more Awen licked, the more they tingled until Mika felt a strange sensation in his fingertips, as if something was pushing up out of them from beneath his skin. It didn't hurt, it felt nice. He lifted his hand to stop Awen licking, and looked at his fingers and watched as tips of green pushed through the skin. There was no blood, no pain, it tickled. He had stems growing out of his fingers, unfurling bright green leaves. When they were the same length as his fingers, they stopped growing, and Mika got out of bed and walked to the window so he could look at his hand in the moonlight – unaware that his parents were standing in the doorway watching him. They'd heard him talking to Awen.

'What's he doing?' Asha whispered, clutching David's arm, as she watched Mika stare at his raised left hand. The collar on his neck glinted and his eyes shone in the milky light.

'He's just sleepwalking,' David replied. 'He doesn't look upset, we should leave him. He'll find his way back to bed in a minute.'

They tiptoed away to their own bed and sat propped up against their pillows whispering in the darkness.

'I wish I could get inside his head,' Asha whispered. 'I want to share his thoughts so I can understand what's going on with him. I feel guilty, David. I wish we'd been more patient.'

David sighed. 'Yeah,' he said. 'So do I.'

'We should have talked to him and tried to understand why he did it.'

'I know, but that fine – I was fuming.'

'The thing is, I know he can't help it,' Asha went on. 'I can see it in his eyes. He's so unhappy and confused. He really believes Ellie's not dead and that they're trying to poison him. But why?'

'I think we should ask Helen to visit him tomorrow,' David said. 'While we're at work, so they can be on their own. Let's see what she thinks. Perhaps he'll talk to her.'

'Good idea,' Asha said.

'Has he gone back to bed?'

'I think so,' David replied.

'Good,' Asha said. 'It creeps me when he wanders around like that.'

7

A DEADLY WEAPON

The space station, the Queen of the North, was the headquarters of the Youth Development Foundation and Mal Gorman's pride and joy. It carried several megatons of people and hardware involved in his new project in orbit around Earth, but although it was large enough to see from the ground, it looked no more than a hole cut out of the stars; an eyeless, silent hulk, her rumbling engines struck dumb by the nature of space.

On board it was past midnight London time and Mal Gorman was still working. In front of the desk in his enormous office, the catering department had laid out a buffet table for his visitors, a group of high-ranking politicians and military personnel, including the Defence Secretary and the Education Minister, who had come to celebrate the launch of the Fit for Life project on Earth. Gorman, as Minister for Youth Development, had spent the evening being told how clever he was, but now he was bored and his guests didn't seem to want to go to bed, and he, being the host, had no choice but to wait up with them. He didn't like people eating in his office and he watched irritably as they stuffed themselves from platters piled high with tank meat and plastic flowers, cheese sculptures, crudités, dips, tarts and wine and droned on about how important they were, whilst dropping pastry crumbs on the floor and discarding their plates of leftovers on his desk.

Eventually Gorman decided he'd had enough of it and called over his butler, Ralph.

'Get the waiters to clear the table,' he said.

'But, sir,' Ralph replied, 'your guests haven't finished eating. I was just about to send for dessert.'

'They're not going to starve to death between now and breakfast,' Gorman snarled, watching the Defence Secretary walk away from the table with a whole platter of canapés. He was one of the youngest and still had a little bit of flesh on his bones.

'Bring coffee,' Gorman said. 'No, scrub that, bring water. Perhaps when they realize the feed is over they'll go to bed. I've got a busy day tomorrow and I want my office back, spotless.'

'Yes, sir.'

After his guests had departed, having said goodbye with tight-lipped smiles, Gorman decided to walk to his rooms via the cargo bay. All the equipment for the Fit For Life project was packed and waiting to be taken down to Earth. The cargo bay was dimly lit and silent, a cavernous hole in the belly of the ship. Gorman's footsteps echoed on the hard black floor. He nodded towards the guards in the office and they waved and took their feet down from their desk and turned off the telly so they looked as if they were working.

The equipment filled the whole cargo bay and was stacked in neat rows on metal pallets ready to be loaded into the freighter bound for Earth the next morning. Every box had the Youth Development Foundation logo, YDF, printed on all sides. The bigger boxes contained uniforms for the project staff. Their type and size were also printed on the box: uniforms for doctors, nurses, security guards – loads of jobs had been generated by the project, and even the people cleaning the toilets had a uniform with YDF printed on the pocket. For weeks the space station had been packed with people under Mal Gorman's watchful eye, training for their new jobs.

The smaller boxes had 'Fit Mix' printed on the side of them and each contained ten thousand small sachets of powder.

Gorman patted them with a bony hand and smiled.

'Mr Gorman, sir?'

Gorman turned to see a man standing behind him.

'What do you want?' he snapped. 'I can't get away from you for a minute.'

'It's Ellie,' the man replied, nervously. 'The lab staff sent me down to find you. She's doing something interesting and they thought you'd want to see.'

They walked quickly towards the maximum-security area along a stark, white maze of corridors. Every twenty-five metres they passed through a door guarded by a security borg who scanned their retinas before letting them pass. Eventually, they entered a room marked 'Opus Three'. It was an observation room, small and dark, lined with desks and equipment and monitor screens. A researcher in a white coat sat in front of a window, which looked out into another room lit by dark red light, where Ellie lay sleeping. The room was empty apart from a bed hollow moulded into the wall. Ellie was curled up on her side with her back to them and a white sheet wrapped around her like a shroud. The top of her head was bound up with tight bandages to prevent her from opening her eyes. It was six weeks since they'd recaptured her, and she'd been kept blind ever since. Gorman wanted to punish her for what she had done to him and, although he didn't admit it to his staff, he was also scared of her. Everyone was scared of her. They knew now that with her eyes uncovered she was a deadly weapon.

'She's asleep,' Gorman observed, impatiently. 'What's there to see?'

'Look above her head,' the researcher said.

Gorman leaned on the desk and stared into the dimly lit room. He could see something moving in the air above Ellie's head, but until his eyes adjusted to the darkness, he couldn't make out what it was.

'Is that a sock shoe?' he asked.

'Yes,' the researcher said, smiling. 'And the other one's on the ceiling, look.'

Gorman looked up to see Ellie's shoe bobbing across the ceiling as if it was on the surface of the sea. 'How's she doing it in her sleep?' he mused.

'She's dreaming at the moment,' the researcher said, pointing at a screen. 'Look at her brain activity.'

'That's interesting,' Gorman said, thoughtfully. He looked at Ellie as if she was a box of chocolates he wasn't allowed to eat. 'I want to know why,' he continued. 'I want to know more. I wish I could trust her; what an utter pain she is.'

'She's promised not to use her eyes like that again,' the researcher pointed out. 'She said when she hurt you it was an accident and she didn't realize what she was doing.'

'I know,' Gorman replied, impatiently. 'But do you trust her? Do you want to be the one to take the bandages off?'

The researcher looked uncomfortable for a moment, then shook his head.

'Let's try threatening her again,' Gorman continued, thoughtfully. 'Tell her we'll kill her family and the monkey. I want to get on with the experiments. I want to know everything about her. Get a security borg to take the bandages off in the morning. When you're sure she's safe around people give her something to do, let her go swimming, she'll like that, and give her a book to read. I've got a book of poems she might enjoy, send someone to my rooms to collect it. Tell her if she's good I'll let her see Puck. Tell her if she's bad I'll kill everyone she knows. And make sure she has an armed guard at all times.'

'Yes, sir.'

'Right, I'm off to bed.'

8
COMING SOON TO AN ARCADE NEAR YOU

Mika was awoken by a bright flash like a bolt of lightning through his eyelids. He was alarmed for a moment, then realized it was the television blinking on at the end of his bed. The light seemed unusually bright as though overnight the veil that had darkened his world for weeks had been lifted. He didn't know that a thousand miles away, Ellie had awoken to find her eyes were uncovered; for Mika it was just another unanswered question to add to a growing pile.

The familiar drone of news voices began, the rush of water – his father in the shower – the metallic yawn of his parents' bed folding up into the wall and the soft sound of his mother's slippers padding on the carpet. Everything sounded normal, but it wasn't. Mika put his hand to his throat and felt the metal collar. No, nothing was normal, he was going to spend the day at home doing the sorting beads and feeling tormented by guilt because he had caused so much trouble for his parents.

'Morning, Mika,' his mother said gently, putting clothes on the end of his bed.

'Morning,' he mumbled warily. His parents had gone to bed angry and he wondered what had changed. He'd thought it would take more than a night's sleep to undo the damage he'd done.

'What do you want for breakfast?' Asha asked.

'I'll do it,' Mika replied, swinging his legs out of bed. 'You've got to go to work; I'm going to be at home all day.'

'I've called Helen,' Asha said, looking at him nervously. 'I asked her to come round – we thought you might like to talk to her.'

'Oh, OK,' Mika said. 'I do, thanks.'

He stepped into the shower, closed the door and turned on the water, leaning against the thin wall. He kept his head up while he washed, because when he bent forward the weight of the detention collar gave him a pain in the back of his neck.

He felt guilty. His parents being nice to him after what he'd done was more difficult to handle than the yelling. He felt he deserved to be yelled at, but he still didn't want to drink the Fit Mix.

He turned the water pressure up so it was blasting his skin and scrubbed himself hard. He wanted to wash them away – Telly Heads, Mr Grey and fellow classmates all down the plughole never to be seen again. As he rinsed his hair he heard a strange voice in the apartment. He opened his eyes and listened, wondering who it could be. He heard the beep of the front door as it slid shut and locked. The person had come in.

'Mika!' His father knocked on the shower door. 'There's a friend of yours out here! You'd better hurry up because he's on his way to school!'

Mika turned off the water.

A friend? He didn't have any friends.

He rubbed himself down as quickly as he could and emerged from the shower half dry with his towel wrapped around him, anxious to see who the 'friend' was.

It was Kobi Nenko, the new boy, and he was soaking wet, wetter than Mika who'd just had a shower, his tangle of black hair dripping on the carpet and his feet squelching in his holey sneakers. He was wearing a long black coat with a spaghetti tangle of wires hanging out of the pockets.

'Hi,' Kobi said, through his hair.

There was a moment of awkward silence.

'Do you boys want a drink?' Asha asked brightly, sensing the tension. She wasn't quite sure what she thought of Kobi with his strange clothes and wires and hair, but she wanted Mika to have friends.

He's got nice hands, she thought, looking at them, long fingers, artistic, nimble, but dirty. His fingernails were filthy.

'No, thank you,' Kobi replied, politely. 'I can't stay.'

'Mrs Fowler asked me to bring you this,' he said to Mika, holding out a blue bag with the letters YDF written on the side. 'It's your goodie bag from yesterday. She said there are things in there you need, including Fit Mix, one sachet for every day you're off school . . . sorry.'

'Oh great,' Mika said sullenly, taking the bag.

'Mika,' David snapped. 'That's not very grateful of you. Your friend has come out of his way to bring you that bag.'

'I didn't want to bring it,' Kobi muttered through his hair. 'I know you don't want it.'

'It's all right,' Mika said. 'Thanks.'

'I've got to go,' Kobi said. 'I'll be late.'

He left quickly, propelled out of the apartment by the awkward atmosphere.

'He's an . . . interesting boy,' Asha said, her eyes fixed curiously on the closed door. 'You haven't mentioned him before.'

'He's new,' Mika said, looking at the bag and wishing he'd been friendlier. 'He comes from The Shadows. I haven't spoken to him much.'

* * *

After his parents left for work, Mika sat on the floor with the containers of sorting beads lined up on the sofa cushions. Everything about the task was designed to be odious and frustrating – the beads were so small, the level in the big container never seemed to go down. They were a nightmare to pick up because their surfaces were smooth, so if Mika held them too tight with the tweezers they popped out of its grip and he lost half of them before he got them to the right colour pot. Some went down the side of the sofa and some landed on the carpet so he had to hunt for them on his hands and knees, rubbing the carpet to make them bounce out of their hiding places in the tuft. He'd been told if he lost even one, he would have to do the task all over again. Sometimes he dropped them in the wrong pot by mistake so he had to hunt for one red bead amongst a few hundred yellow beads or one white bead in a few hundred blues. But despite Mr Grey's intention to torture Mika with the beads, he found the repetitive nature of the task soothing – he liked the quiet 'tap' as he dropped a bead into its right pot and he enjoyed the tidiness he was creating as he worked, because he had no chance of achieving the same result with the thoughts in his head – his thoughts were like the tangled mess of wires hanging out of Kobi Nenko's pockets.

Mika couldn't wait for Helen to arrive. He glanced at the clock every minute, and when he heard the door buzz he jumped up, nearly knocking over the container of unsorted beads and only just managing to rescue it before it landed on the carpet.

He opened the door, and felt happier the moment he saw her – she was wearing a plastic rain bonnet that came down to her eyebrows, an antique pair of yellow rubber boots and a green coat that looked like an old-fashioned camping tent. She could have gone away for the weekend and accommodated several friends.

She rooted around in her handbag and produced a packet of biscuits. Mika was relieved to see it was a fresh packet.

'I brought the biscuits,' she rasped, tottering past him. 'Squashed fly biscuits, my mother used to call them. That lift smells like an old man's toilet. Put the kettle on.' She stopped suddenly and turned. 'Oh my goblin lord! What is that contraption on your neck?'

'A detention collar,' Mika said, grinning. 'The headmaster fitted it yesterday. If I step out of the apartment it gives me an electric shock strong enough to make me wee myself.'

'I'd like to give him an electric shock!' Helen said, her eyes flashing angrily under her rain bonnet. 'See how he likes it!'

She cursed the weather as she slowly peeled off her layers of tent, boots and rain bonnet. Mika removed the containers of sorting beads from the sofa so she could sit down, and put the kettle on.

'What have you been up to then?' she asked, settling on the sofa and wiggling her toes in her woolly socks. 'It sounds like you've been busy.'

'I think I'm mad,' Mika blurted out anxiously, beginning to pace back and forth. 'You've got to help me. Everyone thinks I'm mad, even my parents, and I don't know what to do about it.'

'Stop pacing,' Helen said, waving her hand. 'You're making me feel giddy. Sit down for a minute.'

Mika sat down reluctantly with his knees jiggling.

'For a start,' she said, authoritatively, 'if you think you're mad, you're not. It's a fact that mad people don't know they're mad. I worked with a boy once who thought he was an orange and there was no convincing him otherwise.'

Mika tried to laugh, but it caught in his throat and threatened to transform into tears as a mix of suppressed emotions welled up inside him.

'But I don't understand what's happening in my head,' he said despairingly. 'This woman came to school and I thought she was a Telly Head! I thought she was trying to poison me with a vitamin drink, and look at the trouble I'm in because of it! Even though I knew I was behaving crazy, I couldn't stop myself! My parents have got to pay a hundred-credit fine because of me and today they're not even angry; it's as if they pity me because I'm mad, and at school they're calling me a paranoid freak! Last night in my dream I had trees growing out of my fingers!'

'Slow down and tell me properly,' Helen suggested. 'Make the tea and start at the beginning.'

Mika got up and made tea and she questioned him about everything in detail, about the strange party, the cakes with the YDF logo written on them, the Fit Mix, the Fit For Life nurse, the dream dog, the tree fingers, everything, and he began to feel better. Helen had this magical ability to make even the most terrible incidents seem funny. When he told her about throwing the cup of Fit Mix in Mr Grey's face, she laughed until she wheezed so much she could hardly breathe and had a coughing fit, and Mika was worried for a moment because she looked as if she was going to fall off the sofa. But afterwards she became quiet and serious and looked thoughtfully at the heavy metal collar around Mika's neck.

'What?' Mika said.

'Shhh, I'm thinking,' she replied.

He stared at her, waiting for her to say something, but instead she sighed and Mika could sense she was troubled.

'You agree with me, don't you?' he said, feeling confused. 'I know you do. It's more than just seeing a demon from my nightmares. I feel suspicious, lied to, not just in school, but everywhere, and it's not only Ellie, I'm being lied to about other things too, I can feel it. I know something. In the back of my mind I know something important, but I feel like I'm looking at one of those puzzle pictures – the ones you have to stare at and the picture appears, but I stare and stare and I can't see the picture. I'm sure someone's trying to tell me something.'

Helen gazed into her teacup, her eyes misty, as if she could see distant galaxies in the bottom of it.

'I think we should look in your goodie bag,' she said. 'Let's see what these people gave you.'

'Nothing I want,' Mika grumbled impatiently. He grabbed the blue bag, turned it upside down and shook it. A pile of stuff fell on to the floor. Seven sachets of Fit Mix, a mug with 'Drink Your Fit Mix' written on the side, a white baseball cap with 'Fit Camp is Fun' written across the front, a T-shirt, shorts, a few packets of sweets, a balloon and a memory card titled 'Introduction to Fit For Life!'

'Looks like they've put a lot of effort into this,' Helen said, picking up the baseball cap and putting it on her head. 'What do you think?' Her long, grey hair hung out of the sides like droopy spaniel ears.

'I prefer your rain bonnet,' Mika said, grinning. He left her inspecting the mug and took a sachet of Fit Mix to the kitchen area. He ripped it open and shook the powder into the sink, hoping some miracle would occur, that suddenly he would know the answers to all his questions. But all that happened was the white powder turned pink and slimy and smelled of strawberry as it made contact with droplets of water in the bottom of the sink. He turned on the tap and washed it away with disgust.

No clues there, he thought, throwing the empty sachet down the waste chute.

'Let's watch this,' Helen said, holding up the memory card.

The television screen covered the wall opposite the sofa. Mika slid the card into the slot underneath it and sat down next to Helen. The screen lit up and filled with the image of a large group of children drinking Fit Mix as if it was so delicious they were about to faint with joy.

'This is cheesier than a toothpaste advert,' Helen said, as a skinny girl with goofy ears drank a cup of Fit Mix. A few seconds later she was skipping through a field full of flowers with the wind blowing in her hair, having grown at least thirty centimetres and become twice as pretty.

'It is stupid,' Mika agreed, watching a boy with bulging muscles stride up a mountain.

'But you won't just grow big and strong,' a resonant voice boomed from the screen. 'Fit For Life will make you more intelligent. We've developed a brand new game called 'Pod Fighter' designed to develop your fine motor and lateral thinking skills. Fit For Life is fun, Fit For Life is cool and Fit For Life will make all your dreams come true.'

'Well, it certainly made your dreams come true, Mika,' Helen muttered, thinking of the Telly Head nurse.

The screen became dark and was silent for a few seconds, then it filled with stars so Mika and Helen felt as if they were floating in space.

'This must be the advert for the game,' Mika said.

'Coming soon to an arcade near you,' boomed the deep voice. 'The *ultimate* game experience. A new game that feels so real, you'll forget it is a game. *You* will be in control. *You* will use your skills to protect *your* world against the Red Star Fleet!'

'Play POD FIGHTER if you dare.'

The word 'PLAY' appeared against a backdrop of fluffy, white clouds. It flashed on and off for a few seconds and then it was replaced by the words 'POD FIGHTER', which hurtled through space so fast, all the stars became trails of blurred light.

Then a fleet of real Pod Fighters appeared, crouching like a row of sleek, black panthers on the deck of a battleship. They glinted in the sunshine, their elegant curves menacing and powerful.

A group of children ran towards them and the curved glass windshields slid back. Two children climbed into each fighter, one in the front, one in the back, wriggling down into the low black seats that wrapped around their bodies. They looked happy and purposeful, ramming their black headsets on and adjusting the straps on their harnesses with focused ease. The windshields slid over their heads to cover them, and moments later, the collective roar of engines filled the apartment. The Pod Fighters rose from the deck vertically, in perfect synchronization, to hover over the ship. Then, one by one, from left to right, they tilted their noses towards the sky and shot up so fast they seemed to vanish.

Mika suddenly felt strange – dizzy as if he'd just stood up too quickly. He closed his eyes and found himself climbing into the pilot seat in one of the Pod Fighters. He could feel the sensation of the seat beneath him, curving around the sides of his body – he knew its smell, the feel of the headset over his face – even the brightly lit control panels were familiar.

'You OK?' He opened his eyes to find Helen looking at him curiously. The advert had finished.

'Yeah, fine,' he said. 'So what do you think?'

She was quiet for a moment and she looked as if she was trying to decide whether or not to say something.

'What?' Mika asked, hoping to nudge a reply out of her.

'You mustn't tell anyone how you feel,' she replied darkly, 'not even your parents. They mustn't know. You've got to say you're sorry and that you made a mistake.'

'Why?' Mika asked, feeling angered and scared by her sudden change of mood. 'You *do* agree with me, I know you do, you know there's something weird going on, you just won't admit it! What am I supposed to do about the Fit Mix? I've got to go back to school next week and apologize to Mr Grey and drink it and I don't want to!'

'You must,' she said, severely. 'You don't have a choice, Mika. Just imagine what will happen if you don't. Think about what it will do to you and your parents.'

She looked at him with raised eyebrows and two images flashed into his mind, the first was of his family moving to The Shadows because they were too poor to stay in Barford North, the second was of Detroit Pippin in a prison cell. He shuddered.

'Besides,' Helen continued, looking away from him and gazing out of the window as a bank of iron-grey rain clouds rolled over the apartment block. 'I get the feeling that if you play this game you'll be glad you did.'

'Why?'

'Perhaps you'll find the answers to some of your questions.'

She still wouldn't look at him, and he studied her eyes as she gazed at the clouds. They seemed to be straining, as if they were holding in a secret that wanted to pop out, and she had to look away from him to stop it happening. He realized something. How could he have been so stupid? Helen was the only person who believed him when he said Ellie was alive, so she must have an idea where Ellie could be!

'What do you know, Helen?' he asked. 'Look at me.'

'Goodness,' she said, as if he'd snapped her out of a daydream. She glanced at her wrist, even though she wasn't wearing a watch. 'I ought to get off. I need to pick up some pasta on the way home, or was it nail polish? I can't remember. Still, if I get both I can't go wrong then, can I?'

She began to stand up, very creakily, as if her joints had gone rusty while she was sitting down. Mika jumped up and blocked the path to the door.

'You can't go yet,' he said, as she squashed her rain bonnet on to her head. 'You've got to tell me what you know.'

'Let me concentrate for a moment or I'll put my wellies on the wrong feet,' she grumbled, buying some time. Mika was watching her with a feverishness she'd seen before, in the eyes of lovers and drug addicts, and for a moment she felt terribly guilty and wished she'd lied to him and told him that he was mad, or that he'd gone to another counsellor, one who didn't know what she did, one who'd have convinced him that Ellie was dead. She felt as if she was pointing him towards the cave of a bone-crunching giant.

But, she thought, he was already heading in that direction anyway. At least now he'll trust his instincts and he'll get something out of it. Perhaps he will find her, he's bright and determined enough.

'You should trust your instincts,' she said. 'You're a very special boy. Trust your instincts, play the game, and be careful.'

'What do you know? Please!' he pleaded, as she shuffled towards the door. 'You can't go without telling me!'

She pressed the icon by the door and it slid open.

'That's it! I'm coming with you!' Mika said, looking around

for his sneakers. 'You're going to tell me even if I have to follow you all around the supermarket.'

'You can't,' Helen said, pointing at the detention collar around his neck. 'You'll get an electric shock and you'll pee your pants.'

'Frag!' Mika said, putting his hand to the collar. 'Wait!'

'Take care,' she said, shuffling out of the door.

The door began to slide shut, and Mika's heart sank.

'Please!' he cried. 'You've got to help me! You promised you would, remember? When we first met, you promised!'

She paused and turned and her eyes softened as she remembered that she *had* promised to help him. But she didn't know Mika then, she had met a troubled boy with black eyes, a boy grieving for his twin. But he knew things that were impossible, he had all the pieces of a very dangerous puzzle in his head, and when he figured it out he would be vulnerable. He was angry and passionate. They would kill him.

'Stop the door,' she said.

Mika thumped the lock icon with his fist and it juddered to a halt and began to open again.

'If I'm going to help you,' Helen said, wagging her finger, 'you've got to promise me you won't go charging around yelling at people.'

'I will,' he replied, desperately. 'I mean, I won't, I promise!'

'You won't tell *anyone*?'

'Not a soul,' he said.

'Not even your parents?' she went on.

'Of course not,' he said irritably. 'They don't believe a word I say anyway.'

'You've got to be careful, Mika, if these people realize you know *anything*, they will hurt you.'

'I will, I've promised!' he went on, feeling as if he was going to explode with impatience. 'I'll be good, just tell me what you know.'

She leaned forward and whispered, 'If you play the game, I

think you will find Ellie.'

'How?' he asked urgently. 'How can I find Ellie by playing a game?'

'I'm not saying any more,' said Helen, adjusting her rain bonnet. 'You've nagged too much out of me already. Just play their game and keep your mouth shut. Right. I'm off. I don't think it was nail polish or pasta I wanted, I think it was cream for my bunions.'

Mika watched her shuffle towards the lift, like a tent with yellow rubber legs, feeling waves of relief and happiness wash over him. All the nightmares, the mockery and the paranoia he had been burdened with for so long seemed to lift up and leave him and he felt as if he was floating in the doorway, despite the weight of the detention collar. Helen turned and smiled as she entered the lift and Mika smiled back, the broadest, happiest smile he had smiled for a very long time, and far above his head, Ellie smiled too without knowing the reason why.

9
OR DIE TRYING

Mika realized that Helen's advice to 'play the game' meant more than just learning Pod Fighter in the new arcade – the most important thing he had to do was keep his suspicious thoughts to himself and convince everyone he had changed his mind about the Fit Mix and was sorry. By the time his parents came home from work that day, he was a different person – he apologized for causing them so much trouble, promised to drink the Fit Mix and cooked tea and *tidied up afterwards* for the first time ever. He even tidied the floor in his bedroom.

'So how did it go with Helen?' David asked, watching in amazement as Mika dropped an armful of dirty socks and pants into the laundry bin.

'OK,' Mika replied.

'What did you talk about?' Asha asked.

'Not much,' Mika said, walking quickly towards his bedroom

to get away from their questions. 'I'd better get on with the sorting beads.'

Asha and David looked at each other and smiled and shook their heads.

'That woman deserves a medal,' David whispered.

On Monday morning when Mika returned to school after his exclusion, he drank the Fit Mix while Mr Grey glared at him with eyes like frozen pebbles. It ran down his throat slimy and cold, making him want to gag with disgust, but he knew he mustn't show how he felt. The last thing he needed was to give Mr Grey an excuse to pile on more punishments, and judging by the reluctance the Headmaster showed whilst removing the detention collar, the slightest whiff of dissent and it would be straight back on again. So Mika saved his grimace of disgust until he'd left the Headmaster's office, and then it was no more than a flicker across his face. He was playing this game to win.

'I'm going to find you, Ellie,' he whispered under his breath, 'or die trying.'

His senses were particularly keen that night as he walked to the arcade in the centre of town with Kobi. Every detail felt as sharp as the January frost. He was a week behind everyone else learning how to play Pod Fighter, and he was anxious to catch up.

'What do you think of Pod Fighter?' Mika asked.

'It's brilliantly designed,' Kobi replied, thoughtfully. 'It feels so real you really do forget it's a game, just like it says in the advert. But it's having a weird effect on everyone, half the class have bought the T-shirts already and no one talks about anything else. They're obsessed. And it's really competitive. How come you want to play all of a sudden? A week ago you didn't want anything to do with it.'

Mika shrugged and looked away. He could feel Kobi's intelligent eyes searching his face through his hair. 'Haven't got anything better to do,' he said stupidly.

'I'll help you catch up if you like,' Kobi offered. 'I'll show you everything I've learned.'

'Thanks,' Mika replied, gratefully.

Kobi took something out of his pocket and fiddled with it.

'What's that?' Mika asked.

Kobi held it up so Mika could look at it. It was a tiny giraffe, a mini borg. It blinked at Mika and moved its mouth as if it was chewing leaves. Kobi stood it up on his palm and it walked around. A gust of wind caught it and Kobi only just stopped it falling off on to the walkway. He put it carefully back into his pocket.

'That's amazing!' Mika said. 'Where did you get it?'

'I made it,' Kobi said, 'out of bits of vacuumbot.'

'That's clever—' Mika stopped suddenly, remembering. He wanted to go on, he wanted to tell Kobi how much Ellie would like it, and only just caught the words before they left his mouth. Kobi didn't know about Ellie, he'd never met her, didn't even know Mika had a twin sister, and Mika realized it was better that way. It was easier, less complicated to have a friend who didn't know. But Ellie would have liked Kobi Nenko and his giraffe and Mika felt treacherous not mentioning her.

It was a cold night and the wind was wet and cruel, but Mika noticed there were loads more people out than usual and everyone was heading towards town. Three girls ran past them, then stopped and turned, their eyes bright and their long hair whipping across their faces in the wind.

'Hey, Kobi!' one cried. 'Are you going to the arcade?'

'Yeah,' he muttered.

'Oh good! See you there!'

Mika watched the girls run on, wondering who they were. 'When did you meet them?' he asked, remembering that girls were usually scared of Kobi.

'Last week in the arcade,' Kobi said. 'If you're good at the game, people get to know you.'

'So you're good at the game?' Mika asked.

''Spose so,' Kobi said, shrugging. 'They put up the scores on a screen at the end of the night so you can see how you've done.'

'Who's the best?' Mika asked hungrily, feeling a surge of competitive lust.

'Ruben Snaith.'

At the mention of Ruben's name, Mika felt his face grow hot. 'It would be, wouldn't it,' he said, bitterly. 'Nobody would dare be better than Ruben.'

They entered the town square and Mika saw the arcade for the first time. The building used to be the Bargain Mart store, selling stuff that fell to bits within minutes for one or two credits, but it had been closed for a year. The arcade was twice as tall as the old building and bathed the whole square in pulsing blue light, and for the first time since Barford North was built, forty-three years before, it felt alive. Even the puddles and the stagnant old fountain looked beautiful, and every droplet of water on the rainy glass shop fronts glittered like a jewel. The fluorescent light, in rows of curved neon, rippled up the building to erupt in a cascade of blue at the top, and below, crowds of people were pouring through the great glass doors into the arcade. There was an air of enchantment and anticipation that was contagious, and Mika felt it as a shiver down the back of his neck, enhanced by the cold wind.

As they approached the doors, they were hit in the face by hot air, food smells, shouting and music. Mika let Kobi walk ahead and watched as he was stopped by two men wearing dark blue uniforms with the Youth Development Foundation logo, YDF, on the pockets. One of the men scanned Kobi's retinas then nodded him in. Mika followed, feeling briefly anxious as the hard light searched his eyes. Once inside, he looked around, trying to take it all in. The entrance area of the arcade was a shopping mall, with a polished white floor, open-fronted stores and fast food restaurants on either side: Tank Meat Express, The Banghra Balti, The Kosha Snack Shack and the Ra Ra Shake Bar, as well as stores selling clothes, shoes, sweets, make-up and jewellery. The place was packed and noisy, every store and restaurant playing different music, every table squirming with bodies and laughter. The Youth Development Foundation logo was written on everything: the uniforms of the staff, the backs of the chairs, even the straws in the Fabshakes, and Mika felt a wave of mistrust seeing it. It was weird watching how everyone was behaving and he felt as if he'd been away for a year, not just a week; the atmosphere was so different in this place than school, gone was the lethargy that made people drag their feet and yawn all day, replaced by an almost hysterical excitement. There had never been anything like this for them before and it seemed like a desert mirage – Mika felt as if he could close his eyes, open them again and it would all be gone and he'd be standing alone in the rainy town square. He watched kids shout to each other across the mall, a girl splutter with laughter, Fabshake dribbling down her front. He didn't like it.

'Told you they've all gone nuts,' Kobi said. 'Follow me.' He walked quickly towards a pair of huge, dark doors at the end of the mall. Above them was a screen playing the advert for Pod Fighter. They walked through the doors and paused just inside to let their eyes adjust to the darkness, and as the shadows of the Pod Fighter simulators took shape, Mika felt as if he was looking into a rock crevice full of giant spiders. The eight-legged simulators were eerie and menacing. They were set out in rows with four of their robotic legs fixed to the ceiling and four fixed to the floor, with their egg-shaped black bodies in the middle. Some of the simulators were motionless and silent and looked as if they were hiding in the darkness waiting for unlucky, human-size flies. Others were rocking and rotating, their robotic legs contracting and expanding as the people inside played the game. Mika walked slowly towards them with his heart thumping.

'Weird, aren't they?' Kobi said.

Mika nodded, but couldn't speak.

'They don't look like Pod Fighters on the outside,' Kobi went on, 'but apparently, inside they are exactly the same down to the slightest detail: the control panels, the seats, the headsets, everything – and not only that, they feel the same too, the robotic legs make them move as if you're really flying. But it's when you flip the Pod Fighter into a corkscrew spin that things get really interesting. Watch that one.' He pointed to a simulator that was moving particularly frantically. After thirty seconds an amazing thing happened: the legs detached themselves from the body, leaving it floating in mid-air, and it began to spin. At the end of the spin, the legs locked on to the body again.

'How does it float like that?' Mika asked, watching avidly.

'Magnetism, I reckon,' Kobi replied. 'Similar to that of a hover car: the magnetic force keeps a hover car off the ground by pushing a negative force against another negative force, or a positive against a positive.

'We need to go down the end.' He pointed to the red walkway, which ran down the centre of the arcade and melted into the darkness. Mika began to make out the shadowy forms of people milling around the legs of the simulators. Kobi began walking and Mika followed.

At the far end of the room there were a few motionless simulators and a large group of people standing around them. They turned and watched Mika and Kobi approach, and to his dismay, Mika saw Ruben.

'Ignore him,' Kobi murmured, walking quickly past without allowing himself to be caught by Ruben's glare. 'What a perp. Let's take this one.'

Mika cursed his bad luck. The arcade was easily big enough to avoid Ruben, yet they'd bumped right into him within minutes of arriving. Kobi pressed his ragged foot on a metal plate on the floor next to a simulator and the lower legs contracted so they could climb into the cockpit. Next he touched a dark, almost invisible icon with his pale fingers and the door slid open, but before they had time to climb in, Ruben appeared with a pair of girls behind him.

'You teaching him?' Ruben said to Kobi, jerking his head in Mika's direction.

Kobi ignored him and began climbing into the cockpit.

'Good luck,' Ruben smirked. 'You're going to need it.'

As he walked away Mika felt his chest contract with anger. The girls were laughing, mocking him.

'Get in,' Kobi said. 'Ignore them.'

'I'm trying,' Mika said, climbing into the simulator. But he wasn't doing very well – inside he was burning up with a powerful desire to squash Ruben like a fly. But suddenly, all thoughts of Ruben were extinguished and he faltered for a moment. He had this feeling they were climbing into the cockpit from the wrong angle – that they should be getting in from above, not the side.

'You get in the gunner seat,' Kobi said. 'It's best you learn that before you try to fly, it's a bit easier.'

There were two seats in the cockpit, one behind the other, and Mika climbed into the one at the back. It was higher than the front seat, so he was looking down on Kobi's mop of tangled black hair. As he settled into the seat, he felt it wrap around the sides of his body, holding him down.

'The seats feel freaky,' Kobi said.

'Yeah,' Mika lied – the seat felt comfortable and familiar to him and he was reminded of the way he had felt while he watched the advert with Helen, as if he had experienced this before – but something wasn't right. He looked around.

'Where are the control panels?' he asked. Apart from two pairs of simple hand controls, there was nothing inside the cockpit apart from the seats. Kobi touched a red circle next the door and suddenly there were hundreds of brightly lit icons covering every surface around them, each one with a different symbol.

'Put the headset on,' Kobi said, pointing behind Mika's head to where it was hanging on a hook. The headset was a black helmet with no back and a curved glass visor across the face. It was surprisingly light, the back cut away so it was comfortable to wear when his head was leaned back against the seat. As soon as he put it on, a display appeared on the transparent visor – he could see a grid of green lines surrounded by green icons and he felt a dark thrill looking from one to another. They looked alien, but familiar.

'Don't blink yet,' Kobi warned.

'Why not?' Mika asked.

'You control the icons in your visor with your eyes. It took me a whole day to figure that one out. You have to blink at them.'

'What if you blink without meaning to?' Mika asked.

'Don't,' Kobi replied. 'It's not that hard, you learn not to look at the icons unless you need them.'

'OK,' Mika said, trying not to blink. 'Where are the instructions on how to play?'

'There aren't any,' Kobi said, laughing. 'That's half the fun.'

Kobi touched an icon above his head and the windshield appeared in front of them. Mika could see they were on the battleship landing strip with the sea heaving around them.

'Ready?' Kobi said.

'Yep,' Mika replied, feeling waves of excitement as he gripped the hand controls.

A few seconds later a blistering roar ripped from the engine behind them.

'Whoah,' Mika said.

He felt a rush of air through his headset and the roar built in intensity until his teeth were rattling. They lifted off, hovered over the ship for a moment, then tilted the nose up, and with a sudden jerk, shot into the sky.

'I can feel the drag in my gut!' Mika shouted.

'I told you it feels real,' Kobi said. 'Wait until you see above the clouds – it'll blow your mind.'

There was a solid bank of grey clouds overhead, and as they shot through it they were blind for a second, but when they came out the other side, they were looking down on it and it was transformed by the sunlight into a glistening blanket of pure white snow. It was beautiful. Around them the sky was clear and blue and Kobi hung the Pod Fighter for a moment, slowly rotating, so Mika could enjoy the view. There was so much space around them, Mika felt vulnerable and a little afraid, it felt so real, he'd already forgotten he was playing a game. Kobi pulled back and they shot up again, higher and higher until the pale blue of the sky deepened into the liquid blue blackness of space and they were floating with the stars and looking down on the planet.

'Get ready,' Kobi said. 'We'll get the first assault immediately. Watch out to your left.'

Mika heard them before he saw them. He steeled himself, determined to impress Kobi with a display of natural talent. A high-pitched whine shot past his left ear. He turned to look and saw a bank of red fighters looping round to come back at them.

'What do I do?' he asked, panicking.

'Shoot them,' Kobi said. 'I'm turning.'

It happened too quickly. Mika gripped the controls of the gun and felt over the buttons under his fingers, but by the time he had managed to fire a few bolts of laser fire it was already too late. There was a bright flash, then darkness.

'What happened?' he asked.

'We got hit,' Kobi replied, taking his headset off.

A red 'Game Over' icon appeared on Mika's visor.

'Already!' Mika said. 'Dammit!'

'Don't worry,' Kobi replied, grinning to himself behind his hair. 'It happens to everyone the first thirty or so flights.'

'I want to fly,' Mika said, moodily. 'I'm not enjoying being the gunner.'

'OK,' Kobi replied, patiently. 'Let's swap places.'

They climbed out of the simulator and Kobi swung his long legs into the gunner seat. 'I'll talk you through it step by step,' he said. 'It's a lot harder, flying.'

Mika climbed into the pilot seat and as it curved around the sides of his body, he felt immediately better. He jammed on his headset, jabbed the button above him to turn the windshield view on as he had seen Kobi do, then hit another, which gave them a three-dimensional mapping system in the corner of their visors so they would be able to see everything around them, deep into space. Mika blinked at it and it enlarged to fill the screen, showing about a dozen Pod Fighters drawn in green lines of light, sitting in rows around them ready to take-off from the ship.

'How did you do that?' Kobi asked, looking with surprise at the new mapping system.

'I hit this,' Mika replied, pointing to a triangular icon.

'Cool,' Kobi said. 'That was a lucky guess.'

But it wasn't a guess, Mika thought, feeling confused. I hit it automatically as if I was flicking on the light when I enter my room.

But he didn't say anything; he sensed Kobi would think he was being arrogant if he didn't follow his instructions, despite the fact the mapping system was useful, and for the next couple of minutes he did only what he was told. As the engines began to roar and the Pod Fighter lifted from the deck of the ship he felt pure exhilaration, aware of the power he was controlling through the plethora of buttons under his fingertips and how sensitive the craft was to the slightest error.

'You control it on every plane,' Kobi said. 'So be careful as you tilt the nose, I crashed it into the ship a couple of times; it can spin out really easily. Pull back gently, keeping it level with the ship, and no power yet or you'll end up in the sea.'

Mika did as he was told, tilting the nose of the Pod Fighter towards the sky, and as he gave it the first burst of power and it shot like a bullet towards the clouds, he felt like yelling his head off.

'Careful,' Kobi warned. 'Not too much power or you'll lose control of it.'

But by this point, Mika had forgotten to listen. He decelerated for the briefest moment to appreciate the blanket of snow-white clouds glistening in the sunlight, before tilting up again, and bolting with gritted teeth through the turbulent planet atmosphere into space. The simple fact was, flying the craft made sense to him – the link between the subtle movements of his hands and those of the Pod Fighter seemed to have been made before he ever climbed in it. He didn't know that wherever Ellie was and whatever she did, a little part of him was with her. It just felt like some kind of miracle.

The crafts of the Red Star Fleet on the first level looked like pointed slivers of red glass – so shallow, they must have been crewed by aliens with bodies the width of tortilla chips. They flew in close formation, weaving through space as if they were plaiting their lines of flight together. This strange movement made them hard targets, but the newly discovered mapping system helped – the enemy appeared with lines of red mesh light all around them, and Kobi soon worked out how to control the guns so he could fire at them from every angle. He didn't say much as they fought, but Mika knew what Kobi was thinking: how had Mika just climbed into the Pod Fighter and flown it without all the crashes and messing about everyone else had experienced? But it was at the end of the first level that Mika really surprised Kobi – they had wiped out at least a dozen Red Star Fleet fighters and were feeling in control and a bit smug, when all of a sudden this new thing came at them.

'Whoah! What's that?' Kobi yelled through his headset. 'It's too fast for us!'

It was the first Dragon Fighter they had seen, a beast of a craft in flame colours, with two rows of serrated teeth painted down the sides of its nose. It was twice the size of them, twice as fast, twice as loud, and it fired balls of flame that seemed to move at the speed of shooting stars. Mika felt his backside melt into the seat as he dodged the first.

'We're going to lose it!' Kobi yelled, firing at it frantically, as if he was shooting peas at a Tyrannosaurus Rex. 'We can't fight this!'

Mika looked at the control panel in front of him, and without even thinking about it jabbed three icons in fast sequence and immediately, as if they had the force of a hurricane on their tail, the Pod Fighter leaped forward, emitting a noise so loud, it sounded as if a volcano was erupting in their heads.

'Whhooooo Hooooo!' Mika yelled, the hairs on his head standing bolt upright underneath his headset. 'Feel that!'

'Jeez Chrise!' Kobi yelled.

Within moments the Dragon Fighter was kilometres behind them, and Mika felt elated, so buzzed up he felt like dancing. He rolled the Pod Fighter into a tight corkscrew then pulled up sharply and flew a few elegant loops like a metal dolphin playing in the sea of space, then, having an idea, he banked sharply round and back the way they had come and in seconds they were behind the Dragon Fighter and hard on its tail. Kobi fired a round of well-aimed shots and it exploded like a small star, bathing their faces in light.

An icon appeared in their visors.

'Level One Completed.'

'How did you do that?' Kobi asked.

'I don't know,' Mika replied, grinning.

'Really?' Kobi said, incredulously.

'Yeah, I just . . . knew what to do.'

'You freaker,' Kobi said.

'Yep,' Mika replied, happily, and for the first time in his life he was glad he was that little bit different to everyone else, but his happiness was short-lived; before he'd even climbed out of the simulator, news of his first flight had spread throughout the arcade and his name was flashing at the top of the leader board. As he walked through the mall with Kobi, everyone stared at him. He kept his head down and walked as quickly as he could, feeling suffocated by the attention, and he wasn't able to breathe until they were out on the dark walkway alone, heading for home.

* * *

Awen, the dream dog, slept with him that night, stretched out down the side of the bed, and a couple of hours before dawn, Mika felt the fur across the dog's shoulders bristle beneath his hand. He took his hand away slowly, as Awen began to growl, a low, throaty growl, his soft black lips curling back to reveal two rows of menacing white teeth. Awen's head was right next to Mika's on the pillow and with the glistening canines only inches from his eyes, he found himself unable to move and hardly daring to breathe, praying the dream dog would disappear before he made the full transformation into a nightmare.

'What's the matter,' Mika whispered.

Awen raised his head from the pillow and looked over his shoulder, the growl intensifying, and Mika became aware he was growling at something in the room, not at him. With a mixture of relief and trepidation, he lay still as Awen got up and trod uncomfortably on his foot before jumping over him on to the floor. The dog stood by Ellie's cupboard, his ears pricked forward, the growl still rumbling in his throat and his tail rigid.

Mika quietly pulled back the covers and sat up. Awen looked at him and his tail wagged once, then he turned to the cupboard again and continued to growl.

'What is it?' Mika asked, daring to put his hand on Awen's back. 'What's wrong with you?' He didn't like the gentle dog behaving this way.

'You want me to look in the cupboard, don't you?' He looked at the door, feeling sick and frightened, trying to hear if there was movement inside above the sound of Awen's growling. 'Shhh,' he said. 'Be quiet a minute.' But Awen didn't want to be quiet, and rumbled on like the engine of an old car until Mika got up. Mika stood looking at the door wondering what to do, knowing that whatever was in the cupboard, it was likely he wouldn't want to see it. His fingers hovered trembling over the handle for thirty seconds, then he carefully pushed it down and peered in. The cupboard was usually crammed with Ellie's possessions, showering soft toys and clothes all over the floor when the door was opened, which didn't happen often any more, because it tore open the wounds that Mika's parents were trying to heal. The door had remained locked and the contents untouched for months and it had become a hidden shrine. So the first thing

Mika noticed as he opened the door was the lack of fallout, and as it opened wider, he discovered to his horror that the cupboard was completely empty, even the shelves and drawers were gone. He peered into the darkness with Awen snarling at his side, trying to make out the shadowy outline of something at the back. No, not a something, he realized, someone. Someone with a square head, his face dark, his body leaning forward slightly with his arms hanging at his sides as if he was turned off, as if he was a vacuumbot stored in a cleaner's cupboard. Awen whined.

'Bite it, then,' Mika whispered, trying to push Awen forward. 'What am I supposed to do?' But Awen backed away instead and sat down looking at Mika as if to say, 'You bite it'. Mika was so frightened he could hardly move, but he also felt angry, he wanted to know where Ellie's things were and what the Telly Head was doing in her cupboard. He stepped inside and pressed the button underneath its screen, and the Telly Head blinked on, raised its head and stared at him expressionlessly with cold, grey eyes. It was the Knife Sharpener, the old man who stood quietly at the end of the bed while the other Telly Heads argued about how to cook him. The old man raised one arm and Mika saw he held a cup in his hand, the same kind they drank their Fit Mix from in the mornings. But instead of slimy, pink Fit Mix, it was full to the brim with large, black spiders, and they crawled over his wrinkly old hand and dropped to the floor and scuttled towards Mika's feet. He only just managed to shut the door before the first spider reached him.

10
WE HAVE EYES EVERYWHERE

'Y ou start,' Gorman said, lifting a glass to his lips. He took a sip of blood-red wine and watched Ellie falter in the doorway of his office. Behind her, a man held the barrel of a gun millimetres from the back of her head. She looked cleaned up for the occasion in a new white uniform and sock shoes, and her black hair had been freshly cut in a sharp line at her jaw, but she had dark rings under her eyes and looked too thin – tiny compared to the man with the gun behind her.

The Fit Mix will sort that out, Gorman thought. In a few weeks she won't recognize herself.

Ellie looked around suspiciously.

'Start what?' she asked.

'Our game of chess,' Gorman replied. 'Look.' He motioned towards a pair of sofas with a low table between them. A chessboard had been set up, with a carafe of wine on the black side and a bowl of sweets on the white. Ellie scowled as she walked across the room and sat down behind her pieces. The man with the gun followed and stood behind her.

'Why are you giving me sweets?' she asked.

'I thought you might like to eat them,' Gorman replied clemently, sitting down opposite her. He did this with difficulty; his knees were very painful. 'But you don't have to of course, if you consider yourself too grown-up.' He drained his glass of wine and refilled it. 'I could ask for some savoury treats if you prefer.'

Ellie looked at the bowl of sweets and felt a lump form in her throat. They were just the kind she had liked once – colourful and chewy and shaped like shrimps and shells. But she couldn't eat in front of Gorman. She could hardly breathe in front of Gorman. He looked particularly dead that night – his lips and mouth stained red by the wine and his papery face grey. He looked as if someone had just got him out of his coffin and plugged him in.

'I'm not hungry,' she said.

'Suit yourself,' he replied, smiling.

Ellie shifted uncomfortably. She didn't like it when Gorman was in a good mood; it made her feel afraid. If Gorman was happy, it meant something bad was happening in the world. Someone somewhere was in danger. She glanced over her shoulder at the gun pointed at her head.

'Why am I here?' she asked.

'Because I wanted to see you,' Gorman replied. 'I thought it would be nice to polish our minds with a game of chess and I thought you might be able to help me with something.'

'What?' she asked, sullenly.

'How's your brother, Mika?' he asked. He lifted his eyes to meet hers and she felt her corneas freeze under his glare.

'How would I know?' she asked, her lips trembling. 'What do you mean?'

Gorman sipped his wine.

'Stop playing dumb,' he said quietly. 'What have you told him?'

'Nothing,' she said, confused. 'How could I? I have no idea what you mean. Please, I don't understand.'

'There are two hundred and seventy thousand twelve- and thirteen-year-old children living behind The Wall on Earth,' he said. 'Two hundred and seventy thousand, Ellie. And last week every single one of them drank a cup of Fit Mix in their classroom except Mika Smith in Barford North. Now tell me, why is that? Why was *your brother* the only one to refuse it? It's a bit of a coincidence, don't you think?'

Ellie lowered her eyes and felt a surge of love and pride.

'He didn't drink it because he's not stupid,' she said quietly. 'It's got nothing to do with me.'

'Well, it had better not have anything to do with you,' Gorman snarled. 'The only reason he's still alive is because you were locked in a room with bandages around your head when it happened, but if I find out you've tried sneaking messages to him to warn him about the Fit For Life project, I'll kill him. I'm not having my project ruined by you. Do you understand?'

Ellie nodded.

'I will be watching him,' he added. 'We have eyes everywhere. Now, start the game.'

Ellie picked up a white pawn and moved it forward to clear the path for her queen and bishop.

'Not like that,' Gorman snapped. 'Use your head.'

She sighed and moved the piece back to its starting place, then she stared at it until it began to glow.

11

DESERTED

The next morning was blown in by howling winds that whipped around the towers of Barford North like joy-riding banshees. Mika awoke before his alarm went off and lay with his hands behind his head thinking about the Pod Fighter. How had he flown like that? It had been like dream flying, as if he'd just jumped off the ground and flapped his arms. He got thrills of excitement remembering it and he couldn't wait to go to the arcade that night and do it again.

He was surprised to hear someone knock at the door and he strained to listen as his father opened it and a few words were mumbled. A few seconds later, David stuck his head in the bedroom.

'We've got a letter from Helen,' he said. 'And it's *handwritten*.' He left Mika's room, taking the rare object back to bed to read it.

Helen? Mika sat up feeling uneasy. He was supposed to be

seeing Helen the next day, why had she sent his parents a hand-written letter? In seconds he was at their bedside, watching them read it.

'What does she say?' he asked, impatiently. They didn't reply for a few moments, then his father held out the letter and Mika took it. It was written on real paper that looked about a hundred years old.

Dear Mr and Mrs Smith,

I am writing to inform you that Mika has made such excellent progress with his counselling I feel he no longer needs to see me. I have enjoyed his company very much, and it has been a pleasure to work with him — he is an intelligent boy with a bright future.

Since you paid me in advance for his treatment I am refunding one hundred and twenty credits on the enclosed credit card.

Please pass on my fond regards to Mika.

Best wishes,

Helen Green

Mika's hands were shaking by the time he finished reading the letter and he felt as if his intestines were being yanked out through his belly button. He looked up at his parents. Asha was holding the credit card and her sleepy face was glowing as if she was looking at an angel.

'Thank odd for that,' David said, his shoulders sinking into the pillows with relief. 'We can pay Mika's school fine with twenty credits to spare! We should celebrate tonight! We could have pizza!'

'Good idea,' Asha replied, smiling. 'Let's have a *big* tikka pizza. Two slices each. Oh Mika, I'm really pleased! Well done!'

Mika wasn't pleased. His eyes were as black as a starless night. He threw the letter on the bed, his face twisted with disgust, and stumbled back to his room.

'Mika!' Asha called after him. 'What's wrong?'

He threw himself down on the bed.

She didn't even tell me to my face, he thought bitterly. Helen's the only person I can talk to and she's deserted me!

'Mika?' Asha said uneasily, standing in the doorway. 'Don't be upset. It's good news, isn't it? That you're feeling better?'

'But she knows I still need her!' Mika shouted.

'But she says you don't,' Asha said, 'and you *do* seem better, Mika. You seemed really happy last night when you got back from the arcade: completely different from a week ago.'

'You don't understand,' he said. 'Leave me alone.'

'She sent a packet of biscuits for you,' Asha told him, hoping it might make him feel better.

'I don't care. I don't want them.'

He cried silently, his angry tears soaking into the cover, and Asha crept out of the room and shut the door. A few minutes later Mika appeared, fully dressed and scowling.

'I'm going to see her,' he said.

'What? Now?' Asha replied, watching him with exasperation as he put his coat on. 'You can't go now; it's half past six in the morning! She won't be awake and it's pouring with rain!'

But before she'd finished her sentence Mika was out of the door and running down the stairs.

He arrived at Helen's tower on the other side of town breathless and soaking wet. He hesitated by the door, realizing his mother was right and Helen was probably fast asleep. He ought to go home and return later, but he didn't want to.

What are you supposed to do, he thought, when the person who's upset you is the person you want to talk to?

Halfway up in the lift, he heard a familiar sound. Not sure if he'd imagined it, he stopped the lift and listened. He could hear the beat of his heart and his breath catching in his throat, the wind whistling up the lift shaft and the metal ropes creaking, but he thought he'd also heard Awen snarling as he had done when the Knife Sharpener was in Ellie's cupboard, but now the noise was gone.

I must have imagined it, he thought. Of course I imagined it, the dog doesn't even exist, he's just an invention of my crazy brain.

Feeling stupid, he took a deep breath and pressed the button to start the lift again, but as soon as it began to rise, he heard the snarl for a second time, and although Mika couldn't see him, he felt the warmth of Awen's body pressed against his leg. When the lift door opened on Helen's floor, the dream dog grabbed his sleeve with his teeth and tried to hold him back.

'Stop it,' Mika whispered, impatiently. 'Get off.' But Awen wouldn't let go and Mika had to push him aside to get out of the lift. 'Stay,' he whispered, feeling completely mad because he was giving commands to an invisible dog. But Awen ignored him and Mika could hear the tap of the dog's claws on the floor as he walked towards Helen's apartment.

He was surprised to find the door open and a figure standing inside. Hearing male voices he leaned against the wall just out of sight and listened. Where was Helen, and why were there men in her apartment? He heard a flump as something hit the floor and realized it was one of her books being knocked from the shelves. He felt a wave of protective anger. Helen's books were her friends, 'the kind you invite for dinner in the middle of winter,' she'd told him, 'and spend all night talking and never go to bed'. He heard another book hit the floor and edged closer to the door so he could see in. The apartment was messy; an odd-looking jumble of clothes hung out of the drawers, and there was an assortment of wild-looking sun hats and sunglasses on the table and a litter of bags on the floor. Helen had obviously packed and left in a hurry.

The men were wearing black suits and white shirts and had a skinny, flint-eyed look about them, and as they searched through Helen's things they reminded Mika of magpies. Then Mika noticed a gun on the kitchen work surface next to the teapot; a big black gun. He ducked out of sight and held his breath. Awen tugged desperately at his leg, urging him to leave, and this time he obeyed the dog and turned and ran as quickly as he could towards the staircase, not wanting to risk the lift because the door would make a noise. Then, no longer able to control his panic, he ran down the stairs.

Where had she gone? Had she left because she wanted to or because she was in danger? In his heart he knew the truth and he ran down the stairs consumed by guilt, sure that Helen's departure and the horrible Magpie Men with their guns had something to do with him.

12
FIT CAMP IS FUN!

Mika tried not to think about what the Fit Mix was doing to him, but after a few weeks of drinking it he could no longer deny that his body was changing. He was growing so fast his feet had split the sides of his new sneakers, his T-shirts looked as though they'd shrunk in the wash and his jeans were displaying an unfashionable strip of hairy ankle.

'Come here a moment,' Asha said, as Mika rushed past her from the shower.

'Why?' Mika asked suspiciously, clutching his towel to his chest. He didn't want his parents to notice he was growing and start asking awkward questions, but it had become impossible to hide.

'Stand against the wall,' she said. 'I want to measure you.'

'Can't we do it later?' Mika said. 'I'll be late for school.'

'It'll only take a second,' his mother insisted. 'I swear you've grown another two centimetres since last week. You banged your head again as you came out of the shower.'

'OK,' Mika said reluctantly. He stood against the wall at the side of the television and she was quiet and chewed her bottom lip while she made the mark over his head.

'You have as well!' Asha exclaimed. 'That can't be normal.'

Mika turned and looked at the new mark she'd made on the wall. Beneath it were many more marks made since Ellie and he had learned to walk eleven years before, each one with a date beside it. Ellie's marks finished a long way below his, and he felt a pang as he looked at the last; he'd grown loads since she'd disappeared.

While he was getting dressed, Asha read the mailing she'd been sent by the school about the Fit Mix. Rapid growth wasn't listed under the heading *Abnormal side effects*. Instead it was under the heading *Health benefits*.

'Mmm,' she mused, standing in the bedroom doorway, watching Mika ram his feet into his sneakers. 'You do look healthier, I suppose, and you don't have those black rings under your eyes any more, and your skin's not so pale.'

She didn't sound entirely convinced.

Mika muttered something and left for school. He was feeling more uncomfortable by the day about going along with the Fit For Life programme. Now Helen had disappeared he had nobody to talk to about it or reassure him that he was doing the right thing. Weeks had passed since he'd started drinking the Fit Mix. He'd kept his mouth shut and done what he was told, but he still knew nothing about where Ellie was and why he'd seen a Telly Head in his classroom, and the pressure to keep going along with it all without saying anything was almost too much to bear. Every day he arrived in his classroom to see smiling children drinking Fit Mix on the screen of his workstation, with the message *You are the future! Drink up your Fit Mix!* written underneath, and every day it got harder to drink it; it was as if his body was staging its own rebellion.

'You look a bit green, Mika,' Mrs Fowler said. 'Are you feeling all right?'

'Yes thanks,' Mika replied, trying to stop gagging all over the desk.

But drinking the Fit Mix and almost vomiting every morning was entertainment compared to Fit Camp. Two weeks after Fit Mix started, Mika arrived in school to see *Fit Camp is Fun!* written across his screen. They all got free sandwiches again that day, and a packet of sweets to take home with them, and everyone assumed it would be like normal sports lessons, just longer. They figured they'd run around for half an hour or so every afternoon, climb a couple of ropes, then go home. How wrong they were. How very wrong.

When Mrs Fowler told them to change into their new YDF sports kit, everyone moaned that it wasn't cool and asked if they could wear their own stuff, and Mrs Fowler said, 'Shut up and get dressed,' so they did, grumbling and giggling. Kobi looked the most ridiculous in the new kit because he was so long and bony. His skin looked almost blue from a childhood of light deprivation in The Shadows.

The first surprise they got was when they were told they would not be transported to the leisure centre as they were expecting (it was several kilometres away), they would have to run along the walkways, and since the only running any of them had done recently was up the red walkway in the arcade to get to an empty Pod Fighter simulator, they were half dead by the time they got there, lungs splitting, dripping with sweat and feet covered in blisters. But that was only the start of it.

Their instructor, Mr Blyte, was short and bald with big feet. When he stood next to Kobi, who was taller than the rest of them, the new instructor looked like a hairless gnome. Mika thought this was funny until the man opened his mouth to speak – then everyone shut up and started quivering, even Ruben. Mr Blyte rasped menacingly, as if he had liquid nitrogen for innards.

'Right,' said Mr Blyte, frogmarching back and forth in front of them, swinging his stopwatch, his feet flapping and his eyes ripping them apart. 'Let's see what you're made of.'

He made them run up and down the basketball court until Roland, the Spelling Bee champion, was crawling on his hands and knees. Then they lifted weights in the gymnasium until their arms felt so weak they hung like boneless jelly at their sides. Then they were put on a line of bikes and cycled up a virtual Mount Everest, blinking away tears of pain.

'Faster,' Mr Blyte snarled, the veins on his bald head throbbing like worms. 'Faster!'

At the end of the session, which lasted three hours, they had to run back to school. Most of Mika's classmates crawled, dribbling on the concrete.

'This is outrageous!' Asha gasped, when Mika hobbled through the door and she watched him try to undress for a shower. He was so stiff, he couldn't bend down to take off his sneakers and she had to do it for him. He sat on the sofa wincing while she peeled his socks off. They were soaked with sweat and blood and his feet looked as if he'd contracted bubble disease.

'Chrise,' said Asha. 'Your feet are bleeding! Look at all these blisters! I don't think you should go to the arcade tonight, you need to rest.'

Mika looked up at her, his eyes burning.

'It's all right,' he said. 'I'll be fine in a minute.'

'No, you won't!' Asha insisted. 'You need to rest!'

'But I've been looking forward to playing Pod Fighter all day,' Mika snapped. 'It's what got me home.'

Asha turned to David for support, 'What do you think?' she asked.

David shrugged and grinned, mixing Fab mash for their tea in a bowl. He was pleased to see Mika taking an interest in something normal like all the other kids. 'Let him go,' he said. 'If he can get there.'

'Thanks, Dad,' Mika replied.

It was going to take a lot more than bleeding feet to keep Mika away from the arcade.

13
TERMS AND CONDITIONS APPLY

Mika couldn't understand why nobody else seemed to notice that the arcade felt cold and the staff never smiled. It was as if the YDF put something in the drinks that got rid of common sense. No one seemed to see the mirrors above the shops and the restaurants and on the dark walls of the game room, but Mika saw them. He sensed people behind them, lots of people, watching. What did a bunch of twelve-year-olds have to offer these hidden strangers? The thought of them scared him, but he pretended to see nothing like everyone else.

Just play the game, keep your eyes down and your mouth shut.

He went to the arcade every night, and as the weeks passed it was busier than ever, as if addiction to the place had spread like a virus. The Fabshake makers ran dry, the burger flippers ran out of buns, and most of the crowd wore Pod Fighter T-shirts in a variety of colours and styles.

Everyone knew who Mika was after his first night in the arcade. Everybody wanted to know the black-eyed boy who'd walked in after a week and beaten them all, and for the first few days, he pushed through the crowd beneath the screen displaying the scores and left, not wanting to face them. But he soon discovered that apart from Ruben, who hated his guts more than ever, they were being friendly, they were curious, even respectful. There was no hidden, sadistic agenda, though maybe a tinge of jealousy, which was understandable, but Mika countered this by sharing his knowledge with them. After all, his objective for playing the game was different to theirs, so it was easy to be generous with his help. He didn't care about being the best; he just wanted to find his sister.

Six weeks after the arcade opened, he walked in with Kobi one Monday night, to find several hundred children standing silently in the middle of the mall, staring up at the screen over the game room doors.

'Weird,' Kobi said, burying his hands in the pockets of his long black coat. 'Look at them all.'

They seemed hypnotized, unblinking, the darkness of space and twinkling stars on the screen reflected in their eyes.

'Have you ever wanted to do this . . .' a low cinema voice rumbled, and an image of a Pod Fighter suddenly appeared, skimming over the sea, '. . . for real?' The Pod Fighter shot up into the sky and belted towards a pale full moon. 'The Youth Development Foundation would like to announce the launch of a competition with prizes beyond your wildest dreams! Win a new generation phone companion! Win a holiday for your family! Win a top-of-the-range hover car and a home in the fabulous Golden Turrets of London! And best of all, get to fly a *real* Pod Fighter! All this can be yours if you've got what it takes to win. You've played the game for fun, now play it for prizes. The competition is open to all twelve- and thirteen-year-olds. Entries must be submitted by the end of February. Terms and conditions apply...'

Mika watched images of exotic holiday destinations and Pod Fighters flash across the screen and felt his heart fill with hope and fear. Helen had told him to trust his instincts, and his instincts were telling him that this was what he'd been waiting for; that this was the path to Ellie. He glanced up at the row of mirrors above the shops and restaurants and sensed the strangers watching as the crowd erupted around him, and while everyone started to push and talk loudly, he felt a cold chill. He noticed Kobi's eyes follow his up to the mirrors and Mika looked away.

'Let's get out of here,' Kobi said, as someone shoved into him. 'Everyone's going to be even more bonkers than ever now.'

They entered the game room and joined a group of friends standing around the feet of the simulators in the darkness. A girl called Maddie approached them. Mika had flown with her a few times – she was a good gunner.

'Isn't it amazing!' she cried, grabbing Mika by the arm. 'Imagine if we won and got to fly a *real* Pod Fighter! Who are you flying with? I've read the terms and conditions and we have to compete in pairs.'

'I don't know,' Mika said, looking around. He knew he wouldn't team up with Kobi because they both preferred to fly, and he was aware he must choose carefully.

Maddie's face fell. 'It doesn't matter if you're thinking about someone else,' she said.

There was an awkward pause. Even though she was a good gunner, Mika didn't want to fly with her.

'I'm not sure, Maddie,' he said, feeling mean. 'I haven't had a chance to think about it. I'll let you know.'

In the next few minutes several other people asked him and each time he said 'No'. Kobi teamed up with a boy called Tom. They looked an odd pair, Tom as if his mother scrubbed him in Ultra Supa White and Kobi as if he slept in a skip, but they flew brilliantly together.

'You'd better choose someone soon,' Kobi said. 'Or all the good gunners will be taken. Why don't you fly with Maddie? She *is* good.'

'I might,' Mika said, but he didn't want to. He felt as if he was waiting for someone, and when a girl walked up the red walkway talking into her phone companion, all sounds around him faded and he knew instantly that she was the one. She looked like a fairy; a punk fairy; her body slight and delicate, her jeans ripped at the knees. She had pretty hands and ears, and spiky red hair that framed her elfin face perfectly. She had Irish and Russian blood that gave her eyes shaped like almonds and cheekbones that looked carved from flawless stone. She was beautiful, Mika thought; he had never seen anyone like her. She glanced towards him and her eyes glowed in the darkness as if they were irradiated. He half raised his hand to wave, to beckon her over, then stopped, realizing how dumb that would seem – he didn't even know her. Kobi offered him a sip of his drink and he poured it down his front.

'Dammit,' cursed Mika, rubbing the wet patch on his T-shirt and watching the girl slide her phone companion into her back pocket. He stepped forward, hardly aware he was doing it, and so did one of the girls.

'Hey, Audrey!' she shouted, and the strange girl looked towards them and then walked over. 'Meet Audrey, everyone, she's just moved here. This is her first night.'

She was spooky as her glowing green eyes cast over them, contrasting so vividly with her punky red hair. Her appearance shocked everyone into silence, and soon the sharp pale form of Ruben was drawn out of the darkness to appraise her.

'Your eyes are weird,' he said.

'They're borg eyes,' she replied. 'I was born with empty sockets.'

'Oh,' Ruben said, taking a step closer.

Get away, Mika thought, bristling with anger. Ruben began to circle the new girl like a predator around its prey and Mika burned with jealousy.

'Like wolf eyes,' Ruben continued, staring at her. 'Reflective on your retinas.'

'Yes,' she replied. Her voice was husky, with the trace of a Russian accent. She didn't seem to mind being stared at. Everyone was staring and Mika supposed she was used to it. She was worth staring at.

'Wolves could see in the dark,' Ruben said. 'Can you?'

'Better than you,' she replied. 'It's my payback for being blind for six years.'

'Cool,' he said, and Mika felt the urge to stick his fingers down his throat. Ruben's sickly flattery was worse than his snide insults and it annoyed Mika that he wasn't teasing the new girl for being a mutant just because she was pretty.

'What's your name?' she asked him, her smile illuminating the space around her.

'Ruben,' he replied.

'Hi, Ruben.'

She looked around at the rest of them. At Kobi in his ragged clothes and scruffy hair, then at Mika, her glowing eyes boring into his as if she could see inside his head. It was intense, and he enjoyed it for a moment, but after a few seconds, he felt overwhelmed and had to look away.

'Hi,' he muttered.

The next few minutes were agony. Now other people were talking to Audrey and she was laughing with them.

She's going to think I don't like her, he thought. You fool. I'm going to lose her if I don't do something, and Ruben will get her.

He watched helplessly as Ruben continued to talk to her.

'What do you do?' Ruben asked, as if he was in charge.

'I'm a gunner,' she said.

'You any good?' he continued, his sharp eyes darting all over her face. 'I haven't got a partner yet.'

'I'm OK,' she replied. 'We should fly together and see.'

No. She can't fly with *him*! Mika thought. He had to do

something fast. He stepped forward.

'I'm looking for a gunner too,' he blurted out, 'why don't you fly with me?'

Ruben shot Mika a look like a flurry of poison darts. Audrey smiled at Mika and he thought he detected a hint of relief in her eyes.

'OK,' she said. 'Why not.'

They grinned at each other and Mika felt his face redden.

'What?' Ruben sneered. 'Mika Smith is a perp! You don't want to fly with him! You want to fly with someone who knows what they're doing!'

Audrey's eyes flashed.

'Don't listen to him,' Mika said coldly, staring Ruben down.

Ruben's pale hands made fists and Mika glared at him.

'You'll pay for that,' Ruben snarled, and everyone around watched pensively, shocked by the odd way Mika and Ruben were behaving over the new girl. Nobody confronted Ruben that way, ever.

The group broke up and started walking towards their simulators, leaving Mika and Audrey alone.

'We should get ready,' he said, gruffly.

'OK,' she replied.

He walked ahead of her to an empty simulator with his heart banging, feeling a mixture of joy and foreboding. Ruben didn't make idle threats and Mika realized he *would* pay for what he'd said, but did he care? Not much. He watched Audrey climb into the gunner seat, her eyes glowing and her delicate hands adeptly checking over her controls, and as he climbed into his seat, it was as much as he could do to stop himself laughing out loud.

He had to show off his flying skills, of course, because he couldn't let her believe what Ruben had said about him. He shot off the launch pad seconds after he heard the click of her harness, and they were pirouetting above Earth a full minute before the others caught them up. The control panels lining the walls of the pod shone soft as fairy lights, the stars above glittered, the clouds below were white as heaven, and it was all so quiet. They waited until the others were arranged in formation around them, then tilted again and roared into space ready for the first assault.

'Watch out to the left,' Mika warned.

'I know,' she laughed.

She was good, really good. She shot down the first three Red Star Fleet fighters before anyone else in the battalion had fired a shot, and the longer they fought, the more exhilarated Mika felt, until he *was* laughing out loud, he couldn't help himself, and so was she; whooping with delight every time she hit something. She was a brilliant gunner, and Mika felt that with her, he flew as he never had with anyone else. What an amazing find she was.

They were fighting for over an hour, long after everyone else had been shot down. When they'd taken out all the Dragon Fighters on level three, instead of going to the next level, Mika flew into orbit and they hung to the left of the moon. He wanted to talk to her. They talked about the game first and then about her new school and her move from Plymouth. He loved the way she expressed herself; everything she said was suffused with an energy and enthusiasm that dissolved the concrete of Barford North, silenced the wind and dried up the rain. She made him feel happy.

'So what about you?' she asked.

'What about me?' he replied, warily. He didn't want to blow this new friendship by letting her know he was a 'freaker', as Kobi had so eloquently described him, who slept at night with an imaginary dog on his bed and a Telly Head holding a cup of spiders in the cupboard.

'You look as though you think a lot,' she said.

'Doesn't everyone?' he replied evasively.

'No,' she answered flatly. 'What were you thinking when we met earlier?'

He squirmed in his seat. He didn't want to tell her that she stirred him with her strange beauty and that he felt drawn to her like a moth to a light.

'That you looked like a good gunner,' he replied.

'Oh,' she said, grinning beneath her headset. 'Thanks.'

'We should fly down and have a look at Earth,' Mika suggested, wanting to change the subject.

'Good idea,' Audrey replied. 'We could look over The Wall and see what it's like on the other side.'

They spent the next hour flying over South America. Where people had once lived the streets of the towns and cities were littered with bones, and everything was covered in yellow dust, which clouded the dark windows and piled in drifts in unused doorways. In the Amazon rainforest, nothing remained but the carcasses of trees standing like black skeletons in a desert. Everything was dead.

'They say it's going to be hundreds of years before its safe to come back here.' Mika said, bitterly. 'How could they have let this happen?'

'I wish we hadn't come,' said Audrey, sadly. 'Let's go back, I can't look at it any more.'

Neither could Mika. It made him feel so sad and angry he was struggling not to cry and he didn't want to cry in front of Audrey, even with his headset on.

'It's almost time to go home anyway,' he said. 'Let's finish.'

Audrey took her headset off and her green eyes were the colour of newly unfurled leaves. She said goodbye and he watched her walk away into the darkness, feeling as if she was taking a little piece of his soul with her. A piece he would never want back.

14
THE MADNESS OF
THE QUEST

Awen opened his eyes and lifted his head and Mika stroked him, sensing the dog was sleepily aware of something, but not alarmed. There was no moonlight that night, so the warmth and the feel of the creature was everything.

'What can you hear?' Mika whispered.

The dog rested his head on his paws and with a sigh his body relaxed, but his ears remained half-cocked, so Mika listened. Something was happening in Ellie's cupboard.

I don't want this tonight, he thought. Please go away.

He lay back and pulled the cover over his head and tried to make the dream change, but Awen found a gap in it with his nose and snuffled in his ear.

'Get off,' Mika whispered. 'I don't want to look in the cupboard.'

But the more he tried not to think about what was happening inside it, the more curious he became, until he realized that the dream would not end until he played his part.

'All right then,' he grumped.

Awen stayed on the bed and watched Mika get up. Mika pressed his ear against the cupboard door and listened. The noise didn't sound like a Telly Head. It was gentle and purposeful, as if something was being made. Feeling reassured, he carefully opened the door and his lungs filled with air that was so cold and fresh, he felt as if he had eaten a whole packet of mints in one go. The cupboard was filled, floor to ceiling with a plant that was growing before his eyes. It reached out, waving soft green tips, leaves unfurling and arching back like moth wings. Awen jumped down from the bed and walked into its midst, and as Mika tried to follow, something amazing happened – as he took a step forward, his body folded over and suddenly he was walking on his hands as well as his feet, and when he looked down, he saw in the dim light that they had transformed into paws just like Awen's. He had become a dog. Awen's head reappeared amongst the foliage and he yapped playfully, as if this was a 'chase me' game, and then he disappeared again. Laughing, Mika made to follow but woke up instead.

He gasped.

Dammit! Now he *didn't* want the dream to end. He wanted to play like a dog with Awen.

In reality it was dawn on Saturday morning and the light through the window was grey. He was still in bed and there was no dream dog or plant, just a heap of his dirty underwear against Ellie's cupboard. His heart started to thump as he remembered what he was doing that day; in a couple of hours he would be competing in the first round of the competition. He dressed quickly and crept round the end of his parents' fold-down bed and made himself a sandwich without waking them. Then he lay on Ellie's bed and looked at her pictures while he ate it. He wanted to take something of hers with him for luck, so he took

down her favourite holopic: a picture of a mountain lioness playing with her cubs over rocks, in the shelter of a low-limbed tree.
He stared at the picture for a while, hardly able to believe that
such beauty had once existed, then he slid it into his back pocket,
taking care to choose the one without the hole. Before leaving, he
tried calling Helen. This had become a daily ritual, though he'd
given up hope that she'd ever answer. He just liked to hear her
voice on the recorded message.

They had to go to Reading to compete because the competition was taking place in the big city arcades, which had several
game rooms. The arcades were staying open all weekend, so they
could have gone later in the day, or on Sunday, but they decided
to get up early and beat the crowds.

They arranged to meet outside the train station at half past
seven and Mika was there a few minutes early. But he was disappointed to discover they hadn't beaten the crowds at all – there
were hundreds of kids in Pod Fighter T-shirts already pouring
into the station and every one of them had an expression of
hungry determination. He stood back, watching them pass, and
the madness of his quest suddenly hit him – he was trying to find
his sister by competing in an arcade game against two hundred
and seventy thousand desperate children. Anxiously, he looked
for his friends and saw Audrey first, her red hair and green eyes
beacon bright in the crowd, with Tom and Kobi close behind her.
Mika felt better being with them, Audrey was so excited, her eyes
kept lighting up as if they were getting power surges from the
national grid, and everyone seemed to have made an effort for
the day: Audrey was wearing her favourite padded top, which
was as green as her eyes, Tom looked as if he had ironed his hair
and Kobi had parcel-taped his sneakers so the soles didn't flap.

The crowd stopped moving outside the station because there
were too many people trying to squeeze through the doors and
they had to shove their way through with kids swearing at them
and pushing them back and jabbing them with their elbows. All
six platforms were packed solid with people waiting for the trains

and Mika started to feel anxious again and began to consider the possibility that they might not even reach the arcade and his search for Ellie could end here in a stupid train station.

'What are we going to do?' Tom said.

'Perhaps we should come back later,' Kobi suggested. 'I'm not bothered when we go.'

'No,' Tom said, anxiously. 'It might be worse later. I want to go now.'

'Me too,' Mika said, feeling a wave of panic at the prospect of leaving the station. He felt as though he'd waited for ever for this day. 'What about you, Audrey?'

'I don't mind,' she said, shrugging. 'As long as we get to play, I don't care.'

'Let's go now then,' Mika said. 'We'll have to push our way through. Stick out your elbows and hang on to each other so we don't lose anyone.'

Mika took the lead and pushed forward with Audrey holding on to his coat. They hit solid knots in the crowd and had to work their way round them, and by the time they reached the edge of the platform, the overcrowding was so dangerous, Mika had to hang on to Audrey to stop her being pushed on to the track. A Silver Bullet hissed to a halt on the platform like a glass-eyed snake and the crowd surged forward, crushing them against the train. The doors opened and everyone pushed at once. Mika felt someone grab him from behind and yank him back and suddenly his grip on Audrey was gone and he was drowning in a sea of fists and elbows.

The others managed to force their way on to the train.

'Where's Mika?' Audrey shouted, looking back for him. 'Oh no! Look! He can't get on!'

Tom leaned out of the train and grabbed Mika's hand. He was hit hard in the face by someone's bag and the doors were trying to close on his arms. Mika heard a ripping sound as the sleeve on his coat tore, but still Tom didn't let go of his hand and with brute force he dragged Mika on board the train.

'Thanks,' Mika said, so grateful that the word sounded pathetically inadequate. 'That must have hurt.'

'Doesn't matter,' Tom replied. 'You almost got left behind.'

'I wish I'd stayed in bed,' Kobi said, inspecting a new rip in his black coat.

'That was scary,' Audrey said. 'I thought we'd lost you, and they almost pushed me off the platform.'

Mika put his arm behind her to stop a group of boys pushing into her, then he closed his eyes and sighed with relief.

'I hope the competition is easier than getting there,' Tom said, looking worried. 'That was awful.'

* * *

It was raining hard in Reading as they left the station. They ran all the way to the arcade, trying to get ahead of the people on the train, but when they arrived, they discovered the queue was already right down the block and round the corner, and they had no choice but to take their place at the end of it and wait. The rain pelted them until they were soaked to the skin and shivering. Audrey wrapped her arms around Mika's back and buried her fingers in his pockets. She smelled sweet; of the stuff she used to spike her hair and of herself. He held her cold fingers tight and closed his eyes, feeling as if he was standing in a queue of lemmings about to jump off a cliff.

It was two hours before they reached the arcade doors, and Mika watched, sick with apprehension, as Kobi and Tom had their retinas scanned by black armoured security borgs. Mika felt the hard red light in his eyes, then they were in, waved through by men in YDF uniforms, and walking towards one of the game rooms.

15
LET THEM HAVE IT

The Reading arcade had four game rooms, each containing hundreds of simulators. Mika and Audrey were directed to the second. Just inside the door they were given a number by a man in a dark blue YDF uniform. They searched for their simulator in the darkness with hundreds of the spider-like forms gyrating around them. It was strangely quiet. The place had the atmosphere of an exam hall, with no music playing or the sound of excited voices like in the arcade at home. More men in uniforms wandered through the rows of simulators and their feet squeaked on the hard floor.

'There's ours,' Audrey whispered, spotting it.

She pressed the footplate and the simulator dropped down.

A man walked towards them. 'Mika Smith and Audrey Hudson?' he said, without smiling.

They nodded and he made a tick on the tablet in his hand.

'The object of the game is to complete as many levels as possible,' he said. 'When you're shot down, you must leave your simulator and have your score verified. It is not a timed exercise, so you can begin when you are ready. Do not try to cheat, we will know.'

'As if we would,' Audrey whispered, watching the man walk away.

There was another team starting nearby and they panicked, desperate to wrestle open the door of their simulator. Mika was just about to do the same when Audrey grabbed his arm, 'Remember the game's not timed, let's take it easy and explore the controls.'

'Yeah, sorry,' Mika said.

They climbed into the cockpit, lit up the control panel and put their headsets on, adjusting them to fit comfortably. Mika relaxed a little as his seat wrapped around him. He checked over the control panel and Audrey explored her gun.

'There are a few icons I don't recognize,' Mika said.

'Me too,' Audrey replied. 'But we won't know what they do until we start flying.'

They turned on their headsets and a familiar green grid appeared in their visors. Then Mika pressed the windshield icon and it blinked on, but instead of the familiar battleship at sea, they found themselves in a huge dark hangar that domed high overhead and was open at one end. The Pod Fighter was facing out into space towards a sea of stars.

'I think we're on a space freighter,' Audrey said. 'This is going to be fun!'

An engineer in yellow overalls walked past them. He nodded and gave them the thumbs up, then a green light flashed in their visors.

'Right, I think this is it,' Mika said. 'Are you ready?'

'Yes,' Audrey replied, gritting her teeth. 'Let's go for it!'

He pulled back the controls and the engine roared like thunder as they shot out of the hangar. A rush of air filled the headsets and Mika breathed deeply as he was glued to his seat by G-force.

There didn't seem to be anything around to attack them, so Mika turned the Pod Fighter so they could have a look at the freighter they had launched from. It was enormous, as big as a city, the kind designed to travel deep into space. Nothing happened for a few seconds, Earth glowed in the distance and they waited. Then they saw another craft about half the size of the planet slowly move out of its shadow.

'Frag,' Mika said. 'Look at that!'

The craft was ruby red, a disc-shaped mega city speckled with millions of pus-coloured lights. Across the front edge was a gaping mouth a thousand kilometres long.

'I think we'd better test the gun,' Audrey said nervously, firing off a few rounds.

From the mouth of the ruby red mega city, a few hundred dots appeared.

'Here they come,' Mika muttered, his heart pounding.

The crafts flew so fast, the first were in firing range within seconds. They were similar to those they'd fought before on level one of the normal game: red slivers, like arrow heads, but these crafts had narrow yellow eyes and left trails of flame in their wake. They looked evil.

'OK,' Mika said, 'let them have it.' He dropped the Pod Fighter into a corkscrew spin right into the midst of the attack and his hands began to sweat on the controls as flame bolts flashed past them. They'd never taken on so many enemy crafts at the same time, but they were expecting it to be harder than the normal game and within a few seconds, instinct had taken over and they weren't even aware of the thought processes as they made decisions – they were so lightning quick they just happened. Within ten minutes they were alone again in a sea of silence and floating debris. They'd blasted every one of the Red Star Fleet to smithereens.

'Wow,' Audrey said. 'We're good! There were loads of them!'

'That was only level one, Audrey.'

'I know,' she grumped.

A green light flashed in their visors.

'Frag,' Mika said. 'Here we go again.'

They watched the mouth of the mega city with their fingers trembling on the controls as their next opponents emerged and flew towards them.

'They're weird,' Mika said, with a furrowed brow. They were larger than the flaming arrow heads and there were fewer of them – only twelve. They lined up to face them about a kilometre away.

'They're like origami,' Audrey said. 'They're folding themselves like pieces of paper!'

They were not like any craft they'd seen before, they were a collection of triangular shapes, ruby red and shiny, which folded and unfolded as if nimble fingers were playing with them. Sometimes they resembled dogs or cats, sometimes snowflakes or people. They seemed to be waiting for something.

'OK,' Audrey said. 'So we're supposed to make the first move.'

Mika thought for a moment, watching one unfold at the sides into the shape of an eagle.

'Try firing at one,' he suggested.

Audrey let off a round of laser fire. The targeted shape shifter instantly disappeared and reappeared in a different place and her shots carried off into space without hitting it. Then it fired a reciprocal shot at them and Mika had to drop the fighter suddenly to avoid getting hit.

'Ow!' Audrey cried, 'I banged my head.'

'Sorry,' Mika replied. 'That was close. Try again. I think this is some kind of puzzle.'

Audrey fired another shot and exactly the same thing happened again – the shape shifter disappeared, reappeared, then fired a shot back at them, but Mika noticed this time that it reappeared precisely the same distance and angle away from its starting point as the last one had.

'I've got an idea,' Audrey said. 'Instead of firing directly at the shape shifter, I'll fire at the place it would move to.'

'Just what I was thinking,' Mika agreed. 'Go for it.'

She fired a round but missed and the shape shifter fired back at them again. Once again Mika only just dodged it.

'Aim to the right a bit,' Mika said.

'I know,' Audrey replied irritably. 'I'm the gunner, remember?'

'Keep your hair on.'

She fired again and this time she hit the spot and the shape shifter came apart as if it had been dropped and smashed, sending ruby red triangles spinning off into space in every direction.

'Nice,' Mika said, approvingly.

One by one Audrey destroyed them all, and Mika watched, awestruck, knowing he couldn't have done it. She was aiming at targets that couldn't be seen and hitting them first time.

'I'm good, aren't I?' she bragged, playfully.

'Not bad, I suppose. Bighead.'

'I wonder what we'll get next,' Audrey pondered, watching the red mega city in the distance.

They didn't have to wait long to find out. Before they'd had a chance to collect their thoughts, the green light flashed again to mark the start of level three, and within seconds they heard a hum and whine. It sounded like an approaching swarm of insects.

'I can hear them but I can't see them,' Audrey said. 'Can you?'

'No.'

The hum and whine gained volume until it was deafening. It sounded like a huge fleet of fighters but they couldn't see a thing.

'Look out!' Audrey yelled, and Mika turned to see a stream of fire bolts come out of nowhere towards them. He shot up several kilometres then flew fast loops trying to outrun their invisible attackers and buy themselves some time.

'They're invisible,' Mika said.

'Really?' Audrey replied sarcastically. 'I hadn't noticed. What have you got on your control panel that you haven't used?'

The hum and whine got louder again. 'They're on our tail! Drop out!'

Mika dropped the Pod Fighter like a stone and the noise faded again. He jabbed frantically at the control panel trying all the icons he didn't recognize. All of a sudden they were blind. The glass windshield had turned black.

'Don't do that!' Audrey screeched. 'I can't see anything!'

'There's no need to yell. I'm only fragging in front of you!' he shouted, correcting the control so they could see again. He jabbed a triangular icon and hoped for the best. This time he got lucky. A red icon appeared on their visors and all of a sudden they could see the enemy – transparent red ghosts of pods flying in a swarm behind them, nearly in range.

'Wow,' Mika said. 'They're incredible.'

'There's so many of them,' Audrey said. 'Hundreds!'

'Never mind. Let them have it.'

Audrey started to fire and Mika swooped the fighter in wide arcs, only just dodging the deluge of fire bolts coming at them. For several minutes they eluded the ghost pods, but after a while Mika realized they were surviving on luck more than skill. There were just too many of them.

'We're going to get hit!' Audrey cried. 'You've got to find us something else!'

Mika looked at the control panel again. There were only two icons he hadn't tried. He hit one.

'Anything?' he asked.

'No, nothing! Try something else!'

He hit the other icon.

'Oh my goblin lord!' Audrey said. 'Look at that!'

Mika looked over his shoulder to see a huge net of green light being cast out of the back of the Pod Fighter.

'They're too far off, we missed,' Audrey said, as the net floated away into space. 'We have to draw them closer.'

Mika slowed down, dodging fire bolts and gritting his teeth, expecting to get wasted at any moment.

'Now!' Audrey yelled.

Mika hit the icon again and cast another net of green light.

The emerald threads spread out wide and the swarm of ghost pods flew right into them. Then the net closed up at the end and it spun gracefully through space with the trapped pods thrashing frantically inside. Thirty seconds later the hum and the whine faded into silence and the spinning net was only a pinprick of green light.

'We did it,' Audrey whispered. 'We. Did. It.'

'Yeah, we did,' Mika said. 'I'm sorry I snapped at you.'

'It's OK. It was pretty intense.'

Mika laughed and Audrey caught it as relief washed over them.

'That was *almost* fun,' Mika said.

'Yeah,' agreed Audrey. 'I wish we'd brought a drink though. My mouth is dry.'

So was Mika's, and his throat was sore. He shuddered with nervous energy as the green light flashed again.

They watched the mouth of the mega city, waiting for something to happen, and this time balls rolled out of it: red glass balls, rolling down an invisible alley towards them.

'Move up,' Audrey said, and Mika raised the Pod Fighter a couple of kilometres so they were looking down on them.

'What's that noise?' Audrey said, and Mika felt every hair on his body bristle and he began to feel bad, the euphoria of the previous minutes gone. The noise sounded like children screaming and crying as if they were feeling fear and pain. The balls rolled past beneath them and the sound began to fade.

'What are we supposed to do?' Mika said. 'They're not attacking us. They're rolling away.'

'Let's go closer and have a look,' Audrey said.

Mika dropped the Pod Fighter and flew towards the red spheres. Each ball was about ten times the size of their craft. There were six in all, rolling and rolling down the invisible alley into deep space.

'Oh I hate it,' Audrey said. 'That noise is horrible. Can you see inside them?'

'No.'

'I think there are children inside.'

'This is sick,' Mika said. 'Why would they put something like this in a game?'

'They're beginning to roll faster,' Audrey said.

The balls gained pace and the crying intensified into terrified screams. Mika closed his eyes and lowered his head, trying to block it out.

'I think we're supposed to destroy them before they roll away,' Audrey said. 'Look, before long we won't be able to keep up with them.'

She was right, Mika realized, the balls were rolling faster and faster away from them, until suddenly they were six blurs of light shooting off into the distance.

'We can't shoot them,' he said. 'I don't want to.'

'Yes, we can,' Audrey said, firing the first shot. 'It's a game, Mika. It's just the sound of children. They're not real.' She fired six shots at the disappearing balls and they exploded in flashes of red light. The screams abruptly halted and Mika felt a wave of horror wash over him.

'I feel ill,' he said.

'It's just a game,' Audrey replied.

'Well, it wasn't fun.'

A message appeared in their visors: *Level four complete. Game Over*.

'Is that it?' Audrey said, surprised. 'Have we finished?'

Mika felt a stab of excitement.

'I think we have.'

'We did it!'

They yanked off their headsets and climbed out of the simulator on shaky legs to find a man waiting for them.

'Well done,' he said.

'Are we through to the next round?' Audrey asked.

'It depends on your scores. Go and wait somewhere for an hour. If we want you to come back, we'll send a message to your companion.' He plugged a lead into the control panel of the pod so he could verify their score.

'Looks promising,' he said nodding. 'It's the best score I've seen yet. You can go now.'

* * *

Outside the arcade it was still raining and the people waiting in the queue looked as if they'd gone swimming with all their clothes on. Mika and Audrey had arranged to meet the others in a noodle bar up the road and they walked towards it to the sound of squelching feet.

The noodle bar, 'Oodles of Noodles,' was packed with competitors who had finished and were waiting for a message from the Youth Development Foundation, asking them to return to the arcade. The windows were steamy, pap pop pumped out of the speakers overhead, and the chefs tossed kilos of sizzling noodles in flat black pans. But despite the fact the restaurant was full, the music was louder than the conversations and the atmosphere was subdued. As Mika walked to the counter, he heard the odd comment here and there and realized most people hadn't even got past the second level.

'It wasn't fair that there were so many fighters in the first level; we didn't stand a chance – they shot us down in seconds.'

'Yeah, and the second level was even harder: those shape shifters, they kept moving and we couldn't hit them.'

'Did you find the net?'

'What net?'

Mika bought drinks with the trace of a smile on his face, then felt guilty.

But somebody has to win, he reasoned, and I'm not doing this for myself.

Audrey had found Kobi and Tom sitting at a table in the corner and Mika joined them. The atmosphere was just as bad as it was in the rest of the restaurant. He realized they'd had an argument; Tom was glaring at the table and Kobi was picking grumpily at the hole in the front of his jumper.

'Hi,' Mika said, carefully.

'Hi,' they muttered.

Mika sucked on his drink, wondering what had happened, but didn't dare ask.

'I made you this,' Kobi said to Audrey and he took a tiny metal borg cat out of his pocket and put it on the table in front of her. It was so small, he must have made it with tweezers and a microscope, and it even had tiny wire whiskers and metal pads on its paws. It rubbed its head against her hand.

'Oh, it's *beautiful*!' she cried. 'Thanks, Kobi!'

'That's OK,' he replied. 'I'm going to make it some kittens. You can have some when they're finished. They're quite fiddly.'

Everyone watched Audrey play with the cat, but the atmosphere was still horrible and Mika couldn't bear the tension any more. 'How was your game?' he asked at last.

'A mess,' Tom replied, bitterly.

'Why?' asked Audrey. 'What happened?'

'Kobi didn't want to shoot at those red balls,' Tom replied.

'No, I didn't,' Kobi muttered defiantly through his hair. 'They were *full of screaming children*. It felt like some kind of sick test to see whether we'd kill people.'

'But I told you!' Tom said, angrily. 'It was just a *game*!'

'Well it didn't feel like one,' Kobi muttered.

'So you *didn't* shoot the red balls?' Mika asked.

'He did eventually,' Tom said. 'But I had to beg him and by the time he changed his mind, it was almost too late. We had to chase after them and they nearly got away.'

'We finished, didn't we?' Kobi said grumpily. 'I don't know what you're moaning about.'

'Because I *have* to win this competition!' Tom said, desperately. 'You don't understand!'

'Why do you *have to win*?' Kobi said. 'This is supposed to be a game but it's making everyone behave like idiots! Audrey nearly got pushed off the platform this morning! Mika nearly had his coat ripped off his back, and now you're being a perp, Tom! You say it's "just a game" and yet you're so angry with me! I wish I'd stayed at home.'

Tom dropped his head and his face bloomed scarlet and suddenly he was normal Tom again. 'Sorry,' he said, looking as if he was fighting back tears. 'Please don't drop out, Kobi. My mum is sick and she's working double shifts in the tank meat factory. We can't afford to put the heating on. I want to help her.'

'My mother's dead,' Kobi said harshly. 'She died in The Shadows because of the mould.'

'Oh,' Tom said, sounding embarrassed. 'I'm sorry.'

Kobi was quiet for a moment, then he sighed.

'OK,' he said reluctantly. 'I'll play.'

'Are you sure?' Tom asked, desperately.

'Yes,' Kobi replied. 'For your mum.'

The companions waited silently in the middle of the table. The tiny borg cat sat amongst them and licked a metal paw, then it curled up and fell asleep on a noodle. The minutes gathered and dripped as slowly as the raindrops on the windows.

Beep! Beep! Beep! Beep!

The messages from the Youth Development Foundation arrived and everyone picked up their companion, hoping for good news.

16

HUNTER AND PREY

Mika's fingers trembled as he picked up his companion. All four screens on their table were glowing and the borg cat was sitting up again, awoken by the message alerts, but Mika didn't dare believe they were the lucky ones until he'd read the message three times.

'Congratulations, Mika Smith! Your team has been selected to compete in the second round of the competition! Please return to the arcade immediately! (Terms and conditions apply.)'

His relief was so intense he couldn't smile or move or do anything.

'We did it!' Audrey cried, leaping up with excitement.

'We'd better go back,' Tom said, enthusiastically dragging on his coat. 'Come on, Kobi!'

The disappointment of all the other competitors was heavy in the air and everyone stared at them as they walked towards the door. It felt awful, but on the street Tom and Audrey rushed ahead, unable to contain their excitement.

'Good luck,' Kobi said as they approached the security borgs outside the arcade for the second time.

'Thanks,' Mika said, feeling so nervous, he had to remember to put one foot in front of the other. The borgs stepped aside to let them in without scanning their retinas.

'Cool!' Tom whispered, striding past them. 'Just think, by the time we go home today we could have won a companion *and* a holiday!'

They were directed into a game room and told to stand in line at the edge of the red walkway. It was utterly silent.

'Look who else is here,' Audrey whispered.

Mika followed her eyes down the line of teams and felt his heart miss a beat as he saw Ruben and his game partner, Yee. Ruben whispered something in Yee's ear and she smiled, nastily.

'What's he got on his head?' Audrey said, stifling a giggle. Ruben was wearing a black bandana. 'What a perp.'

Ruben glared at Mika as if he wanted to rip his legs off, and Mika looked away and tried to ignore him. He didn't like it in the quiet arcade with the watching strangers behind the mirrors. He could feel them, sense their interest and greed, and his heart was beating so madly, he felt sure it would explode and redecorate the black walls with his blood.

A man came in and stood in front of them. 'Congratulations,' he said, in a flat voice. 'You have reached the second round of the competition. This game will be different to the first, so listen carefully so you understand what you have to do. The first instruction regards your team. We want you to swap positions, so whoever was pilot last time is gunner this time. Does everyone understand?'

There was a wave of shocked whispers down the line and Mika and Audrey looked at each other, panic-stricken. Swapping roles seemed like a death sentence; she had always been the gunner when they flew – it was the way they worked.

'Oh no!' she hissed. 'What are we going to do?'

'We've got no choice,' Mika whispered. 'You can fly, can't you?'

'Yeah, of course I can, but what about you? Can you gun?'

'I'm a bit rusty,' he said. In truth he hadn't flown as a gunner for weeks.

'We've got to try not to panic,' she said. 'We've all got the same disadvantage.'

'Quiet!' the man said and a sickened silence fell. 'And listen carefully. When you put your headsets on, you will find yourself on the mother ship again, as you were at the start of the last game. However, this time you will not be fighting the Red Star Fleet, you will be fighting against each other. Each of your Pod Fighters has a number. Your task is to shoot down one Pod Fighter while another pursues you. Imagine you are a link in a chain of Pod Fighters – you destroy the link in front of you, while the link behind attempts to destroy you. The aim of the game is to survive. Does everyone understand so far?' Everyone nodded. 'Good. You may not destroy *any* Pod Fighters other than the one you have been told to shoot down. If you do, you will be disqualified.'

'Does that mean we can't fire at the Pod Fighter chasing us?' someone asked.

'Exactly. You can't fire at anyone except the Pod Fighter you've been told to shoot down.'

'So how do we protect ourselves?'

'That's for you to figure out. Only the best will survive. You have forty-five minutes and your time starts . . . now!'

The teams turned and ran towards their simulators, and Mika's hands were shaking so badly as he put his headset on, Audrey had to help him tighten the strap. When they were belted into their harnesses and ready, two Pod Fighter icons appeared in their visors with numbers underneath. One was marked 'Prey' and the other was marked 'Hunter'.

'So we have to shoot down number five and stay away from

number fourteen,' Audrey said.

'This is going to be a nightmare,' Mika said. 'How are you going to understand all the controls?'

'Tell me now,' Audrey replied confidently. 'Show me a few and the rest I'll have to guess.'

Mika began to tell her, prioritizing the most important, and through the windshield, the familiar domed hangar of the mother ship appeared. They were not alone on the launch strip this time; on either side of them were the other competitors' Pod Fighters. Mika could see the teams inside, adjusting their headsets and preparing for take-off. A green light flashed indicating the start of the game.

'Ready?' Audrey said.

'I suppose so,' Mika replied, nervously.

Their ears filled with the roar of thirty engines and Mika grabbed the gun controls as Audrey prepared for take-off. They felt the familiar rush of air in their headsets as they shot off the landing strip, out of the mother ship and into space.

'Don't forget,' Audrey said, 'we have to shoot number five and avoid number fourteen.' She dropped immediately so they broke away from the group. 'Start looking for them.'

Above them, the other Pod Fighters looped around each other trying to find their prey amongst the swarm. The first unlucky victim went out within thirty seconds in a sudden flash of light.

'I can't see their numbers,' Mika said. 'We need to get closer.'

'Give me a minute to get used to flying,' Audrey replied. She dropped the Pod Fighter again, looped in a sharp corkscrew, then shot up and stopped dead.

'That was good,' Mika said.

'Of course,' Audrey replied.

Suddenly a Pod Fighter shot towards them from the right and Mika's heart missed a beat.

'It's OK,' Audrey said. 'It's not our hunter, it's number eight.'

The Pod Fighter flew a playful arc around them and shot off

towards the main group again. The group was slowly dispersing and spreading out as hunters found their prey and set off in pursuit. Occasionally there was a flash of light as another team was shot down.

'OK. Let's go for it,' said Audrey. Mika gripped the gun hard and they flew directly into the mass of Pod Fighters, searching anxiously for numbers five and fourteen, but everyone was moving so fast, they couldn't see the numbers and within seconds they had someone on their tail.

'Oh no, it's our hunter!' Audrey cried. 'How did they find us? I can't see the numbers!'

'Neither can I,' Mika said. 'There must be some kind of display. Try the control panel. Try everything!'

Audrey dropped the Pod Fighter and looped, trying to evade their hunter while she jabbed at the icons on the control panels. Nothing happened; their hunter kept up and began to fire.

'The controls aren't doing a thing! Nothing!' she yelled.

'Try them in sequence or pairs!' Mika said. 'They must work somehow! Hurry! We're going to get wasted!'

Their hunter was good; its hail of laser bolts was only just missing them, despite Audrey's excellent flying. Twice Mika closed his eyes thinking, this is it, they've got us this time, only to open them again to find that by some miracle, they were still in the game. Audrey cursed as she stabbed at the icons and tried to keep them alive at the same time. Then all of a sudden an icon appeared in Mika's visor, and as he looked at each Pod Fighter its number appeared.

'That's more like it!' he said. They were silent for a few moments while they looked at the display.

'We must be number thirty,' Audrey said. 'Look, you can see our hunter, number fourteen, following us. So where's our prey?'

They searched the display for it.

'I've found it,' Audrey said, and she made a sharp U-turn back towards the mother ship with their hunter hard on their tail. 'Top left. Eleven o'clock.'

The Pod Fighter they had to eliminate, number five, was hiding from them above the mother ship.

'It must have destroyed its prey already,' Mika said. 'They didn't waste any time, they must be good.'

'Doesn't matter,' Audrey said. 'We'll get them anyway.'

Mika wasn't so sure; they weren't even in firing range when number five suddenly vanished.

'No way! How did they do that?' he exclaimed.

Their hunter fired a spray of laser bolts and they were forced to drop suddenly under the mother ship, losing their pursuer in the shadow of its bulk.

'There must be an invisibility shield around our prey,' Mika said. 'In the last round we found a display for the invisible fighters, remember? They appeared like red ghosts.'

Audrey punched desperately at the control panel with one hand and wove the Pod Fighter through the shadow of the mother ship with the other. Suddenly another Pod Fighter appeared on the display. It was transparent and red, just like the ghost pods in the first round. When Mika looked at it, a red number five appeared.

'OK, so we can see them now, that's good.'

Their prey was a couple of kilometres away, hanging motionless in space. Audrey veered right and hurtled towards it, losing the protective shadow of the mother ship. Their hunter was on their tail again within seconds and firing at them.

'This is impossible,' Mika said.

'No it's not, I'm still looking for the invisibility shield,' Audrey said, flying with one hand. 'If our prey found it, we can.' Moments later she said, 'Yes!' and a second red ghost appeared on the display.

'That's us!' Audrey yelled, nearly deafening Mika through the headset. 'Number thirty!'

Mika watched the display as their red ghost shot towards number five.

'You're a genius,' he said, watching their hunter falter in

confusion and surprise, then veer off in the wrong direction.

A few moments later, number five shot up, realizing it had been seen.

'Game on,' Audrey said, and shot after it.

It was not easy following an invisible target, they could see nothing through the windshield, only the red ghost on their display, and Mika was impressed with Audrey's flying skills, which kept them right on target. However, actually hitting the craft was going to be a different matter entirely, and when Mika began to fire, his shots missed it by hundreds of metres. It was like trying to catch a fly in his hand with his eyes closed.

'It's like the shape shifters in the first round, you need to anticipate where it will move,' Audrey said.

'I know,' Mika said, irritably, shooting another couple of pointless rounds. 'But you could predict exactly where the shape shifters were going to move, you can't predict this.'

He watched the red ghost of number five for half a minute as it looped, dropped and corkscrewed through space without firing a shot and tried to figure out if there was a pattern to the way it flew.

'Come on! We've only got five minutes left!' Audrey said.

'Give me a chance.'

Mika suddenly realized that the Pod Fighter always took a right-hand loop out of a corkscrew and all he had to do was wait for them to do it again.

'There are only four Pod Fighters left,' Audrey said, anxiously.

'Three,' Mika said, and fired a round. Number five was just pulling out of a corkscrew, and just as he'd predicted, they took a loop to the right. There was a blinding flash of light. When they could see again, only fragments of the shattered ghost remained, slowly spinning and spreading out into space.

They screamed and jumped in their seats.

'You did it!' Audrey yelled. 'I can't believe it!'

'Thanks,' he said sarcastically, feeling a little offended by her lack of faith.

'No, I don't mean you're a bad gunner, they were just so good!'

'I hope that was Ruben,' he said.

'Yeah, so do I,' Audrey replied. 'It would serve him right. Fancy coming here wearing a black bandanna, as if he's the King of Kung Fu. He's so arrogant.'

'How much time have we got left?' Mika asked.

'Just over a minute.'

For that minute they hung in space and watched their hunter fruitlessly search for them. At one point the Pod Fighter passed so close, they held their breath.

A 'Game Over' icon appeared and they climbed out of the simulator and took their headsets off. Audrey's eyes sparkled as if she had green fireworks exploding inside them, and her fairy face and red hair were gleaming with sweat.

They grinned at each other. They'd done it.

* * *

The teams stood in line and the simulators loomed around them like a silent jury in a courtroom. A man walked out of the darkness and read from the tablet in his hand. 'Three teams have made it through to the third round,' he said. 'Please step forward when your number is called.

'Thirty . . .

'. . . eight

'. . . and nineteen.'

Mika and Audrey stepped forward, then another team they didn't know, and last of all, Ruben and Yee. Immediately Mika turned to look at Kobi and Tom, realizing he hadn't even thought about his friends for the whole game. Tom, who had risked his own safety to drag him on to the train. Kobi, who had been his first and only friend since Ellie had disappeared. He hadn't thought about them once and he felt an uncomfortable tightness under his heart. They walked away with the losing teams and the door closed behind them.

'Oh no!' Audrey whispered. 'How could Ruben win, but not Kobi and Tom! Tom's going to be devastated! This is terrible. I hope they wait for us outside.'

'So do I,' Mika said, 'because I've just thought of something really bad.'

'What?' Audrey asked. 'Tell me.'

'Remember how good number five was?' he said. 'How smart they were and how hard they were to catch?'

'You don't mean . . .' Audrey whispered, '. . . we shot down Tom and Kobi? That they were number five?'

'I hope not,' Mika said. 'But they were so good, I can't help thinking it was them. Tom will never forgive us.'

A woman walked towards them with a white box in each hand.

'Well done,' she said. 'These boxes contain capsules we want you to add to your Fit Mix. Take one a day. Just pull them apart and stir them in.'

Audrey and Mika stuffed the boxes into their bags without even looking at them, their eyes on the door and their hearts outside with their friends.

* * *

Outside the arcade, the rain was falling like grey rods that melted on to the pavement, then coursed like silvery ropes down the drains. Mika and Audrey ran into the street and searched frantically for Tom and Kobi. There was still a long queue waiting to go in and the road was littered with hunched-shouldered shoppers. Eventually, they saw their friends standing in the doorway of the cinema opposite, with film trailers playing behind them on a row of wet screens. Kobi's black hair hung in rat-tails over his face, and Tom licked the rain from his lips and hugged himself as they crossed the road.

'Hey,' Tom said, trying to look pleased to see them, but Mika knew the truth the moment he saw his eyes.

'We were your hunter,' he said. 'Weren't we?'

'Yes,' Tom replied, looking away.

'Oh no!' Audrey cried. 'We didn't realize!'

'It's OK,' Tom said. 'We know it's not your fault.' He began to walk away.

'We didn't know!' Audrey called after him.

Tom walked on, heading in the opposite direction to the train station.

'Where are you going?' Audrey yelled.

'Leave him,' Kobi said. 'Don't worry, I'll talk to him. He doesn't blame you, he's just worried about his mum.'

They watched Kobi lope off down the street, a bundle of wet rags with his feet exploding like bombs in the puddles, and Audrey began to cry.

'What's going to happen to Tom's mum?' she said desperately. 'Now he can't help her!'

'We didn't know,' Mika said. 'It's not our fault.'

They walked to the station in silence and Audrey's eyes had the faraway look of someone too exhausted to think. They sat on the platform while they waited for a train and Audrey took Kobi's cat out of her pocket and let it play on her hand. Mika was glad she was quiet. He had a war raging inside him between three overwhelming emotions: relief, dread and guilt. But when he got home and told his parents he'd won them their first ever holiday, his father's eyes lit up with amazement and Asha skipped around the sofa with glee, and he felt a little bit better and wished he could tell them what he was *really* competing for.

17

ANIMALS WERE BEAUTIFUL

On Sunday mornings, Mika and Audrey usually went to the arcade to practise, but that Sunday Audrey called to say she had to go to her auntie's for lunch, so Mika stayed home. He didn't mind; after a day of competing in the Reading arcade, the last thing he felt like doing was playing Pod Fighter and he was also curious about the prizes he had won and wanted to be at home when they arrived. To pass the time, he tried to mend his coat, but when he tried it on, he realized he'd sewn the sleeve together by mistake and couldn't get his arm into it.

'You'd have looked like Frankenstein's monster in it anyway,' Asha said, as she unpicked his ugly black stitches. 'I'm really annoyed with the boy who did this to you, now you don't have a good coat.'

Mika had lied about the rip in his coat, because he knew she'd freak out if she knew the truth and he watched, guiltily, as she neatly mended the hole.

Just as she finished, the plague siren started as it did every Sunday morning, to test it was working. Barford North's was on the top of the tank meat factory and for three awful minutes the sound of it paralysed their minds and froze the blood in their veins. Afterwards Asha was always irritable.

'And you don't just need a new coat and jeans and sneakers,' she said, banging around in the kitchen. 'We need to get you a new plague suit, too. Yours will be useless the amount you've grown recently.'

'Don't bother,' Mika said. 'I'm never going to need it.'

'You might,' she said.

'Why?' he said. 'It's forty-four years since the Animal Plague. Everything is dust on the other side of The Wall, and besides, the suits are so thin I can't see the point of them. If an animal bit you, its teeth would go straight through it.'

'They're designed to protect you against *saliva*,' Asha said, impatiently. 'Not bites.'

'So I'll be all right if an animal *licks* me,' Mika said. 'That's OK then.'

'Don't make jokes about it,' Asha said, impatiently. 'It's not funny. You have to have a plague suit that fits, it's the law.'

Mika threw himself on the bed and looked wistfully at Ellie's animal pictures.

'And I wish you'd get rid of those,' Asha said, following him into his room. 'They're creepy. I don't understand why you want to look at them. They're only centimetres from your face when you're going to sleep. I'm surprised they don't give you nightmares.'

'It's not animals that give me nightmares,' Mika said. 'It's people. I like the pictures, they remind me of Ellie. Animals were beautiful.'

'You wouldn't say that if you'd been around during the plague,' Asha said.

'You weren't,' Mika pointed out. 'You were just a baby and

you got evacuated before it was anywhere near you.'

'Well yes, but we saw it all,' Asha said. 'They were broadcasting it twenty-four hours a day on television. You grew up watching cartoons. *I* grew up watching dogs biting babies in their prams and ripping windows from their frames. If you'd grown up seeing *that* you wouldn't want pictures of animals centimetres from your face.'

'Well, I'm not getting rid of them,' Mika said, scowling. 'They make me feel happy.'

Asha huffed and stomped out of the bedroom and Mika began to wish he'd gone to the arcade after all. Staying in and arguing with his mum wasn't half so much fun.

Luckily, a few minutes later, his prizes arrived so they had something else to think about. He heard the door buzz and a clown roly-polyed into the apartment and crashed into the back of the sofa. Asha gasped and put her hand to her mouth.

'Are you OK?' she asked, not feeling as polite as she sounded. She was in the middle of her Sunday morning cleaning spree and the last thing she wanted was a clown sprawled all over the floor. It was a creepy-looking clown too; its face was painted with a big red smile but the mouth beneath the makeup looked sour. They watched it scrabble around on the floor looking for its nose, which had rolled under the sofa.

'Here,' David said, finding it and giving it back.

'Thanks,' replied the clown, squidging it into place. Then it stood up and cleared its throat. 'Congratulations, winner!' it cried. 'You have successfully completed the first two rounds of the competition!'

The clown waddled to the door, nearly tripping over its blue feet, which were as long as flippers, then, huffing and puffing, it dragged a large box with a red ribbon tied around it into the apartment. 'Your prizes,' it said, panting. 'And information about your holiday. Have fun!'

Seconds later, it was gone and Mika and his parents were left staring at the box.

'It's very big, Mika,' Asha said. 'What did you say you've won?'

'A phone companion,' Mika replied, still dazed by the clown experience. 'And a holiday.' He pulled the ribbon, there was a sudden explosion and the three of them fell back, blasted in the face by a storm of silver confetti. Asha choked in shock and spat bits out of her mouth. Mika picked a piece off his jeans and looked at it. The confetti was shaped like the Youth Development Foundation logo, YDF, and the force of the explosion had plastered the silvery pieces to everything, even the curtains and walls.

'Look at all this!' David said, peering into the box. 'There's *real* food in here and party stuff!' He began emptying it on to the floor: there were YDF banners, balloons, napkins and party hats. There was a large cake with YDF iced on the top of it and several cartons of food, including tank meat steak and *real* strawberries, and at the bottom, Mika's phone companion.

'Well, I'll be blowed!' David exclaimed, his eyes shining with wonder.

'Man's Best Friend' was written on the front of the box. 'Model two one five phone companion with Lilian character sim.'

'Jeez,' David said. 'Not even my boss has one like this. They cost a bomb!'

Mika was surprised – he knew the prize would be a phone companion, but not one like this. Even rich kids didn't have companions like Lilian, while most of the kids at his school had old companions handed down from their parents, with stupid cartoon characters. Mika had sat on his over a year ago and it had a big crack across the screen.

He opened the box and slotted the sim card into the side and it booted up. The screen buzzed and Lilian appeared. She was very pretty and her eyes shone as she leaned forward to have a look at him. She was an impossible, enviable age, in her late teens, maybe.

'Hello!' she said. 'Pleased to meet you. I'm Lilian, your new companion. Are you ready to initiate?'

'What do I have to do?' Mika asked.

'You have to initiate her so she knows you,' David replied enthusiastically, itching to get his hands on her. He loved gadgets although they couldn't afford any. 'The new generation companions only work for their owner. They're the nearest thing you can get to a human servant. Anything you want to know, she'll find out for you. She can make appointments, make sure you get to school on time, don't miss birthdays, all kinds of things.'

'Would she do my homework?' Mika asked, mischievously.

'If you asked her to,' David said, looking alarmed. 'But you're not to do that, OK?'

'OK,' Mika replied, smiling.

'When you initiate her, she'll ask you lots of questions and learn to recognize your voice,' David said. 'Here. Give her to me.' He took the companion from Mika's hands and fiddled with it.

'David,' Asha said gently. 'You just said Mika has to do it.'

'Oh yeah,' David said, looking sheepish and giving it back. Lilian yawned.

'She's tired,' Asha said. 'I expect she needs charging. That's an impressive prize for a kids' competition. What else can you win?'

'A hover car, and a home in the Golden Turrets,' Mika said.

'Seriously?' David said, his eyebrows raised. 'You can win a *hover car* and a *home in the Golden Turrets* playing Pod Fighter?'

'Yeah,' Mika replied.

'Chrise,' David said. 'Wish I was a kid. How are we going to find out about the holiday you've won?'

'I can tell you that,' Lilian said. 'I've already got a message for you; hang on a sec . . .'

A moment later, Lilian's pretty face was replaced by a man in a straw hat.

'Hello, Mika Smith!' the Hat Man cried. 'You are one of only a hundred competitors to reach the third round of the competition!'

'One of only *a hundred*,' David interjected. 'That's impressive.'

'The prize you have won is a week's holiday in an exclusive *offshore* resort! The date of your departure is two weeks from today! So prepare for the time of your life! What fun you will have, Mika Smith! While your parents are sunbathing and drinking cocktails, you will be competing in the third round of the competition!'

The man spun his hat, trumpets tooted and then he disappeared.

'It's a shame you have to compete while you're on holiday,' David said.

'I don't mind,' Mika said. 'While you're enjoying yourselves, I might win a hover car.'

'Well, if you're sure,' David said, smiling happily.

'I am,' Mika said. 'Just imagine if I won . . .'

His parents' eyes turned misty and they gazed at the floor as if it was scattered with diamonds instead of the Youth Development Foundation confetti. Asha's companion beeped. The Youth Development Foundation had sent her more information about the holiday.

'Oh, wow,' she said. 'The holiday is on a Caribbean-style resort! That's where all the rich people who live in the Golden Turrets go! And wait, there's more, they're giving us money to buy holiday clothes, and there'll be palm trees and beaches and everything!'

Then her smile was replaced by a frown. 'They say I've got to remind you to take the capsules. What capsules?'

'Oh, those,' Mika said, looking for his bag. He found the white box he'd been given the day before and put one of the capsules on the palm of his hand so his mother could look at it. It was bullet-shaped, transparent and full of white powder.

'What's in it?' Asha asked, taking it from his hand.

'Nutrients,' Mika said, vaguely.

'More nutrients?' Asha replied, looking concerned. 'I hope they don't make you grow any more . . .'

'I'm sure they won't,' Mika said, taking it back quickly, keen to stop her asking any more questions. 'Look, you've got confetti in your tea.'

'Oh yeah,' Asha replied, looking in her cup and seeing several YDF logos bobbing around in it. 'I suppose I ought to ask the vacuumbot to clean the ceiling and curtains again.'

The vacuumbot refused to come out of its cupboard.

'You stupid thing,' said Asha. 'Why won't you do what you're told? Can you win a vacuumbot in this competition, Mika? I think this one has given up the will to live.'

'No,' Mika replied. 'Only hover cars and apartments. But remember, you can sell the hover car if I win it. You could buy several hundred vacuumbots with the money from a hover car.'

'We could, couldn't we?' Asha said, her eyes lighting up as she began to imagine what it felt like to have money. 'Oh, wouldn't it be great, Mika. Just imagine what we could do.'

She found a dustpan and brush and started brushing the curtains. They were so old and ragged, big lumps started falling off them, but Asha didn't seem to notice, she continued brushing with a rapturous smile on her face. Mika quickly found a cup, filled it with water and stirred in a sachet of Fit Mix and the contents of the capsule.

'Here's to you Ellie,' he whispered, as he raised the cup to his mouth.

Afterwards, he plugged Lilian into her charger and lay on the bed feeling wracked by guilt. Because of what *he* wanted, people who cared about him were being hurt; Helen was gone, Tom couldn't help his mum and now he had started lying to his parents so they didn't get suspicious. And although he knew he had no choice, the guilt was a heavy burden to carry along with his fear and his love for Ellie, and he wondered whether he was really strong enough to do it.

18
LIGHT TRAILS

In Barford North on Monday morning, the mood in school was subdued. The wind blew through the dark, damp playground, but instead of warming themselves with talk of Pod Fighter and dreams of living in the Golden Turrets, everyone shivered in their thin coats and sucked miserably on yellow YDF consolation prize lollipops. Mika felt too awkward to face their disappointment, especially since he was thinking they'd had a lucky escape, so he hovered by the school gates until the bell rang and they were all inside. When he arrived in class, everyone was drinking their Fit Mix and Mrs Fowler looked at him reproachfully for being late.

He took off his coat and sat next to Kobi. They hadn't seen each other since Tom had left them outside the arcade.

'How's Tom?' Mika whispered.

'Not good,' Kobi said. 'He's really disappointed.'

'I'm sorry,' Mika said, earnestly.

Kobi nodded. 'I know. Anyway, I don't care, I was only playing for Tom.'

Mika looked up to find Mrs Fowler watching him. She nodded towards the sachet of Fit Mix and the cup of water on his desk, so he made it up and mixed in one of the capsules with Kobi watching him curiously.

* * *

After school, Mika met Audrey in the Ra Ra Shake Bar. It was Audrey's favourite place, the colours as acid bright as her eyes and the music funky. They sat on high stools looking out over the mall and because so many people had been knocked out of the competition it was unusually quiet; the loudest noise was coming from the air conditioning units above their heads, which were pumping away as if there were hundreds of kids beneath them, not just the few milling around. The staff in the shake bar looked bored, and in the game room the simulators were as lifeless as spiders in a room with no flies.

'Everyone in school was miserable today,' Audrey said, gazing down the empty mall. 'I didn't want to tell anyone we'd got through. I hope they start playing again tomorrow. It's not going to be much fun if we're flying on our own all the time.'

'I'm sure they'll come back soon,' Mika reassured her. 'They'll miss the game.'

'Do you think Tom and Kobi will come back?' she asked, sadly. 'It won't be the same without them.'

'I don't think Kobi will,' Mika said. 'He says he wants to make music with his new companion because it's got a better composer than his old one. I don't know about Tom.'

'I hope he comes back,' Audrey said. 'I like him.'

'So do I.'

They only had two weeks to prepare for the next round of the competition so they talked about what they were going to do, but after a while, Mika realized Audrey wasn't listening properly. Kobi's borg cat played on the table between them and she stared at it with a furrowed brow while it patted the straw from her drink.

'What's the matter?' he asked.

'I don't know,' she replied, blinking. 'My eyes have gone weird; I think I might have to go to the borg doctor tomorrow and get them checked.'

'What's wrong with them?' Mika asked, curious to know what it was like to have the eyes of a robot.

'I can see light trails on things when they move,' she replied. 'It started earlier when I was in school and it's making me feel ill.'

'Do you want to go home?' he asked. 'I won't mind if you do.'

'No way,' she said. 'We need to practise.'

But she couldn't practise. Within minutes of take-off, she felt so sick, they had to abandon the game and Mika walked her home.

'It's like you're drunk,' he said, holding on to her arm to stop her bumping into the fountain in the town square. 'You're all over the place.'

'I feel awful,' she said, miserably. 'I think I must have caught a bug.'

He left her at her door and walked home. It was still early, so Asha was at work and David was just sitting down to watch a movie. As Mika walked in, he noticed the packet of biscuits Helen had sent him next to the sofa. They were digestives, the same kind he'd eaten with her many times, and looking at them made him feel sad.

'You don't mind if I eat them, do you?' David asked, taking one out of the packet. 'I thought they'd go nicely with my film.'

'No,' Mika said, gloomily. 'I don't want them.'

David walked to the kitchen area to put the kettle on for a cup of tea and Mika hung up his coat. But as he turned to face his father again, his eyes widened with shock as he saw that the biscuit David was holding had something stuck to the bottom of it.

'You OK?' David asked. 'You look as if you've seen a ghost.'

'Yeah, course,' Mika replied, trying not to look at the biscuit. His father hadn't noticed. 'What's the film about?'

'I dunno, some adventure thing,' David replied. 'Someone at work lent it to me.'

He turned away and searched for a cup in the cupboard and Mika tried to get a closer look at the biscuit. Whatever was stuck to the bottom of it was square and white, but he couldn't see it well enough to work out what it was. He opened the saucepan cupboard next to his father's legs so he could crouch down and look at the biscuit from below. His heart leaped. The square thing was a piece of paper folded up many times and his name was written on in it in Helen's inky handwriting. It was a letter! A secret letter from Helen stuck to the underside of the biscuit!

'Why do you want a saucepan?' David asked, and Mika looked up to see his father frowning at him. 'It's a bit late for cooking.'

'Sorry,' Mika said, standing up again. His heart squirmed painfully in his chest. That most precious object, *a letter from Helen*, had been sitting unnoticed in the cupboard for weeks! How stupid he felt, how frustrated. And how could he get the letter away from his father? As David placed his cup next to the kettle, his movement caused the paper to unfold a little, so Mika was able to read the first tantalizing sentence;

'Dear Mika,

Last time we met, I wanted to tell you a secret but I was scared for you, so I didn't dare. However, I've changed my mind because you are in terrible danger and you need to know the truth . . .'

Mika's heart began to thump madly. He couldn't see any more of the letter because of the way it was folded.

What secret? What terrible danger and truth? Suddenly it seemed all the things he needed to know were in his father's hand!

'Look!' Mika said, pointing towards the window, hoping David would be distracted enough to put the biscuit down.

'What?' David replied, turning. He stared out of the window

at the drizzly darkness for a few seconds. 'I can't see anything,' he said.

'Oh, it's gone now,' Mika replied. 'It was one of those big freighters.'

'Really?' David said, still holding the biscuit and feeling perplexed; Mika hadn't been interested in 'big freighters' since he was three years old. He looked at his son with a furrowed brow and started to raise the biscuit to his mouth. Desperate to stop him, Mika knocked the sugar sub over so it spilled on the carpet.

'What's wrong with you?' David said impatiently. Helen's letter was now dangling from the biscuit, but he still hadn't noticed it. 'How did you manage to do that?'

'Sorry,' Mika said again.

'You'd better clean that up,' David said. 'Before your mother gets home.'

He raised the biscuit to his mouth for the second time and Mika winced, unable to think of any other tactic than grabbing it from his father's hand and running away with it, and he was just about to do exactly that when David said, 'Eww, I think this biscuit is mouldy, it's got white stuff all over it.' He took a step towards the waste chute.

'No!' Mika yelled. But it was too late; the biscuit left his father's hand and flew like a mini Frisbee into the waste chute and Mika could do nothing but listen to it bang down the tube to the crusher in the basement feeling as if he was being strangled.

'What's wrong?' David asked. 'It was mouldy. It was so furry, you could have given it a hairdo.'

'Nothing,' Mika choked. He grabbed the packet of biscuits from the floor and ran to his room with them.

'Don't eat those, Mika!' David called after him. 'They'll give you food poisoning! And what about the mess in here? There's sugar sub all over the floor!'

'I'll do it in a minute!' Mika shouted, tipping the rest of the biscuits on to the bed. He searched through them frantically, praying for another letter, but all the rest were just plain old mouldy biscuits. 'You idiot!' he hissed to himself. 'You perping, fragging noodle brain!' Helen had sent him a letter and all he'd seen was the beginning: '. . . I wanted to tell you a secret . . . you are in terrible danger and you need to know the truth . . .' At last she had decided to tell him what he craved to know but her letter had sat in the cupboard for weeks in a packet of mouldy biscuits and now it was in the rubbish crusher and he couldn't get it back.

How stupid he felt. How he hated himself. And the fragment of Helen's message he'd read didn't help him at all; it just made him feel more confused and afraid. What secret did she want to tell him? What terrible danger did he face?

* * *

Later that night, unable to sleep, Mika lay in the darkness listening to a song Kobi had sent him when they first became friends playing Pod Fighter together. Darkness was right for Kobi's music; it was melancholy yet so beautiful Mika felt himself lift out of his body, fly through the window and up into the night sky. The sleeping hulks of the towers beneath him looked like megaliths on an ancient plain. Higher and higher he rose until he was floating amongst the stars. When the song ended, he asked Lilian to play it again. At the end she said, 'Do you want it again?'

'No thanks.'

He opened his eyes and leaned out of bed to plug Lilian into her charger, and that's when he saw it for the first time. As his hand moved towards the floor to feel around for the cable, it left a trail of golden light in its wake. He forgot about the charger and moved his hand again, waving it fast in front of his face. As it moved it seemed to emit light, as if light was leaking from it. He held his hand still and it became dark, but around it was an aura like a halo. It was as if he could see the heat escaping from his skin. He drew patterns in the air, circles, zigzags, spirals, then more circles again, and then he began to feel scared. He connected Lilian to her charger and buried his hands beneath the cover.

* * *

By the next morning, Mika was seeing light trails on everything that moved: on his mother's hand as she mixed his Stir and Serve, his father's as he combed his hair, and on his own as he tied up his laces so it took him twice as long to do it as it usually did.

'Are you all right?' Asha asked, as she watched him struggle.

'Yeah, fine,' he replied, but not feeling it.

He left for school and staggered along the walkway as if he was drunk. Every person that passed him left a trail of hilly light in their wake and when he reached school and walked across the dark playground, the sensation of motion sickness was heightened as thousands of kids moved around him. He closed his eyes and leaned against a wall, feeling its dampness through his clothes, resting his head until the bell rang for class.

When he reached the classroom he felt a little bit better; the light trails were still there, but his eyes were becoming accustomed to them. However, he still bumped into several desks on the way to his.

'Hey,' Kobi said, with a sharp look. 'What's wrong with you?'

'Nothing,' Mika mumbled, almost falling into his chair.

'Right, class!' Mrs Fowler shouted. 'You know what to do! Everyone drink your Fit Mix!'

Mika mixed the powder with water in the plastic cup, then emptied a capsule into the drink. He felt his stomach spasm looking at it and he thought he was going to vomit.

'What's that?' the girl sitting behind him asked.

'Nothing,' Mika said, irritably, trying not to be sick.

'Why have you got a capsule and the rest of us haven't?' she asked, enviously.

He heard the scraping of chairs behind him and suddenly he was surrounded.

'Yeah, what is it, Mika? What makes you so special? Hey

look! Ruben's got one as well. What's it for? It's something to do with the competition, isn't it? Look everyone!'

Mika couldn't breathe with them crowded around him, and their moving heads and hands were a blinding light show.

'Go away,' Kobi said, pushing them back with his hand. 'What's wrong with you? Leave him alone.'

'Class!' Mrs Fowler yelled. 'Settle down! Everyone back to your desks and drink your Fit Mix or I'll send for Mr Grey!'

* * *

That afternoon, Mr Blyte introduced a new exercise to their fitness programme. They arrived at the Complex Leisure Centre to find an assault course had been built in the biggest gym hall.

'Oh no,' Roland Spelling Bee whispered, when they saw it for the first time.

Mika just looked at the assault course and felt his stomach lurch. There were ten-metre walls to climb with only the smallest hand and footholds. A tank full of water covered in green nets. A maze of metal tunnels, jumps, rope ladders and slides.

'Good afternoon!' Blyte bellowed. 'Everyone grab a backpack and put it on!'

There was a pile of backpacks on the floor. A girl tried to pick one up and it was so heavy, she nearly fell over.

'What a pathetic display!' Blyte roared. 'Pick it up, girl, and get it on you!'

She tried again and hauled the straps on to her shoulders with difficulty.

'Right!' Blyte snapped, his eyes sharp as knives. 'If this exercise doesn't sort you lot out I don't know what will! Twice round the assault course everyone, then five kilometres on the treadmills. The first one to finish gets a voucher for a kebab in Tank Meat Express!'

'I swear this is full of concrete,' the girl muttered, as she staggered towards the start, and she was right – Mika could feel hard lumps through the fabric of his backpack. His head spun as he put it on but he managed to keep going until he was climbing up the second wall. Kobi was just beneath him and Mika could hear him breathing hard as he struggled not to lose his grip. Moments later he saw him over to his right, the muscles in his arms glowing gold with the strange new light and pumped up with the effort of the climb. Mika faltered, feeling dazed, and he watched the blood pulsing through a vein on Kobi's forearm and thought he could hear it, boom boom, boom boom. He felt mild surprise as he began to fall and was unconscious before he hit the ground.

* * *

When Mika opened his eyes again he was lying on a bed surrounded by a white curtain. Of all the ways to wake up, this had to be the worst for Mika; he panicked, inhaling sharply as he saw the corner of the curtain twitch where someone grabbed it from the other side. But it wasn't a Telly Head, it was a woman in a white coat with the letters YDF embroidered on the pocket.

'Where am I?' he asked.

'In the health bay in the Complex Leisure Centre,' she replied softly. 'How do you feel?'

He watched golden light dance from the ends of her fingers as she pulled the curtain back.

'Weird,' he said.

'Weird in your body or weird in your head?' she asked.

'Both.'

'Are you seeing light trails?' she asked, sitting down on the end of the bed.

He nodded, cautiously.

'It's because of the capsules,' she said. 'It's nothing to worry about, Mika. The way you're feeling is just your body acclimatizing itself to change. In a few days' time, you'll feel much better.'

'Good,' he said.

'You'll be glad you're taking them soon, believe me,' she went on, smiling as if she knew a fantastic and interesting secret.

'Why?' Mika asked.

'I can't tell you,' she answered, as if he was a cheeky toddler. 'It's a surprise. Like on birthdays. But you'll be glad you took them, just give yourself a few days to settle down. OK?'

'OK.'

'I'll get you something to eat and drink and then you can go home.'

'Thanks.'

'And we don't need to worry your parents by telling them, do we?'

'No,' he replied, heartily agreeing with her.

'Good boy,' she said.

He glared at her back as she walked away, resenting her for looking at him as if he was an object and talking to him like a baby.

As he left the health bay, Ruben was brought in, supported on one side by Mr Blyte and on the other by one of the men who worked in the gym – a hulk of a man with legs and arms like fake-tanned tree trunks. Ruben's head rolled on his shoulders as if his neck was a rubber band, and his feet dragged on the floor. Mika stepped aside to let them pass, embarrassed that only an hour before he had been in the same state and niggled that Ruben had taken longer to collapse than he had. Then he prayed this wasn't a prediction of their performances in the next round.

19

A GOLDEN BIRD

The two weeks before the holiday passed slowly for Mika because it was so hard to conceal the fact that he saw light trails on everything – they were so beautiful, a couple of times he forgot himself and said, 'Wow!', which was confusing for the people around him who could see nothing, and made him look even more bonkers than they already thought he was.

People left trails of golden light when they moved, while objects left trails of the palest blue. When it was dark, the sky was filled with streamers of gold and blue light: blue from the flying pods and gold from the people sitting inside them. It was so beautiful it made his heart swell with wonder and he regretted the fact he couldn't tell anyone what he could see. He didn't even mention it to Audrey, even though he knew she could see them too. She never talked about the light trails after that first night in the Ra Ra Shake Bar and he was glad. Although he was still afraid, for the first time there was beauty in his world and a little part of him was excited and looking forward to finding out why. He even saw the light on Awen, and sometimes, when it was dark in his room, that was all he saw of him; a golden glow down the side of the bed.

The day before Mika and Audrey left for their holiday and the third round of the competition, Mika's class had a surprise visit from Mr Grey in Fit Camp.

'I want everyone in proper kit!' Mr Blyte yelled in their faces, spraying them with bits of his lunchtime burger. 'Anyone without it, see me! If any of you let me down you'll be doing press-ups until the sun sets on the day you DIE!'

They dressed quickly in silence with their backs to him. Mika had a chilli sauce stain on his T-shirt so he spat on his finger and rubbed it.

'Smith!' Blyte yelled. 'What the frag are you doing? Come here!'

Mika walked towards him.

'What did I just say to you? Are you stupid?'

He threw a clean T-shirt at Mika.

'I want that back after the lesson!' he shouted. 'Get dressed!'

He made them stand in a line while he inspected them, then he led them into the gym hall and told them to wait for Mr Grey.

He looked particularly grey that afternoon, as if he'd just had a fresh coat of grey paint – his suit, his skin, his hair, his pale grey eyes and lips. For the past few weeks the Headmaster had been nothing more than a nodding grey shadow that moved along the walls in school. Mika felt his skin crawl the moment he heard his footsteps enter the gym hall. He stood in front of them holding two pieces of plastic paper.

'Good afternoon, class,' he said, filling the gym with his train station breath.

'Good afternoon, Mr Grey,' they chanted.

'It's nice to see you all,' he continued. 'Unfortunately, I've not had time to come down and see what marvellous work you've been doing here in the Complex Leisure Centre before, but I must say how impressed I am by how fit and strong you all look – Mr Blyte has obviously trained you well. I hear your average growth since starting Fit Camp is fourteen centimetres.'

He nodded to Blyte, and Blyte smiled and rolled back on his heels looking pleased with himself.

'I have special awards to give out today,' Mr Grey continued, 'to pupils who have made Barford North School very proud. We have not just one, but two of our boys through to the third round of the competition. Mika Smith and Ruben Snaith, step forward.'

Mika felt a hundred eyes on him and he didn't want to move.

'Mika,' Mr Blyte snapped.

He stepped forward so he was standing next to Ruben in front of Mr Grey. Ruben's proximity made the skin down his left side prickle. He stared at the floor wishing he could dive into it.

'On behalf of Barford North School,' Mr Grey said pompously, 'I'd like to award these certificates to commemorate your progress in the competition. I'm sure everyone would like to join me in congratulating you on your remarkable achievement.' Then in a quieter voice that was menacing enough to cut through Mika's borrowed T-shirt, 'Especially *you* Mika, after *your* difficult start.'

He handed them the certificates and everyone started to clap and the noise sounded like a flock of pigeons trying to escape the gym.

'But I must say this,' Mr Grey continued, when the clapping had subsided, 'every one of you should feel proud of your achievements over the past few weeks. You look magnificent. You are icons of health and fitness and I have no doubt that very soon, every one of you will prove yourself a fine citizen of the northern hemisphere. Give yourselves a round of applause.'

The clapping started again, but this time it sounded confused; after all, they were only twelve. They still had six years of school to survive before they had to think about becoming fine citizens of the northern hemisphere. Mr Grey handed out more Youth Development Foundation consolation prize lollipops and the children left with furrowed brows.

Mika dropped his certificate and lollipop in the bin on the way home and didn't waste any time thinking about Mr Grey's strange talk about fine citizens of the northern hemisphere. He could see light trails on everything that moved, he had lost Helen's letter, the only thing that could have helped him, and the next day he would be competing in the third round of the competition – he had enough to worry about.

* * *

Mika shared a dream with Ellie that night. She opened her eyes in her white room on the Queen of the North and saw a golden bird sitting on her knee where it was raised beneath the cover. It glowed in the darkness, filling the small space with warm light. It was a garden bird, a Jenny Wren, with a round breast and short tail. Ellie tried not to move so it wouldn't be afraid and they looked at each other with interest.

I wish I was you, she thought, able to fly like a ghost through the wall of my prison.

The wren's head cocked to one side and its tail bobbed. Then, as if it was a wishing bird, it took off and Ellie found herself flying with it; through the wall with a soft thrup of feathers into the observation room, past the men in white coats and out the other side. Then through locked doors and lots more walls until they had left the spaceship behind and were diving together through space towards Earth. Through the bird's eyes, Ellie could see The Wall and the grey outline of Europe. Down, down, they flew, until they were skimming the tops of the towers of Barford North, and then, like a missile aimed at Mika, the bird flew through the wall of their tower and into their tiny bedroom.

Hearing the flutter of feathers Mika opened his eyes just in time to see the bird land on Awen's head. The dog made a rumbling noise in its sleep but didn't stir. Dog and bird bathed the room in golden light and Mika felt his heart swell with love.

'I know you,' he whispered.

He put out his hand, hoping the bird would hop across on to his finger. It did and they looked at each other. The bird's eyes were bright and intense, and as he gazed into them he felt waves of emotion: the deepest love, the most palpable relief, then, such desolate anguish and loneliness he felt as if he was being crushed by it.

'Ellie,' he whispered.

There was a noise through the wall in the next apartment; the flush of a hygiene unit. The bird startled and took off and flew through the door of Ellie's cupboard.

Mika jumped up and opened it, hoping to find the bird inside, but to his horror, he discovered that the Knife Sharpener had caught it in his hand. The bird's light guttered and flickered, like a candle trying to burn without oxygen, then the Knife Sharpener tightened his grip and the light faded until Mika could see nothing but the flickering face of the monster.

20

A NEW BREED OF HUMAN

Gorman glared at Ellie through a sheet of fortified glass. She was standing in the middle of an empty room in full body armour with her arms crossed defiantly. All he could see of her face were her eyes glowering back at him through the slit in her helmet.

'Tell her to do it again!' Gorman ordered. 'And again and again until we know how she does it!'

'But she's been in there six hours, sir,' a scientist replied, politely. 'And she says she's got a headache.'

'I don't care!' Gorman yelled. 'I want a scientific explanation for what she can do by the END OF THE DAY! NO EXCUSES. TELL THEM TO BRING IN ANOTHER ONE!'

'Bring in another piece of asteroid,' the scientist said into his com, and a few seconds later, two men entered the room pushing a hover trolley carrying a large chunk of asteroid.

'I can't do it again!' Ellie cried. 'I've got a pain behind my eyes! I can hardly see!'

Gorman watched one of the men talk to her, issuing threats, telling her Puck wouldn't be fed if she didn't obey his commands. Afterwards, the men placed the chunk of asteroid in the middle of the room and left, locking the door, so Ellie was alone.

'Are you sure she's wired up properly?' Gorman asked.

'Yes,' the scientist replied. 'She has receptors monitoring every single chemical impulse in her brain. The inside of that helmet looks like a bowl of spaghetti.'

'OK,' Gorman said. 'Tell her to do it.'

'When you're ready, Ellie,' the scientist said.

Ellie sighed. The chunk of asteroid was twice the size of her head and ten times heavier than it looked. She stared at it for a split second and it exploded, making the walls of the room and the reinforced glass of the window bow out. For a few moments it sounded as if there was a hailstorm going on in the room as thousands of tiny fragments of asteroid fell to the floor. Ellie sank on top of them, too tired to stand up any longer.

'Can I go now?' she shouted at the window.

'Did you get anything?' Gorman asked the scientists who were staring at the computer screens. 'Do you know how she does it?'

'No, sir,' one replied, shaking his head.

'So what *do* you know?' Gorman said, angrily. 'What am I paying you all for?'

'We know her brain is larger than a normal human's,' one of the scientists offered, 'and she is clearly capable of doing things we can't, but we don't know how. We're beginning to wonder if the mutants aren't simply normal humans gone wrong, but something new.'

'You mean a new breed?' Gorman asked, sceptically. 'Of human?'

'It happened in prehistoric times,' the man replied. 'Only thirty-five thousand years ago two species of human coexisted, the Cro-Magnon and the Neanderthals.'

'But that didn't happen all of a sudden like this,' Gorman scoffed. 'Did it?'

'No,' the scientist admitted. 'But we were wondering whether the thirty-year gap when no babies were born might have something to do with it.'

'You were wondering?' Gorman sneered. 'You thought, you pondered, you guessed. What sort of scientist are you? Wondering and pondering! You don't know anything, do you?'

'Not really,' the scientist muttered, hanging his head.

'Well she's not going to bed until you DO!' Gorman roared.

'Yes, sir.'

21
BLUE SKY

Asha was so looking forward to the holiday, she packed several times in the days leading up to it. The Youth Development Foundation had given the winners credits to spend on holiday clothes, so nearly everything they were taking was new. Mika thought his mother looked the best she had since Ellie had disappeared; more often than not she was smiling or looked as though she was thinking good thoughts. She packed on the floor, kneeling in front of the sofa with the television ignored in the background, wearing a plain white sari with her long hair tied elegantly at the nape of her neck, her cowgirl costume in the cupboard so she didn't have to look at it. Mika watched her lay everything out in neat piles: sandals, shorts, sunglasses and swimming costumes, all with their shop tags still on.

'I think you could do with another pair of shorts,' she said. 'I'll have to pop into town before the shops close and get you some.' She smiled, pleased by the prospect of another excuse to go to a shop and buy something without worrying they would have to starve for a week to pay for it. 'Oh and perhaps something else for the evening,' she added. 'There are bound to be a couple of meals and we don't want to wear the same thing every night. I'll try on that ruby red sari I saw and I'll get you a shirt. What do you think?'

'Yeah,' said Mika, not really paying attention. He was watching her hands make patterns of golden light from the floor to the case as she put the things back into it. There were subtle differences to people's light trails, and he was beginning to recognize these as echoes of their character. His mother's light trail moved sinuously: warm and smooth and the colour of honey. Audrey's was bright and fractious, broken up sometimes when she was excited or moved quickly, like sparks from a fire. Kobi's were strong as if he had a force field around him, and Tom's were confused and sometimes darkened as Mika approached him, even when he looked friendly, which made Mika wonder whether the light trails showed emotions too, even those people chose to hide.

They had three false starts leaving for the holiday. A chauffeured pod waited for them on the roof of their tower but the lift was broken as usual, so they had to climb the stairs with their cases. The first time they had to go back because Asha had forgotten to pack their toothbrushes; the second time, David wanted to check he'd turned off the air con, and the third time, Mika had forgotten Ellie's holopic of mountain lions, and even though they'd struggled up the stairs and had nearly reached the roof, he insisted on going back for it. Their chauffeur looked grumpy and impatient by the time they'd climbed into the pod and he didn't help with the bags.

The pod had an egg-shaped interior; the chauffeur sat at the front with a glass divider behind him and in the back was a comfortable curved seat for the passengers. They put their luggage in the middle between their legs and Asha got out the box of sandwiches she'd made for the journey.

'We haven't even left yet,' David said, smiling, as she offered him one.

'I know, but they are nice,' she replied, sheepishly.

They flew north across the whole length of Britain, over towns and cities they'd never seen before. The last time they were in a pod, Mika had been choking to death, so it felt great to be doing something pleasant in one.

The air roads were marked at either side by air buoys – brightly lit balls that hung at twenty-metre intervals. They had messages on them, one word on each, so you read the whole thing as they flashed past. Some told you how far the centre of the next town was – Leamington Spa. 2km. Some gave you the weather forecast – Thirteen. Degrees. Cloudy. Rain. Wind. SW. Moderate. Most were advertizing. Miracle. Hair. Grow. Grows. Hair. Like. Weeds. Centimetres. Per. Week. Guaranteed.

Mika watched them until he got bored, then he looked down on the passing towns, all exactly the same as theirs with the hundreds of towers of fold-down apartments punctuated by factories and sewage plants, the heart of each town marked by an enormous yellow plague siren on the tallest building. He looked across the landscape and the yellow sirens in the distance looked like buoys on a concrete sea.

The real sea was not what Mika was expecting – in Pod Fighter it was calm and blue, but off the north coast of Scotland it was a restless mass of iron-grey water that hurled hundred-ton waves at the cliffs and made the tiny pod feel as fragile as a bath bubble. Mika watched the colour drain from his parents' faces as the land shrank behind them, and it was several anxious minutes before the outline of the domed shell of the Caribbean World Holiday Complex appeared on the horizon.

'Chrise, look at that,' David said.

The dome was huge, at least as big as Barford North, and higher than the tallest skyscrapers they had passed on the way. It seemed impossible that such a large thing could float on the sea, but there it was, camouflaged partly by its mirrored surface, which reflected the cresting waves around it and the grey sky overhead.

As the pod flew over the dome, a hole appeared in the top to let them in. They hovered for a moment, then quickly descended, allowing them a brief glimpse of a tropical island surrounded by a friendlier sea, sapphire blue and twinkling in the light of a warm sun. They landed in the middle of the island on a pod strip surrounded by gently wafting palm trees.

'Look at the sky!' Asha exclaimed. 'It's blue!'

'What did you expect?' laughed David. 'Red?'

'You know what I mean!' she retorted, slapping his arm. 'When was the last time we saw blue sky? It's so beautiful! Look at all the *trees*.'

The pod door opened and the tropical heat hit them like a bucket of hot sand. They staggered with their bags on to the pod strip to be greeted by a man in a brightly coloured shirt. He smiled in a friendly way as he loaded their bags on to a hover trolley, then he escorted them to a grass-roofed building nestled amongst the palm trees.

'He was a nice man,' Asha said, as they watched him walk away.

They stood by the door of the hut and tried to take in their new surroundings. After forty-three years surrounded by mouldy concrete and floodwater, the Caribbean World Holiday Complex was a bit of a shock to the senses. All around them greenery rustled in a coconut-scented breeze and it was difficult to accept that even the flowers by the door to the hut and the sun beaming down on them were fake. Everything was made of plastic, even the sand.

'Look at this,' Asha said, touching a fragile-looking flower. 'It looks so real!'

She screeched suddenly, making them jump.

'What's wrong?' David asked, looking nervously at the flowers.

'A ... a ... a ... oh!' Asha spluttered and a moment later, a crab scuttled towards them. She screeched again and hid behind her husband.

'It's not real!' Mika laughed, picking it up. 'Look, Mum, it's made of plastic and it's got a switch on the bottom.' He flicked the switch so the crab's legs stopped wiggling and held it out. Its pincers and legs went floppy so it looked sad.

'Don't,' she said, covering her face. 'Please, Mika, I can't bear it.'

Mika reluctantly turned the crab back on and put it in the flowers. He heard flapping in the tree overhead and looked up to see a parrot and he felt happy suddenly, even though he knew it wasn't real.

The hut looked as if it was made of roughly hewn wood with woven grass walls. Inside there were fifty tables, some occupied by competitors and their families who had arrived before them and some empty. The atmosphere was cheery; a Caribbean band played steel drums in one corner and waitresses in colourful skirts with flowers in their hair shimmied around the tables. One greeted them at the door and led them to a table where Audrey and her mother and aunt were waiting. They leaped up. Mika liked them immediately; their light trails were bright and warm and they threw their arms around them as if they were happily reunited with old friends. He could see Audrey in their features; they both had the same Russian lines with a hint of oriental blood, but instead of red, their hair was black.

'Good to meet you at last,' Audrey's aunt said. 'I'm Tasha.'

'And I'm Una,' her mother added, kissing Mika's cheek.

There were hugs and kisses all round and David blushed and cleared his throat as he weathered a hurricane of lipstick, but he sat down happily enough and Mika was relieved to see them all getting on. Audrey was quiet. She looked incongruous with her punky red hair and borg eyes in that place: an alien elf in Eloper sneakers. She looked around the hut and he realized she was searching for evidence of the game.

'The arcade must be close,' he said.

'I want to go and look for it,' she replied. 'I hope we don't have to stay here long. It's boring.'

Their waitress came to the table with a tray of cocktails that were so full of fruit, plastic palm trees, flamingos and umbrellas, they had to remove half of it to get their lips near the drink. This amused the adults, but Mika and Audrey fiddled with theirs pensively and they didn't feel better until everyone had arrived and there were signs of progress. A man took to the wooden stage. It was the Hat Man from the message they had been sent by the YDF. He was wearing a straw hat and an orange, flowery shirt and he looked impossibly happy as if someone had superglued the corners of his lips to his cheekbones.

'Welcome everybody to the Caribbean World Holiday Complex!' he cried. They heard a trumpet fanfare, he made a flourish with his hand and a pair of wooden doors swung open to reveal a black hover car on a revolving platform. Then, with a second trumpet fanfare, lights flashed on above it and everyone gasped as they caressed the car's elegant curves and shiny paintwork.

'It's a Jaguar!' David whispered.

'What do you think of that?' the Hat Man cried. 'As you can see, the prize for the third round of the competition is a top-of-the-range hover car with built-in widescreen televisions and heated wraparound seats! And we have twelve of these beauties to give away, so you're in with a good chance of winning one, kids, so what do you think?' He raised his arms as if he was expecting riotous screams of joy, but the hundred competitors responded with self-conscious silence. 'Come on! Let's hear you!' he insisted, waving his hands above his head.

Mika gritted his teeth and Audrey rolled her eyes as some of the others joined in a half-hearted chorus of 'Yeaaaah.'

'How embarrassing,' Audrey muttered with her head down.

'OK!' the Hat Man said. 'Glad to hear you're all still alive! Listen carefully now, competitors. As you've already been told, you will be competing in the third round of the competition while you are here! And we're not going to keep you waiting! In just a few minutes, you will be leaving your parents and going to our *special competition centre* on the island, where you will spend the rest of the day! And then tonight, you will rejoin your parents on the beach for a delicious barbeque! Won't that be fun, everyone! Then, for the rest of the week, you will be training for a new game! So I hope you haven't forgotten to bring your swimming costumes, kids, because you're going to need them!'

'What?' Audrey whispered. 'What does he mean, new game? When are we going to play Pod Fighter?'

'Where's the arcade?' one of the competitors shouted.

'There isn't one,' the Hat Man said. 'You won't need an arcade for this round.'

'So how are we going to play Pod Fighter?' someone else asked.

'You won't be playing Pod Fighter,' he replied. 'But the water games we have arranged will be just as exciting!'

There was an uncomfortable silence and Audrey looked at Mika angrily.

'I can't believe it,' she whispered. 'All that time we've spent practising and we're not even playing Pod Fighter!'

'Calm down,' her mother said, touching her arm. 'Don't you think it would be nice to do something different? You've spent every night in the arcade for weeks. You hardly see any light. Whatever you do it will be enjoyable in a place like this.'

'I want to play Pod Fighter,' Audrey said, scowling angrily. 'That's why I entered the competition in the first place.'

'Now then!' the Hat Man bellowed. 'Parents! What will *you* be doing this week? Eh? Eh? Well I'll tell you – nothing, unless you feel like it!'

He raised his arms again and the adults cheered enthusiastically.

'If you want to try something new,' the Hat Man cried, 'you can use *all* the facilities. There are windsurfing and scuba diving lessons, scores of pampering beauty treatments and much, much more. But if you fancy lying on the beach all day drinking cocktails and soaking up the sun, feel free! It's entirely up to you!'

Waitresses began to walk through the tables with baskets in their hands, which had gold ribbons tied to the handles. The adults started talking loudly, and as baskets were given to Asha and Una, Mika began to realize that the prizes in this round were for the parents, not for them. After all, what use was a hover car to a twelve-year-old boy? He wondered uncomfortably why the YDF would need to bribe their parents.

'Look at this!' Asha cried, when she'd untied the ribbon on the basket. 'It's full of *real* food! Look, Mika! Bread!'

'Wow,' Mika said, trying to sound enthusiastic.

'And soy cheese!'

'Right then, everyone!' the Hat Man shouted. 'It's time to take the competitors to our *special competition centre,* so say goodbye to your parents and follow me!'

The Hat Man left the stage and walked towards a door at the back of the hut.

'Goodbye, darling,' Asha said, holding a piece of cheese in one hand and her cocktail in the other. 'Good luck!'

'Thanks, Mum,' Mika said. 'I'll see you later, on the beach for the barbeque.'

He walked with Audrey through the door at the back of the hut feeling as if they were passing through a portal into another world – on one side, warm and colourful, and on the other, cold and blank. They found themselves in a white room that contained nothing but grey plastic chairs, and when the door closed, the happy sound of their parents' laughter abruptly halted.

22

HAVE A NICE HOLIDAY

In the white room, the hundred competitors were told to sit on the rows of chairs and wait for their names to be called. Audrey left first and she looked at Mika anxiously as she was led away by a man in a YDF uniform. Mika felt his stomach twist as the door closed behind her and it suddenly occurred to him that they weren't competing as a team any more – they were on their own. With her gone, he felt darkness draw in on him as if his nightmares were showing through the fabric of the day and he heard the mutter of the Telly Heads, watching.

He was glad when his name was called. He followed a man through the door and they walked along a shrub-lined path bathed in fake sunlight towards a pair of metal gates with razor wire at the top.

'After you,' the man said, as the gates swung open. He put his hand on Mika's back, encouraging him to walk forward towards a low white building, its mirrored windows reflecting the surrounding shrubs and palm trees. It looked formal and secretive, and inside the smell was medical. The man left him in a room that reminded him of his doctor's surgery in Barford North, only there wasn't any mould on the walls and everything was new.

There were two people in the room, a man and woman in white coats. They didn't introduce themselves. They fitted him with a yellow wristband, which had a bar code on it, then told him to stand in a glass cubicle that looked like a shower. He heard a whining noise and a slice of light moved slowly down his body. It didn't hurt, but he felt it right inside him, hot and prickly. After this he was told to pee in a bottle, which he found very difficult. He had to think about dripping taps and gushing fountains while they huffed outside the door.

After his pee was labelled and put in a fridge, they looked at his webbed feet. He had to lie on a metal bed while they stared at them and whispered, and this was even more embarrassing than peeing in the bottle. By the time they'd finished, a three-dimensional model of his webbed toes rotated on a screen.

'Is that it?' Mika asked, desperately, as they dropped their gloves down a waste chute.

'Not yet,' the woman said. 'Wait here.'

As she walked out of the door, Awen appeared and nipped her on the backside. The dog disappeared instantly, but Mika could hear him snuffling around the floor as if he was doing some detective work. Mika sat on the edge of the bed, wondering why the YDF were interested in his mutation. It was nothing compared to some, like Lara with her sweetcorn teeth, and Audrey, who was born without eyes. While Asha was in hospital giving birth, the woman in the bed next to her had a baby covered in fur and they had to shave her to see what she looked like.

Awen sneezed as if he had fluff up his nose, then rubbed his muzzle against Mika's leg.

A man entered.

'Come with me,' he said.

Mika followed the man deeper inside the building and into a dark room. In the middle of the room was a reclining chair, like those used by dentists, but this one was black and had straps hanging off the arms. Mika looked at it and felt beads of sweat break out on his forehead. Another man in a white coat stepped forward to greet him.

'Hello, Mika,' the man said. 'Relax. You've got nothing to worry about.'

Yeah, right, Mika thought, looking at the straps on the chair. He wondered what his parents would think if they could see him at that moment. They were probably only a few hundred metres away drinking cocktails on the beach thinking he was playing a game. Strange game.

'I want you to lie on the chair and make yourself comfortable,' the man said.

Mika tried to do as he was told; he lay on the chair, but there was no way he could make himself comfortable on it, his body was rigid with fear.

You'd better be grateful for this, Ellie, he thought. You'd better be nice to me after this.

'Relax,' the man insisted, seeing the distrust and fear in Mika's eyes.

Mika took a deep breath but tensed again as he felt the man's hands on his head.

'I'm going to attach a few electrodes to your forehead but they won't hurt, OK?' the man said.

'OK,' Mika replied, but as he felt the cold electrodes press on his forehead, he wanted to rip them off and run away.

'Right, that's good,' the man said, stepping back to admire his work. Mika could see wires in front of his eyes. The man moved them so he had a clear view of a screen on the ceiling above him.

'I'm going to put the straps on now,' the man said. 'They're only to stop you moving so our equipment can look in your eyes, so don't worry about them.'

Mika gritted his teeth as he felt the first strap tighten over his forehead. Then his arms were strapped to the sides of the chair, his legs to the end and another strap was tightened over his chest.

'Can you breathe all right?' the man asked.

'Yes,' Mika replied, shakily.

This is how I feel when the Telly Heads are standing around my bed, he thought: paralysed and about to be eaten.

'I'm going to show you a film now,' the man said. 'It's going to be like the cinema but with no popcorn.'

Mika considered making a sarcastic comment like, 'Oh good, how fun,' or, 'I hope I haven't seen it before,' but swallowed instead and tried to ignore his heart, which was throwing itself around in his chest as if it was trying to break out. The man walked away for a moment and Mika tried to turn his head to watch him, but was unable to move. When the man returned he was holding a syringe.

'What's that?' Mika asked.

'I'm going to give you an injection,' the man said. 'You'll feel a slight prick from the needle, but don't be afraid, nothing bad is going to happen to you.'

Before he had the chance to speak, Mika felt the needle pierce the skin on his arm and the contents of the syringe enter his vein with a sickening cold sensation as if it was ice. He felt it move up his arm towards his shoulder and bit back the tears, feeling absolutely terrified.

'How do you feel?' the man asked.

'Fine,' Mika lied.

'Are you ready for the film?'

'Yes.'

'OK, I'm going to leave you now. The film will start in a few moments.'

Mika heard the door click gently and the screen above his head lit up and the film began. At the beginning, it was like watching someone's memories speeded up, fragmented like snapshots and film clips. He saw a birthday party with lots of small children with balloons, a herd of antelope on a grassy plain, a man and a woman cutting a wedding cake, a baby in a hover buggy with the rain cover down, a concrete wall covered in graffiti and a woman in a kitchen slicing tank meat. The images came faster and faster and they began to mix up and distort: he saw the birthday party again, but in the centre of the room amongst the children was a snarling plague dog. A hand peeled the skin off an orange, and the fruit was full of maggots. He saw a boat sailing on the sea with the sun setting behind it, then he realized there were dead fish floating on the water. A small child fell over on the walkway and when he got up, he was holding a gun and waving it around as if it was a toy. The images were horrible, sinister, and they began to flash past so quickly his brain screamed with the effort of trying to keep up with them. He tried to close his eyes to shut them out, but found he couldn't, and even when the pictures moved so fast he was no longer able to make sense of one image before it was replaced by another, he knew he was seeing things he didn't want to see, bad things. His breathing got faster, he pushed against the straps trying to break out of them, but there was no escape, he was stuck there until the film ended. Eventually the screen turned blank and the man came back into the room and leaned over him.

'Well done,' he said.

'Let me out,' Mika replied, flatly.

'OK,' the man said, smiling as he loosened the straps.

'Can I go now?' Mika asked. 'Back to the beach?'

'Yes,' the man replied. 'You'll be just in time for the barbeque.'

'What time is it?' Mika asked.

'Six o'clock,' the man replied.

'How long have I been here?' Mika asked.

'A few hours,' the man replied, vaguely. 'It didn't feel that long, did it?'

'No,' Mika said, feeling a surge of panic as he realized what they'd just done to him. They'd given him a drug, then, while he was semi-conscious, they'd been inside his mind while he had no control over his thoughts. What had they seen? Did they know how suspicious he was? As he climbed out of the chair he felt weak with fear.

'Are you all right?'

The man was watching him.

'I feel tired,' Mika replied, trying not to meet his gaze.

'You'll feel better in a few minutes,' the man said reassuringly. 'Don't worry. A man will take you to the hut to meet your friend, then to the beach so you can join your families. But first I want you to make me a promise.'

'What?' Mika asked, nervously.

'I want you to tell your parents you've been playing puzzle games today. Do you understand?'

'Yes,' Mika said.

'There will be another test tomorrow morning,' the man continued. 'We'll send someone to collect you after breakfast. Make sure you're dressed and ready, and again, you'll need to tell your parents you're doing puzzles. Don't forget.'

'OK,' Mika replied.

'Have a nice holiday,' the man said.

As Mika walked back to the hut, he was half expecting men in white coats to come running after him because they'd found all the suspicious thoughts in his mind. It was a horrible feeling, especially with the sun shining and the sound of the sea in the distance, and he was immensely relieved to reach the hut and Audrey.

She was drinking fruit juice from a glass full of plastic tropical fish, which swam around frantically as she sucked through the straw. They exchanged a look that communicated the horror of the past few hours, but they couldn't speak because there were men everywhere, watching them, and one insisted on walking with them to the beach, even though there was a signpost outside the hut with a big, red arrow on it.

The path was wide and sandy and the sunlight filtering

through the palm trees was as warm as the embers of a dying fire. They took off their sneakers when they reached the sand, so they could feel it on their skin, and Audrey saw Mika's webbed feet for the first time.

'You're a mutant,' she remarked, smiling.

'Yeah, a web-toed freak,' he said. 'At least, that's what Ruben calls me.'

'Charming,' Audrey said. 'I wonder what he calls me.'

'Wolf eyes,' Mika replied, his face darkening at the mention of Ruben's name.

Audrey's eyes flashed as she decided whether she approved of this nickname, then she shrugged and smiled. 'I quite like it,' she said.

'So do I,' Mika admitted. 'It suits you.'

They walked along the beach looking for their families. It was perfect: the curve of clean white sand, the gentle sapphire sea, the rustic huts, so neatly spaced, and the shrubs and palm trees behind them. There were cocktail waiters walking along the beach, filling up empty glasses, and Mika found his mother lying on a sun lounger having her nails painted. He hadn't seen his parents look so happy since Ellie disappeared.

'You're just in time for the barbeque,' David said cheerfully, with a glass of champagne in his hand. 'And I'm Head Chef.' He had no shoes on and he was wearing shorts and a baseball cap. 'What have you been doing?' he asked.

'Puzzles,' Mika said, avoiding eye contact.

'You look tired,' Asha commented.

'I am,' he replied. 'They were difficult.'

'Never mind,' David said, kindly. 'You can relax now. You can help with the barbeque if you like.'

'OK,' Mika replied, guiltily. He hated lying to his parents, especially when they were being so nice to him.

The manicurist finished Asha's nails and left.

'Look!' Asha said, holding up her hand. She had tiny palm trees painted on the nails.

'Lovely,' Mika said, grinning.

'They're awful, aren't they?' she said. 'I did want something a little more dignified, but the manicurist said all she could do was palm trees, parrots or coconuts and I felt sorry for her. But it was nice to be fussed over.' She closed her eyes and lay back on the sun lounger, her white beach sari rippling in the breeze. 'I can't believe you won a holiday to a place like this,' she sighed. 'It's heaven.'

* * *

Later, Asha showed Mika around their hut, which was large and comfortable, and as the fake sun set and his father cooked, he swam in the sea, punishing his lungs with dive after brutal dive. Below the surface was the only place he felt safe. He'd seen cameras in the palm trees above their hut and he was still worrying about what the YDF had discovered about him that day. Audrey had been lingering around as if she wanted to talk to him, but he avoided her. What was happening to them was too weird for words – what could he say?

When it was dark he returned to the huts and ate with everyone. It was a beautiful night; all along the beach, barbeques glowed and the sound of laughter carried on the breeze. The trees were hung with thousands of fairy lights and the sky above twinkled with stars. It all looked so perfect, but over the aroma of cooking food, Mika could smell danger as if it was rotting around the back of the hut.

23
YOU ARE NOT TO TALK
ABOUT WHAT YOU DID

The next morning, Mika awoke to the sound of his mother singing. He got up and padded barefoot on the warm wooden floor to find her flitting around the kitchen, her hair tied loosely so it swung as she moved with her light trails dancing behind her. Just the kitchen in the hut was bigger than their whole fold-down apartment at home and there were so many cupboards, Asha said she was breathless by the time she'd looked in them all. On the worktop was another basket of food and he could smell fresh bread and coffee.

'I wanted to make sure you ate breakfast before you left,' she said. 'There are bananas in the basket, why don't you try one?'

Mika had never eaten a banana before. He pulled one off the bunch and bit into the top of it.

'Yuck,' he said. It was bitter and rubbery.

'You're supposed to peel it first, silly!' laughed Asha. 'Here. Let me do it. Eat half and I'll put the rest in a pancake. No, on second thoughts, you may as well eat the whole thing, there are loads! I keep forgetting we're not at home! All this real food! We'll have to take some back with us for the neighbours. Go and sit at the table outside and I'll cook your pancakes.'

Audrey was already there with her mother and aunt. She seemed happier than the day before and she crunched an apple with her toes buried in the sand and gazed at the sea.

'Isn't it beautiful, Mika?' she said, lifting her pointy chin into the breeze. 'Look at it.'

'Yeah,' Mika nodded, watching the morning sunshine glitter on the gentle, lapping waves.

'Just think,' she went on. 'How *lucky* people used to be. They had all this beauty for free and it was *real*.'

Before they'd finished eating, a man arrived to take them away. They all looked the same, the men: bald and grumpy, with their stomachs hanging over the waistbands of their dark blue YDF uniforms – they could have swapped lives for a weekend and their wives wouldn't have noticed. This man looked uncomfortably hot in his shirt and tie and he was sinking as he struggled across the sand towards them in his smart black shoes. Audrey stifled a giggle.

'They could have let the poor things wear shorts and flip-flops,' Una said, watching him nearly fall over as she munched on a bread roll.

Mika and Audrey found their shoes and said goodbye, then followed the man away from the beach, through the razor wire gates and into the low white building. Seeing the place again, they shuddered, remembering the black chair and the needle.

Inside, they were split up and taken to different rooms, and this time Mika found himself in a small, white room containing a table, two chairs and a man in a white coat.

'Hello, Mika,' the man said. He looked intelligent, Mika thought, his hair burned off by intense brain activity and his eyes bright and penetrating. 'Please sit down.'

Mika sat.

On the table in front of the man was a marble. Mika wondered what it was for.

'Have you been taking the capsules we gave you?' the man asked.

'Yes,' Mika replied. The man wrote something on his tablet. Mika tried to see what, but he was too far away.

'Have you noticed anything different about your vision since you've been taking them?'

'Yes,' Mika said. 'I see light trails on things when they move. Gold trails on people and blue trails on objects.'

'Good,' the man said, making another note.

Mika felt himself bubble up like a volcano of questions. He was aware he ought to be careful what he said, but his hunger for knowledge overwhelmed him.

'Don't other people see them?' he asked.

'Not many,' the man replied.

'Why not?' Mika asked.

'They just can't,' the man said. 'But we're here to talk about you, not other people.'

'Sorry,' Mika said. 'What is the light?'

'Energy,' the doctor replied. 'It was always there, you just couldn't see it before.'

'I thought so,' Mika said.

The man picked up the marble and waved it in front of Mika's face.

'What do you see?' he asked.

'I see a gold trail on your hand and a blue trail on the marble,' Mika replied.

'Good.' The man wrote on the tablet again. 'OK. Now I want you to try something else.' He put the marble on the table between them. 'Now look at it closely and tell me what you see.'

Mika stared at the marble until his eyes were blurred and he could no longer focus properly. After a minute the man asked him if he saw anything.

'No,' Mika replied, feeling disappointed. 'My eyes blurred and I couldn't look at it properly.'

'OK,' the man said, patiently. 'Try again. This time relax. Look at the marble but don't stare at it. You're straining your eyes. Take a deep breath and relax. OK?'

Mika nodded and looked at the marble again, trying not to care what happened so he didn't mess up, and this time he saw a faint blue light in the centre of the marble. It was the first time he'd seen the light while he was awake when something wasn't moving.

'I can see it!' he said.

'What can you see?'

'I see a blue light in the centre of the marble.'

'Brilliant, Mika, that's what we want.' The man wrote vigorously on the tablet and Mika watched him, feeling excited.

'Now I want you to try something else,' the man said with his eyes intent. 'I want you to look at the marble until you see the light, then I want you to try to move it with your eyes as if you are pushing it across the table with your finger. Do you understand?'

'You want me to move the marble with my eyes?' Mika repeated, incredulously.

'Yes.'

'But that's impossible.'

'It's not impossible, Mika,' the man said. 'But it is very difficult. The drugs we've given you in the capsules will help, but even so, only very few people can do it. I believe that you may be one of them. I want you to stay relaxed, but focus. Try not to worry about failing or think about anything else, OK?'

'OK.'

'Give it a go then.'

Mika looked at the marble. For the first few seconds his head was spinning with all the questions he wanted to ask and he had to force them all out so he could concentrate. After thirty long seconds he saw the light in the marble again. He was so pleased he lost his concentration and it faded.

'Sorry,' he said, 'I lost the light.'

'Try again.'

The man sat back in his chair so he was further away from Mika and this helped. Mika tried to pretend he wasn't there – that this wasn't a test and he was on his own. The light appeared and he gently tried to drag it to the left. He felt a pain at the back of his eyes as he did this and he nearly lost it again, the light began to fade, but he focused and built it up until it was glowing. For over a minute he tried until suddenly he felt a tug between his eyes and the marble as if they were connected and it slowly rolled a couple of centimetres to the left. Mika jolted and gasped, shocked by what he had done. He looked up at the man and the spell was broken.

'Well done!' the man said, beaming at him. Mika watched him scrawl a big tick on the tablet.

'How do you feel about the competition, Mika?' he asked, serious again.

Mika thought for a moment, not wanting to say the wrong thing.

'It scares me,' he replied.

'Why does it scare you?' the man asked. 'Are you scared of what you have just done?'

'No,' Mika said. 'I'm scared I won't win.'

'What do you want to win more?' the man asked. 'The home in the Golden Turrets or the chance to fly a real Pod Fighter?'

'I want both,' Mika said. 'The home for my family and to fly a Pod Fighter for me.'

'Good,' the man said, writing on the tablet again. 'Now listen carefully, Mika. You are not to talk about what you did in this room with your parents or anyone else. Do you understand?'

'Yes.'

'Did you tell anyone about the light trails before you came here?'

'No. Well, yes, but only a YDF woman when I fainted.'

'OK,' he said, nodding. 'That's fine. But you mustn't tell anyone else. When you go back to your parents I want you to say you've been doing puzzles again. Do you understand?'

'Yes,' Mika said.

'Good,' the man said. 'Because this test is a very important part of the competition, so if you want to win the prizes, you have to keep it a secret. Sign here.'

He pushed the tablet towards Mika.

'What's this?' Mika asked, seeing a document and a space at the bottom for his signature.

'The Official Secrets Act,' the man replied. 'Just so we're clear about our agreement.'

Mika signed, feeling as if he was writing his name in blood. The man took the tablet back and looked at his signature.

'Excellent,' he said, scribbling without looking up. 'Right, that's the hard bit over. For the rest of the week you'll be learning how to play a new game in the sea, and on Saturday there'll be a contest. Relax and enjoy yourself; it's going to be fun. And well done, Mika, very well done.'

Mika stumbled back to the beach, hardly looking where he was going, dumped his clothes on the sand in front of the hut and ran into the sea, feeling as if he would explode if he stayed above the surface a second longer.

What had just happened in that room? Had he really moved something just by looking at it? It seemed too incredible to be true, it was a miracle, and yet he remembered how hard it had been to do it, how it hurt his eyes and tugged at his mind. He felt astounded and terrified in equal measures. As if another person was waking up inside him and although they shared the same body, they were strangers.

When he resurfaced for the tenth time, he found Audrey treading water beside him. They swam further out. Her eyes were dark and scared.

'I've just moved something with my eyes,' she whispered. 'Did you?'

He nodded. They were quiet for a few moments and looked anxiously towards the beach.

'I don't like it,' she said. 'I did while I was doing it, but now I'm scared. What do you think they want from us?'

'I don't know,' Mika replied, feeling his chest tighten.

'They're watching us,' she whispered. 'There are cameras in the trees.'

'I know,' he replied. He looked around, wondering if they could be heard, even so far from shore. 'Come on, let's go back,' he said. 'I don't think we should talk about it. It's not safe.'

24

TARGET PRACTICE

The next two days were like a real holiday. In the morning, Mika and Audrey ate their breakfast in front of the huts and afterwards they joined the other competitors in the big welcome hut, where they were split into teams and taken out on boats. They learned to play water polo and had swimming races and dived for shells. The sea was only six metres deep, so it was light from the surface down, and the first time Mika dived off the boat and found himself swimming over a coral reef, he was staggered by its beauty. It teemed with borg fish, all sizes, shapes and colours. Everywhere he looked there was movement. To a boy who had grown up thinking water was naturally brown and slimy, it was beauty beyond imagination, and he had to keep reminding himself that it was fake, the fish had switches on their bellies, the coral was plastic and hollow inside and the seawater was actually blue if you put it in a glass and they'd been strongly advised not to drink it. There were cameras on the boats and in the water and he'd even spotted one in the lid of a food basket that contained their lunchtime sandwiches. But just like in the arcade, he pretended to see nothing.

Five boats went out in the morning, each carrying twenty competitors. They were white fishing boats, with wide decks, awnings and comfortable places to sit. They cruised around the island at a relaxed pace, passing the beach where the parents were eating their breakfast. Then, with the beach out of sight, they dropped anchor near a crop of rocks and a man stood amongst them on the deck and gave instructions. Mika and Audrey's team was led by Justin – a serious man, but not unpleasant like Mr Blyte. He smiled sometimes and listened attentively to their questions.

On the third morning, as the boat prepared to leave, several long black boxes were loaded on deck. After they had dropped anchor, Justin opened one and took something out.

'This is a harpoon gun,' he said, holding it up so they could all see. 'The barrel holds thirty titanium-tipped bolts and has a firing range underwater of fifty metres.'

The harpoon gun looked dangerous but really interesting, and the competitors whispered with excitement.

'Needless to say,' Justin continued, 'anyone caught disobeying instructions or messing around while you learn to use them will be sent back to their parents on the beach. I think we're all bored of diving for shells, don't you agree?'

They all nodded and looked hungrily at the gun.

'Good,' Justin said. 'Over the next two days you will also learn how to scuba dive, so on Saturday, you can use your new skills to compete against each other.'

They were split into smaller teams of four, and first they were taught how to use the scuba diving gear. They stood on the deck while the men moved from one competitor to the next, showing them how to put on their stab jackets, tanks and masks. Then they spent a few hours learning what each piece of equipment did and how to breathe through it and speak to each other underwater. The masks covered their faces, and Mika felt happy when he put his on and saw the display was similar to that in a Pod Fighter headset, with targeting and mapping systems and eye-sensitive icons around the sides.

'Feel the weight of it,' one of the instructors said, handing Mika a harpoon gun. It was very light. 'Now feel the weight of this,' he said, taking the gun back and giving Mika one of the titanium-tipped bolts. It felt as if he was holding nothing. He rolled it on his palm and touched the tip of it with his finger.

'Now watch this,' the man said. He took the bolt from Mika's hand and slid it into the barrel until it clicked. He pressed a couple of icons on the control panel on the side of the gun, then aimed at the crop of rocks near the boat and fired. The bolt shot off with a whisper and penetrated the rock like a hot knife into butter.

'Pretty good, eh?'

Mika nodded.

'Now I want you to take the gun,' the instructor continued, 'and feel it over with your eyes closed. In the water with the mask on, your vision is limited so you need to get to know the gun with your hands. Practise loading and unloading the bolts, and feel your way on the control panel. Use the map in your visor to aim and let your hands do the rest.'

He watched Mika feel over the gun.

'And be careful. Make sure your gun is locked all the time until you've been shown how to use the controls. You'll be taken down for target practice on the seabed, and only then, under strict supervision, are you permitted to fire.'

'OK,' Mika said.

The men dived down to the seabed to set up targets. When they returned to the surface, they told the competitors to swim down and stand on the red markers, which had been set out in a line at five-metre intervals. Twenty metres away were targets like those used for archery with a red bull's-eye in the middle.

The instructors stood behind them and talked to them through their masks. When everyone was ready, they were given the order to release the safety catch on their guns and to fire. They had to shoot thirty bolts, and the first competitor to hit the bull's-eye would win a special prize. Mika had just fired his first shot and missed the target by a metre, when a man said, 'Well done, Audrey, you've just won your family two hundred credits!'

* * *

'Two hundred credits!' Una exclaimed, when they'd walked back to the huts and Audrey had given her the prize money. 'What did you have to do to win that?'

'Shoot at targets under water,' Audrey said, enthusiastically. 'I was the first to hit the bull's-eye.'

'What with?' Una asked.

'Harpoon guns,' Audrey said. 'With titanium-tipped bolts.'

'You are kidding,' Tasha said, horrified. 'You've been using a harpoon gun? I thought you said you were diving for shells!'

'That was a couple of days ago,' Audrey replied. 'But don't worry, they've borrowed instructors from the army.'

'So let me get this straight,' Una said, incredulously. 'They've got a hundred twelve-year-old kids under water with harpoon guns shooting titanium-tipped bolts?'

'Don't be like that, Mum,' Audrey said. 'It's fun. And they've told us if we muck about they'll send us back to the beach. It's safe, I promise.'

25
IT'S ALL FAKE

'**R**ight,' Justin said. 'Let's learn how to do something new.'

He flipped open the lid on one of the black boxes to reveal the rows of neatly packed harpoon guns.

'Now you can hit a static target,' he said, 'we're going to try something more interesting. Today you will be learning how to hit one of these.' Justin opened another box and lifted something out with both hands. It was a silver fish, about thirty centimetres long.

'What can you tell me about this fish?' he said, holding it up.

'It's a borg,' someone said.

'Yes,' Justin replied. 'But it's not like the other borgs here in the holiday complex, this is a very sophisticated piece of equipment. It thinks it's a fish and behaves like one, but it's a lot more than that, it can tell us who hit it and from how far away. If any of you manage to get one I'll be very impressed; it's not easy, they're devils.'

Justin handed the borg fish round the group, and when it

finally got to Mika he felt his arms tense under the weight of it. It was a mean-looking beast with serrated fins, a row of needle-sharp teeth sticking out of its fat lips, and eyes that glowed red.

'Watch this,' Justin said. He touched his tablet and the fish suddenly sparked into life and thrashed in Mika's hands. Mika felt a sharp pain in one of his fingers and he let the fish fall. It dropped to the deck with a clunk and flapped frantically, gasping as if it was drowning in air. Justin grabbed it by the tail and threw it over the side of the boat, and they heard a heavy splash as it hit the water. Mika sucked the blood from his finger and cursed.

'OK,' Justin said. 'Get your scuba gear on and the other instructors will come down and help you find your markers on the seabed.'

They changed quickly, dropped into the water and swam down to find the markers. They were different to the ones of the previous day. Each had an arrow on it pointing in the direction of the crop of rocks. Mika stood on the marker next to Audrey and waited for instructions from the men who stood in a line behind them.

'OK, everyone. Make sure you're all facing in the direction of the arrows. You may only shoot towards the rocks. When you see the fish, fire.'

Mika undid the safety catch on the harpoon gun without looking down, then felt it over with his hands to remind himself of the controls. He activated the target map by looking at the icon in the corner of his display and a grid of green lines appeared before his eyes with a red dot indicating where the harpoon gun was pointing. He watched the crop of rocks, waiting for the fish. A crab scuttled towards them making clouds in the sand, fronds of weed as fine as mermaid hair wafted in the warm water and the sunlight cast ripples on his arms and hands and the seabed. He felt as if he'd waited hours when a flash of silver darted out from behind the rocks. It was fast and erratic, darting to the left and right, and he felt the water warp around him as everyone raised their guns and fired. The bolts shot away leaving trails of white bubbles and blue light. When the water cleared the fish was gone.

'You missed,' a man said in Mika's headset. 'Wait for it to come back.'

A minute later it appeared again, glinting silver and darting playfully this way and that as if to say, 'You don't stand a chance.' Again Mika felt the water warp with the sudden movement around him. He paused for a moment this time, determined to get a good sight on the fish before firing his shot, but before he'd even lined it up with the red dot the fish fell, suddenly limp, with a bolt embedded in its side. Someone else had hit it.

'Audrey, well done,' a man said.

Mika watched the man swim over to the fish and retrieve it, and for the first time he considered the possibility that Audrey would get through to the final round of the competition but he wouldn't. He wasn't good enough. He was going to lose, and Ellie would be lost for ever.

'Are you all right?' Audrey asked, as they were walking back to the huts along the beach. 'You just trod on that lady's hair.'

'Oh, sorry,' Mika said, looking back to see an angry sunbather glaring at him.

Darkness fell and the still night air filled with the clink of glasses and the smell of barbequed tank meat. Everyone seemed to be enjoying themselves, but Mika's mood was bleak and their laughter made him irritable.

'I remember nights like this before the Animal Plague,' David said, piling tank meat on his plate. 'The meat was real then, of course. It wasn't grown on sticks in tanks of yellow fluid in the old days.'

'I can't believe people used to *eat* animals,' Mika said. 'How could they look at a living, feeling creature in the same way as a loaf of bread?'

'Everyone did,' Asha said. 'I know it sounds strange now all the animals are extinct, but even you would have eaten meat if you were born then.'

'No I wouldn't,' Mika said contemptuously. 'It's barbaric.'

Everyone went quiet and wondered why Mika was so angry. He stomped off and sat on his own to chew on a lump of bread.

When the meal was over, he walked down the beach. Audrey followed him and they lay on a blanket eating a bunch of grapes she'd brought with her.

'You are good enough,' she said, after ten minutes of surly silence.

'No I'm not,' Mika said. 'I'm rubbish.'

'You wouldn't be here if you were rubbish,' Audrey insisted. 'You're just being negative because you've had a bad day.'

'Mmm,' Mika said.

'Look at the stars,' Audrey said, dreamily. 'They're so beautiful! Do you think they're in the same position as the real ones?'

'No,' Mika replied. 'Look over there, the pattern is repeated, and there, and there.'

'Oh,' she said. 'That's a shame, but they're still lovely.'

'It's all fake,' Mika said, irritably. 'Nothing's real any more.'

'I'm real,' she said. 'Apart from my eyes.'

He could see her smiling in the darkness and suddenly realized he was being horrible to her and yet she was still being kind to him.

'I'm glad I met you,' he said, quietly.

'Really?' she replied, sarcastically.

'Of course I am, noodle brain.'

He threw a grape at her mouth and it missed and hit her nose. She laughed as it dropped on to the blanket and she felt around for it with her hand, then she paused, sensing someone. They looked up to see a light trail moving towards them.

'Who's that?' Audrey whispered.

Mika felt a chill run down his spine. The person's light trail was tinged with red. He'd never seen that before and he didn't like it.

'It's *Ruben*!' Audrey whispered, her borg eyes identifying him before Mika's could.

Ruben stopped a few paces away and sneered down on them,

his face dimly lit by the fairy lights hanging from the trees.

'Mutant freaks,' he said, then kicked out with one foot and hit them in the face with a spray of sand. It was so shocking and unexpected, for a few moments they did nothing but gasp and rub their eyes while he laughed at them. But as he walked away, Mika felt a tidal wave of rage and he leaped to his feet ready to run after him and pulp him into the sand.

'My eyes!' Audrey cried out. 'Help me, Mika!'

Mika stopped at once, turned back and pulled her to her feet. 'Let me look,' he said, prizing her trembling fingers away from her face. 'I'm going to kill him! What a fragging perp!'

'I can't see!' she cried. 'Perhaps they're broken!'

'I'm sure they're not,' he said, trying to comfort her. 'They're just full of sand. Come on, let's go back to the hut and you can wash them.'

Their parents were still sitting around the table talking and laughing. When they saw Mika and Audrey approach, they stood up quickly so the champagne slopped from their glasses.

'What happened?' Una asked, anxiously.

'Ruben!' Mika raged. 'He kicked sand in her eyes! I want to punch his fragging lights out!'

'Who's Ruben?' Asha asked. 'Why would he do that?'

'I don't know!' Mika ranted. 'He's a psycho!'

Una took command of the blind Audrey and led her into their hut, while Mika paced the sand with his blood boiling. He didn't understand it – how could someone do that to a blind girl?

'She'll be fine in a minute,' David said, kindly. 'Don't let this boy get to you. It sounds like he's just trying to wind you up because you're competing tomorrow. It's just a game, Mika, and he's playing nasty; it's not worth it.'

But it's not just a game, Mika thought, desperately, it's much more than that; and he was unable to calm down until Audrey re-emerged, smiling again and able to see.

26
A CLOUD OF RED SMOKE

Mika was still thinking of Ruben as he fell asleep, and he dreamed he made a river with his own angry blood. It poured out of his mouth and down a mountainside in a raging torrent that ripped pylons and towers from the earth to form heaps of bloody concrete and twisted metal at the bottom. When the torrent subsided, he wondered if he was dead. He felt empty, as if there was no blood left in his veins and his anger had burned up his insides so he was only a shell. He watched his hands as they crumbled to dust and the wind blew them away.

In the morning, he remembered the dream and what his father had said about Ruben, and realized he could not allow him to affect the way he played the game. He sat with Audrey outside the hut and ate two banana pancakes so he wasn't competing on an empty stomach.

'You can do it,' Audrey said, watching him frown at the sea. 'I know you can.'

'It's OK,' replied Mika. 'I feel better today. How are your eyes?'

'Fine,' she said.

Their parents wished them good luck and they walked to the Welcome Hut to meet up with the other competitors. The atmosphere inside was horrible and everyone looked as if they were about to have all their teeth removed with no anaesthetic.

They were split into teams of ten for the game and three teams had assembled and left when Audrey's name was called. She walked up to the stage and moments later, Ruben joined her, and the first thing he did was look at Mika and smirk. Mika felt it like a punch in the stomach, but he watched them walk away knowing there was nothing he could do but try not to think about it.

Mika's name was called in the fifth group and so was Ruben's game partner, Yee. She walked to the front, swinging her hips and pouting as if she was on the catwalk in a fashion show. Mika took a few steps back so he didn't have to stand next to her.

'Leo Curtis.'

The boy stood up and Mika felt himself spark with interest as he had done the day he met Audrey. He was gold – not just his light trails, but his body too. He had golden skin and dreadlocks, which hung to his shoulders like rope. He was wearing a plait of black cord on his wrist and a gold ring on his finger, and as he wove through the chairs leaving twists of bright light in his wake, he had an air of quiet confidence that drew everyone's eyes.

But not arrogant, Mika thought. Leo smiled at Mika, and his startling blue eyes brought the sea into the room.

'Hey,' Mika said.

'Hey.'

On the boat, the men helped them into their stab jackets as they cruised around the island. Their boat dropped anchor by a red buoy with the number '5' on it and in the distance Mika saw the boats that had left before them, dotted at regular intervals.

On the closest beach he saw a pair of ambulance pods, the paramedics sitting on the sand with their faces tilted towards the sun.

The men spent a long time checking over the equipment. Mika's harpoon gun was found to be faulty and taken away and replaced with another. They tested the displays in his mask and checked his breathing equipment.

He watched the gold boy, Leo, tie his dreadlocks at the nape of his neck. The boy was joking with the men in a warm Canadian accent as their fingers worked deftly on his equipment and Mika wished he could feel so confident.

When they were ready, the ten competitors stood in line, waiting for instructions.

'You will swim down to the ten markers on the seabed and stand facing in the direction of the arrows,' said one of the men, his eyes scanning them seriously. 'Your targets will be borg fish. The object of the game is to shoot as many fish as you can in ten minutes. You are not to leave the marker until you are told to do so by one of us. If you leave the marker without permission, you will lose your points. You can communicate with us through your masks if you have any problems during the game. Are there any questions?'

Nobody spoke.

'OK. Let's get on with it.'

The markers were set out in a curve on the sandy seabed and the arrows pointed towards a cluster of coral teeming with fish. The water was the palest green, rippled like marble by the sunlight on the surface. The visibility was good and Mika could see at least a hundred metres beyond the coral. He chose the marker at the right end of the curve and Leo took the one next to him, his dreadlocks wafting out of the back of his headset like snakes. Mika watched the gold ring on his finger glint as he adjusted the straps on his headset and enabled his gun. A few moments later the men took their positions behind them and Mika felt the tension in the water rise until it was almost unbearable. He looked down the row at the other competitors.

Apart from their wafting hair and the streams of bubbles rising from their masks, they were completely still, rooted to the markers, their eyes fixed on the cluster of coral in front of them, guns raised and fingers hovering over the triggers.

A voice spoke in his headset.

'Mika, are you ready?'

'Yes,' he replied.

'The game will begin in thirty seconds.'

A clock appeared in the corner of his display and he watched it count down. The sea looked like an empty film set waiting for the action to begin. Five, four, three, two, one. The clock reset itself and began to count down from ten minutes. Mika gripped the harpoon gun, struggling to control the anxiety that threatened to paralyze him. He remembered he had Ellie's holopic of mountain lions in the pocket of his swim shorts and dared to remove his hand from the gun for a moment to touch it through his wetsuit. He breathed deeply and focused on the light-rippled water before him.

At first sight, the shoal of borg fish looked like glitter dust; so far away, it was no more than fragments of light. Bright as stars one moment, then gone the next, the shoal made lightning-quick, synchronized twists and turns through the water towards them.

Mika supposed there were a couple of hundred. They were fast and erratic with no pattern to their movement, and all he could do was try to guess when the shoal would turn to be side on to him so he had a chance of hitting one. He waited until the shoal had reached the coral before he fired, then shot twenty bolts in as many seconds. For a fleeting moment the fish were close enough for him to see their needle-like teeth and glowing red eyes, then they snapped round and darted away, leaving several falling to rest on the seabed with bolts embedded in their sides. The ten competitors were a blur of motion as they reloaded their guns from the cartridge of bolts strapped to their thighs. Mika reloaded his then checked his hit counter. He'd hit one fish. Only one.

'Frag,' he muttered.

They had eight minutes left. Mika watched the shoal glitter and shift in the distance and prayed it would come back soon. The moment it turned the other competitors began to fire, but Mika waited until it had crossed the coral. He had only seconds before the fish snapped round and darted off, but this time he hit four.

Six minutes left. He had a strategy now and he waited eagerly for the shoal to return, but nothing happened for over a minute. He had an itch on his nose, which made it difficult to concentrate. Then something appeared in the distance: a mass of dark shapes cast shadows on the seabed. They moved slowly through the water and as Mika began to make out their forms he felt confused – they weren't fish, they were mammals. They had mottled brown and black fur and flippers, bulbous heads and snouts covered in rolls of loose skin. Their silent, rhythmic movement was eerie and they looked so heavy it seemed a miracle they could swim. As they reached the coral Mika recognized them from one of Ellie's pictures; they were elephant seals. He wondered what to do. They had been told to shoot fish, not mammals. Some of the competitors began to fire, but he lowered his gun so it was hanging at his side and he glanced over at Leo and was relieved to see he had done the same. Some competitors fired one shot then stopped, unable to make up their minds, some let off the entire contents of their barrels. Nine of the elephant seals fell and Mika felt the vibration in his feet as they hit the seabed.

He was expecting the rest of the herd to swim away as the shoal of fish had done, but they kept coming and Mika froze on his marker as their enormous hulks passed silently through them. Leo reached out his hand to touch one and Mika was so distracted by this gesture, he didn't notice what was happening in the distance until Leo's head suddenly snapped round and Mika followed his gaze.

Another shoal was swimming towards them and this time

there was no doubt in Mika's mind what they were; the ghostly, pale forms of white sharks, each at least three metres long. They wove quickly through the water, their snouts jerking from side to side, and as soon as they reached the herd of elephant seals, they attacked. Mika gasped and felt his head spin as he got an overdose of oxygen and the water suddenly became a boiling mass of teeth, borg bits and fragments of fur. A shark swam within metres of him to attack a seal, shaking its head like a dog as it ripped it to pieces. He got a close-up view of its dead, black eye and was so scared he nearly peed in his wetsuit. Remembering he'd been told not to move from the marker, he struggled to control his instinctive urge to get away from it. He looked around to see several of the other competitors had left theirs and were firing wildly into the midst of the chaos.

They're not real, Mika thought desperately. This is a game. He aimed and fired and shot the closest shark through its eye. It went crazy, whipping the water milk-white as it tried to shake the bolt from its head. It was dangerously close, but Mika kept his feet firmly rooted to the marker hoping it would swim away, and eventually it did, still lashing its head from side to side until it froze and sank to the sand. Immediately Mika's hit counter shot up twenty points and he prepared to fire again. His next target was further away, its razor-sharp teeth ripping into the flank of an elephant seal that seemed dead already and swung limply in the water as it was savaged. He shot the shark through the gills with the first bolt. It jerked with shock, let go of its prey and snapped round to swim straight at him as if it knew who had shot it. Rigid with fear Mika shot it again in the mouth, closing his eyes as it continued to come towards him, its nose jerking from side to side and strips of ripped skin wafting from its teeth, and at that moment he felt a terrible pain in his leg, so sickening, he almost vomited in his headset.

He opened his eyes and looked down to see blood pumping out of his thigh into the water. He felt confused. The shark wasn't real, how could it have bitten him? He had no idea what had happened and felt so shocked, he could do nothing but watch as the ribbons of blood pumping from his leg transformed into a cloud of red smoke in the water. Later he remembered thinking that his leg looked as if it was on fire.

He felt something touch his arm and looked up to see Leo's worried face through his mask, his mouth moving, though Mika couldn't hear any words. Moments later he was surrounded by men.

'What happened?' he asked dreamily. He felt disconnected, foggy and a bit tired. He wanted to lie down on the seabed and go to sleep for a while.

'Someone shot you, Mika,' one of the men said. 'We need to get you out of the water because you're losing a lot of blood.'

'Shot me?' Mika repeated, confused. He looked down again and this time he saw a bolt sticking out of the marker just behind his left leg. It still had bits of his flesh attached to the end of it and they were waving around like pink and red seaweed. It had gone straight through his thigh and out the other side.

'Come on,' the man said, holding his arm.

'No,' Mika said, feeling himself well up with panic. 'If I leave the marker I'll lose the game.'

'The game's over, Mika. You can leave now.'

They grabbed him by the arms and dragged him away from the marker to the surface.

* * *

The first thing Mika heard when his head broke the water was screaming.

'Get off me! Get off! I want to go home! I hate you! I'm not doing this any more! You're psychos! You're trying to kill us!'

Strong arms came over the side of the boat to drag him on board. He heard himself slap wetly on the deck and was vaguely aware of motion around him. He struggled with his mask and someone helped him get it off and he took a lungful of warm air. A man's face appeared.

'Stay calm, OK?' he said. 'The ambulance pod is here. The paramedics are going to look at your leg.'

He felt tugging on his legs and he struggled to lean up on his elbows so he could see what they were doing to him. One of the paramedics was cutting the wetsuit off his leg and another was pressing something on the wound. Blood spurted between his fingers and spattered his sunglasses.

'Lie down and try to relax,' said the paramedic. 'Don't watch.'

Mika didn't want to lie down. He didn't trust them. But he felt too weak to sit up so he lay back and turned his head in the direction of the screaming. It was Ruben's game partner, Yee. She was pinned to the deck by two men and thrashing around like the sharks, her wet hair lashing their faces.

'Stop screaming, Yee. It's over,' one said, but she didn't stop screaming and she struggled even harder.

'What's wrong with her?' asked Mika anxiously.

'She freaked out down there. She's the one who shot you. It's all right, they're going to give her something to calm her down.'

Moments later Yee fell silent. Mika watched her eyes lose focus and close, her body relax. She sighed as if she was lying down in a warm bath. Mika closed his eyes. The pain from his leg was everywhere – he felt it from the tips of his toes to the top of his head and it washed over him in delirious waves, sweeping up his body, and he wanted it to stop.

'Make the pain stop,' he muttered.

'OK.'

He felt a brief prick on his arm.

'My holopic,' he whispered. 'The lions in my pocket.'

'Don't worry, we've found it. We'll keep it for you.'

A second later he was falling with Yee into a warm bath of nothing.

27
KEEP THE BOY IN THE GAME

Mal Gorman sat forward in his chair. A close-up image of Ellie's brother lying in a hospital bed filled most of the screen on his desktop, but in one corner was the image of a man with whom he was discussing Mika's accident.

'He looks just like his sister,' Gorman said, thoughtfully. 'What is it about this boy? He was the only one to refuse to drink the Fit Mix and now he's got himself shot. Looks like trouble runs in the family.'

'And so does talent,' the man said. 'He's one of the best, sir. He could be just what you're looking for.'

'Really?' Gorman was quiet for a moment, not sure if this was good news or bad. 'Well, he'd better not be as difficult to handle as his sister. One stroppy little bog rat is quite enough.'

'He seems calmer than Ellie,' the man said. 'And he works incredibly hard; his scores for focus and perseverance are the highest in the group. There is one thing though . . .'

'What?' Gorman asked.

'When we did the memory scan on him we hardly found anything. It was as if he was fighting against us even though he didn't know what we were doing to him. He must have an incredibly strong will. The few scraps of memories we did find are so dark, we can't work out what's happening.'

'Let me see them,' Gorman demanded.

'It's hardly worth it, sir. They're no more than a couple of hours of moving shadows.'

'I don't care,' said Gorman. 'Send them to me.'

'Yes, sir,' the man replied. 'What do you want us to do about his parents? They've been yelling their heads off since the accident and they want to take him home as soon as possible. It was chaos in here; the mother was screaming, there was blood spattered up the walls – when we took the compress off the blood was pumping out the wound like a fountain. The harpoon bolt severed the main artery at the top of his leg.'

'Why did you let the parents see that?' Gorman said, angrily. 'What were you thinking?'

'We had no choice, sir,' the man said, defensively. 'The boy needed his father's blood; without it he would have died. But now, of course, they don't want him to compete any more.'

'I don't care what they want,' Gorman said, coldly. 'Think of a way to shut them up and keep the boy in the game. If he's as good as you say he is then he must compete in the final round. We can make the parents disappear if necessary. If they haven't changed their minds in a few days, let me know and I'll arrange it. And don't forget to send me those memories; I want to see what's going on in his head.'

'Yes, sir.'

28
THE HEALING CHAMBER

Mika heard a hum, a warm comforting sound, and he felt vibrations in his leg. He tried to open his eyes so he could look at it, but he felt as if his lids were glued shut and after a while he gave up. He could hear talking somewhere, quiet voices, and for a while he allowed the sound of the conversation to merge with the hum and he didn't try to listen to what was being said. The vibrations in his leg tickled and as his mind drifted further into consciousness he remembered the blood and the pain and felt a sting of panic as his head filled with sharks, their jagged teeth wafting strips of skin, and their dead black eyes metres from his own. But the pain was gone and the light through his eyelids was warm and bright. He tried to move his hand but couldn't and had no choice but to relax and feel relieved that the nightmare was over. But was it? The voices belonged to strangers, a man and a woman. He decided to listen to their conversation and the first sentence hit him like a bucket of ice water so he was instantly alert, praying they didn't realize he was conscious.

'His parents want to take him home as soon as he wakes up.'

'Do they?'

There was a moment of silence.

'But Mal Gorman said we have to keep him here, whatever it takes. He has the potential to be one of the best.'

'So what do we do? The parents are already suspicious; they'll go ballistic if we tell them they *can't* take their son.'

'We don't have to say they can't take him. We just need to buy some time. If we can keep them here until after the prize-giving dinner so they realize they've won a hover car and are in the running for a home in the Golden Turrets, they should change their minds. What if we tell them it will take until tomorrow evening for his leg to heal? They're poor, they're not going to know how fast the healing chamber works – they're still using stitches and bandages in the refugee town hospitals. We'll let him out today in a hover chair, but we'll tell the parents he has to come back tomorrow after the prize-giving dinner for another treatment.'

'Good idea.'

'Look.' The voice sounded closer, as if the woman had moved nearer the bed.

Mika's heart started to race.

'His fingers twitched, do you think he's coming round?'

'Possibly. His heart rate's gone up. We'll talk more later.'

Mika listened to the squeak of their shoes on the floor as they walked away, and his first response to what he'd heard was anger. How dare they speak so disrespectfully about his parents? As if they were stupid because they were poor and wouldn't realize they were being tricked! But when his anger subsided, he felt a dark thrill.

They think I'm one of the best, he thought. I'm still in the game! He smiled inside, relief and happiness crowding out his fear.

But what about his parents? What would he do if they didn't

change their minds and they refused to let him continue?

Mika worried himself to sleep and several hours later opened his eyes to see a white fan gyrating above him, bathing his face in cool air. He turned his head to see Ellie's mountain lions leaning against a jug of water by the side of the bed and he felt relieved he hadn't lost it.

A nurse stepped quietly towards him with a tablet in her hand.

'Hello,' she said. 'Can you feel any pain?'

'No,' he replied. 'It tickles.'

Mika lifted his head to look at his leg. It was encased in a glass bubble.

'Good,' said the nurse. She looked at the control panel on the glass bubble and pressed a couple of icons.

'What is that?' he asked.

'A healing chamber,' she replied. 'It's a sort of microwave oven for wounds. It heals in super-quick time.'

'How long will it take?' he said, waiting for the lie.

'You'll be able to go back to the beach today, but you'll need another treatment tomorrow night before you go home,' she replied, without looking at him.

'Oh,' said Mika, thinking what a bad liar she was.

'That wound would have taken weeks to heal a couple of centuries ago,' she continued. 'That's if you hadn't bled to death to start with. And then you might have got gangrene and had it chopped off.'

She grinned.

'That's a nice thought,' said Mika.

'You were lucky. The bolt clipped the bone but didn't break it. You lost a lot of blood, but luckily your father was on hand. You've got half a litre of his. Remember to be a good boy and say, "thank you".'

'Where is he?' Mika asked.

'In the waiting room, with your mother.'

'Can I see them?'

'Of course, I'll tell them you're awake.'

Asha's eyes were red and her face was blotchy from crying. David looked pale and angry.

'Oh Mika!' Asha cried, grabbing his hand. 'Tell me exactly what happened!'

'A girl shot me by mistake,' he replied. 'It was an accident, Mum. I'm fine.'

'But what were you doing? I thought this was supposed to be a game!'

'We were just shooting targets,' Mika said flippantly. 'We've been training for days. It was just a freak accident.'

'Well there won't be any more "freak accidents",' David said angrily. 'Because we're taking you home!'

The nurse stepped forward and said the doctor wanted to talk to them, and they left reluctantly. Mika could see them through a window, but couldn't hear what they were saying. At first the conversation looked heated and his parents looked angry, but by the end of it, they were nodding with resigned expressions on their faces.

'We can't take you yet,' David said, when they'd come back to his bedside. 'But as soon as you've finished your treatment tomorrow night, this is over. Even if you have got through to the final round, you're not competing any more, it's not safe.'

Mika left the hospital unit in a hover chair. His leg didn't hurt at all because it was completely healed – he'd checked when he was in the toilets, and there wasn't even a scar to show where the bolt had ripped into his leg, but he made a show of wincing now and then to corroborate the lie his parents had been told. All he could do was pray that when they found out about the hover car they would change their minds.

He zipped along in the chair and they found an ice cream hut and asked for strawberry cones. Mika licked his once and the ice cream fell off the top and landed on the sandy path with a splat.

'Frag,' he said.

Asha laughed. 'That happened when you were little; it was so tragic you cried your eyes out!'

She walked back to the ice cream hut and got him another one, and he watched her from his hover chair feeling guilty. When they reached the beach Audrey ran across the sand to meet them.

'Cool chair!' she said. 'Let me see your leg!'

Mika pulled up his shorts so she could see the bandage and her eyes widened with morbid curiosity.

His parents walked ahead to talk to Tasha and Una by the huts.

'How many sharks did you kill?' Audrey whispered.

'Two,' he said, grinning.

'And me,' she said, with her eyes shining.

They shared the details of their games in hurried whispers as they moved towards the hut, then Audrey fell silent and Mika realized she'd had the same kind of problems with her mother and aunt, and that it was not a good idea to talk about flesh-ripping borg sharks, harpoon guns and nearly bleeding to death in their company.

On the steps of their hut, David found a basket left by the Youth Development Foundation. On the handle was a card. The message said, 'The Youth Development Foundation would like to apologize for the inconvenience caused by your son's accident. We hope you enjoy the rest of your holiday.' There were plastic flowers and perfume for Asha, a Youth Development Foundation baseball cap and pen for David, and another pen for Mika.

'Fantastic,' Mika said sarcastically, clicking the pen so the nib shot in and out.

'Yuck,' Asha said, sniffing her perfume with her nose screwed up.

29

JUST TRY AND STOP ME

The Welcome Hut looked beautiful for the prize-giving dinner; hundreds of orange lanterns had been strung through the rafters, the tables were decorated with garlands of plastic flowers and when the food arrived, it looked so lovely on the plate, Asha took a photograph so she could remember it when she got home.

Everyone was dressed in their best clothes and Mika thought his mother looked amazing; her skin glowed in the candlelight and the beads on her new red sari glittered like rubies. But there was a hard edge to her smile and she looked impatiently towards the door now and then as if she was keen to leave as soon as possible. His father hardly touched his food and didn't speak a word for the whole meal and Mika realized the hover car was going to have a hard job changing their minds.

The waiters cleared the desserts from the tables and the Hat

Man took to the stage.

'Hello, everyone!' he shouted, throwing his arms in the air. 'So this is it! The moment of truth! In a few minutes you will know if you are going home with a top-of-the-range, Jaguar hover car!'

The wooden doors swung open to reveal the hover car again, and this time it had a teddy bear sitting in the pilot seat.

'Just imagine driving that, dads!' the Hat Man said.

'Dads?' Una whispered irritably. 'What does he think I'd do with one? Paint my nails in it?'

'Twelve competitors will win a hover car and go through to compete in the final round! But on behalf of the Youth Development Foundation, I would like to say well done to everyone for getting this far! You have all been fantastic competitors and every loser will be getting one of these amazing consolation prizes!' He held up a box and everyone tried to see inside it. 'A luxury, four-piece cutlery set! Engraved with the Youth Development Foundation logo! We hope you treasure this gift as a memento of your wonderful time here!'

'A cutlery set?' David repeated, angrily. 'I think Mika deserves more than that!'

'I don't know,' Asha said, sarcastically. 'We could do with some new cutlery.'

Mika would rather have had a metre of stinking floodwater in their apartment than a Youth Development Foundation cutlery set, but he kept his thoughts to himself.

The Hat Man called the losers to the stage and one by one they collected their cutlery set and left with tears in their eyes.

'This is painful,' said Una, 'Do we have to watch eighty-eight kids go through this?'

'Looks like it,' Asha replied. 'Surely they could have given them the cutlery set later and not made them walk to the stage in front of everyone.'

'They're so big, you forget how young they are,' Tasha mused, gazing at Audrey with misty eyes.

It was a strange experience for Mika watching it all knowing he had won. As the tables emptied around them Audrey gripped his fingers tighter and tighter until he had to prize them off and tell her she was hurting him.

'Sorry,' she said.

Eighty-three. Eighty-four ran out of the hut without collecting his cutlery set. Audrey and Leo were still there but so was Ruben. Please let eighty-five be Ruben. No. Please let eighty-six be Ruben. No. Eighty-seven. No.

The last losing name was called.

'Mark Thomas!'

Poor Mark Thomas; he walked sadly to the stage as the winners began celebrating. Some climbed on the tables and danced, some ran across the hut and threw themselves on the bonnet of the hover car, and before Mark Thomas had left the stage with his Youth Development Foundation cutlery set, a team of waiters were pushing an ice sculpture of a dolphin into the centre of the room and all around the bottom, sitting in glittering diamonds of ice, were bottles of champagne with Jaguar key cards tied to them.

But amidst the joy, three people remained in their seats: Mika, stuck in his hover chair, and his parents.

'You did it,' David said quietly, watching one of the dads throw the teddy out of the hover car and climb into the pilot's seat.

'So?' Asha said, angrily. 'What price did he pay? I don't care about the hover car; this changes nothing. I mean it, David, he is *not* going to compete in the final round.'

One by one the winners' names were called by the Hat Man and they walked up to the ice sculpture to collect the bottle of champagne and the key to their hover car, which would be delivered later to their homes. Some faltered for a moment, their faces bathed in icy light while they decided which bottle to choose, which was dumb, because they were all the same. Ruben grabbed his and shook it as if he was a racing driver. Audrey hugged hers to her chest and bounced back to their table like Tigger. Leo took his quickly and slipped away to the corner of the room. Mika was so overwhelmed by the intensity of his feelings he couldn't remember how he got there in the hover chair, let alone how he picked up the bottle. His mother's last words were ringing in his head: 'He is *not* going to compete in the last round.'

Well you just try and stop me, he thought.

30
BACK TO REALITY

After the prize-giving dinner, the holiday was over for everyone else and the competitors and their families had to return to the real world of mould, work and school. Every few seconds, the hole in the dome opened and a pod shot out carrying a family away, but Mika and his parents couldn't leave with the others, because he had to go back to the hospital unit so the doctors could pretend to finish healing his leg.

They walked there in silence, with David and Asha looking as if they had hours to live. The healing chamber hummed over his leg. Asha drummed her palm tree painted fingernails on the arm of the chair and David paced around the bed huffing impatiently until they left. Asha had already packed their suitcases, so they went straight from the hospital unit to the pod waiting to take them home. The hole in the top of the dome opened to let them out and the pod flew like a bee into a thunderstorm.

'Jeez Chrise!' David cursed, grabbing hold of Asha so she didn't fall off the seat as the pod lurched sideways. Mika looked out of the window and before the view was completely obscured by rain he saw black waves that could have swallowed Barford North in one gulp. Bolts of lightning flashed through the clouds and stabbed the monstrous sea like spears.

'Back to reality,' David said grimly as thunder shook the pod.

Barford North looked more horrible than ever when they landed on the roof of their tower. The plague siren on the tank meat factory was hit by a bolt of lightning that lit up the town like a camera flash and it looked dreary, depressed and unwelcoming.

'Quick!' David shouted, his words snatched by the wind as he dragged their cases out of the pod. They hauled them down the stinking concrete stairs trying not to breathe through their noses. It felt bitterly cold in the tower after a week in the holiday complex, and outside the door to their apartment water dripped on their heads while Asha looked for the key. Her handbag was full of apples, bananas and soy cheese she'd brought home for the neighbours. She dumped it all in Mika's hands so she could see what she was doing.

'The key must be in here somewhere!' she said, up to her elbows in her bag. 'I swear this bag's got a magical trap door in it for anything important.'

The fold-down felt as cold and gloomy as the rest of the building when they walked in and it smelled of mildew because the air conditioning had been turned off for a week. There was a new patch of black mould around the window frame where rainwater had seeped in. David felt it and sighed.

'It'll seem better when we've unpacked and put the cases away,' Asha said, trying to sound cheerful. She turned on the lights and the air conditioning and brushed the frayed arm of the sofa as if that would make it look better. The air con unit started making a noise as if it was trying to eat chopsticks, then it stopped and the apartment filled with a burning smell.

'Pooh!' Asha said. 'What's wrong with this stupid thing? I despair with this apartment, I really do. As soon as we fix one thing, something else goes wrong.'

'Just imagine how different it would be if we lived in the Golden Turrets . . .' Mika said, seizing the opportunity to make them change their minds.

'No,' Asha snapped, bashing the control panel on the air con unit. 'I will not imagine living in the Golden Turrets. What sort of people organize games for children that involve borg sharks and harpoon guns?'

'But it was just an accident,' Mika insisted. 'Please let me try to win the apartment. We'd never have to worry about money again, there'd be no rent to pay, just bills. You wouldn't have to wear the cowgirl outfit. Please, Mum.'

'Just an accident?' Asha snapped. 'Your blood was spattered on the ceiling! What do you think that was like to see?'

The front fell off the air con unit and smoke began to pour out of it.

'It must have been awful,' Mika said, reasonably. 'But I'm fine now.'

He did a little jig to show how perfectly fixed his leg was. David opened the window to get rid of the smoke and a freezing cold, rainy wind blustered into the apartment.

'This place is our home,' Asha continued, with her teeth chattering. 'And that's that.'

'Dad, please!' Mika said.

'No,' David replied, putting his dressing gown on over his coat. 'And don't ask again, the subject is closed.'

David turned his back on Mika and filled the kettle at the sink and Asha pretended to busy herself with the cases. Mika felt so angry and frustrated he wanted to yell at them. He knew they were right to want to stop him competing, he agreed with them completely; he'd almost got killed when it was supposed to be a game, but how else was he going to find Ellie? He had got so far, he couldn't stop now, he just couldn't.

But, he remembered, anger would do nothing for him in a situation like this. The angrier he was, the angrier they all were; it always achieved exactly the opposite result to the one he wanted. He thought for a moment. There had to be something he could do. There *was*. It was cruel and definitely a last resort, but the moment he thought of it, he knew it would work. He leaned against the wall, thought of Ellie and silent tears began to run down his face. The instant his parents noticed, the expressions on their faces softened and their eyes filled with pain. He felt mean making them upset but he knew he had no choice and could only hope that whatever price they paid now, they would consider it worthwhile in the end. He cried desperately and it wasn't hard. All he had to do was imagine never seeing Ellie again and despair overwhelmed him. He told them how much he missed her and that the game helped him cope with her death and by the time they went to bed, they had said he could compete, but only if he absolutely promised not to get involved in any dangerous games. He promised and crossed his heart, then lay in Ellie's bed feeling terrified.

31
THAT BOY WILL BE SCARED OF ME

In the early hours of the morning, after Mika and his parents had gone to bed, Mal Gorman sat at the desk in his office on the Queen of the North, staring at the screen. He didn't know what time it was, only that supper had passed long ago and his butler, Ralph, had gone to bed. The office was almost dark, lit only by the clean light of planet Earth, glowing through the window and the much dimmer light cast from the screen that covered his desktop.

The man had been right about Mika's memory recording; it was so dark, Gorman had to watch it in darkness to see anything and most of it made no sense whatsoever. All he could make out were a few shapes moving around and static, then the odd birthday cake or smiling face, just childhood stuff, so he'd spent a boring evening frowning at it, waiting for something interesting to happen. Then, right at the end, he found what he had been waiting for, a memory so vivid, Mika hadn't been able to suppress it, and just as it shocked and frightened the boy, so it shocked and frightened Gorman. He couldn't believe what he was seeing and he watched it over and over again for hours as if that would make it better. Lurking in the shadows of a place where dark walls seemed to press in all around was a man in a black suit with a television for a head. It was an inbetween moment, a moment in which nothing much happened and yet it was horrible. The man's face flickered in black and white on the curved glass screen and his eyes gazed blankly out of it as if he was feeling nothing, as if he had no soul. He just stood there in the darkness crushing a bird in his hand that was struggling feebly to get away. But it wasn't the bird's plight that scared Gorman, or the darkness or the blank-eyed face on the flickering screen, it was the fact that *he* was that man. Somehow, a refugee child from Barford North had a memory of *him* in his head, looking like a freak, a monster.

He woke up his butler and asked for hot chocolate. Ralph arrived looking sleepy in his dressing gown with his grey hair fluffy on top.

'Good evening, sir,' Ralph said politely, placing a small tray on the desk. 'Is there anything else I can do for you?'

'Yes,' Gorman grunted. 'Watch this.' Gorman pushed the tray aside and played Mika's memory again so Ralph could watch it.

'Is that me?' Gorman asked when it had finished.

'It does look quite like you, sir,' Ralph replied, nervously.

'But that's impossible!' Gorman shouted, immediately flaring up. 'How could I be in that boy's mind? He's never met me! He's just some scruffy urchin with holes in his sneakers! How dare he think such a thing? How dare he have me in his head looking like that?'

Gorman tried to lift the cup of chocolate to his lips but his hand was trembling so much he had to return it to the saucer.

'Then it must be somebody who looks like you, sir,' Ralph said, carefully. 'How can it be you if you've never met the boy?

In fact, now I look at it again, the nose looks altogether the wrong shape.'

'Really?' Gorman asked, hopefully. 'You think so?'

'Without a doubt,' Ralph lied.

Ralph took away the tray of chocolate and returned to bed and Gorman stood up and walked towards the window and gazed at Earth wondering why he was scared of a memory in the mind of a twelve-year-old boy.

And it isn't even me, he reassured himself. But perhaps I should get rid of the boy just in case.

No, I can't do that, he might be one of the best.

But how would he feel, knowing he had to deal with a boy who had an image like that in his head? Gorman needed these special children; they were the only ones who could do the job he had planned for them. But he had assumed they would be scared of him, not the other way round. How could he control a boy he was scared of? It would be like having a pocket full of fireworks that had started going off. He remembered what Ellie had done to him while she was lying in that coffin in The Shadows and felt his heart palpitate. But, he reminded himself, they're just children, and until I tell him, Mika Smith will have no idea what he can do.

I am Mal Gorman and that boy will be scared of *me*.

32
FLOATING PANTS

Mika and Audrey went to the arcade the first night after they returned from holiday, but instead of the warm welcome they were hoping for from their friends, everyone rushed off to start Pod Fighter games without even saying hello.

'What's wrong with them?' Audrey whispered. 'We haven't seen them for a week, why are they ignoring us?'

'I dunno,' Mika replied, watching them curiously – they seemed excited and he realized something must have happened while they were away.

They played a couple of games on their own and still nobody invited them to join in and it wasn't until the end of the night that they discovered the reason why: that coming weekend, there was a special event at the arcades for all the children who had not qualified in the competition. The YDF were giving away loads of prizes including a thousand credits and vouchers for real food, and clothes and sneakers.

'So they don't hate us,' Audrey said, as Tom walked straight past as if they were invisible. 'They're just hopeful again.'

* * *

Mika and Audrey would be competing in the final round of the competition the next weekend so Mika decided to practise his new trick in bed at night, just in case he was asked to do it again. He didn't have a marble so he used a frozen pea, which he smuggled from the freezer into the bedroom in his hand. He sat in bed for half an hour staring at it and willing something to happen and when nothing did, he began to wonder if he had just imagined doing it before, because the pea just sat there, defrosting on the cover. But just as he was about to give up because his eyes were getting tired, the pea began to glow inside. Feeling excited and a little afraid, he lost his concentration and it faded again. It was like trying to make a fire by rubbing sticks together over a bit of fluff – you had to blow on the ember very carefully so it made a fire but didn't go out. It was another quarter of an hour before he made the pea glow again and this time he moved it, only a bit, it rolled once and stopped, but he did it. He jolted and hit his head on the bunk bed above him, then lay in the darkness with his eyes wide open feeling afraid of himself. But the next night his heart thumped with excitement each time the pea began to glow, and once he got the hang of it, his progress was fast; after a couple of hours he could make it roll through the valleys in Ellie's cover. By the end of the third night, he could lift it into the air so it rolled in front of his face as if it was boiling in water, and by Thursday morning, he had progressed to larger objects. Asha walked into his room unexpectedly to find a pair of pants floating in the air. Mika panicked and broke eye contact so the pants dropped to the floor and tried to look busy with Lilian.

'I swear I just saw your pants floating in the air,' Asha said.

'What?' Mika replied, screwing up his face as if he had no idea what she was talking about.

'Your pants . . .' his mother said doubtfully. She stared at them on the floor for a moment. 'I must be going mad,' she muttered, and left the bedroom shaking her head.

33
CAPE WRATH

When Mika awoke on Friday morning, he felt a pain in his thigh as if it was remembering what had happened to it. He got up and dressed and looked out of the window at the clouds feeling uneasy. He sensed something, an expectant stillness, tense and concentrated like a cat about to pounce and he felt tired and wanted nothing to think about, to just be a normal kid getting up on a normal day. But they were coming for him later, so it was far from a normal day and he was far from a normal kid; he could move things with his eyes. He turned to see Ellie smiling at him from a holopic. A seven-year-old Ellie with gappy teeth and a scab on her chin where she'd scraped it falling over. He took a deep breath, stood up and got ready for school.

His classmates were excited because the new event was starting that night, and Mika noticed that Mrs Fowler was behaving strangely. She didn't tell anyone off, even though they were shouting, and while they were drinking their Fit Mix, she welled up with tears and hastily left the classroom muttering something about needing to check the litter bins. In the afternoon, she wished them all good luck before they left for Fit Camp with a wobbly voice and a tissue crushed in her hand. Mika met her eyes and realized she was crying for them.

'Good luck, Mika,' she said, touching his arm gently as he passed her. 'I hear you're going away tonight to compete in the final round?'

'Yes,' Mika said. 'Someone's coming for me at six o'clock.'

'Well, take care and have a nice time,' she said, her eyes shining with tears.

'Thanks, Mrs Fowler,' he replied.

He couldn't be angry with her. Whatever happened, it wasn't poor old Mrs Fowler's fault; she had known them all since they were five years old. She loved them.

* * *

After Fit Camp, Mika's classmates ran into town to the arcade. They were all so fit now, they sprinted the three kilometres and weren't even breathless when they got there. Mika walked home in the opposite direction to pack his bag. His parents had left work early so they could spend some time with him before he left, but Mika wished they hadn't; Asha talked incessantly, fretting over what he was taking with him, and David wouldn't sit down and kept walking round the sofa.

'They haven't even told us how long the journey is,' Asha complained, holding sandwiches in her hand. 'How am I supposed to know how much food to give you?'

Mika felt as if he had a big hole where his stomach used to be, so food was the last thing on his mind.

'That's plenty,' he said, taking the sandwiches and putting them in his case. 'They'll probably feed us when we get there anyway.'

'I wish they'd tell us where they're taking you,' David said, grumpily. 'I don't like not knowing.'

'It's only for two days,' Mika said.

'Call us as soon as you get there,' David continued, firmly.

'If I can,' Mika replied.

'And don't talk to any strangers,' added his father.

'But they'll all be strangers, Dad,' Mika pointed out.

'You know what I mean,' David grumped. 'And don't do anything dangerous.'

'I won't,' Mika said. 'I've already promised. No harpoon guns or dangerous games.'

'Remember to pack your wash bag,' Asha said.

'I've already done it,' Mika replied. 'I don't want to get disqualified for smelling.'

'There's no need to be cheeky, Mika.'

Their fussing got on his nerves and he didn't want to have an argument with them just before he left, so he hid in the hygiene cubicle so he could be on his own, but just as the door slid shut, Lilian called out from his pocket.

'What do you want?' Mika whispered, irritably. 'I'm in the loo.' And he got her out of his pocket just so he could glare at her.

'Sorry,' Lilian said, looking sheepish in a very pretty way. 'Helen wants to talk to you.'

'Helen?' Mika said, disbelievingly. 'My Helen?'

'Yes.'

'Quick!' Mika urged. 'Put her on!'

He was hugely relieved to see her face, but he was shocked by her appearance; she looked completely different; her witchy, long grey hair had been cut short and styled in neat curls and she was wearing pearl earrings and a flowery dress with a lacy collar. In fact she looked just like the normal old ladies who lived in her tower, who glared at him disapprovingly as if boys shouldn't be allowed. He couldn't believe she was looking like that by choice. She was also wearing an odd looking metal bracelet that didn't match the rest of her outfit and she was crouching down as if she was hiding. Beside her was an ornate table with a frilly tablecloth covering its legs, and behind that Mika could see a few other old people with party hats squashed on to their heads.

'Hello, Gorgeous,' whispered Helen. 'Good to see you.'

'You too,' Mika said, quickly. 'Where are you?'

'At a birthday party,' she whispered. 'But you're not missing much. Half the guests are asleep and the other half don't know they're here. Did you get my letter?'

'No!' Mika whispered frantically. 'My father opened the biscuits and it got thrown in the bin!'

Helen's face fell.

'Oh no,' she said, looking worried. 'So you don't know The Secret?'

'No!' he said hungrily. 'Tell me now!'

'There isn't time,' she said hurriedly. 'Are you still in the competition?'

'Of course!' he replied. 'You're scaring me, Helen. What do you know?'

'You're in *terrible danger*,' she said.

'Yes, I know that bit, tell me more!' he insisted.

'You must drop out of the competition,' she said, looking nervously over her shoulder, '. . . and *stay away from the arcades*!'

'I can't!' Mika replied frantically. 'I've reached the final round and they're coming for me in less than an hour. If I don't go I won't find Ellie!'

Suddenly two pairs of chunky legs in brown tights and white skirts appeared behind Helen and she looked over her shoulder.

'Drat!' she hissed. 'I've got to go!'

'No!' Mika said, desperately. 'Tell me The Secret! Tell me where you are!'

A beefy hand appeared and grabbed Helen firmly by the shoulder and Mika heard a voice. 'Tut, tut, Mrs Gelt. What are you doing hiding behind the table? Now let's get you back to your chair, there's a good girl, and we'll see if there's a lovely piece of birthday cake for you.'

'Get off me, you brute!' Helen said, slapping the beefy hand that was holding her shoulder in a vice-like grip. 'How dare you!'

'Now, now, Mrs Gelt,' the voice said, threateningly. 'If you don't do as you're told you'll have to sit on the naughty step. Be a good girl and give me the companion.'

'No!'

Mika could hear a tussle and a lot of swearing, then Helen's companion flew through the air and landed in the middle of something white and squidgy and he realized it was the birthday cake because he could see a mess of iced flowers and broken candles.

'Mrs Gelt!' an outraged voice shouted. 'My goodness! What disgusting behaviour! You've just ruined that beautiful cake! That's ten minutes on the naughty step!'

'Save yourself!' Helen yelled as she was dragged away. 'Get away from them!' Then the screen fizzed and blanked and she was gone.

For thirty seconds, Mika stared in bewilderment at the blank screen. Where on Earth was she? And why were they calling her Mrs Gelt? Her name was Helen *Green,* not *Gelt.* He was really worried about her but he couldn't help feeling annoyed too, because for the second time she'd tried to help him and just made him feel more afraid without telling him anything useful. He wasn't going to the arcade anyway, and he couldn't drop out of the competition, because that would mean giving up on Ellie. He would rather she'd told him other things, like this secret she kept going on about and where she was. Why did she tell him to stay away from the arcades? What was going to happen there? He thought about the new event taking place that weekend and felt a surge of panic. He stuffed Lilian in his pocket and left the hygiene room and ran past his parents towards the door.

'Where are you going?' Asha asked, sharply. 'You can't go out now! They're coming for you soon!'

He could hear his mother yelling as he ran down the stairs, but he blocked it out and ran faster. He had to speak to Kobi before he left to make sure he stayed away from the arcade. He tried to call him, but there was no reply.

'How much time have I got before they come for me?' he asked Lilian.

'Fifty-three minutes,' she replied.

He began to run towards Kobi's tower, pounding along the walkway. It was the quiet time of night when most people were at home. There was no wind and in the stillness he felt as if the clouds were pressing down on him and the low buzz of pylons made the air feel like gas. Everything felt primed for a huge explosion. On the other side of town, he saw a solitary figure on the walkway and as he got closer to it, he realized it was Tom walking towards the arcade. He skidded to a halt, but Tom's feet didn't miss a beat and he walked on as if he hadn't even seen him.

'Tom!' Mika shouted after him. 'Wait!'

Tom turned and his light darkened which made Mika feel uncomfortable.

'What do you want?' Tom asked, impatiently. 'I'm on my way to the arcade.'

'Are you competing in the new event?' Mika asked

'Yes,' Tom said. 'And I'm already late because I had to help my mum; she's in bed, sick. What do you want?'

'To help you,' Mika said.

Tom blushed and looked away.

'I want to give you some money,' Mika said. 'We're going to sell the hover car I won.'

'You hardly know me,' Tom said, uncomfortably. 'You can't do that.'

'But I want to,' Mika said. 'If it wasn't for you pulling me on to the train that day, I wouldn't even be in the competition. Just think of it like chips or noodles. You really want them when you're starving hungry, then halfway through, you're full up, so you offer them around.'

'Money's not like chips or noodles,' Tom said. 'Anyway, I don't need your help, I can win a thousand credits this weekend on my own.'

Tom began to walk on, but Mika grabbed him by the arm and held him back.

'Please don't go to the arcade,' Mika said. 'Take the money from me and go home to your mum.'

'What's wrong with you?' Tom replied angrily, shaking Mika's hand off him. 'You're being weird.'

'Please,' Mika said.

There was an awkward silence and Mika felt the cameras on the walkway watching them. It was awful. He wanted to tell Tom he was in danger and to stay away from the arcade, but he didn't dare. One wrong word spoken in haste could make him disappear, like Ellie.

'You don't think I'm good enough to win, do you?' Tom said.

'Of course you are,' Mika replied adamantly. 'That's not what I'm trying to say.'

'Well, what are you trying to say?' Tom asked. He looked offended and confused and didn't wait for the reply that Mika was unable to offer him. 'I've got to go,' he said. 'I can look after my mum; I don't need your help.'

And Mika watched him walk away with the horrible feeling he would never see him again.

* * *

Kobi opened the door with his hair tied back and a light strapped to his head. For the first time ever, Mika saw his eyes, nose and mouth all at once. He had a noble look about him and for a second Mika pictured him riding like a prince across a desert on a horse.

'Hey,' Mika said.

'Hey,' Kobi replied with a surprised smile. He had a strange-looking pen tool in one hand and a half-eaten bagel in the other. He stepped aside to let Mika in and Mika walked past him, picking his way through the rubble of borg bits strewn across the floor. He'd never seen so much stuff crammed into one fold-down, even Helen's looked tidy compared to this. There were heaps of dismantled borgs everywhere, even in the kitchen all over the work surfaces, and instead of a sofa and a television, there was a table with a bright work lamp shining down on it.

'I'm making those kittens,' Kobi said. 'For Audrey.'

'Is your dad home?' Mika asked, looking towards the bedroom door.

'No,' Kobi said, 'he's at work.'

Two of the kittens were finished and they were playing together, scampering across the table, while the third lay still, waiting for its head to be attached.

'I don't know how you do that,' Mika said, admiringly, looking at the tiny borgs.

'Patience,' Kobi said. 'My dad started me off when I was little. Apparently I wouldn't stop screaming unless he gave me a bit of wire and a screwdriver. He was studying industrial robotics before the plague. Now he fixes Maid Maud borgs – you know, the ones that go round offices selling raspberry popperade.'

'That's a shame,' Mika said.

'Yeah,' Kobi replied. He sat down at the desk and took a bite of his bagel. Something moved in the corner of the room and Mika realized there was a silver raven sitting on one of the piles of borg bits watching them with beady eyes.

'That's Nevermore,' Kobi said. 'He can't fly yet but one day he will. Come here Nevermore.'

The raven spread his wings and jumped across on to the table, then frogmarched around it proudly with the kittens trying to attack his feet.

'Hello, Nevermore,' Mika said.

'Craaark,' Nevermore replied in a friendly way.

'So?' Kobi said, watching Mika carefully. 'Aren't you supposed to be leaving soon?'

'Yeah,' Mika said.

Kobi stared at him. 'So what are you doing here?'

'Nothing,' Mika replied, shrugging. 'I just wondered whether you were going to the arcade this weekend.' He held out his finger and Nevermore gently nibbled it with his metal beak.

'Of course not,' Kobi scoffed. 'It's full of loons. Have you come here just to ask me that?'

'I just wondered,' Mika said.

Kobi gazed at Mika as if he was trying to crack a code, then he rooted around under a pile of wires and found an ink pen and a scrap of plastic paper and wrote:

'If you can't say it, write it.'

Mika stared at the words on the paper and felt tears well up inside him. Kobi watched him for a few seconds then wrote something else:

'I know you know things. So do I.'

Mika took the pen and wrote on the paper:

'Something bad is going to happen in the arcades.'

They looked at each other and Kobi nodded and ripped the paper to shreds.

* * *

Mika ran home and made it just in time; a man arrived at the door of the apartment at the same time as he did. While they were saying goodbye, Asha hugged him so hard she pulled his T-shirt out of shape and he had to prize her fingers off his neck so he could leave.

'I'll see you on Sunday,' he said. He looked into her eyes hoping it was true and his heart swelled with pain as if he was never going to see her again.

'Good luck,' David said, his voice thick with emotion. 'Knock 'em out.'

'I'll try,' Mika replied, swallowing sharp tears.

Perhaps next time I see you, he thought, I'll have Ellie with me.

He put his hand in his back pocket to check her lions were there. The holopic was beginning to look a bit battered – as well as fighting sharks with it in his pocket, he'd been sitting on it for weeks and some areas of the picture had faded.

The door to the fold-down slid shut and the man walked towards the stairs up to the roof.

'Where are you taking me?' Mika asked.

'Cape Wrath,' the man replied. Then he walked on in silence, with Mika following nervously behind.

34
THE IMPLANTERS

Mal Gorman caught a glimpse of his own reflection in the window of his chauffeured pod and his heart missed a beat. Since watching Mika's memory recording, he couldn't look at himself without imagining he had a television for a head. He rummaged for his Everlife pills and tried to take one but it missed his mouth and rattled to the floor.

'Drat,' he cursed, trying to bend down. It was too far away and his knees hurt, so he glared at it angrily while he found another one.

He was on his way to one of the big arcades in Birmingham to watch the launch of the new event.

'Looks like you've got a good turn out, sir,' the chauffeur said as they descended to land on the roof of the arcade. 'It looks like every twelve-year-old kid in the city is here and I'm sure all the other arcades will be the same.'

'They'd better be,' Gorman grunted.

He looked out of the window. It had started to rain, but despite this, the area around the arcade was crowded with children. The blue light pulsing up the front of the arcade gave them a ghostly hue and their pale faces pointed skyward like wet pearls on a dirty plate.

There was a group of people waiting on the roof to greet Gorman. The local headmasters, the mayor, the Arcade Managers and the Fit Camp Instructors huddled together, grimly holding on to their umbrellas to prevent them being carried off by the wind. Gorman ignored them all, climbed out of the pod, and walked to the edge of the roof to look down at the children below. He checked his watch. There was less than a minute to go before the arcade doors opened.

'Good,' he said, when at precisely seven o'clock, the crowd surged forward.

'Excellent,' Gorman added, as he watched a girl being pushed down into a puddle. 'That's the spirit.'

He entered the arcade through a door on the roof and the huddle of local important people followed. They were to join him for a guided tour and afterwards, for a celebration supper. It was busy and hot inside the arcade and the staff were rushing to and fro making last-minute preparations as the children poured in. The tour was led by the Arcade Manager, who showed them everything from behind the secret windows. They looked down on the shopping mall from above the Ra Ra Shake Bar and watched the children enter the game room from a window over the doors. Gorman was soon bored; the other visitors were seeing an arcade for the first time but he knew every millimetre of them inside and out, so a guided tour was no use to him. The only place he wanted to visit was the Implanters' room.

'Why are you showing me this?' he asked impatiently, as the Arcade Manager led them into the staff canteen. 'Do you think I'm interested in where you eat your lunch? Stop wasting my time and take me to meet the Implanters.'

'Yes, sir,' the Arcade Manager replied, his face reddening. 'This way, everyone.'

The Implanters' room looked cold and clinical. It had a long metal table down the middle, a row of metal sinks on one side and shelves for storage on the other. The Implanters were wearing long white gowns and they were unpacking boxes of equipment on the table. As Mal Gorman and the other visitors entered, they fell silent and turned to face them. Gorman studied their features, looking for signs of weakness. What they were about to do to the children was not going to be easy if they had an atom of compassion. He looked at their details on a tablet and noted with satisfaction that three were retired traffic wardens.

'Do any of you have children or grandchildren who are old enough to come to the arcade?' he asked, casting his grey eyes over them.

They shook their heads.

'Good,' Gorman said, 'I know you've been asked that already, but I wanted to be sure. You know how important it is that the implants are fitted correctly?'

They nodded.

'I hope so, because if any of these children die, you won't be paid. I want to control them, not turn them into vegetables. Several were ruined while the tests were being done because of stupid mistakes that could have been avoided.'

He continued to scrutinize the Implanters' faces. His eyes fell on a woman at the back of the group whose features looked softer than the others. He looked at his tablet and discovered that she used to work in a children's nursery.

'You,' he said, pointing at her. 'Get out!'

She jolted with shock. 'Why?' she cried. 'What have I done?'

'I don't like the look of you,' he replied. 'Leave now.'

'Please!' she pleaded. 'I need this job! I need the money!'

'Tough,' Gorman said, dismissing her with a wave of his hand. She ran from the room sobbing and he carried on assessing the remaining men and women. Then he nodded as if he was satisfied that they were as emotionless as they appeared.

'Someone tell me what you will be doing on Sunday,' he demanded.

A woman Implanter stepped forward. She was a peculiar-looking creature, Gorman thought, with no eyelashes or eyebrows and small, childish teeth with big gaps between them.

'All twelve- and thirteen-year-old children,' she said, 'except the mutants, will be fitted with an implant.'

'Yes,' Gorman said. He already knew this, but he wanted to hear her say it so he could be sure she understood her job. 'Tell me exactly how.'

'We've put a screen up in front of the arcade doors,' she continued. 'It looks like a big advertisement for the new event, but really it's there so the children waiting outside can't see what's happening behind the doors. On Sunday, they'll come in expecting to win lots of money and prizes and we'll implant them then. It takes less than three seconds per child, so by the time they've realized something's wrong, it will be too late. And afterwards of course, they won't care. After they're implanted, they won't even remember their names, they'll just do exactly what they're told. Then they'll be given a number and a polystyrene helmet and we'll tell them to walk up the stairs to the roof. They should just follow each other like sheep. The freighters will take them a hundred at a time packed in crates to Cape Wrath and we should be finished by eight o'clock.'

'Good,' Gorman said, contentedly. 'Tell me what you have to do with the mutant children.'

'The mutants can't be implanted,' the woman continued, 'because their brains are different to a normal child's so the implants don't work.'

'So what are you going to do with them?' Gorman prompted.

'When a mutant child comes through the doors, we have to inject them with a tranquilizer to make them fall asleep, then they can be transported to Cape Wrath on a stretcher and locked up.'

'Good,' Gorman said. 'Be very careful not make any mistakes

with the mutants, they are extremely valuable. Let me see an implant.'

The woman held one out on the palm of her hand. It was a round, silver disc, about the size of an old-fashioned five pence coin, with six vicious-looking spikes sticking out if it. Underneath the disc was a tiny motherboard and a single wire, the width of a hair.

'Once it's embedded in the forehead of the child, it's very neat and tidy,' the woman said. 'The spikes dig deep into the skull keeping it in place and the wire self-locates, so in less than two seconds it has found the right part of the brain and attached itself.'

'The wonders of modern science,' Gorman said, turning the implant over in his hand. 'For the first time in history, children will do as they're told. We should have invented these things years ago.' Then his face clouded and he continued irritably, 'But it's a shame they don't work on the mutants.'

He gave the implant back to the woman with a sigh. 'You seem to know what you're doing,' he said. Then he turned to the Arcade Manager. 'How do I get out?'

'Don't you want to stay for the celebration supper, sir?' the Arcade Manager asked, trying not to look relieved.

'No,' Gorman replied. 'I'm moving my staff to Cape Wrath tomorrow morning, I have more important things to do.'

'I'll get someone to show you, sir,' the Arcade Manager said.

Alone again in his chauffeured pod, Gorman put his head back and closed his eyes. The pod began to rise into the night sky and he drifted with it towards sleep, but before he was completely there, he felt something strange in his mouth. Half asleep, he let the object fall on to his palm, where it sprang open, green and supple. It was a leaf, a large leaf, almost as big as his hand. For a few seconds he stared at it in astonishment, then he blinked and it was gone.

35
HELL

Mika realized Cape Wrath was not going to be a holiday complex with wafting palm trees and golden sands, but he wasn't expecting to feel as if he'd arrived in hell – Cape Wrath was a fist of land punching the sea on the northern coast of Scotland. It had cliff faces of jagged black rock and no beaches, so the waves and the boulders collided in a constant, booming assault. There was a hint of green to the narrow strip of land that rolled away from the cliff top, but it was only a hint, and it died out as it approached a monstrous, black fortress as if the roots of the new structure had poisoned the earth around it. It was Mal Gorman's pride and joy; one of ten new gargantuan ring fortresses built across the north. A doughnut of black metal with a thousand eyes of yellow light pricking through its skin, the towers of Barford North looked like gingerbread houses compared to this behemoth on the cliff top. Its walls rose higher than the clouds and the tiny pod transporting Mika had to climb steeply to get over them. The pod dipped over the top and the inner wall curved all around them, circling a great hole in the ground where the rock had been hollowed out to create a giant underground hangar.

Mika heard a noise loud enough to crack the sky and a pair of Pod Fighters rose from it like black wasps from a nest. He'd never seen a real Pod Fighter before and he felt the hit of adrenalin as it entered his veins. In a second the fighters were out of sight and carving through the clouds.

'Wow,' he whispered.

The pod dropped into the hangar like a pebble into a well and they landed. The door opened and Mika stepped down into the dimly lit space. There were hundreds of Pod Fighters in neat rows all around him. They looked new, fresh out of the packet, as if they'd never been flown before, and their elegant curves gleamed in the low light.

He could hear the boom of waves as they hit the cliffs only metres away from him, and the wind was briny and bitter, even though they were below ground. He shivered and thought he could not imagine a more hostile and unwelcoming place than this. A man in uniform stepped forward. He had three gold stripes on his shoulders.

'Welcome to Cape Wrath,' the man said, politely. 'Please follow me.'

'What about my bag?' Mika asked, looking anxiously back at the pod.

'Don't worry,' the man replied. 'Someone will bring it for you.'

They walked through the lines of Pod Fighters to a lift in the far rock wall. It was gloomy and functional inside and had a metal grille instead of a door. Mika stepped into it reluctantly and it seemed to go up for ever before it finally stopped, but he was happier when it opened again and he found himself in a warm, well-lit space. It was all white and had the feeling of a new house that nobody had moved into yet. The shiny white floor didn't have a single scuff and he felt as if his feet were the first to touch it.

They walked past lots of doors before entering a large area enclosed by a glass wall. Mika thought uncomfortably that it reminded him of an animal enclosure in the old zoos before the plague. There was even a guard on the door. He looked round for windows on the outside but there were none. In the centre of the area was a communal living space containing white, curvy tables and chairs and a few plastic sofas in front of a screen on a wall. Around this area were hygiene rooms and twelve other doors leading into smaller rooms. The man took him towards one of these and Mika felt a chill as he read his name in letters of red light and realized he had been part of Cape Wrath even before he'd arrived. The man opened the door and stood aside to let him in.

'You can change into your uniform,' the man said. 'Then I'll come and take your clothes.'

'OK,' Mika replied.

Mika walked into the small room, and as the door shut behind him he felt overwhelmed by claustrophobia. There was a bed, a cupboard and a desk with a mirror over it and everything was white. There was no window and the air came through a vent over the door. On the bed, neatly laid out, were a tray of food and the uniform he had been told to put on. Awen appeared, sniffed the food and disappeared again and Mika wished he could do the same; the meal was some kind of curry but it looked like sick. He put it in the cupboard so he didn't have to look at it.

Even the uniform was white, with a black line down the arms and legs. It was made of a thin, stretchy fabric designed for ease of movement. There was also a pair of shoes that looked like socks with rubbery soles. They were the most ridiculous footwear Mika had ever seen, but holding them in his hands, he sensed Ellie. His pulse quickened and he looked round as if he would see her standing behind him, cheered by a wave of optimism. He changed quickly and the man came to take his clothes, leaving him with nothing of his own but the holopic of mountain lions.

'Eat up and get an early night,' the man said. 'You're going to be very busy tomorrow and we want you to sleep.'

Mika didn't feel like eating or sleeping. He lay on the bed; it was hard and the pillow was thin and had the Youth Development Foundation logo printed on it. He folded it in half and put it behind his head, then looked up and saw a camera on the wall watching him.

There's no pretence we're on holiday now, he thought, grimly.

A few minutes later, there was a gentle tap on the door. He opened it and was relieved to see Audrey.

'Hey! Nice shoes!' she said, grinning.

'Great, aren't they,' he replied, raising one foot and looking at it. 'I think I'll ask to keep them and wear them at home.'

She laughed. She looked different in her white uniform with the black stripe, older and more serious, but she soon ruined this impression by taking off her sock shoes and jumping on the bed.

'Not very bouncy,' she said, with an impish glint in her eyes.

He watched her jump up and down on the bed like a demented fairy and wished he could be like her, so untroubled and optimistic and defiant. But, he thought, she's only behaving this way because she doesn't know anything.

'That camera's watching you,' he said, pointing at it. 'You'd better behave yourself.'

'I don't care,' she said, sticking her tongue out at it. 'Wasn't that food horrible? It looked like sick. I haven't eaten it.'

'Neither have I.'

'Tell them in the kitchen,' she said to the camera, 'I liked the food we had on holiday. I want bread, soy cheese, apples and salad.'

'You're crazy,' Mika said.

'No, just relieved,' said Audrey, her eyes bright with happiness. 'I can't believe how slowly last week went. I thought I was going to die of boredom. Do you think we'll get to fly the Pod Fighters tomorrow?'

Mika shrugged.

'I hope so,' she said, dreamily.

She flopped down on the bed and stared at one of her sock shoes and it lifted into the air and drifted towards her hand.

'It's good being able to do this,' Audrey said, putting it on. 'I don't have to move to pick stuff up any more.'

* * *

Audrey went to bed, but Mika felt too nervous to sleep. He wanted to have a shower, but he could hear Ruben and some other people messing around in the hygiene rooms. He waited for ages, then their shouts and laughter abruptly halted and he heard a stern voice rapping out commands and he figured they'd been told to stop mucking about and go back to their rooms. He waited a few minutes to be sure the coast was clear then walked quietly through the communal area with his towel and wash bag. He passed a couple of other competitors and they smiled.

'Hey,' Mika said.

He heard water running in the boys' shower and stuck his head round the door to see Leo, the golden boy with dreadlocks who'd helped when he was shot. He was tilting his face into the stream of hot water and it ran through his hair and down his gold back to his . . . tail. Leo had a tail – a short, skin-covered tail that twitched lazily as he rubbed shower gel over his face. Mika felt embarrassed, as if he'd seen something he shouldn't have seen, and he wanted to go before Leo noticed him. He made to leave, holding his breath, but Leo sensed his presence and turned to halt Mika with his sea-blue eyes.

'Hey,' Mika said, feeling a complete idiot as he stood there with his wash bag and towel clutched to his chest.

'Hi, Mika,' Leo replied. 'How's your leg?'

'Fine. Thanks. I mean thanks for helping me when I was shot. I owe you.'

'No you don't,' Leo replied, simply. 'You would have done the same for me.'

He turned away again and squirted shower gel into his hands

from a dispenser on the wall and lathered it on to his arms. Mika realized he'd look stupid if he left without showering, so he stripped and washed beside him. Leo was quiet and Mika felt self-conscious, and after Leo had dried and left he cursed himself under his breath for being such a perp.

He's only a boy like me, he thought.

But is he? There was definitely something different about Leo besides the fact he had a tail. He wondered whether all the finalists were mutants. He and Audrey were, Leo clearly was, but what about Ruben? Mika had never noticed anything different about Ruben's body and he bullied mutants so how could he be? But Mika knew some people concealed their mutations because they were embarrassed about them. Some people, like Ellie, had operations to remove them, and some had them on the inside where they couldn't be seen. If they were all mutants, it would be a strange twist of fate that the children who had always been teased for being different would end up winning a competition. The idea made Mika feel uneasy. Was it because they were mutants that they could see the light trails and move things with their eyes? Again he sensed the stranger inside him and he didn't like the idea that the YDF knew more about this person than he did.

36

STUPID OLD MAN

Eventually sleep took Mika and luckily it was dreamless, but thousands of miles above him, on the Queen of the North, Mal Gorman was not so fortunate. Caught in a nightmare he saw himself with a television for a head standing in the middle of a concrete car park, the sort that had existed when everyone drove petrol cars with wheels, many years before. He was holding a set of old-fashioned keys in his hand and he turned around as if he'd lost his car and was hunting for it. But there was nothing else in the space, no cars, no people, nothing but concrete marked with worn white parking spaces as far as the eye could see.

Then the ground began to tremble and the Gorman Telly Head looked down and huffed as if he was thinking it had no business behaving that way while he was trying to find his car. Then it began to heave and bend and bow as if a giant was turning over in its sleep beneath it. It happened so quickly,

Gorman only just managed to stop himself falling over by spreading out his arms to keep his balance, and when the giant came to rest again there were hills and valleys beneath the concrete crust, and the car park with its worn white parking spaces looked like an enormous crumpled duvet. The Gorman Telly Head was angry and he started to shout at the ground beneath his feet.

'How am I supposed to find my car when the car park keeps moving about?' he yelled. Fine cracks appeared in the concrete crust, spreading quick as lightning over the hill. He jumped as one formed between his feet and skittered backwards in his haste to get away from it. The face flickering on the screen wasn't quite so angry now, it was beginning to look scared – and for good reason – because out of the hole grew several green vines, quick as the cracks and slithery as snakes, and finding his feet they began to wind up his legs. He kicked at them violently and shouted some more, waving his car keys as if the vines would care that he couldn't find his car. But it made no difference how much he complained; in less than a minute, his whole body apart from his television head was bound in vines like a mummy wrapped in bandages in a tomb. Then the fearful expression on the screen face transformed into panic as a gush of black and white vines writhed violently around his throat and he began to choke. Then they smashed through the screen and they began to wind around the television set and within seconds he was covered in them from head to toe like a fly cocooned on a spider's web. Then another crack appeared beneath his feet and the earth ate him with one vast gulp, vines and all, and Gorman was so terrified he woke up with his hands around his throat, gasping.

It was quiet in his bedroom and very dark. He thought he could hear the vines slithering across the floor.

'Light,' he gasped, and it came on. 'Brighter!' he said. 'Brighter! Brighter!' And soon the bedroom was as bright as a supermarket.

Gorman looked at the floor and felt silly. There were no vines, only normal, daytime carpet and his slippers by the bed.

'You stupid old man,' he whispered. 'And anyway, that thing with a television for a head isn't even you.'

37

HE'LL BE GOOD, I PROMISE

Very early the next morning, the man with the gun entered Ellie's room. Looking at her, he thought she was asleep, so for a few moments, he stood next to her bed with the gun held softly in his hand, feeling sorry for her. Tucked up in her pyjamas, with her hair spread out on the pillow, she looked like a normal child. Then her eyes opened, making him jump.

No, he thought, there is nothing normal about this child.

He reminded himself what she'd done to Mal Gorman in The Shadows – the incident on the salvage boat had become legend amongst the men. This child's dark eyes had the power to cause pain, maybe even death. He held his gun with a firmer grip and pointed it at her face.

'What do you want?' asked Ellie. She'd seen more guns than any other object in the past few weeks, but it still wasn't nice to wake up and find one poking up her nose.

For days she'd realized something important was about to happen. There was more activity on the ship, more freighters going to and fro from Earth. But nobody would tell her what was happening, despite her frequent questions, and she was worried about Mika.

'Get up and get your things,' the man with the gun said, coldly. 'You're moving.'

'Where?' she asked.

'Earth,' the man replied.

'Why?'

'Because Mal Gorman says so.'

'Really?' she said, hopefully, leaning up on her elbows. 'Where on Earth?'

'Not where you're thinking,' the man said, firmly.

'I'm not stupid enough to think I'm going home,' she said indignantly, pushing back the covers. 'Tell me where.'

'Cape Wrath,' the man replied.

Ellie had visited Cape Wrath with Mal Gorman, just after it was built. She shrugged.

'I suppose it's better than this boring space bin,' she said. 'What about Puck? He can't stay here on his own.'

'He's coming,' the man said.

'Good,' she said, relaxing a little.

'Get your things then,' the man said impatiently. He looked around the bare, white room.

'I haven't got any things,' she replied, quietly. 'Just this.' She picked up the book of poems Mal Gorman had given her and put it on the bed. Despite the fact it was a gift from the man she hated most in the world, she read it every night. Her escort waited outside the door while she dressed and she put on extra layers, a wrap over her uniform and a white padded coat that came down to her knees. She knew how cold it was at Cape Wrath.

'Ready!' she shouted.

The man re-entered. 'Come on then, Trouble,' he grunted, motioning with the gun towards the door. 'Grab your poems and let's go and get that scallywag of a monkey.'

They walked deeper into the spaceship along corridors that felt like the tunnels of a huge, smooth white worm.

All the staff rooms on the ship were the same size and shape except Mal Gorman's quarters, with white plastic walls, ceiling and floor and an egg-shaped hollow for a bed. But Puck also had a white plastic tree in his room and this was the only familiar shape around him. When Ellie was away, he cuddled the white plastic tree while he slept, and if he was alarmed by a sudden noise or the appearance of a strange face at his window, he retreated into its plastic branches as if it would protect him. His days had been long, lonely and boring since they'd been caught, and he was never let out. Through the window in his door he could see the staff walk past, and twice a day he was fed a measure of monkey chow. This would be his life if Ellie didn't come.

A few minutes before she arrived, Puck leaped on to the closest branch to the door and pressed his black palms against it. Then he craned his neck and pressed his cheek to the glass so he could look down the hallway. He could feel her coming.

Ellie began to run.

'Walk!' the man with the gun shouted after her. 'Ellie! I said WALK!'

Ellie stopped running, but walked almost as quickly, forcing the man to do the same to keep up with her. She hadn't seen Puck for three days because Gorman had been in a bad mood, and she knew how lonely and depressed he would be. She reached his door and he leaped around his white plastic tree for joy. She pressed her hands against the glass and breathed deeply. The monkey dropped to all fours and walked along the branch to the window. Then he put his small, black hands next to hers.

'Come on then,' the man with the gun said gruffly. 'Let's ask for a carrier to put him in.'

'We don't need a carrier,' Ellie said. 'I can carry him. He'll be good, I promise.'

'I don't think so,' the man replied, sceptically. Puck was looking the picture of innocence at that moment, all fluffy and cute and hooting with happiness, but the man had plenty of scars to remind him how this bundle of fluff transformed into a screeching vampire. 'I'd rather arrive at Cape Wrath with all my fingers,' he added. 'If you don't mind.'

38
THE CRACKLE BECOMES
A ROAR

Mika's dreamless sleep lasted a couple of hours, then the Telly Heads stood around his bed licking their wrinkly lips. A few times he half awoke and panicked in the windowless room. There was no bunk above him, no Ellie pictures to anchor him in reality, and it was almost a relief to slip back into the nightmare and find himself faced by something familiar. But this time the dream was different, this time it went further than ever before. The Telly Heads were quiet, they had decided how they wanted to eat him, and now they were going to cut him up. The Knife Sharpener stepped forward and placed the blade on the fragile skin of his inner arm and Mika watched, unable to move, as the tip of the blade, like a violin bow, drew the first drop of dark blood. He tried to shake his head to wake himself up, but couldn't. He opened his mouth to scream, but no noise came out and he realized that if he didn't escape the nightmare in the next few moments, he would die of fright.

He was saved by Ellie. The moment her foot touched the ground in the hangar, something coursed through the fabric of Cape Wrath and into Mika's body through the bed. He awoke, knowing she had arrived with as much certainty as if she'd walked into the room and tapped him on the shoulder.

'Ellie,' he whispered.

His first impulse was to break out of the glass enclosure and search Cape Wrath for her, but he remembered that even if he did manage to get out, the fortress was the size of a town with thousands of locked doors and guards and he had no idea where she was. He would have to be patient. He sat up in bed feeling rushes of happiness and trepidation. She was so close now and every atom of his being ached for the moment he would see her again.

* * *

Mika washed and ate and waited on his bed for the day to begin. A man came for him and they walked through the fortress past scores of empty rooms that felt, like him, as if they were waiting. Eventually, he found himself in the doorway of an occupied room, a room that contained a table, three chairs and Ruben Snaith. He came to an abrupt halt in the doorway as if he'd hit an invisible wall and cursed his bad luck. He did everything in his power to avoid this boy, but fate kept throwing them together.

'Nice to see you too,' Ruben sneered, responding to Mika's contemptuous look.

'Go in,' the man ordered. The door slid shut and Mika faced Ruben across the table. Ruben glared at him, his pale eyes as hard as frozen floodwater.

'I see you don't like each other,' the man said. 'I hope you don't let this affect your concentration; you are being watched.'

Mika looked up to see a camera on the wall. He sat down and tried to pretend Ruben wasn't there.

The man took some things out of a bag and put them on the table – a plastic maze, a few silver balls and a couple of toy cars with old-fashioned wheels. One of the cars started to roll and Mika caught it with his hand as it fell off the edge of the table.

'Who did that?' the man asked, sharply.

'I did,' replied Ruben, proudly, then he looked at Mika and smirked.

'I don't remember asking you to begin,' the man said icily. 'I'll tell you when to start.'

Two patches of colour appeared on Ruben's cheeks and Mika smiled.

Maybe competing with Ruben won't be so bad after all, he thought. He could feel his dislike of the boy killing off all other emotion inside him and firing his determination to win. He wouldn't have felt that way if he'd been sitting opposite Audrey.

Their first task was to race silver balls through a maze. It wasn't easy; Mika could feel his brain aching with the effort of it and he realized almost immediately that Ruben's ball was moving faster than his. He started to panic, thinking he would lose, but luckily he found a better route through the maze and finished first. He looked up as his ball rolled out of the maze to see beads of sweat on Ruben's forehead and it occurred to him what a horrible world Ruben inhabited – a place where nothing mattered more than proving he was better than everyone else. Ruben, the bully, who only had friends because everyone was frightened of him.

'Good,' the man said, scribbling on his tablet. 'Let's try something else.'

He put the maze aside and took a red plastic ball out of the bag and placed it in the middle of the table. It was about the size of a tennis ball, light and solid.

'Right,' the man said. 'I want you both to concentrate on the ball at the same time and tell me when you can see the light.'

Mika stared at the ball. He found it difficult to concentrate with Ruben there, so he couldn't focus properly.

'I can see it,' Ruben said, smugly.

'What about you, Mika?'

'Not yet.'

'Concentrate.'

Mika stared at the ball and eventually the inside began to glow with a blue light.

'I can see it,' he said.

'Good,' the man said. 'Now I want you both to lift the ball into the air.'

The silence was absolute while Mika and Ruben concentrated. Mika felt a pain behind his eyes because although the ball didn't look heavy, it felt heavy in his head. After a minute Ruben looked away.

'It's making my eyes hurt,' he said.

'Don't worry,' the man reassured him. 'I think you're both too tense. Let's have a break for a minute.'

They both drank a cup of water before trying again. Mika looked up to find Ruben's pale eyes glittering with real, murderous hatred.

He's insane, Mika thought. He looks like he wants to kill me.

It occurred to Mika that Ruben's malice could stop him finding Ellie, and his anger and hatred began to swell.

'OK,' the man said. 'Let's try again.'

This time they did it; the ball rose from the table and rolled in the air between them.

'Well done,' the man said. 'Don't lose it. Hold it there for a minute . . . OK, now I want you both to push it away from you. Mika, push it towards Ruben. Ruben, push it towards Mika. Let's see who's the strongest.'

The ball stopped rolling and shook in the air as Mika and Ruben tried to push it in opposite directions. Mika was surprised how easy it was now he was angry, and he was aware of a new noise in his head like the crackle of a fire. He felt suddenly strong and tried to propel the ball forward with his hatred, but the force of Ruben's resistance was powerful and after a few seconds the ball did something no one was expecting – it melted and warped mid-air and began to flicker with flames. Both boys continued to stare at it, neither willing to give in, so it shuddered between them, filling the room with black smoke.

'Stop!' the man shouted, but they couldn't stop, their eyes felt glued to the ball.

'STOP!' the man yelled again, thumping the table. Mika dragged his eyes away and the lump of burning plastic fell. A fire alarm started to go off and their lungs filled with toxic fumes.

'Get out of the room!' the man said urgently, waving his tablet around in the air. 'Wait outside!'

Mika staggered through the door and headed for a row of chairs, coughing desperately, but before he got there, he felt a sharp tug on his collar and he was off his feet and flat on his back. He looked up to see Ruben standing over him.

'You fool,' Ruben sneered. 'You'll never beat me.'

'You want to bet?' Mika snarled.

'Yes,' Ruben laughed. 'And do you want to know why?'

'I'm sure you're going to tell me, Ruben,' Mika said, 'so get on with it.'

'Because you're weak,' Ruben said.

'No I'm not,' Mika replied.

'You are,' Ruben snarled, his face contorted by disdain. 'You're damaged. I can smell it, Mika. I smell everything you feel, your confusion and your paranoia and fear. My mutation is useful, not like yours, web-foot. Your love for your sister has crippled you.'

'So you *are* a mutant!' Mika said, angrily. 'You nasty, pointy little frag. Poor Lara. How could you spend years teasing Lara about her teeth when you're just the same yourself. I hate you and so does Audrey. Can you smell that? Can you smell how much Audrey dislikes you? And her pity? She thinks you're messed up and she doesn't want anything to do with you.'

The sensible part of Mika knew it was madness to bait Ruben this way, but he had gone beyond the point where he could stop himself. The crackle of a fire in his head had become a roar and he watched the sinews in Ruben's face and arms turn rigid and felt glad. Ruben lifted his foot to stamp on Mika's chest but Mika rolled to the side, and the next few seconds were a blur of floor as Ruben threw himself on top of Mika and tried to hit him in the face. Mika saw red, literally, it was as if his eyes filled with blood as his anger and hatred haemorrhaged into them. He hit Ruben hard on the mouth and his lip split and blood dripped on to Mika's face. Then Ruben put his hands round Mika's throat and started to squeeze. Mika pulled his knee up and gave him a sharp jab in the stomach, thinking that would get him off, but it didn't work, Ruben was still squeezing and his grip felt so strong it was as if his hands had turned to stone. Mika couldn't breathe and his head felt hot and he began to feel dizzy. He pushed on the side of Ruben's head, yanked at his uniform, tried to roll to the side to get him off, feeling increasingly panic stricken. Then a hellish fear gripped Mika. He could hear his mother crying, Ellie calling for him, and what he felt was beyond terror. He fought against Ruben with animal ferocity, the roar filling his head, then suddenly their eyes locked and he felt something powerful surge out of his. Ruben immediately screamed as if Mika had stabbed him in the eyes and he fell sideways on to the floor. Feet pounded down the hallway. Mika clutched his throat and sucked in air. A man held out his hand and pulled him up.

'You OK?' he asked, pulling Mika to his feet.

'You psycho!' Mika panted, glaring at Ruben, who was still lying on the floor. 'You've got a serious problem!'

'And you haven't?' Ruben sneered, without looking up. 'Don't pretend you're so fragging perfect after what you just did.'

Mika saw a hygiene room across the hallway.

'I want to wash,' he told the man. He had Ruben's blood on his face and he wanted to get it off.

'OK. But don't be long.'

Mika staggered into the hygiene room with the roar still filling his head. He washed his hands and splashed his face and tried to calm down. He turned to see Awen cowering in the far corner with his ears back and the tip of his tail wagging nervously against the wall.

'Come here,' Mika called softly, crouching down and putting out his hand. But the dog backed further away with his tail between his legs and the fearful whites of his eyes showing. 'Come, Awen,' Mika pleaded. 'Please.' But Awen turned and disappeared into the wall and Mika leaned against it and cried with shame.

The smoke cleared, a new ball was found, and half an hour later Mika had to sit opposite Ruben again and pretend nothing had happened. It wasn't easy; in the middle of the table was a hole where the first ball had melted through it and Ruben was looking at him as if he still wanted to strangle him.

For Ellie, Mika thought, breathing deeply. You're doing this for Ellie.

39
A FIRE CATCHING

The last time Puck had been away from the Queen of the North, he was shot down in a Pod Fighter, almost drowned at the bottom of the river and locked in a coffin for several hours before finding himself back on the spaceship with only his plastic tree for company. From his point of view the whole experience had been utterly pointless torture, so it was understandable that when his carrier was loaded on to the space freighter, he spent the whole journey screeching his head off with fear. He was in the cargo hold so he couldn't even see or smell Ellie – he was all alone and utterly distraught.

Ellie went to see him as soon as they arrived at Cape Wrath with her breakfast in her pocket and the man with the gun behind her. But to her dismay, she found Puck already had a visitor and not one he wanted; Gorman was there waving a banana at the monkey through the glass wall at the front of his new enclosure and Puck was sitting in the far corner, ignoring him.

'That creature is spoilt,' Gorman sneered, handing Ellie the banana.

'He probably doesn't feel very hungry,' Ellie snapped. 'How would you like it if you'd been taken away from home without any explanation and left on your own in a strange place?'

'He's got a bigger room,' Gorman said. 'What's wrong with him? A lot of refugee families would be happy to have that much space.'

'If he was with his family,' Ellie said, 'he *would* be happy.'

'Don't start that again,' Gorman said impatiently. 'I came to see how you're settling in, and I'm very busy, so be polite.'

'Lucky me,' muttered Ellie, opening Puck's door. He leaped into her arms and clung to her. 'Hello,' she whispered, fussing his head. 'Do you want to play a game?'

She looked around his new space. The glass wall let in plenty of light and the room *was* much larger than his old one, much better for games, Ellie realized, because she wouldn't have to crawl under the plastic tree to play with him. The new tree had its trunk in the right-hand corner of the room and its white branches spread across the roof and over the walls, so the middle area was unobstructed. She gave Puck her breakfast muffin, which had nuts on the top, then she took a bag of letter tiles out of her pocket. Gorman sat down and watched them through the glass wall and the man with the gun stood next to him.

'Just ignore them,' Ellie whispered to Puck.

She had a question she wanted to ask and it felt like a stone in her stomach. Mika was in Cape Wrath, she could feel him and she wanted to know why, but she was scared to hear the answer. Puck realized something was wrong and he put the muffin on her lap after only one half-hearted bite and this made her feel even more wretched. She had to ask about Mika, if not for herself, then for Puck.

'My brother's here,' she said quietly.

'Yes,' Gorman replied, after a surprised pause.

'Can I see him?' she asked, her eyes welling up with tears.

'No,' replied Gorman. 'He's busy.'

'What is he doing?' she asked. 'Why is he here?'

'Damn you!' he said, impatiently. 'Why do you ask so many annoying questions? Haven't you learned anything? You should know by now it doesn't pay to irritate me. Now shut up!'

She got up and walked towards him until they were facing each other through the glass.

'I want to know what's happening to my brother,' she persisted, glaring at him with bold dark eyes. 'Tell me.'

'No,' he replied, trying not to flinch. 'Don't push me, Ellie, or you'll regret it.'

For a few seconds she felt like she wanted to kill him. She wanted to melt every bone in his dried-up body and the roar filled her head quickly, like a fire catching in a field during a drought. It was the second time she had faced Mal Gorman feeling this way, but this time she knew what she could do and how easy it would be. But the man with the gun stood next to Gorman with his fingers tense on the trigger. He would shoot her without hesitation, or even worse, Puck. Besides, she didn't want to kill, never, not even this evil man. Ellie turned away from him and closed her eyes and breathed deeply until the roar subsided. Then, feeling calmer, she sat on the floor.

'Come on, let's play,' she said to Puck. He sat up on his haunches and looked expectantly at the bag of letter tiles she held in her hand. This was his favourite game. She shook them out in a heap on the floor and spread them around with her hand so he could see the letters on each one. The tiles were white and the letters were black. She took a deep breath and Puck watched her face, his fuzzy eyebrows twitching impatiently. She concentrated and thought of the letter T and a few seconds later Puck picked it up with a small black hand, moved a short distance away and put it on the floor. Then he scampered back and waited to see if he was right.

'Good,' Ellie said. 'Well done.'

She was quiet again and the game was repeated. Puck searched with his eyes over the letters and picked up an H. Gorman watched, feeling frustrated and intrigued. After more than a year of experiments, his scientists still couldn't explain how Ellie communicated with the monkey. The words formed a sentence in a spiral around her as Puck ran backwards and forwards, making happy noises as he worked. Ellie sat quietly, her legs crossed and her eyes burning with concentration.

When they had finished, Gorman stood up and read what they had written.

'The bark of the elder makes whistles for the children

To call to the deer as they rove over the snow.

'I was born in the dark,' says the Green Man,

'I was born in the dark,' says he.

'Where did that come from?' Gorman asked uneasily.

'It's a verse from a poem,' Ellie replied. 'From the book you gave me.'

'I gave you?' he repeated.

'Yes,' she replied. 'When you took the bandages off my eyes.'

He thought for a moment and remembered. 'Oh yes,' he muttered. 'So I did.' He turned and Ellie watched him walk away, knowing her brother's fate was in the hands of a volatile and unpredictable man.

40
A PARCHED MAN IN THE DESERT

After an entire day of moving stuff with their eyes while people stared at them and scribbled on tablets, the twelve finalists of the competition were given a special treat. It was a rare clear night, so they were taken to a room at the top of Cape Wrath to watch the aurora borealis, the northern lights. The room was large and empty with a glass wall overlooking the North Sea. There was food on a table behind them but everyone except Ruben picked at it with little appetite, feeling anxious and wary. They had all sensed something when Ellie and Puck arrived, as if the empty fortress was filling up with pain.

The light of the aurora borealis looked like coloured silks wafting in the darkening sky and Mika thought of his mother on the beach with the breeze licking the folds of her holiday sari. He watched, wondering if he was imagining the silken lights and the moon-tipped waves. The barrier in his mind between dreams and reality had been dissolving for weeks, but since his fight with Ruben earlier that day, he felt as if it was about to disappear altogether. Ellie was so close and he felt like a parched man in a desert.

When he managed to sleep, he dreamed the black water of Barford North was rising, and as each floor was flushed out by the tide, tatty old sofas floated out the windows and he could hear people crying.

He didn't feel better when he awoke. He opened his eyes, instantly fearful. It wasn't yet morning, and in the darkness he saw two discs of silvery light: wolf eyes. At first, he thought he was still dreaming, then someone whispered, 'Are you awake?'

'I don't know,' he replied.

'Mika, I want to go home!'

It was Audrey. He reached out and touched her hand to be sure and it felt warm and solid. Yes, it was real, daytime Audrey, sitting on the end of his bed in the darkness, and the reflective retinas of her borg eyes were all he could see of her.

'What are you doing?' he whispered, glancing anxiously at the camera on the wall. 'You might get in trouble.'

'I had a nightmare,' she whispered. 'I was scared.'

'Come here,' he said, and she shuffled along the bed so he could hug her in the darkness. Awen appeared and put his head on her lap, and although only Mika could see him, the three friends comforted each other.

'Thanks,' Audrey whispered, pulling away when she felt better.

'That's OK. Go get some sleep.'

The chink of light in the door expanded and contracted as she went through.

'Night, night,' she whispered.

'Sweet dreams.'

41

IF THEY SMELL FEAR

On Sunday morning, Cape Wrath was blasted by gale force winds and the sea and the sky touched. Centuries ago such menacing conditions would have sunk a score of ships and plucked planes clean out of the sky, but Cape Wrath had survived millions of years of such treachery and the howling wind and monstrous waves were hardly noticed by those inside. All night, freighters stacked up and dropped down to lay their cargo like eggs in the fortress and its empty chambers had been filling up with people and equipment. The curving corridors now clattered with footsteps and one by one, the lights flicked on as if many eyes were opening. Cape Wrath was waking up.

As Mika washed with the other boys, he tried not to look at himself in the mirror. He had a ring of bruises around his neck where Ruben had tried to strangle him, and on the way out of the hygiene room Ruben blocked Mika's path.

'Watch it,' Ruben snarled, as Mika bumped into his shoulder.

'Get out of my way,' Mika said, pushing past him.

Mika ventured from his room for breakfast and joined Audrey and Leo at one of the curvy white tables. They ate quietly from ration trays. A girl stood in front of the television, brushing her hair. A boy sprawled on one of the sofas, reading something on his companion. In their new uniforms they looked as if they belonged in the place. Mika struggled to eat, his throat hurt.

'You look as if you had fun yesterday,' Leo commented, looking at Mika's bruises.

'Yeah, Ruben is a laugh a minute,' Mika replied, sarcastically.

'I don't trust him,' Leo said, quietly. 'There's something wrong with him.'

After breakfast, they were told they had only one more test to do before the competition winners were chosen. Sick with nerves one by one they were taken below ground to the lowest level of the fortress, where they walked through low corridors of barely lit, unpainted concrete. When it was Mika's turn he realized the moment he got out of the lift that he was moving towards Ellie. Their guide walked quickly ahead and Mika followed, feeling the urge to open every door they passed to look for her. Then they entered a maximum security area and Mika paused, feeling as though Ellie was so close to him he could reach through the floor or ceiling and touch her. Awen appeared briefly and wagged his tail and snuffled at the wall to the left, then he walked through it and was gone.

There! Mika felt a surge of happiness, as if a thousand flowers had bloomed in his heart, and he put his hands on the wall.

On the other side, Ellie was sitting in Puck's new enclosure with the monkey on her knee. She had stroked him until his eyelids drooped and he swayed, almost falling asleep where he sat in her lap. She had her head leaned against the wall and she was wondering how she could feel so bored and frightened at the same time, the two emotions didn't seem compatible, like lemon juice and milk, but that's how she felt waiting to find out what Gorman was doing to her brother. Then she sensed him.

Mika!

She held her breath and her heart began to beat in sore punches. He was close! Very close! Puck's eyes flashed open as if someone had prodded him with a stick. He stood on his back legs with his curled tail twitching and looked towards the wall at the back of the room. They both saw the dog, but only for a split second, a skinny creamy dog which walked through the wall with its tail wagging as if it was pleased to see them. Puck scampered towards it, but it vanished before they met and he jumped up and across one of the branches of the white plastic tree instead. Mika was there on the other side of the wall! Puck ran to and fro along the branch and Ellie jumped up and put her hands on it, her heart swelling with love and pain.

Mika.

She pressed her body against it, trying to get as close to him as possible.

Ellie.

He was smiling, she could feel it.

'What are you doing?' asked a cold voice.

Ellie turned to see the man with the gun watching her suspiciously through the glass.

'Nothing,' she said. She took her hands away from the wall and turned her back to it.

'Why were you leaning on the wall?' he asked.

'I was just playing with Puck,' she replied.

'Let's go,' the man said.

'No!' said Ellie. 'Please let me stay a bit longer.'

He shook his head. He didn't like the way Ellie and the monkey behaved sometimes, he didn't understand it and it frightened him. 'Come on. Now.'

* * *

The twins were led away in opposite directions and felt fresh pain where they tore. Mika walked blindly through the concrete labyrinth and suddenly found himself standing on the edge of a pit in a large, poorly lit room. He felt shocked, as if he'd woken up whilst sleepwalking. He'd completely forgotten about the competition, all his thoughts and feelings were still in that stretch of corridor with his sister and he realized he needed to drag himself into the present or he was in trouble.

The pit was five metres square, lined with battered metal plates and looked as if it had been built to restrain a velociraptor, maybe several very angry velociraptors – the grids over the lights were warped and bent and the floor was cracked in several places. There was a large steel door leading into the pit, maybe three metres tall, and it was so badly dented, it looked as if a bomb had exploded on the other side. Two men appeared wearing black body armour and helmets and the man who had come with Mika left quickly, as if he wanted to get away from the pit as quickly as possible. Mika looked up to see four cameras pointed into the pit, and to his right, there was a man-size cage on a chain. There was a long gash in the ceiling above it, so the cage could be moved and dropped down into the pit. It didn't take a genius to figure out what was about to happen to him.

'What do you want me to do?' Mika asked, trying to control the terror that was melting his brain.

'Stay calm,' one of the men advised. 'That's the most important thing. If they smell fear, it will make them worse.'

'If *what* smell fear?' Mika asked, looking down into the pit. He heard something heavy throw itself against the door and he gulped as another big dent appeared in the thick metal. Whatever was behind that door was desperate to get out. The man took a blindfold out of his pocket and Mika cursed under his breath as it was tied around his head.

Thank frag my parents can't see me now, he thought, frantically. My mother would die of fright. What are they going to learn from doing this to me?

He breathed deeply.

They're not going to kill me, he told himself. What would be the point?

The blindfold was tight and he couldn't see a thing. He felt the men's hands on his arms guiding him towards the cage and stepped inside. The only solid part of it was the floor. He listened as they fastened the door with several locks.

'They can't get you,' one of the men said, 'if you keep your arms and legs inside the cage. Whatever you do, don't put anything, not even a finger, through the bars, OK?'

'Yes,' Mika replied, shakily.

'We can fix cuts and broken bones,' the man went on, 'but we can't grow new hands or feet.'

'OK,' Mika said, feeling as if he'd already got the message.

The cage began to move and he crouched down and put his hands on the floor to keep his body steady as it rocked. In the pit below, he heard the grind of heavy bolts as the locks on the metal door were released. The door slid back with a groan and the creatures were out. There were several, Mika could tell by the sound of their feet on the concrete floor, running round in circles beneath him. They made heavy clicks, and whirrs and low whines and he knew from this that they were some kind of borg. He heard a snarl, not loud, but so ferocious he felt it rip into his gut like shark teeth, but that was just the start of it, within seconds they had realized he was above them and they launched into a rabid frenzy. Snarling and growling, they leaped into the air, their metal teeth snapping at the cage, and the image that flooded his mind was of ripped skin and spattered blood, slips of silver and evil red eyes. Suddenly the cage lurched and tilted as one of them managed to get a grip on the side with its teeth and Mika felt himself slip down towards it. He grabbed desperately in the opposite direction, trying to hold the other side of the cage, then remembered he couldn't put his fingers through the bars. The beast was yanking with its head, its whole body weight pulling down one side of the cage, and Mika was sliding towards it. Terror paralysed him for a few seconds. Blind and helpless he slid down until his foot went straight through the bars by its snarling jaws. Survival instinct kicked in and he yelped and pulled back and luckily, at the same time the cage hit the bottom of the pit and the jar of impact made the borg lose its grip. Mika lay on the floor and panted. It was quiet then, oddly quiet considering the madness of the last minute. He lifted his head and tried to get a sense of what was happening outside the cage. He could hear them, their feet clicking on the floor. They were pacing around him, their movements slower now, and he wondered what was supposed to happen, what the people watching through the cameras were hoping to see. How he wished *he* could see. He wanted to know what they were, he could hear them sniffing through the bars and it was maddening being able to hear them but not see them. He stood up and concentrated, trying to build a better picture in his mind from the sounds he could hear. They were like dogs, he was pretty sure of that because of the sounds they made, but they were enormous, at least as tall as him if not taller. They were moving lazily now and their heavy footsteps sounded relaxed. He heard one sit down right next to him with a big sigh and the others followed, resting against the wall of the cage. He felt the urge to touch them, to connect physically with them, but just as his fingers passed through the bars of the cage, one of the men above shouted at him angrily. 'Oi! You fool! Don't do that! That's enough, pull him up!'

The chain jerked on the top of the cage and Mika felt it start to rise.

42
LIKE PURGATORY

Mika walked away from the pit feeling as if he'd spent days dragging a boulder up a mountain and when he returned to his room, he fell asleep as if someone had unplugged him the moment he lay down. He awoke feeling cold and saw needles of light in his eyes. Awen was close, nuzzling his hand and he fiddled with the dog's silky ears and listened to the sound of leaves rustling. Then he heard another noise in the distance like woodpeckers or hammers and eventually realized someone was knocking on the door. Awen spooked and left and Mika opened his eyes to see Audrey jittering in the doorway like an electrocuted imp, as if she'd spent the time he was asleep licking an electricity pylon. She had a bruise on her jaw.

'You look terrible,' she said. 'Your face looks like tank meat.'

'Thanks,' he replied. 'You don't look so great yourself.'

She flopped on his bed and Mika inspected his face in the

mirror over the desk. His eyes were puffy, he had red pillow marks on his cheek and the bruises on his throat had deepened in colour.

'You'd better splash some cold water on your face,' she said. 'A man just said they're taking us for the prize-giving dinner in a minute. We're going to find out who's won.'

'I think I need more than cold water,' Mika replied, frowning at his reflection.

'We haven't got time for a head transplant,' she said.

They were quiet for a minute, both aware they were balanced on a pair of scales and in the silence they felt Cape Wrath, waiting.

'I don't like this place,' Audrey said, uneasily. 'I'm glad we're going home soon. Why do you think they lowered us into that pit?'

Mika shrugged and looked meaningfully at the camera to remind her people were listening. She fell quiet again and they both thought about their experience in the pit. They had grown up in a world with all kinds of borgs everywhere doing things for them: the vacuumbots in their homes, the Ghengis Borgs on The Wall, the animal borgs they had seen on holiday, but all these borgs had one thing in common; they were as empty-brained and empty-hearted as a toaster or a kettle. You could flick a switch and turn them off and they wouldn't know any different. But these dog borgs felt special; the way they moved and behaved felt *real* somehow, as if they were alive. Who had made them? Where did they come from? Why had twelve children been lowered into a pit with them? The competition had become more bizarre with each round, but now it was nearly over and there was no time to think about dog borgs, only about whether or not they had won. 'Are you going to wash?' Audrey asked.

'Yes,' Mika replied.

Then he grabbed a towel and went to the hygiene room to stick his head under a tap.

* * *

The finalists of the Youth Development Foundation's competition were taken to Gorman's private suite on the top level of the fortress for their last meal together. It had been fitted in an old-fashioned style, like a grand old house before the plague, so when the lift doors opened, they found themselves in a great hall with a marble floor. A crystal chandelier hung from the ornately plastered ceiling and a staircase wound its way round walls adorned with paintings of men in tights with curly hair and women in dresses that looked like cakes. The children huddled together nervously; three contestants had disappeared since that morning and the remaining nine were busy imagining hands and feet slipping through bars and the snap of metal teeth.

They were led into a long dining hall with oak panelling on the walls. Down the middle of the room was a banqueting table also made of oak and it was the first time most of them had seen real wood. They touched it curiously, feeling its warmth. Another, smaller oak table made a cross at the top and both were laid with silver cutlery and candlesticks. Scores of priceless candles burned even though it was afternoon, and behind the top table, a gas fire blazed in a stone fireplace. Over the mantle hung an oil painting: a view of Cape Wrath hundreds of years ago, punching green and proud from the rugged Scottish landscape. They were told to sit down. Five girls and four boys remained. Mika waited for Ruben to choose a chair near the top table before taking one at the other end. Audrey sat on his left with her eyes glued to the painting and Leo sat on his right with a girl called Iman; a striking black cat of a girl whose lines were as elegant as those of a Pod Fighter. She smiled at Mika and he tried to smile back, but couldn't. He watched the candles flicker with a horrible feeling something bad was about to happen.

It's nearly over, he reminded himself. You're so close to *them* now. And the closer you are to *them*, the closer you are to Ellie.

But it felt like waiting to be burned. Like standing next to a fire, knowing he would have to reach in to pull his sister out.

* * *

Gorman sat on a gold chair before another fire in his dressing room. The Minister for Youth Development had bigger, grander rooms than this, but the dressing room, with its red velvet curtains and antique rug, was the warmest. Still he shivered; nothing seemed to shake the cold from his bones in Cape Wrath.

His dinner suit hung freshly pressed over the arm of the butler, who stood in the corner, waiting for the doctor to finish examining his master.

'What's wrong with me?' Gorman asked the doctor irritably. 'I haven't got time to be ill, I've got too much to do.'

'Your heart is beating erratically, sir,' the doctor replied. 'Are you particularly stressed or worried about anything?'

'No,' Gorman snapped. 'I'm just not sleeping very well and I feel cold. I thought perhaps I'd caught a chill.'

'You need to rest,' the doctor advised. 'Perhaps you shouldn't go to this prize-giving dinner.'

'Don't be ridiculous,' Gorman said. 'I'm giving the prizes and I want to see the children. Just give me a pill or something. And hurry up, I've only got a few minutes.'

Gorman rose to his feet and held out his arms so the butler could put on his jacket. The doctor sighed and looked in his case at his bottles of pills and medicines. He shook out two large blue tablets and left them with a glass of water on the table next to Gorman's chair, but he wasn't sure they would help. Hearts were not designed to keep beating for a hundred and eight years, even with Everlife pills, and Mal Gorman needed to be more careful with his.

As Gorman left the dressing room, he felt his pulse quicken as if someone had turned up the speed dial on his heart. He paused for a moment and with one bony hand resting on the banister, he looked down the stairs towards the dining hall, wishing he didn't feel so uneasy about sharing a meal with a few children.

They will be scared, he reminded himself, there is nothing for *me* to fear.

He took a deep breath, straightened his back and walked down the flight of stairs.

* * *

The butler entered the dining hall and rang a gold bell, then he said, 'Please stand for Mal Gorman! The Minister for Youth Development!'

Mika stood with the others and looked towards the door. Then he gasped before he could stop himself as the second Telly Head walked out of his nightmares into reality. But this one was much more frightening than the sneering nurse with her plastic cups, for here was the Knife Sharpener, the demon who'd lurked in the darkness of Ellie's cupboard crushing her in his hand, the monster who'd pressed a blade against his arm and smiled as the first drop of blood appeared.

But he wasn't the only one to gasp as the old man walked in. What a scary sight Mal Gorman was, even to those who'd never dreamed about him. Thirty years of Everlife pills had made him look like a walking corpse. Skeleton hands hung out of his jacket sleeves and faded eyes protruded from a skull face of bone and papery skin. A few strands of grey hair still grew from his scalp, but they looked parched as grass trying to grow on the edge of a desert. Audrey reached for Mika's hand and a shudder passed through them like a Mexican wave.

'This is weird,' she whispered. 'I want to go home.'

Gorman walked towards the top table and a waiter pulled out his chair. As he sat down he looked at the nine children as if he was a collector of fine jewels and had opened the box to admire them. But there was no love in his eyes, only a cold glint, because he wasn't appreciating their beauty, only how much they were worth.

Mika stared into his lap, still recovering from the shock of seeing Gorman while he was awake. He'd dreamed about this man for months . . . but how was that possible when they'd never met? *Mal Gorman, the Minister for Youth Development* had stood in Ellie's cupboard in Barford North with a cup of spiders in his hand. It was too creepy for words, but he couldn't deny it, the features of the old man's face were burned on his brain as well as those of his parents. But Mal Gorman's appearance was not the only shock in store for Mika. The butler rang the bell again and eleven more people walked out of his nightmare to join Mal Gorman at the top table.

They were announced as politicians involved in the Youth Development Project but Mika knew nothing about politics, all he knew was that these monsters with their papery skin and bulging eyes had spent months arguing about how to eat him, and now here they were, sitting at a dining table, tucking their napkins under their chins. Waiters waltzed around the dining hall placing enormous silver platters on the tables, and although Mika was relieved to find he was not on the menu, it was a grim meal; the Telly Heads gorged and guzzled and stared at the finalists with gravy on their lips while the children shuddered and wished the event over as quickly as possible. They were immensely relieved when, after the second course, Mal Gorman rose to announce who had won the competition.

'I'm going to announce the winners before dessert,' Gorman said. 'Then, perhaps, some of you might want to eat it.'

His mouth smiled but his eyes remained cold. Nobody laughed at his joke. Mika could barely breathe for fear and longing.

I can't believe I'm doing this, he thought. I'm actually hoping to win a competition organized by the Telly Heads.

'But first,' Gorman said, 'I want to say how much pleasure it gives me to see you all here. This competition has been a journey of discovery for all of us and you have exceeded our expectations, well done.'

The Telly Heads nodded and smiled and raised their wine glasses in agreement.

'You have bright futures ahead of you,' Gorman continued, 'whether you win this competition or not, so don't be disappointed if your name isn't called today. You will all be rewarded for your efforts. But now I will announce the winners, so please stand up when I call your name.'

'Iman.'

The black cat of a girl stood up and the Telly Heads clapped.

'Santos.'

A skinny cheeky boy with a shaved head and old-fashioned glasses got up from his chair.

'Leo.'

The Lion Boy.

He rose to his feet with calm eyes and the slightest trace of a smile.

'Colette.'

A French girl stood up, blushing through a mass of chestnut hair.

'Audrey.'

Mika nudged her with his elbow and she looked at him as if an eagle had landed on his head.

'Me?' she said.

'Yes, you, noodle brain,' whispered Mika.

'Me?' she repeated, looking at Mal Gorman.

'Yes,' Gorman replied. 'Unless there's another Audrey hiding under the table.'

Her eyes glowed as she stood up and the Telly Heads clapped their bony hands.

'You next,' she whispered to Mika.

Five contestants now stood and four remained seated. Mal Gorman paused for a moment and the room became as still as a holopic. But his pause wasn't intended to add drama to the scene, he was having last-minute doubts about his final choice. It had taken him a long time to select the last child. He'd been forced to choose between the two most promising children, as he knew if he took both he wouldn't be able to control them. The previous day these two boys had burned a hole in a table and tried to kill each other. Ruben Snaith and Mika Smith were incredibly

powerful but keeping them together would mean ongoing problems, like owning two dogs who constantly fought for leadership
of a pack. In his dressing room, Gorman had tried to make his
decision logically, based on the results of the tests, but he couldn't
disregard Mika's dream memory. Because of Mika Smith, every
time he looked in the mirror, he saw himself with a television for
a head. How could he have that boy around when he had dreamed
such a thing? And then there was his sister, Ellie, to consider.
Those dark eyes of hers had nearly killed him. That moment in
The Shadows had been the most painful and terrifying of his life
and although he was constantly reminding himself they were just
children, he didn't want two like Ellie, his heart couldn't take it.
Gorman had stared into the fire in his dressing room and decided
that although Mika Smith had done better in the tests, the last
winner of the competition, the final chosen one, would be
Ruben Snaith.

But that was before Gorman saw Ruben Snaith. What a
peculiar-looking boy he was. In the silence, Ruben was glaring at
Gorman with a sneer on his face and his fists clenched on the
table, as if he was threatening him, insisting his name was called.
He looked like a bleached rat, Gorman thought, his nose was too
pointy and his skin too pale as if he had milk for blood, no not
milk, something more venomous than that, snake venom, white
and viscous. By contrast, Mika Smith, sitting at the other end of
the table, looked sensible, modest and calm.

What should he do? Was he over-reacting about Mika? They
were only dreams, after all. He remembered that his men had
told him Mika worked hard and would be easier to control than
Ellie. Easier to control . . .

Gorman's heart slowed right down, then speeded up, as if it
couldn't make up its mind whether to stop dead or beat so fast it
exploded. Everyone was watching him and the silence felt like
purgatory.

'The last winner is . . . Mika Smith.'

Somehow Mika managed to stand, knowing Gorman had

only chosen him in those last awful moments.

'Mika?' Ruben sneered, jumping up from his chair to face Mal Gorman. 'Mika Smith? You chose *Mika* instead of *me*?'

'Sit down, Ruben,' Gorman said.

'No!' Ruben shouted, stepping back so his chair fell heavily on the floor, his face grotesque and gargoyle-like in the candle-light.

'Ruben,' Gorman said, his eyes cold as ice. 'Control yourself and sit down or you will regret it. You will not leave here with nothing.'

Ruben's face bloomed scarlet with humiliation and anger.

'What are you going to give me? A YDF cutlery set? A conso-lation prize lollipop? You've made a mistake and you know it! You weren't sure, were you? You chose me then you changed your mind!'

'How dare you question my judgement?' Gorman said quiet-ly, trying not to flinch under the boy's evil glare. 'Sit down or I'll have you removed.'

'NO!' Ruben yelled. 'I'm not a child! And I won't be treated like one! Change your mind or you'll regret it!'

Mika didn't think he could be shocked by anything else that day, but as Ruben rose up into the air to float eerily above the table, he watched in stunned silence with the others. Ruben's light trail turned completely red and spread out in mist-like tendrils around him, and his eyes began to glow with a blood-red haze. He looked so utterly evil, the Telly Heads seemed like cheery old grandparents in comparison and they shrank back in their chairs as Ruben cast his glowing red eyes over the table. Iman screamed and stepped sideways as a fork flew through the air towards her, narrowly missing her eye. Then all at once, cutlery, carafes and glasses rose into the air and began to spin in a deadly, bladed whirlwind. Glasses smashed into each other sending lethal shards flying through the air and knives shot with a whoosh towards faces, necks and backs. Waiters used their trays like shields and the Telly Heads hid behind their high-backed chairs.

Mika and Audrey threw themselves under the table, then they were joined by Leo, his hand to his face and blood running through his fingers. He had a gash down his cheek from eye to jaw, where the skin had been sliced like a melon. Above them they heard Gorman yell, 'Kill him, NOW!'

From beneath the table, Mika saw several pairs of army boots run into the room and heard the click of safety catches. In an instant he knew what he had to do; he scrabbled out from beneath the table. Audrey tried to grab him with her free hand and hold him back, but he broke away, climbed on to a chair and with a flying tackle, launched himself at Ruben and dragged him out of the air. A shot rang out and they fell and landed with a crash on to the table. There were screams. Cutlery and glass rained down on them. Mika's mind blanked as if someone was surfing his channels and he waited to feel the first wave of pain, sure that the bullet had hit him. But it didn't come. Instead he heard Ruben swearing and trying to push him away.

'Get off me!' Ruben yelled.

He shoved Mika roughly aside, climbed off the table and tried to run for the door, but he was grabbed by several men who covered his eyes and dragged him away.

Mika rolled over on to his back to find Audrey glaring at him. 'They nearly shot you!' she said, furiously. 'Why did you do that?'

'I don't know, they were going to shoot him,' he replied.

'So you thought you'd let them shoot you instead?' she cried.

'But they didn't,' he said, smiling. 'I'm fine. We won!'

'Won what?' she cried. 'This is supposed to be a game! This morning they put us in a pit with those dogs and now they just tried to shoot a boy! I want to go home!'

He looked at her, not knowing what to say. After all, this was a game run by Telly Heads.

The men with guns returned and started shouting, telling them they had to go back to their rooms. They were escorted in silence and locked in so they couldn't talk to each other. Mika sat on his bed, shaking. He had Leo's blood spattered all down his front and a shard of glass embedded in his hand. He gritted his teeth and pulled it out, watching the blood run in rivulets off his palm, but he felt no pain, only a delirious, exhausted happiness. He had won the competition, he could reach into the fire, and every moment of fear and pain was worth it to feel so close to Ellie.

43
REACH INTO THE FIRE

Half an hour later a man entered the room.

'Are you hurt anywhere?' he asked, looking at Mika's bloodstained clothes.

'Just my hand,' Mika replied.

'Let me see,' the man demanded and Mika held it up briefly to show him.

'That's deep,' the man commented, looking at the cut. 'We'll have to heal that . . . and do something about your throat, too; you look as if you've been strangled.'

'I have,' Mika replied.

'Well you can't go home looking like that,' he said. 'You'll need half an hour in the healing chamber.'

'Home?' Mika repeated, welling up with panic. 'I'm going home . . . already?'

'Soon,' the man replied. 'Mal Gorman wants to talk to you

before you leave. He's with Audrey at the moment, but he won't be long.'

Mika paced by the side of the bed panicking, feeling as if he'd been pushed away from the fire. They were going to send him home before he'd found Ellie but what possible excuse could he use to stay? The competition was over and they didn't want him any more. But he was shocked by this, he'd expected more, there had to be more than this.

Please let there be more.

Mal Gorman appeared in the doorway and held out a bony hand. Their eyes met and to Mika's horror, he felt a spark of recognition pass between them, as if Gorman knew he was the monster from Mika's nightmares. For a fleeting moment, he sensed doubt and fear and a quiet danger like poison or gas. The knife was there; Mika couldn't see it but he felt the cold metal pressing on his skin. What did Gorman know? The old man had chosen him and yet he didn't seem to trust him. Mika's mind returned to the black chair where he had been strapped down while his memory was searched and he felt an icy chill. There were many things Mika didn't want Mal Gorman to know about him. Many things. Struggling to stay calm, he took the old man's hand and shook it. It felt dry and hard.

'Sit down,' Gorman said quietly.

Mika obediently sat on the bed and felt his stomach tighten as Gorman sat next to him. He smelt of nothing, Mika thought, as if he'd been freeze-dried fifty years ago.

'How do you feel?' Gorman asked.

'Fine,' Mika replied.

'Good,' Gorman said, with a cold smile. 'You were brave earlier when you tackled Ruben. The Education Minister is grateful to you; apparently he was almost hit in the chest by a knife. I hope you weren't hurt.'

'Not really,' Mika said, closing his hand. He felt a pang of relief that he had done something Gorman liked, even though his gratitude was misplaced; after all, the last thing Mika was thinking about when he saved Ruben was protecting the scumbag Telly Heads.

'You seem to have taken the events of the past hour very well considering you were almost shot and you didn't get your pudding,' Gorman said.

'I know what Ruben's like,' Mika replied, carefully. 'He doesn't like it when he doesn't get his own way.'

'So I see.'

Their eyes met again and this time Mika observed a more confident look as if Gorman felt reassured by their talk.

'I was right to chose you,' Gorman said thoughtfully. 'You deserve it.' He removed a gold card from his jacket pocket and placed it on the bed between them.

'What's that?' Mika asked.

'The key to the apartment you've won in the Golden Turrets,' Gorman replied. 'Your parents will be there when you arrive.'

'Will they?' Mika asked, surprised. 'So I'm going straight to London, tonight?'

'Yes,' Gorman said. 'It's all arranged. After you've gone to the healing chamber you'll be flown there by a chauffeur. Your parents will travel in a removal freighter – we've already sent men to your old apartment to pack up your things. The other winners and their families will be living on the same floor in the Golden Turrets and tonight, you'll be having a party to celebrate your success.'

Mika felt the colour drain from his face.

I must seem grateful, he thought, this is supposed to be what I want.

He struggled to think of something appropriate to say, like, 'Oh good,' or, 'Thank you,' but his lips wouldn't move. He was being sent away without his sister to a new apartment he didn't want. It was all going wrong.

'Your parents will be proud of you, Mika,' Gorman said. 'You have achieved the impossible; you've moved your family from a fold-down apartment in the refugee town of Barford North, with stinking floodwater all around it, to the *Golden Turrets* in

London – the most beautiful homes in the new world. You've got an amazing future ahead of you, you are very lucky to be chosen.'

'What do you mean?' Mika asked cautiously. 'The competition is over.'

'Yes,' Gorman replied. 'But your life isn't, is it?'

'No,' Mika said, trying to say the right thing.

'And,' Gorman went on, quietly, 'I have a *special prize* for you.'

'Really?' Mika said, feeling a spark of hope.

'But to get it you'll have to prove I can trust you,' he continued.

'What is it?' Mika asked.

'Something you believe was taken from you,' Gorman said. 'Or rather someone. Have you any idea who I'm talking about?'

Gorman's words pricked Mika like hot needles. He knew exactly who Gorman was talking about and he felt as if the old man had taken another key out of his pocket and placed it on the bed and this time it was the key to Ellie.

He looked at Gorman, his eyes pleading with him and tears burning his throat.

'You know she's with me, don't you?' Gorman said.

Mika nodded and dropped his head. He could feel great sobs of relief swell inside him but he didn't want to cry in front of this man.

'I thought so,' Gorman said.

'What do I have to do?' Mika asked, desperately. 'I'll do anything.'

'Good,' Gorman said, simply. He stood up and began to walk towards the door.

'Wait!' Mika said. 'Tell me what I have to do!'

Gorman turned in the doorway to face him and his eyes were hard. 'I've already told you. I want you to prove I can trust you.'

'How?' Mika asked, hungrily.

'Make me a promise,' Gorman said.

'Anything,' Mika replied.

'Promise me you'll come back tomorrow,' Gorman said. 'And do whatever I tell you.'

Mika was shocked by this request, but he agreed to it immediately, because he knew this was his chance to reach into the fire. 'OK,' he said.

'At half past eight tonight,' Gorman continued, 'while you are with your parents at the party, they will receive a message telling them you are coming back. They'll be upset and angry and they'll probably ask you lots of questions because they're going to want to know why. But you must tell them nothing. They must not know what you can do. Promise me.'

'I promise,' Mika said, with his heart thudding. This was hard, he could already imagine how upset his parents would be when they discovered Mal Gorman wanted him to return and he refused to talk to them about it. But what choice did he have? Ellie was suddenly within his grasp.

'And,' Gorman continued, 'you must stay in your new apartment tonight. You are not allowed to go anywhere else. My men will be watching you and I will be very angry if I hear you've disobeyed me. Promise me you'll stay in the apartment.'

'I promise,' Mika said, nervously.

'Give me your companion,' Gorman demanded, holding out his hand.

'My companion?' Mika repeated, hesitantly.

'Yes.' Gorman replied. 'I don't want you making any calls.'

Mika found Lilian and silently placed her in the old man's hand, wondering if she knew anything that might make the old man more distrustful. He remembered Helen's call, warning him he was in danger, and felt a suffocating grip on his heart.

But calls aren't saved, he reminded himself. Gorman won't find out about that.

Nevertheless, he didn't want to give him Lilian.

'Repeat your promise,' Gorman said, dropping the companion into his pocket while Mika watched anxiously.

'I must stay in the apartment tonight,' Mika replied. 'And come back to Cape Wrath tomorrow. And I must not tell my parents what I can do.'

'Good,' Gorman replied. 'Are you sure you can keep this promise?'

'Yes,' Mika said, feverishly.

'You'd better,' Gorman said. 'I've told the other winners I'll make them homeless if they don't do as I say. I'll take their new apartments away in the Golden Turrets and dump them in The Shadows. I don't need to threaten you in the same way, do I?'

'No,' Mika replied, feeling his blood run cold.

'Because if you don't keep your promise, you will never see your sister again.'

44
DON'T FORGET WHERE
YOU CAME FROM

As Mika left Cape Wrath, he felt a sudden and overwhelming wave of sorrow and a tear rolled down his cheek. He caught it on his index finger and rubbed it thoughtfully between his finger and thumb, thinking it had been cried for Ellie because he was leaving her behind. But he was wrong; the tear had been cried for thousands of children, not just one.

As he flew away from the giant ring fortress, a line of freighters approached it. In the darkness, they looked like a string of black beads that stretched all the way to the distant horizon. They were carrying children; thousands of children from refugee homes, who had been lured into the arcades by a lie. Instead of rushing home with their pockets full of money or vouchers for real food or clothes, they had left with an implant buried in their foreheads. A round metal disc attached to their brains by a fine wire that now controlled everything they did, except feel. They were unable to speak or move but inside they were tormented by fear and confusion.

Mika was too tired to cry more than one tear, even though he felt like crying a river. He put his head back and closed his eyes, feeling weak and sick and wishing Ellie was coming home with him.

* * *

Half an hour later he opened his eyes to see London. He'd only ever seen it on television before and he was dazzled by its scale and beauty. The Golden Turrets shone like a heap of hot treasure on the horizon, bathing the night sky with a warm orange glow. Each turret was sliced into thousands of luxury apartments, and their lights twinkled like diamonds. All around on the air roads, pods whooshed towards the city like bees towards a hive, leaving trails of blue and gold light in their wake.

'Lovely innit?' the chauffeur said. 'You're a very lucky boy.'

'Yes,' Mika said, thoughtfully.

They flew through the city and descended on the edge of New Hyde Park. The golden street, which formed a ring around it, was clean and wide and softly lit by lights set in the curbs. The people walking past were dressed for the night. Jewels glittered on their hands and their bodies were wrapped in cloaks of expensive fabrics that looked like fur, wool or silk.

The chauffeur opened the door to let Mika out. Immediately he heard a strange sound.

Boom. Boom.

'What's that?' he asked as his feet hit the pavement. It sounded like the heartbeat of an enormous beast, as if a dragon was sleeping beneath its treasure, instead of on top of it.

Boom. Boom.

'The Shadows,' the chauffeur replied. 'Haven't you heard?'

'No,' Mika said. 'What's happening?'

'The mould is getting worse,' the chauffeur replied grimly.

'Hundreds of people are dying every day. And they say the government won't help them because it's cheaper to let them die.'

Mika looked at the ground beneath his feet and shuddered. He'd just eaten dinner with several members of the Northern Government, and it didn't surprise him at all that they'd do such an awful thing. He remembered how they'd gorged themselves while they'd stared at him with greedy eyes. Their light guttering, barely human, barely alive.

'But the people in The Shadows won't be ignored,' the chauffeur said. 'So they're banging on the pillars holding up the Golden Turrets with huge steel balls on chains. All day and all night they swing them – one time for every person who's died. It was driving people crazy up here when it started on Friday night, but apparently you get used to it.'

Boom. Boom.

'I don't think I'll get used to it,' Mika said. He gazed at the pavement and tried to imagine what was below, all that darkness and water and millions of people trying to stay alive and balls on chains swinging against the pillars.

'Creepy innit?' the chauffeur said. 'I'm glad I don't live down there.'

'So am I,' Mika agreed.

Boom. Boom.

He looked at the people walking past. They were talking and laughing as if they couldn't hear it. He watched a woman apply lipstick with a small gold mirror in one hand, and the boom vibrated through her red stiletto shoes.

'When everyone moved behind The Wall,' the chauffeur said, 'we were all the same for a while, because we were united by tragedy and loss. But not any more, not since the Golden Turrets were built. It's amazing how quickly people forget where they came from. But I suppose that's the way it's always been. Some people have nothing and others have everything. Anyway. Enough of politics. You've just won yourself a new home and I don't want to make you feel bad about it. You make the most of it, lad. Just don't forget where you came from.'

'I won't,' Mika said, firmly.

He watched the pod rise and loop up around the turrets before disappearing into the night sky. A full moon was hanging like a gong amongst them, huge and pale. It looked down on him as if it knew everything and Mika wished he felt the same.

His turret was one of the biggest and most beautiful in the city and it towered over New Hyde Park like an elegant sculpture with a gently tapered dome at the top. The scale of it was breathtaking; the cylindrical base was the same size as their old refugee tower, but it was at least three times as tall and seemed to go up forever. His neck ached as he tried to look at the top of it.

The curved apartments inside the turret had balconies and glass walls. Inside the ones near ground level, he could see rich people talking and laughing and this made him feel as if he was watching an advert on telly. The breeze picked up and blew a fine mist from the fountains in the park across his face. It felt fresh and smelled of perfume. By the doors were a pair of security guards in smart black uniforms, and they watched him with contempt as he walked up the shallow marble steps.

'You must be from the competition,' one said, eyeing Mika's filthy sneakers and jeans.

'Yes,' Mika replied, dropping his bag with its broken strap on the step in front of them. They looked down their noses while he searched for the gold key card, but when they saw it glinting amongst his socks, they stepped aside to let him in.

Just inside the foyer there was an ornate marble fountain with nymphs sitting around it bathing their feet and combing their hair. Mika walked up to the edge and trailed his fingers in the cool clear water, feeling astonished by its extravagance. In their old foyer the walls were covered in slime and the wind whistled through in a ghostly lament as if people had frozen to death in its corners.

He heard footsteps behind him and turned to see two boys and a girl. They were the same age as him and yet they looked as if they came from another world. A perfect world where people were warm and ate real food, but their lights were dark, revealing their hostile thoughts, and the girl looked at Mika as if his ragged clothes made her feel sick.

Boom. Boom.

He looked at the floor, remembering The Shadows, but the rich kids ignored the sound and continued to stare at him.

'Who are you?' the girl asked, haughtily. 'How did you get in?'

'I live here,' Mika replied.

'No you don't,' one of the boys scoffed. 'People like *you* don't live *here*. You must have come in with the cleaners.'

'And you're touching our water,' the girl said, 'Don't. You'll make it dirty.'

Mika almost retaliated. His anger surged up with the crackle of the roar and he wanted to punish them for their prejudice and wipe the haughty sneers from their faces. How easy it would be to humiliate them with the powers he now knew he had. Then he remembered his promise to Mal Gorman and knew this was not the time to be showing off to arrogant strangers, however horrible they were. He turned from them and picked up his bag and walked towards the lift. He heard the boys laugh and say something as the door closed but he clenched his teeth and blocked it out.

Remember Ellie.

Boom. Boom.

The lift began to rise and he slumped against the wall, dreading the moment when he saw his parents again. It wasn't going to be easy to keep that part of his promise to Mal Gorman. How could he get away with not telling them anything? The bruises on his neck and the cut on his hand were gone but he felt different. Since he'd left home on Friday, he'd been strangled by Ruben, almost killed him by looking at him, then saved his life, been lowered into a pit full of strange borg dogs, met the Telly Heads, won the competition and found, but not seen, his supposedly dead twin sister. He felt as if he'd been playing all the parts in a very strange soap opera and now he had to face his parents and say nothing. And then, at half past eight, while they were supposed to be enjoying a party, they would get a message from Mal Gorman and find out he had to go back to Cape Wrath in the morning. They were going to be mad as hell and very upset. They would ask lots of questions he wouldn't be able to answer. It was going to be awful.

But worth it.

* * *

He would never forget the vision that met his eyes as the door to their new apartment opened; his mother stood barefoot on a luxurious carpet in her blue celebration sari and behind her, the Golden Turrets glowed through their very own wall of glass.

'Mika!' She ran towards him and threw her arms around his neck. He breathed into her hair and felt a spasm in his chest as he overflowed with love for her. Then she pushed him away so she could look at him.

'You seem different,' she said, her eyes scrutinizing his face with maternal sharpness.

'I've only been gone two days, Mum,' he said. 'Are you going to tell me I've grown again?'

'Have you been hurt?' she asked, narrowing her eyes.

'No,' he replied, nervously. 'Why do you ask?'

'I don't know,' she said. 'You just seem ... different. I'm so glad you're home.'

'So am I,' he said.

'I just said "home", didn't I?' she said, sounding confused. 'I can't believe it! Look at the view!'

She gestured towards the glass wall. There was a door to one side that led out onto the balcony and Mika saw his father leaning on the railing with a glass of wine in his hand. He walked out and stood beside him and they gazed down into the park. It was laid out in a pattern of gold paths and pools, their fountains rising and falling in elegant plumes.

'I can't believe you won us a home here playing a game,' David said, shaking his head. He looked at Mika and smiled. 'I'm so proud of you.'

'Thanks,' Mika replied.

'Has your mother shown you around yet?' David asked.

'Not yet,' Mika said.

'She will,' he went on, smiling.

'Does she like it then?' Mika asked, tentatively. 'Here?'

'Well, it was a bit of a shock when they turned up three hours ago with packing cases and said we were moving. But I have to admit the place is growing on me and it's only twenty minutes on the train to Barford North for work and friends. But that noise . . .' he paused and they listened to it:

Boom. Boom.

'I don't think I'll get used to that. It makes me feel guilty. I don't think I'd want to stay here if the government don't do anything to help them down there. I suppose we could sell the apartment if we decide we don't like it. You know, several government ministers live above us in this turret.'

'Do they?' Mika asked, looking up.

'Yeah,' David continued. 'Right at the top, in the dome. The apartments up there are even bigger than this.'

'Mika!' Asha called. 'Come and look at the kitchen!'

David grinned and sipped his wine. 'I'll leave you to it,' he said, 'There's only so much I can say about cupboard doors and spice racks.'

The main living area led onto an open-plan kitchen with highly-polished pretend wood cupboards. Mika let her show him everything, the acres of cupboard space, the fancy fridge full of champagne and party food, the polished stone worktops and the lovely shiny taps.

'Look at the air conditioning!' she enthused, showing him the control panel. 'We can choose from three different smells: summer meadow, sea breeze or bluebell wood.'

There were two bedrooms and their doors opened on to the living area from the left and right and each had its own bathroom and glass wall overlooking the city. Mika's room was as big as their whole apartment in Barford North and the walls were panelled with smooth pretend wood. In his bathroom he had gold taps and a warm air cubicle to dry in. There were small soft lights embedded in the walls and on the floor, a thick cream carpet.

'Where's the furniture?' Mika asked, looking around.

'There isn't any,' Asha replied. 'Not even a television. All we've got is our old sofa.'

'Never mind,' Mika said. 'I don't mind sleeping on the floor. The carpet is soft.'

'There are wardrobes,' Asha said. 'So there's no excuse to chuck your clothes everywhere. We've got under-floor heating and room service – just like in a hotel and a new vacuumbot and a swimming pool and gym and a restaurant, although we probably can't afford it . . . look in this cupboard! It's a dry laundry unit! You hang your dirty clothes in here and fifteen minutes later they're clean! Why don't you clean what you're wearing now before everyone arrives for the party?'

She sighed and sank to the floor.

'What's wrong?' Mika asked.

'Nothing,' she said. 'It's just a bit overwhelming. We got home from shopping this afternoon and I was making a cup of tea and wondering whether we'd eaten all the Fab mash when there was a knock on the door. Two hours later we were here. I suppose I'm a bit shocked. It's so . . .'

'Good,' Mika finished for her, sitting down and taking his sneakers off. 'Like another holiday, but for ever.'

He wiggled his toes in the plush pile of the carpet.

'Those are definitely going in the laundry unit,' Asha said, eyeing his sneakers and socks with disgust. 'Pooh.'

He could feel her eyes on him again, searching.

'What's wrong, Mika?' she asked. 'What happened while you

were away?'

'I won the competition,' Mika replied, carefully avoiding eye contact. 'There's nothing wrong.'

* * *

Asha went to the kitchen to prepare food for the party. Mika shoved his clothes and sneakers in the laundry unit, dimmed the lights and sat cross-legged on the carpet in front of the glass wall. The air roads were busy with early evening traffic and in the street surrounding the park, the pedestrians looked like ants running in and out of golden holes. There was a police pod hovering opposite and he sensed them watching him. Only a few weeks before he'd seen the police outside his window and felt terrified, but now they didn't bother him at all. He'd found Ellie and all he had to do was get through one night without leaving the apartment or letting his parents find out what he could do and he would be with her again. How he wished he could tell them.

That would make the party go with a bang, he thought.

Little did he realise, this party was going to go with a lot of bangs and his promise to Mal Gorman was not going to be as easy to keep as he thought.

45
LOOK NORMAL

Mika grabbed his clothes from the laundry unit, warm and clean and smelling of spring, and dressed quickly, ready for the party. He found his mother in the new kitchen with two maids sent by the YDF. Mika smiled, watching her follow them around, trying to help them while they helped her.

'What can I do?' she asked, wringing her hands and looking lost while they laid out gold trays of party snacks and white china and cutlery. 'Perhaps I should make tea. Would either of you like a cup of tea before everyone arrives and a little rest, or coffee if you prefer ... a glass of wine?'

'No thank you, Mrs Smith,' they replied, primly.

'Why don't *you* have a glass of wine, Asha?' David suggested. 'Don't worry about the food, have a glass of wine and relax until everyone arrives.'

'I suppose I could,' she replied, pensively. 'Isn't this lovely?'

'*You* are lovely,' David said, kissing her, and they embraced with the Golden Turrets glowing behind them.

If only this was it, Mika thought, the fairy tale ends with a kiss in the fairy palace and everyone lives happily ever after.

He wondered how Ellie was feeling at that moment and suddenly the night seemed torturously long. He checked the time, it was only half past six; two hours before Mal Gorman's message would arrive and twelve hours before he was due to return to Cape Wrath. He tried to relax, after all there was nothing he could do but wait until morning. What could possibly go wrong?

The guests began to arrive and soon the apartment was full of people laughing and making friends. Mika liked them all, particularly Leo's father, who was a huge man with dreadlocks as thick as rope and a deep belly laugh. Iman's little sister was the cutest baby he'd ever seen, and she ran around the adults' legs with handfuls of food in her party dress. Everyone seemed happy to celebrate their new homes, but Mika and the children who'd won them gathered on the balcony where they could be alone. The French girl, Colette, sat on the floor hugging her knees and the rest leaned on the balcony and gazed at the Golden Turrets, their healed wounds like invisible lies on their skin.

Audrey's green eyes were bright with fear. 'I don't understand why Mal Gorman wants to take us back again,' she whispered. 'This was supposed to be a game!'

'It hasn't felt like a game for a while to me,' Santos said, polishing his glasses on his T-shirt. 'I think being asked to sign the Official Secrets Act was a big clue.'

'I'm scared about the promise we made,' Audrey said. 'What if something happens and we can't keep it? Our families will be dumped in The Shadows! They might die!'

'We will keep it,' Mika said quickly. 'Whatever our parents ask us, we'll say nothing and the second part is easy – all we've got to do is stay in the apartment.'

'There are five police pods watching us now,' Leo said. 'Look at them. They're all around the park.'

'Gorman doesn't trust us,' Audrey whispered. 'Perhaps he thinks we'll try to run away so we don't have to go back tomorrow.'

'And *willingly* make our parents homeless?' Leo scoffed. 'How could he think we'd do that?'

'Because he's judging us by his own standards,' Santos said.

'I'm scared,' Iman whispered. 'I don't want the apartment or the hover car. I hate it here with that booming noise. I just want to go home and be normal. I want to see my friends. Now they've taken our companions, we can't even tell them we've moved. What are they going to do to us? I wish I'd never entered this competition.'

'We wouldn't be safe anyway,' Leo said. 'Mal Gorman was looking for us. The competition was about finding us.'

'Why?' Audrey said, desperately. 'So we can move toy cars with our eyes? Why do we have to go back tomorrow? I don't understand.'

'I think we can do more,' Mika said, darkly. 'And Gorman knows.'

'Like what?' Audrey asked, fearfully. 'It must be something bad if those government skeletons are interested in it.'

'I think we can hurt people,' Mika whispered. 'I did it by accident to Ruben while he was trying to strangle me. I made him scream just by *looking* at him.'

'I set fire to my bed,' Iman said, her eyes wide. 'After we got back from holiday I was trying to turn the pages of my book by looking at them and they burst into flames!'

'Ruben lifted his own body,' Santos reminded them. 'If he can do that maybe we can too.'

He bit his lip and screwed up his eyes.

'Not now, you perp!' Leo said. 'The last thing we need is our parents seeing *that*! Look. Mika's mother's watching us.'

They turned to see Asha eyeing them suspiciously through the glass wall.

'We need to look normal,' Mika whispered, anxiously.

'How?' Santos asked.

'I dunno, smile a bit, look as if we're having fun and don't float or set fire to anything.'

46
HARVESTED FOR WAR

'What time is it?' Mal Gorman asked.

'Twenty-seven minutes past eight, sir,' Ralph replied. The butler was on his knees in front of the dressing-room fire, toasting a crumpet for Gorman's supper, and his master sat in the gold chair with a blanket around his shoulders.

'Only three minutes now,' Gorman said quietly, staring at the fire. 'Before the poor find out what we're doing to their children and I become the most hated person on the planet.'

'Surely they won't *hate* you, sir,' Ralph said. 'You're only doing your job.'

'I know,' Gorman replied. 'But I don't think they're going to see it that way.'

'But aren't you giving them all a thousand credits?' Ralph asked.

'Yes,' Gorman replied, pulling the blanket tighter around his shoulders.

'Well that's very generous, sir,' Ralph said, diligently buttering a crumpet. 'I'm sure they'll be grateful for that. They'll be able to buy some food.'

'They ought to be grateful,' Gorman said. 'But for some reason I've found poor people would rather starve to death than lose their children, so I'm sure there'll be a few complaints.'

'But the police will deal with those, won't they, sir?' Ralph said, in his most reassuring tone.

'Yes,' Gorman replied.

He thought about the prison complex off the north coast of Ireland and hoped it was big enough.

They can always build another one, he thought. And anyway, parents are not my responsibility any more, I have what *I want*.

'Do you want honey sub on your crumpet, sir?' Ralph asked. 'Or jam?'

'Honey,' Gorman replied. 'And two crumpets. Then send for Ellie, I suppose I ought to tell her what's happening to her brother.' He shivered suddenly and leaned closer to the fire.

'Are you sure seeing Ellie is a good idea?' Ralph asked, solicitously. 'She can be rather stressful.'

'She won't be today,' Gorman said, confidently. 'I've got good news for her.'

'Well if you're sure, sir,' Ralph replied, sceptically.

'And when you've done all that,' Gorman added, 'make the fire hotter.'

'Very good, sir,' Ralph replied, wiping sweat from his brow.

Gorman picked up his companion and sent his message to the parents of two hundred and seventy thousand children while Ralph spread honey on his crumpet.

* * *

Boom. Boom.

Gorman's chosen ones lay on the balcony staring at the moon.

'Are we all mutants?' Iman whispered.

'Yes.'

'I was normal when I was born,' she said. 'But I started growing horns when I was three. Feel my head.'

They touched the black girl's scalp through her finely plaited corn rows.

'Oh yeah,' Audrey said, curiously. 'I can feel them. What did they look like?'

'Scary,' Iman replied. 'Like a goat's. My real parents were so frightened they gave me up for adoption.'

'No!'

'I don't mind now,' Iman said. 'My new parents love me and they wouldn't care if I had hooves as well as horns.'

The French girl, Colette, sat up, and they watched with fascination as she peeled the skin off her left hand. It came off like a glove from the wrist, and beneath it, silver fingers glinted in the moonlight, fingers moved by complex joints and ligaments. Then she peeled the skin off her right hand, and held them out and turned them over so they could look at them.

'They're beautiful,' Santos said admiringly, adjusting his glasses.

'An artist made them,' Colette replied. 'I was born without hands and feet. There's no circuitry in them, I control them with my mind just like you do when you move things. I've been able to do it since I was a baby but I kept it a secret, only my parents knew until now. I thought I was the only one, but I'm glad I'm not.'

Santos pulled up his sleeves. He had spurs on his wrists like those of a bird of prey, each with a single long curved claw. Leo showed them his skin-covered tail, Mika his webbed feet and Audrey her eyes.

'I wish we knew why Mal Gorman wants us.' Audrey said.

'I'm sure whatever he's planning to do with us, it's not going to be what we want to do,' Leo said. 'For the past few weeks I've felt strange, restless, as if I'm supposed to be doing *something*. I'm sure we can see the light for a good reason, not just to move and kill things.'

'I agree,' Colette said. 'I wish we knew more.'

Awen snarled and Mika felt the hairs on the back of his neck bristle.

'Something's wrong,' he whispered.

They all sat up and listened, but it wasn't a noise they heard, but an eerie silence, as if millions of people were holding their breath at the same time.

Inside the apartment, David was about to pop the cork on another champagne bottle, but he too sensed a change and turned down the music.

'Listen,' he said.

'How strange,' Una commented, after a few tense seconds. 'They've stopped banging on the pillars.'

They listened again and waited as if the dragon sleeping beneath its treasure was well-loved and they were worried about it. They listened to hear it breathe again, to hear its heart beat, but instead, they heard a terrible sound that pierced them through like shards of glass as a wail rose from the black water of The Shadows; a wail more terrifying than the plague sirens.

'What was *that*?' Asha gasped, looking at the floor. 'What's happened? Something terrible must have happened down there. It sounds like thousands of people wailing in agony!'

The children ran in from the balcony to join their parents in the apartment and everyone stared at the floor, listening to the terrible noise. Moments later, a companion called for its owner and one of the maids screamed.

'What's wrong?' Asha cried, rushing to her side.

'They've taken my son!' the maid wailed. 'They've stolen my boy!'

Everyone gathered around her and David read the message from Mal Gorman on her companion.

'All twelve- and thirteen-year-old children,' he said disbelievingly, 'were taken this afternoon by the YDF from the arcades!'

'Why?' Asha asked. 'What for?'

'For *an army*,' David replied, his face contorting with horror.

'For an *army of children*! The government's sending the children to war!'

Suddenly, all the other companions called out for their owners and every parent discovered they'd been sent the same terrible message.

'No!' Asha screamed. 'Not Mika! Not after Ellie, PLEASE!'

'They're taking the children who won the competition tomorrow,' David said numbly, his hands shaking as he read the message again on his own companion. 'They're all going to war.'

Asha turned to look at the six children, standing together by the glass wall. They looked strange, she thought, their skin luminous as if they'd spent a few hours in the wrong room of a nuclear power plant, and for the first time she noticed the similarity between them; despite their different skin colours and features, they looked as if they had been carved from the same piece of stone.

'You knew something,' she said to Mika, 'didn't you?'

He looked at the floor, not daring to speak, and Audrey began to cry.

War.

The Youth Development Foundation had been building an army of children.

Mika felt the blood drain from his face as he realised how obvious it was: Fit Mix to make them grow faster, Fit Camp to make them strong, Pod Fighter to teach them how to fly, and the competition to put them through selection tests for an army of children. No wonder Mr Grey was talking about 'fine citizens of the Northern Hemisphere', they all knew! Even Mrs Fowler! He and his friends had been grown like a crop! Harvested for war! He remembered how the Fit For Life nurse and the teachers had humiliated him the day he refused to drink the Fit Mix and felt so angry he wanted to smash everything around him. They'd punished him! They'd told him he was mad! They'd convinced him he was a paranoid freak, when all the time he was right and they knew it!

How Mika hated Mal Gorman at that moment as the promise he'd made took on new resonance; he had promised he would go back in the morning and do whatever he was told. He had promised to go to war.

'Why didn't you tell us?' Asha cried. 'How could you come home and not tell us what they were doing to you?'

'We didn't know,' Mika said quickly. 'Not about the army or the war.'

'But you knew *something*!' she cried, angrily. 'Didn't you? I realised the moment you came home! What's happened to you? If this competition was about building an army, why did you win it? What can you do that's so special? You've got to tell us!'

Mika hung his head.

'We can't tell you,' Leo said.

'What?' his father shouted. 'Of course you can! We're your parents! Why do they want you?'

'Sit down, now!' David bellowed at Mika. 'And tell us everything that's happened while you were away!'

'No,' Mika said. 'We're not allowed.'

'Don't be ridiculous!' David yelled. 'How can you be not allowed to talk to your *own parents*! This is insane! You're going absolutely nowhere tomorrow! I'm not having my twelve-year-old child sent to war. How could they possibly believe that a thousand credits would make *that* alright! Now we've got a lovely new home and some money for *furniture!* Well they can STUFF IT. I FORBID YOU TO GO TO WAR AND THAT'S THE END OF IT!'

'Please, Dad,' Mika said. 'Don't be angry with us, we thought we were playing a game.'

'I'm not angry,' David said, his shoulders falling. 'I'm *devastated,* Mika, I can't believe it! Just when our lives seemed to be getting better!'

'It's not his fault,' Santos's mother said, gently. 'We've all been tricked.'

'Please, talk to us,' Una begged Audrey. 'Perhaps we can help.'

'No Mum,' Audrey sobbed. 'You can't help. We promised we wouldn't talk to you. You don't understand.'

'Oh this is AWFUL!' Una cried, putting her arms around her daughter. 'You poor things! To think you were playing a game and to have *this* happen! You'd tell me if you could, wouldn't you?'

'Yes,' Audrey cried miserably. 'We want to tell you the truth but we can't.'

Iman's baby sister began to wail desperately as she realised the party had stopped and everyone was crying instead of laughing. The cake she held fell from her hand and her father picked her up and cuddled her.

'It's OK, sweetie,' he whispered, kissing her cheek. 'They won't take you.'

'They're just children,' Una cried, desperately. 'How could the government do this?'

'Because we're too old to fight,' David said bitterly. 'No babies were born for thirty years so the youngest of our generation is forty-three.'

'But how could there be a war?' Asha said. 'There hasn't been a war since The Wall was built. Surely we would have seen something on telly if we were on the brink of war, it doesn't make sense. We haven't got any enemies; there's nobody to fight.'

'The government must have kept it a secret,' David said. 'Until the children were ready.'

'Perhaps the enemy are in a place we don't hear about much,' Leo's father suggested. 'Like the Arctic.'

'But surely we'd still know something about them,' Una said. 'There's no room for secrets any more, there's not even enough room for people since we moved behind The Wall, even in the Arctic.'

'This is crazy,' Asha said. 'What are we going to do?'

'What *can* we do?' Una cried. 'How can we argue with the Northern Government? They make the laws and if they say our children have to go to war, then they have to go!'

'I've just had a thought . . .' David said, stiffening with anger. 'The government haven't taken *all* twelve- and thirteen-year-old children; I saw some earlier in the park.'

'Yeah,' Una said. 'Come to think of it, so did I.'

Mika remembered the two boys and the girl he'd met in the foyer and realised they were right.

'So how come they're still here?' Asha asked.

'Because the government isn't sending the *rich* children to war,' David said, angrily. 'Just the *poor* ones.'

'Listen,' Audrey said, as her keen ears picked up another noise in The Shadows. 'Can you hear that?'

'Oh my odd,' Asha whispered. 'What's happening now?'

47

A RUMBLE FROM THE SKY

They rushed to the balcony and looked down into New Hyde Park. For a few minutes they couldn't see the mob coming up from The Shadows, but its roar was so loud, they could feel the vibrations through their feet. Iman's baby sister began to sob with fright and her father covered her eyes and carried her into the apartment so she couldn't see what was about to happen, but she would hear it and she would never forget.

There were six vertical tube stations around the perimeter of the park and they formed the main links between the two levels of the city. The people of The Shadows began to pour out of their doors like lava from a volcano.

'Look at their light!' Audrey whispered. The mob moved like a swarm with an angry red haze around it. Within seconds it had filled the park and was surging through the streets, eyes mad with sorrow, faces twisted with hatred and hands gripping baseball bats and iron bars and lumps of rust-streaked concrete. They heard a smashing sound as the first windows broke and as if this was the signal for the riot to begin, the mob roared even louder and lurched like an injured beast towards the turrets.

'They've come for their children!' Asha cried. 'They're going to rip this place apart!'

'They must know there are government ministers above us,' David said uneasily. 'They're going to come in here.'

'But we can tell them who we are,' Una said fearfully, as the mob began to batter against the doors. 'Surely they won't hurt us if they know we're on their side.'

'How are we going to do that?' Asha cried desperately. 'Look how angry they are! They'll never believe it! Look at our clothes! We're in the Golden Turrets drinking champagne! They're going to think we're part of the government!'

'Watch out!'

David ducked as a lump of concrete flew past his head and hit the glass wall behind him. A large crack appeared, like a spider's web. Moments later they heard another loud crash as the heavy glass doors to their turret were shattered. They looked over the balcony to see the security guards running away and the angry mob pouring into the foyer.

'We have to get out of here as quickly as possible,' David said. 'Before they reach our floor.'

'No!' Mika said, feeling a surge of panic. 'We can't leave the apartment! We promised Mal Gorman we wouldn't!'

'Don't be ridiculous!' David shouted impatiently. 'There's a mob in the turret about to rip it to pieces, Mika! We have to get out of here!'

'Please, Dad,' Mika pleaded, 'don't make me leave!'

David ignored him and turned to the other parents, and they quickly discussed how they were going to escape from the turret.

'We ought to call the police,' Una suggested.

'I've tried,' Leo's father replied. 'But I couldn't get through. Everyone in the turrets must be calling them right now, we're going to have to save ourselves.'

'OK,' David said, purposefully. 'Then we need to go up the building to the pod strips.'

'Yes,' Una agreed. 'We can wave for help and get someone to rescue us from there.'

'OK, quickly,' David said. 'Everyone grab your coats. It's going to be cold.'

Mika watched desperately as they prepared to leave the apartment.

'Mika?' Asha said. 'Find your coat.'

'No,' he said.

'Oh for odd's sake, Mika!' David shouted. 'Don't start being difficult now! Forget about your promise to Mal Gorman! He wants to send you to war!'

'I don't care,' Mika said, scowling. 'I'm not leaving.'

'Yes you are!' David yelled. 'Now get your coat!'

With his parents watching him and feeling increasingly desperate, Mika found his coat and put it on and Ellie seemed to slip away as if he was losing grip of her hands over the edge of a cliff. Maybe Gorman would understand that he had to leave because of the riot, but Mika was scared that he wouldn't. He remembered the spark of recognition between them, that fleeting look of doubt and fear in Gorman's eyes. Mika didn't know why the old man didn't trust him, but keeping this promise would be the only chance he'd get to prove himself. His one chance to reach Ellie. Yes, it was madness to stay in the apartment with a riot moving up the building, but the pull he felt towards his sister was stronger than ever, as if it wasn't just love dragging them towards each other, now there was another, equally powerful force at work. He felt as if he was caught on a fishing line with the hook buried in his heart and the pain when he tried to move against it was intolerable.

The door opened and everyone rushed out. It was chaos in the hallway and their group was quickly swallowed by the tide of people pouring out of the luxury apartments and making their way to the top of the building. It wasn't difficult for Mika to lose his parents; the moment they took their eyes off him, he dropped back and leaned against the wall while the crowd rushed past. Only Iman's baby sister noticed; she reached out over her father's shoulder as if to wave him goodbye, then she was gone with the others; swept away by the fast-moving crowd. With a lump in his throat but feeling hugely relieved, Mika returned to the apartment.

Audrey. He was surprised to find her facing him as he walked through the door.

'I knew you were going to do that!' she cried, her green eyes bright with fear. 'Come on, Mika! We don't have a choice! We have to leave!'

'I can't,' he insisted. 'You go, Audrey. Quick, before the others are too far away to catch up.'

'I'm not leaving without you,' she said, stubbornly.

'Well I'm not letting you stay,' he replied, trying to push her towards the door. 'It's too dangerous. Go!'

'No,' she said. 'If I'm going, then you're coming with me.'

'I can't,' he repeated, turning away from her.

'Why not?' she cried. 'I don't understand!'

'My promise to Mal Gorman is different to yours,' he said painfully.

'How?' she asked.

He was quiet for a moment and she waited.

'What's wrong?' she said.

Again he was quiet and he looked away from her. He knew this was the moment he had to tell her about Ellie, but he was scared. Afraid that if he told anyone before he saw his sister, it might jinx it somehow and it would all go wrong. Then he felt a pang of guilt. Audrey was risking her life to stay behind with him; she deserved to know. He hit the lock icon so the door slid shut, sealing them in the apartment.

'If I break my promise,' he said, hesitantly, 'I'll never see . . . my . . .'

'What?' she urged impatiently.

'Sister.'

Audrey was speechless for a few seconds, her eyes wide with astonishment.

'Sister?' she repeated softly. 'You've got a sister?'

He nodded. 'Her name is Ellie,' he said. 'She's my twin.'

'Why didn't you tell me before?' Audrey asked with a hurt voice.

'I couldn't,' Mika replied. 'I wanted to.'

'Where is she?'

'Cape Wrath,' Mika said bitterly. 'The YDF took her. A year ago. And told us she had drowned.'

'No!' Audrey said, her eyes flashing with anger.

'But I could *feel* her,' he said desperately. 'I didn't believe their lies. And now I know Mal Gorman's got her. He told me I can see her if I keep my promise.'

'So she must be like us,' Audrey said, darkly.

'Yes,' Mika replied.

'No wonder you don't want to leave,' she said. 'Poor Ellie, poor you. But surely Gorman won't expect you to stay in the apartment with a riot in the building?'

'I don't know,' Mika replied, doubtfully. 'He doesn't trust me. He seems to feel threatened by me and I don't think he'll be reasonable if I leave, he'll think I've run away. You don't understand. I can't take the risk.'

Suddenly, the whole apartment began to vibrate and they heard a gut-rattling rumble coming from the sky. They ran to the balcony and looked up.

'Oh my odd Mika!' Audrey cried. 'But you can't stay! You'll die!'

48
INTO THE NIGHT

Twenty million people were left to rot in The Shadows when the Golden Turrets were built, and their anger had been rising up to boiling point since the day the sky was taken. And that's just what it looked like to Mika and Audrey when they ran out onto the balcony; a boiling mass exploding through the lid fitted over it. The mob had doubled in size and was still pouring out of the stations and in the Golden Turrets across the park they could see it moving up through the floors like a human tornado. The glass walls were being smashed out from the inside and the luxury apartments were quickly flooding with desperate people, roaring their lungs out for their dead loved ones and lost children and smashing to pieces the opulence that had made their world so awful. From the top of the turrets a constant stream of civilian pods shot up into the sky as the residents fled to safety.

But the angry mob didn't scare Mika and Audrey half as

much as what now hung over it. They looked up to see dozens of army freighters hanging in perfect square formation over the park, their lights blinking and their engines rumbling as their enormous mouths opened to let the soldiers out.

'We have to go now,' Audrey said. 'Or we'll get caught in the middle of a battle.'

Heavily armed soldiers dressed in riot gear began to drop down on lines into the mob. Mika knew she was right and felt a wave of despair.

'Please, Mika,' she pleaded. 'You won't be much use to Ellie dead.'

'OK,' he replied, reluctantly. 'But let me write a note for Gorman telling him where we're going.'

'Then you'll leave?' Audrey asked, hopefully.

'Yes,' he agreed.

'OK quick,' Audrey said, running back into the apartment. 'Find a pen.'

'I wish Gorman hadn't taken our companions.'

They searched frantically through the party debris for an ink pen so Mika could write a note for Mal Gorman.

'Where do you keep them?' Audrey asked, opening and closing the drawers in the kitchen.

'I don't know,' Mika said, putting his hand down the side of the sofa. 'We only moved in today. This is ridiculous. Why can you never find a pen when you need one?'

He felt one with his fingertips amongst the fluff and lost things in the sofa, but when he pulled it out it, he found it was broken and completely useless.

Something crashed against the door of the apartment.

'What was that?' Audrey said.

'I don't think it's room service,' Mika replied.

For a moment they stood together frozen, wondering what to do, as the rioting mob began to bludgeon the outside of the apartment. Within seconds they heard a loud crunch and a hole appeared in the wall next to the door.

'We're trapped!' Audrey cried.

'Come here,' Mika said tugging at her frozen arm.

He pulled her into the kitchen and opened the biggest cupboard, suddenly grateful for the tour his mother had given him earlier. It was a corner cupboard meant for storing the vacuumbot and just large enough for both of them. Mika pulled it out and Audrey crawled in first and he followed, closing the door just as the mob began to climb through the hole in the wall. Inside the apartment they exploded as if a match had been struck in an old-fashioned gas station.

It was terrifying. Folded up in the tiny space, Mika and Audrey could do nothing but pray they weren't discovered as the mob smashed the apartment to pieces around them. Audrey pressed her cheek against Mika's shoulder and gripped his arm and he heard Awen whimpering nearby. But worse than the violence and the fear of being discovered was the roar. Mika put his hands over his ears and closed his eyes tight, desperate to block out the feelings of the people around him, but their anguish and hatred seemed to bypass his senses and seep through his skin like osmosis. And in those awful moments he saw snapshots of their lives, the dark, filthy water, the barely edible food, the people coughing their lungs out in damp cold beds and children weeping for parents who had died and left them alone and it was so distressing he found himself gasping with pain. He was saved by an explosion in the apartment, followed by the crash of falling crockery and for a moment the roar was replaced by a shocked silence. Mika heard a familiar sound: a Pod Fighter engine, and he opened the cupboard door a tiny crack to see it hovering over the balcony pointing its guns into the apartment and the mob, with only bats and bars to protect them, running for their lives.

The soldiers climbed out of the Pod Fighter onto the balcony and ran after them and Mika quickly shut the door as a spray of bullets punctured the floor of the kitchen.

'What are we going to do now?' Audrey whispered.

Mika could feel her trembling with terror.

'Don't worry, we'll think of something,' he whispered.

He waited until the gunfire sounded further away then cautiously opened the door again and looked out. There wasn't much left of their smart new home; the glass wall was gone, the kitchen lay in splinters and all the lights were broken so the apartment was dark but for the reflected glow of the nearby turrets. A bitter wind blew through the space finding the holes in the walls. The Pod Fighter was hovering silently over the balcony, waiting for the soldiers to return.

Suddenly Mika had an idea.

'We could take the Pod Fighter,' he whispered. 'We don't have to go far and we could use the communication system to tell Mal Gorman what's happened to us.'

'Do you reckon we'll be able to fly it?' she asked hungrily.

'What else have we been doing for the past few weeks?' Mika replied. 'And the YDF did promise us a flight in a real Pod Fighter and we haven't had it yet.'

'Yeah, they did,' she said, bitterly. 'Shame they didn't tell us we'd have to go to war to get *that* part of the prize.'

'Quick, before someone comes,' Mika said.

He crawled out of the cupboard and Audrey followed. Then they ran across the living area onto the balcony and climbed up on to one of the Pod Fighter's curved, black wings so they could see into the cockpit.

'How are we going to get in it?' Audrey asked. The windshield was shut and the lock icon on the outside was glowing red.

'We'll have to unlock it from the inside,' Mika replied.

He moved round so he could clearly see the icon that opened the door in the arcade simulators.

'Quick!' Audrey said. 'Before someone comes!'

'Shhh,' he said. 'I'm trying to concentrate.'

He gazed at the icon through the windshield until it glowed with a pale blue light. Then he imagined pressing it down with his finger. It didn't take long; after thirty seconds of intense concentration, the windshield slid back with a hiss and they were in. The helmets were waiting for them on the seats and the control panels were active, ready to go.

They fitted their harnesses quickly and the seats wrapped around them ready to fly. Mika closed the windshield and it sealed with a hiss.

'OY!'

They looked back into the apartment to see two men in riot gear pointing guns at their heads through the windshield.

'Frag,' Mika muttered. He quickly turned the Pod Fighter ninety degrees clockwise and shot up into the night sky.

49

FIGHTING SMOKE

The moment Ellie entered Mal Gorman's dressing room and saw his eyes, she knew the YDF had taken Mika. She felt the urge to vomit with horror all over his slippers, then weep with desperate relief. After living like a ghost for so long, she was about to be brought back to life.

But don't hope for anything good out of this, she thought. If you get a glimpse of happiness, Gorman will suck it out of you then laugh in your face, and he'll use Mika to manipulate you, just like he does with Puck. Mika will suffer, everyone will suffer – except Mal Gorman.

But we'll be together, a desperate voice cried inside her, everything will be easier together.

'Sit down,' Gorman said.

Ellie looked around the dressing room for a chair, but there was only one and Gorman was sitting on it, so she sat at his feet on the rug in front of the fire. Like everything else in the dressing room, the rug looked borrowed from another time, a Celtic knot of rambling rose with thorns and orange blooms. The man with the gun leaned against the wall in the shadowy part of the room and melted into the darkness until he was almost not there. She gazed into the fire as it leapt and curled, aware that several Mal Gormans were watching her; the one in the gold chair with the blanket around him and others on the mantelpiece, all in uniform. From schoolboy to Minister of Youth Development, they frowned down on her from photographs and holopics. Gorman was the only person she knew who kept only pictures of himself.

He held out a silver bowl, so she took it. The bowl was also patterned with roses and it was full of plump pink and white marshmallows. In her other hand he placed a skewer. It was about thirty centimetres long and made of silver, with a gold handle shaped like a koi carp fish. She rolled it on the palm of her hand and thought it would make an excellent weapon.

'It's sharp, so be careful,' Gorman said, watching her nervously.

She wondered what she was supposed to do with it.

'Have you never toasted a marshmallow?' Gorman asked.

'No,' Ellie replied.

'Really?' he said. 'Let me show you.' He took the skewer from her hand and impaled a pink marshmallow on the end it. She noticed his fingers trembling; he looked particularly frail that night. His hand almost dropped the skewer he was holding out over the fire, as if it was too heavy for him. They both watched the marshmallow as it was licked by the flames.

'You know what I have to say,' Gorman said. 'Don't you?'

'No,' Ellie replied, cautiously. 'What?'

'Mika's coming to stay with us,' Gorman said. 'He's one of six new children I've chosen. He's with your parents tonight, but he'll be coming back to Cape Wrath tomorrow. So if you're good, you might see him. Here,' he continued, holding the skewer so she could take the toasted marshmallow from the end. 'Mind you don't burn your fingers.'

She pulled the sticky, hot marshmallow from the skewer and Gorman watched her face as she ate it. Her happiness was so intense, he almost remembered what the emotion felt like, but the flicker of warmth in his heart was snuffed out immediately by a tap on the door.

'What?' Gorman shouted, making Ellie jump.

Ralph entered, looking peevish. 'There's a man here, sir. He wants to talk to you and he says it's important.'

'They always say that,' Gorman snapped. 'Tell him if he's any longer than thirty seconds, I'll hang him on the outside of Cape Wrath with a cloth and a tin of polish.'

'Yes, sir,' Ralph replied.

A few moments later, the man entered the dressing room as if he was being pushed from behind. Anticipating bad news, Gorman's eyes froze. 'Spit it out,' he said coldly.

'We have a problem, sir,' the man said. 'There's trouble in London; the Shadows people are complaining because they want their children back.'

'So?' Gorman snapped. 'That's not my problem. My job was to collect the children and prepare them to fight, not deal with their moaning parents. Get the police to do it. Arrest them all and throw them in prison.'

'The police are trying, sir,' the man continued nervously. 'And the army. But there is rather more trouble than we were expecting. The people have come up from The Shadows and they're rioting in the Golden Turrets.'

'Are they?' Gorman asked, and his heart began to gallop like a horse with a broken leg. 'How many?'

'Over a hundred thousand,' the man replied. 'And more are coming up by the minute.'

'Let me see,' Gorman demanded.

There was a screen on the wall facing the fire and the butler quickly found a news report. They watched the human tornado as it ripped the golden city to pieces.

'My children,' Gorman said. 'Where are they?'

'Well, that's why I'm here, sir,' the man replied. '*That's* the problem . . .'

'What's happened?' Ellie cried. 'Is Mika in danger?'

'Shut up!' Gorman snapped, turning to glare at her. 'How dare you interrupt!' Then he fixed the man with a look that shrank him to half the height. 'Where are my children?' he snarled.

'We've found *four*, sir,' the man replied hopefully, as if Gorman should be glad they'd found so many. 'They were with their parents at the top of the building on one of the pod strips, waiting to be rescued.'

'Four?' Gorman yelled. 'FOUR? I don't want FOUR, I want SIX! Where are the others?'

The man's face bloomed scarlet with embarrassment. 'We're not sure, sir,' he blustered. 'The riot happened so quickly, you see. All of a sudden there were thousands of people running around smashing everything, and the police you sent to watch the apartment got distracted and—'

'Stop waffling, man!' Gorman roared. 'Just tell me where my children are!'

'We think they've run away, sir,' the man said sheepishly. 'In a . . .'

'What?' Gorman snapped impatiently.

'In a Pod Fighter, sir,' the man muttered.

Mal Gorman gripped the marshmallow skewer and held it up as if he wanted to stab the man through the heart with it. 'In a *Pod Fighter*?' he roared. 'HOW THE FRAG DID THEY GET A POD FIGHTER?'

'Our men left it on the balcony of the children's apartment,' the man replied, quickly. 'But it was locked. It should have been safe. No normal person could have stolen it; the children must have used their special powers to undo the lock from inside. Their parents didn't know anything about it. They thought the children had followed them up to the roof with the others.'

'So these two thought they'd sneak off, did they?' Gorman roared. 'And run away while no one was looking! Which ones are missing? I'll skin them alive!'

'Mika Smith and Audrey Hudson, sir,' the man replied.

Gorman was silent for a moment and Ellie watched the fire-light flicker in his eyes. She had never seen him look so angry before.

'No!' she cried, frantically. 'Mika wouldn't run away, and he's never stolen anything! There must be a mistake!'

'I thought I told you to SHUT UP!' Gorman roared, throwing the skewer like a dagger and just missing her eye. It clattered on to the hearth, and as he watched her shrink away with a sob, the darkness of her brother's dream closed in on him. He saw the face of the Telly Head reflected in her tears, heard the slither of vines coming from the fire and suddenly he was engulfed by a terrible sense of foreboding. He closed his eyes for a second and saw Mika looking down on him, with a smile on his face.

'Your brother has betrayed me!' he yelled. 'I knew I shouldn't have trusted him!' Then he turned to the man and shouted, 'Find those children and KILL THEM! And get this girl OUT OF HERE!'

* * *

High above the Golden Turrets, Mika and Audrey hid in the darkness while Mika tried to figure out how to use the communication system so he could tell Mal Gorman where they were. It was quiet above the city, but chaos still reigned below. The mob had reached the upper floors of the Turrets and was smashing out the windows of the government minister's homes. But in the streets below, the army was gaining control, beating back the mob with their electric batons and shields and pushing it towards the tube stations, where it could be forced back down to The Shadows.

'It looks like they're fighting smoke from up here,' Audrey

whispered, as she watched the mob swarm backwards through the golden streets. It looked as though the stations were sucking it in.

The Pod Fighter's com wasn't as easy to use as they'd hoped.

'Why does it keep asking for a stupid code?' Mika said, jabbing the control panel impatiently. 'It won't work without a code! Frag! I've tried everything I can think of. What are we going to do?'

'We might be able to go back soon,' Audrey said. 'They're forcing the people down into The Shadows.'

'How soon?' Mika said anxiously. 'If Mal Gorman finds out we've taken a Pod Fighter, before we can tell him we're not trying to run away, he'll go ballistic.'

'But we didn't have a choice,' Audrey reminded him. 'At least we're still alive. Look, is that a police pod flying towards us? Perhaps we could ask them for help.'

'How are we going to do that?' Mika asked irritably. 'The com doesn't work, remember?'

'Damn.'

They saw a flash of light to the left.

'They're firing at us!' shouted Audrey.

'Oh, great,' said Mika. 'Now we're in trouble.'

He flew under the police pod and banked steeply up behind it. By the time it had turned to look for them, they were two kilometres away.

'They'll be able to track us with their mapping systems,' Audrey pointed out, 'like in the game. We'll never get away from them.'

'I think we should go back to the apartment,' Mika said. 'This was a really bad idea.'

'OK,' Audrey said, fearfully. 'Quickly, before they find us again.'

But as Mika flew down towards the Golden Turrets, they saw a squadron of Gorman's men waiting for them. Within seconds, they were being chased by dozens of Pod Fighters and the air around them was blistering with laser fire.

'Go down!' Audrey screamed. 'Fly through the Turrets!'

* * *

Ellie rocked on her bed in the darkness, tugging at the roots of her hair, and as she wondered desperately what was happening to Mika, she felt the dark noise between her mind and his dissolve. It was what she had wished for since the day they were parted, it was as if she was retuned like a radio so that suddenly, she was right there with him, seeing what he could see: the Turrets glowing like a heap of hot treasure, the air roads winding streamers of gold and blue light around them and the Pod Fighters chasing him like a flock of carrion birds. She felt what he felt like a flicker book of emotions: the rushes of adrenalin, the brief moments of fear, panic and relief and his utter desperation to cling to life, not just for his own sake, but for those he loved. His mind was as sharp as a scalpel, but his heart was falling to pieces and she was worried he would make the same mistake she had and try to escape through The Shadows. She had a better idea; she knew a safe place he could go. It would be risky trying to get there with Mal Gorman's men chasing him, but he had a much better chance of survival than trying to escape in The Shadows. So she did what she could to save him by reciting a silent mantra.

'Mika, please, go over The Wall. *Go over The Wall.*'

* * *

After ten minutes of flying with a squadron of fighters on their tail, Mika knew it was only a matter of time before he made a mistake. He was blinded by laser fire and they faced death at every turn, and not just from Mal Gorman's men; the whole city had been stirred up by the riot; horns blared, sirens flashed and the air roads had broken apart so all the traffic was flying in the wrong direction. Civilian pods kept dropping like stones right in front of them and buildings full of rioting people appeared out of nowhere.

'I can't do this much longer!' Mika shouted. 'I'm going to hit something!'

'Watch out!' Audrey yelled, and she closed her eyes and bit her lip as they shaved the roof off one pod then swerved to avoid hitting another. 'Hide somewhere!' she cried. 'Find somewhere to hide!'

Mika shot down to ground level and they flew along New Regent Street towards New Leicester Square. The riot was still in full swing below them like a boiling mass of batons and fists. But as Mika banked down the curved street, the mob froze and ducked and covered their heads as he nearly scalped them at two hundred kilometres per hour.

'Oops,' Audrey whispered.

In New Leicester Square, he stopped dead.

'They're right above us!' Audrey said, looking up. 'Go in there!' She pointed towards the foyer of a large cinema. The doors had been smashed by the mob leaving an opening large enough to fly through. Slowly and skilfully, Mika manoeuvred the craft inside the foyer with only centimetres to spare. Inside everything was broken and the floor was strewn with sweets.

'What are we going to do now?' Audrey said, desperately. 'They'll find us in no time.'

'I don't know,' Mika replied, 'but I can't keep flying through the city like this, it's too dangerous.'

'I wish there weren't so many people around,' Audrey said. 'I'm afraid to use my guns in case I hurt someone. But we'd be safer if I could destroy the weapons on the Pod Fighters chasing us. Perhaps we should leave the city. There won't be so many people outside London so we'll be able to defend ourselves better.'

'We could,' Mika said, hesitantly. 'But where can we go? If we leave the city we'll be over refugee towns. There won't be so many people, but they'll be able to get a better shot at us.'

'Why don't we go down to The Shadows?' Audrey suggested. 'We could use the pillars for cover and try to hide until the riot is over. When we know it's safe, we could fly back to the apartment so Gorman realizes we weren't trying to run away.'

'I'm not sure,' Mika replied. He closed his eyes and found himself in a dark place.

Ellie. He could hear her. For the first time he felt as if he was sitting right next to her and she was whispering to him. Rocking in the darkness. Pulling her hair.

'So what should we do?' Audrey asked. 'Where will we be safe?'

Mika opened his eyes and rotated the Pod Fighter so it was facing out of the cinema.

'Over The Wall,' he replied.

He pulled back, the engine roared and the Pod Fighter shot through the doors like a bullet, banked sharply up the back of the New National Gallery and into the night sky.

* * *

As they left the glowing city behind them, Mika felt increasingly anxious. The further he flew from his new apartment in London, the further he felt from his promise to Mal Gorman. But at least now they could defend themselves; over the concrete spread of refugee towns Audrey faced out of the back of the Pod Fighter and took out the guns of those chasing them with surgical precision. The damaged Pod Fighters dropped and looped away to inspect their wounds, but there were always more to replace them and Mika and Audrey flew and fought as if their lives were balanced on a knife edge.

It took only minutes to reach the south coast of England, and soon they were flying into milky darkness, the moon low, silver tipping the waves.

'They're falling back,' Audrey said, surprised, watching the Pod Fighters drop away. 'Why are they doing that?'

* * *

'Mr Gorman, sir, we think they're heading for The Wall.'

'The *Wall*?' Gorman repeated, pressing his temples. 'How could they know?'

'They don't know. I think they're just desperate and looking for somewhere to hide.'

'Dammit!' Gorman cursed. 'This is the worst thing that could happen, the WORST! Why on Earth would they want to go over The Wall?'

'What do you want us to do, sir?'

'You've *got* to kill them before they get over it and see what's on the other side,' Gorman said.

'But what if we can't stop them, sir? What if they do get over?'

'Then you'll have to follow them.'

The crackling of the fire filled a shocked silence.

'A lot of men will die, sir.'

'I don't care,' Gorman replied. 'If a thousand men die going over The Wall to stop those children finding out The Secret, it will be worth it. Tell them I'll send their wives a medal.'

* * *

For a while The Wall looked like a grey ribbon and the moon hung over it as if it had come to watch.

'They're catching up with us again,' Audrey said, seeing a mass of Pod Fighters suddenly appear to the north. 'Fly faster.'

Mika accelerated until the clouds above them and the waves below merged and they felt as if they were slipping through a silver-threaded void. The Wall grew until the moon and the sky disappeared and all they could see in front of them was a looming mass of salt-stained concrete with guard towers and razor wire along the top of it. Mika slowed down, suddenly plagued by doubt. They were going over The Wall and he knew that because of all the chemicals used to kill the animals and plants on the other side, it was so poisonous they'd die just touching the barren dust. His hands began to tremble and his guts churned and he bit his lip so hard he made it bleed.

But Ellie told you to go there, he thought, desperately, she must know something we don't.

Then everything happened at once – The Wall was upon them, and so were the men behind, and the night air lit up with laser bolts. For a fraction of a second, Mika saw the enormous metal Ghengis Borgs in the guard towers as they swung their guns and began to pump what looked like balls of lightning towards them. Audrey screamed and everything came together like elements in a chemical bomb. For several terrifying seconds they couldn't see anything but flashes of light and spinning fragments of Pod Fighter as most of the men on their tail were blown to pieces. They almost crashed into The Wall – Mika pulled up, gagging with fright, so close to it, they fried its salt-crusted surface. Up, up, hugging the concrete with the Ghengis Borgs pumping above them, then with a flick and a spin they were over like a dolphin through a hoop.

The moon. On the other side of The Wall they saw the moon still watching them over a calm sea.

50
OVER THE WALL

It was so quiet. No, not quiet, Mika thought, their Pod Fighter engines were hardly quiet, more . . . peaceful, calm. It was a still night, barely a cloud in the sky and no wind. The sea rolled as if it was half asleep in a rocking chair. The sky above looked as deep as it was, and they had never seen so many stars – they were accustomed to looking up at the sky through a haze of light pollution that ruined the view over Barford North even when there were no clouds. And there was no traffic, no factories, no televisions.

'We're alone,' said Audrey, quietly, scanning the mapping system for red dots. 'We made it.'

'I don't understand why the Ghengis Borgs tried to kill us,' Mika said. 'They're supposed to be there to protect us.'

'Well, that can't be true,' Audrey said. 'They killed all Gorman's men. I don't think they were protecting us, they were trying to stop us getting over The Wall.'

'But why?' Mika wondered. 'If there's nothing over here but poisoned dust, what are they protecting?'

'Maybe there is something over here,' Audrey suggested.

Their hearts began to beat faster as they turned this idea over in their minds.

'Let's look,' Mika said.

They were flying south over the Atlantic. He turned east and made for the coast of southern France.

'Damn,' Audrey said, seeing a cluster of red dots in her visor. 'There's a squadron of Pod Fighters just west, about three hundred kilometres. More of Gorman's men have come down from space.'

'Game on,' Mika said, grimly.

'Stop!' Audrey yelled. 'Stop! Stop! Stop!'

Mika brought the Pod Fighter to an abrupt halt so they were hovering over the sea.

'What's wrong?' he asked, fearfully.

'I saw something in the sea!' Audrey said. 'Go back a bit.'

Mika hadn't seen anything, but he remembered that Audrey's borg eyes could see better in the dark than his.

'What was it?' Mika asked, turning the Pod Fighter back the way they'd come.

'I don't know,' Audrey said, excitedly. 'But it was huge and it rolled over just beneath the surface of the waves.'

Curiosity overwhelmed caution and they spent a whole precious minute searching for the strange object in the sea.

'We shouldn't be wasting time doing this,' Mika said at last, scanning anxiously for Gorman's men.

'It's gone, anyway,' Audrey said, disappointed. 'We'd better go.'

* * *

'I need to sleep,' Mal Gorman said. Even though everything had gone wrong and he had just given the order to kill two of the children he'd spent weeks trying to find, his eyes felt as heavy as bowling balls and he was struggling to keep them open. It was as if his brain couldn't cope with any more stress and was shutting him down like an overheated hairdryer. 'Just half an hour, Ralph. Wake me up in half an hour and let me know what's happening.'

He walked unsteadily from the dressing room fire to his bedroom, and the butler followed at a respectful distance, ready to catch the old man if he fell. The bed was a huge antique, salvaged from a stately home that had been knocked down to build refugee towers, and Gorman looked small sitting on the edge of it, like a skeletal Tom Thumb. He shivered, pulled open the drawer on the elegant bedside cabinet and took out a knife with a long blade.

'Do you want me to look after that, sir?' Ralph asked, eyeing it nervously. 'I expect Chef's missing it from the kitchen.'

'No,' Gorman said. 'Go away.'

Ralph left the room, shutting the door quietly, and Gorman got into bed with the knife clutched to his chest.

* * *

'Land,' Mika said, seeing a dark strip on the horizon. They gained on it quickly. The moon had disappeared, so it was just a featureless black mass to Mika, but Audrey gasped.

'What can you see?' Mika asked impatiently.

'I must be dreaming,' Audrey replied.

'Tell me then, noodle head!'

'Trees?' Audrey said, cautiously. 'At least, they *look* like trees. I can just see the tops of them, like humps, and there are loads, really close together.'

'You mean – a forest?' Mika asked.

'Yeah, one of those!' Audrey replied. 'Like in history programmes.'

They were quiet for a moment.

'But that's not possible,' Audrey said, unable to accept what her eyes were telling her. 'All the trees are dead. They told us they were killed by poison during the plague.'

'They told us lots of things,' Mika replied sceptically. 'Like Fit Mix is good for us. Let's fly lower and have a proper look.'

He slowed down and cruised over the dark, lumpy landscape and as his eyes adjusted to the darkness, his heart began to pound. It was impossible, but true; they *were* trees! He could just make out the leaves and branches of the forest canopy stirring as they flew over it.

'I can see them,' he said, quietly. 'You're right. It's all forest. As far as I can see.'

'And look!' Audrey said. 'What's that over there?'

They could see patches of light in the distance, spread out like glowing fires through the forest. They flew quickly towards them, their hearts pounding faster by the second.

'Houses,' Mika said, incredulously. '*Huge* houses. There are people *living here!*'

They flew towards the nearest house and Mika slowed down as they passed over an enormous pair of gates. It was built in the style of a French chateau, with turrets, courtyards, fountains, landscaped gardens with topiary and mazes and five swimming pools, two of which had pink water and bubbled like jacuzzis.

'How can this be possible?' Audrey said. 'How can there be trees and houses and people here? It's supposed to be poisoned dust!'

'It's not possible,' Mika replied angrily. 'But it's true. We've been lied to, Audrey, about everything.'

They flew over another enormous house, this one more modern in style, like a huge heap of white cubes with a beautiful garden around it. 'Look at it,' he said angrily. 'People are dying in The Shadows because there isn't enough space, while on this side of The Wall, people are living in mansions surrounded by forest!'

'Oh no!' Audrey cried. 'Gorman's men have found us!'

On their visors they watched swarms of red dots flying towards them from every direction.

'We're surrounded,' Audrey said.

'Don't panic,' Mika replied. 'We'll wait for them, then move in at the last moment and take them by surprise.'

With their hearts in their mouths, they waited, but just as the first of their pursuers flew over the dark horizon, something completely unexpected happened.

'Oh frag!' Audrey cried. 'WHAT are *they*?'

They rose from the dark forest, their metal wings arched and their talons reaching forward as if to pluck their Pod Fighter out of the air like a sparrow. They were giant eagle hawks, but a hundred times bigger and more powerful than the real birds they were designed to mimic. On the outside they were coated with silver flex metal, which was impenetrable to all weapons, and they moved with deadly speed and agility. Mika rolled the Pod Fighter and only just managed to escape a closing pair of metal talons. Red eyes blazed, they heard an angry screech, and then came the familiar sound of laser bolts. Gorman's men had arrived, and over the dark forest, their laser fire looked like strings of luminous spaghetti.

Mika banked sharply, just in time to see one of the giant eagle hawks catch a Pod Fighter in its silver beak, bite it in half as if it was a jellybean and drop the pieces into the forest below. Then more giant eagle hawks came, their great silver wings carrying them up from the dark trees. Mika took advantage of the distraction and flew a few kilometres away, turned off their lights and hid in the darkness so they could watch a battle more bizarre than anything they could have imagined.

The Pod Fighters swarmed around the giant hawks, which flashed in the darkness as bolts of laser fire hit them and bounced off again. Some of the hawks hovered over the fray, then dived and plucked the Pod Fighters clean out of the air, squashing them like bean cans with their talons. Others thrashed in the midst of the battle, their beaks taking chunks out of the fighters that flew past them.

'They make our borgs look like toys,' Mika said.

'They're guarding the mansions,' Audrey observed. 'The people living here are so rich they've got giant borg hawks for security. Those poor men! And look what's happening to the trees!'

They watched in horror as the forest began to burn where the Pod Fighters crashed into it and exploded like bombs as they hit the ground. They were so distracted by watching the battle, they forgot they were part of it: a solitary Pod Fighter snuck up behind them and they didn't even notice. It was a terrible mistake – the first bolt of laser fire took out their engine, the second, their left wing, and the third, their right. Both wings burst into flames, and as the Pod Fighter plummeted towards the forest like a black Icarus, the cockpit began to fill up with deadly smoke.

* * *

Gorman heard the vines slither under the bedcover like snakes, but before he'd had the chance to move a muscle, they'd found his ankles and wound around them with anaconda ease. He began to lift his head, then heard two more coming for his arms. He lashed out with the knife and cut and sliced and cried for Ralph to save him.

Ralph was making tea in the dressing room. He was just about to wake Gorman from his nap. He heard his master's cry, set down the teapot and ran quickly to the bedroom. The first thing he saw was blood, blood everywhere, all over the bedcover, all over the floor and all over his master, who was sitting in the middle of a big puddle of it holding the knife. He had deep cuts all over his arms and legs that were bleeding profusely, and the first thing Ralph felt was surprise that so dry a carcass could contain so much fluid.

'The pollen-ripe bees are plundering the catkins,' Gorman whispered, with a faraway look in his eyes. 'You must stop them!'

'Yes, sir,' Ralph replied, gently removing the knife from Gorman's hand. 'But I think I ought to call a doctor first.'

Gorman woke, suddenly, as if his soul had returned to his body.

'I've killed that boy,' he said. 'And I needed him.'

51

ONE FOOT IN DEATH

The burning Pod Fighter fell nose down into an oak tree. The smaller branches at the top gave way immediately, crack, crack, crack, as the burning craft fell through them, but fortunately, although the tree was old, it was also strong and its lower boughs were as thick as giant's arms. The tree caught the Pod Fighter about five metres above the forest floor and broke Mika and Audrey's fall with a gentle bow.

Mika hung face down in his harness for a few moments, panicking as he fought for breath. The hard yank of the straps as the Pod Fighter hit the tree winded him and his lungs were full of smoke he couldn't exhale. Then, as if he was drowning, he breathed out then dragged in another lungful of poisonous smoke. He hadn't taken a breath of clean air for far too long and he felt his brain and his body scream. He could feel the heat of the fires, hear the sound of the tree burning and for the second time since he was shot through the leg, he visited the place where you stand with one foot in life and the other in death. Audrey was silent and Ellie was crying. Blinded by smoke he reached forward and bashed the icon to open the windshield. It juddered back about ten centimetres then caught on the dented body of the fighter, but air came in, and he coughed and coughed and was born again. He could see the forest floor beneath him as the dying fires flickered light over the fallen leaves, and he felt as if they'd crashed on an alien planet, so strange a sight it was. He pushed the windshield fully open, undid his harness and stood in the nose of the cockpit. The Pod Fighter creaked against the branches as he shifted his weight. Then he pulled himself up and over his seat so he could reach Audrey and take off her headset. Her arms dangled limp as she hung from her harness and he felt like Peter Pan when Tinkerbell's light began to fade, as if his heart was cracking like the old wood of the tree. Her pale elf face was smudged with soot from the smoke and her eyes were closed. Mika patted her cheek, loving her so much he felt his legs melt.

'Audrey!' he said. 'Wake up! Oi! Noodle brain!

'Audrey?'

He heard the roar of an engine and looked up to see the Pod Fighter that had shot them down, sweeping a searchlight through the forest canopy. His heart missed a beat as the light froze on them and the Pod Fighter hovered, directly overhead.

'Audrey!' He shook her by the shoulders, knowing if she didn't wake up now, she never would. He also knew he couldn't leave her, so they would both die in this dream place and never go home. He shook her again, roughly this time, and still she hung like a rag doll until he had a jolt of inspiration and pushed her up so her chest was released from the pressure of the harness. She gasped. Her eyes shot open, startling him with their nuclear brightness.

'Hello?' she croaked, as if she was wondering why he was staring at her. 'What are you doing?'

'Trying to keep you alive,' he said, smiling with relief.

'Where are we?' She put her hand to her throat – it hurt from breathing smoke.

'In the forest,' he whispered. 'We landed in a tree. Quick! Get out of your harness! If we don't get away from here in the next ten seconds, we're dead.'

Coughing violently, she fumbled her arms out of the harness. The men in the Pod Fighter had flown a short distance away, found a clearing and landed. Mika and Audrey hung nervously from the broad branch of the oak then dropped the five dangerous metres to the forest floor. Thankfully it was soft and they landed unhurt. They ran into the dark forest, frightened by its silence, trying to suppress the coughs that would give them away, but their lungs had been scoured raw by the smoke and the night air was cold and they choked on its freshness. For an eternity they ran, with the crash of men's feet behind them, Audrey in front, because she could see the trees. Mika saw nothing unless he looked up at the black branches against the night sky, so he ran blind behind her, feeling all the time more frightened and further from Ellie.

How are we going to survive this, he thought frantically, as he tripped on the root of a tree. How will we ever get home?

Eventually Audrey stopped and leaned over and panted with her hands on her hips. 'I think we've lost them,' she said. 'I can't hear them any more.'

They listened for a moment, trying to pant quietly, and Mika felt the darkness wrap around them like a cloak. They heard a twig snap nearby and much further away, a sound that turned their blood to ice – a howl.

'Did you hear that?' Audrey whispered, clutching his arm.

'Yes,' Mika said, quietly.

'It sounded like . . .'

'A wolf?'

Then they heard another sound – a scream. It was a long way away, but every noise in the forest seemed blown all around it by the wind. Mika shuddered with cold and fear.

'It can't be wolves,' Audrey said. 'They're extinct.'

'Like trees and mansions?' Mika replied. 'I think it is wolves.'

They heard another scream, closer this time and curdled by blood.

'They're killing Gorman's men!' Audrey said. 'We have to get away!' She started to run again and Mika blazed after her, and they ran as if the wolves were already chasing them. Audrey, now blinded by fear, coursed into trees, fell down holes and scrambled forward, leading them deeper and deeper in the vast and silent darkness. But trying to flee was pointless, because they were already surrounded. A pair of red eyes appeared directly in front of them and they stopped dead, hoping the darkness and silence would protect them. But more red eyes appeared, with blue light trails behind them. The lights circled Mika and Audrey, flicking through the trees, gradually closing in until they were near enough for Audrey's borg eyes to see the animal shapes behind them.

'You won't believe this!' she whispered. She could see a dozen or so silver forms slipping through the trees. 'I think they're the borg dogs from the pit! They were *wolves*, Mika! And they're huge!'

Mika watched one melt out of the darkness only three or four metres away. It was as tall as a man at the shoulder.

'Frag,' he whispered, trembling from head to toe.

'Stand still and let it smell you,' Audrey whispered.

'I don't think I've got much choice,' he replied.

Its metal fangs were as long as his fingers and dripping with fresh blood. Its muzzle rippled back in a terrifying snarl as it crept towards him with its head down and its red borg eyes glowing. Mika closed his eyes and prayed as he felt its cold nose on the back of his hand. Nothing happened for a few seconds, so he opened his eyes again and found, to his astonishment, that the whole pack had come forward. A dozen giant silver wolves with blood on their muzzles were walking lazy circles around them. One sat down, another yawned, some looked over their shoulders into the dark forest as if it was time to move on to other business.

'They move as if they're alive.' Audrey whispered, touching one as it passed her. 'They must have been built by the same people who made the eagle hawks. They're guarding the forest.

'I wish Kobi could see them.'

'Yeah, he'd think they're great,' Mika replied grimly, still not daring to move. 'He'd probably have one living in his fold-down so he could figure out how it was made.'

'He wouldn't get many visitors,' Audrey remarked. 'Those teeth are sharp as knives.'

One of the wolves pricked up its silver ears, raised its nose to the sky and sniffed the air. The others followed and a few seconds later, as if something was calling them across the forest, the pack trotted off into the darkness.

'I wonder why they didn't kill us?' Mika said.

'I think they actually *like* us,' Audrey replied.

'It's as if they don't know we're human,' Mika observed. 'I don't understand.'

They sank to the ground and leaned against the trunk of a tree and touched earth for the first time. It was damp and soft and smelled clean. They gazed into the darkness for a while, wondering whether the wolves would return. It was cold and their breath came as clouds of vapour and they shivered in their thin clothes. But after a few minutes they weren't much aware of their bodies any more, because in the stillness, with their special sight, the cloak of darkness lifted and the forest began to reveal itself in forms of golden light. And this was not the fairy gold of manmade turrets and taps, it was the light of life. It was early spring and the trees began to glow from their waking roots to their fat blossom buds and unfurled leaves. And spread across the forest floor, where the sunlight could reach its fingers during the day, a carpet of bluebells was coming into flower. But that wasn't all! There was movement! They could see movement everywhere! Audrey picked up a handful of rotten leaves and it was swarming with small, gold forms.

'Woodlice,' she whispered.

A mouse scampered across a rotten tree stump. Birds stirred in the branches of the trees. Mika and Audrey gazed at them in shocked wonder, trying to come to terms with the miracle of their existence.

'There can't have been an Animal Plague,' Audrey said faintly. 'It never happened, did it?'

'It doesn't look like it,' Mika replied.

'It was all lies,' Audrey said.

'I knew it,' Mika said. 'I always knew we were being lied to! All this time we've been living behind The Wall in those horrible concrete towers, eating food made of mould and surrounded by stinking floodwater while on the other side, it was like *this*.'

'It's as if there's *another* level of London,' Audrey said, looking around. 'A secret, invisible level, above the Golden Turrets, where even *richer* people live. The people in the Golden Turrets have got their fancy apartments, but they've got *nothing* compared to this. These people have huge mansions and forests and *animals*!'

'How could they keep such a huge secret?' Mika said. 'How could everyone live behind a wall for forty-three years without realizing *this* was on the other side of it?'

'No one ever comes here,' Audrey pointed out. 'We're reminded all the time how horrible and dangerous it's supposed to be. Even in the game it looked like poisoned dust.'

'Our poor parents!' Mika said furiously. 'They lost everything when they moved behind The Wall! And the whole thing was a lie!'

'I wonder why nobody asked questions,' Audrey said.

'Why would they?' Mika replied vehemently. 'They saw the plague on television.'

'Oh yeah,' Audrey sighed. 'My mum believes everything she sees on television.'

'So does mine,' Mika said, bitterly. 'Whoever did this to them must have faked the news reports.'

'So the plague sirens must be fake, too,' Audrey said.

'It's all fake,' Mika replied, disgusted. 'Those stupid paper plague suits, I always knew they were useless.'

'All those history lessons we did. We learned more about the plague than anything else.'

'Lies.'

'And the posters in our classrooms of animals foaming at the mouth with blood in their eyes.'

'Just to scare us so we wouldn't want to come here.'

'They've treated us like idiots.'

'They've lied to us about *everything*.'

Pale dawn light began to filter through the trees and its opaque beauty awed them into silence for a while. Birds began to sing and Awen appeared and sniffed contentedly through the leaves at Mika's feet.

'But isn't it *beautiful*?' Audrey whispered. 'I used to cry myself to sleep when I was little because all the animals and plants were dead. It seemed so unfair, when I knew *I* would have looked after them, but I'd never get the chance because they'd been killed by the people born before us. But look, Mika! They're *still here*! And more beautiful than I ever imagined! I don't know how to feel. I'm so angry and happy at the same time.'

'Me too,' Mika said. 'I feel as if I'm waking up from a nightmare.'

'Yeah,' Audrey agreed. 'A nightmare in which humans kill every living thing except themselves, so there's nothing left but concrete and floodwater. Thank odd it's not true.'

'But this part of the world belongs to someone else now,' Mika pointed out. 'And we're not supposed to be here. Those eagles and wolves should have killed us.'

'This must be what the war is about,' Audrey said grimly. 'Mal Gorman and the government must know the plague never happened and that it's beautiful here.'

'I think you're right,' Mika agreed. 'Our parents said the enemy had to be in a place we didn't know about, and we certainly didn't know about this. And a few weeks ago, my friend Helen disappeared and I couldn't find her, but before she left, I told her I felt as if we were being lied to. She tried warning me that we were in danger. She wanted to tell me a secret. This *must* be it. It all makes sense now. Maybe she's here, on this side of The Wall.'

'I wonder if your sister knows,' Audrey pondered, looking up the trees as if they'd disappear if she took her eyes off them.

'Ellie,' Mika said, anxiously. 'It's morning, Audrey. What are we going to do? We're stuck in the middle of a forest on the other side of The Wall! And if I don't go back and convince Mal Gorman I haven't betrayed him, I'll never see her again! How are we going to get out of here?'

'The Pod Fighter,' Audrey said as if it was obvious.

'It's burned out,' Mika replied impatiently. 'It's useless.'

'Not that one,' she said. 'The other one; the one the men came down in.'

'Oh yeah!' he said, his eyes lighting up. 'You're a genius.'

'I know,' Audrey replied. She stood up and carefully brushed down her legs so she didn't hurt any bugs. 'Let's go and find it.'

They walked quickly, taking care not to step on the plants, as the sun poured colour into the forest. The pollen dust of spring flowers floated through the air. Bright new leaves filtered the light so it dappled gently over the carpet of bluebells. Awen led and Mika followed, with Audrey close behind; so enchanted by the beauty around her, she didn't think to ask how Mika knew the way.

They reached the oak tree that had caught the Pod Fighter in its arms.

'Oh no,' Audrey said sadly. 'Look what we did to it.'

One side was covered in buds and new leaves, but the other was a mass of charred, broken branches, with the Pod Fighter still suspended from its boughs; a buckled, smoking carcass. Mika felt a lump form in his throat as he noticed a bird's nest on the ground by his feet where it had been knocked out of the tree by their fall. He crouched down and found an egg amongst the leaves and turned it over in the palm of his hand. It was beautiful; pale blue and chalky smooth, with a dusting of soft brown speckles. But there was no light inside it.

'It's dead,' Audrey said sadly behind him.

Racked with guilt, Mika gently returned the egg to its nest.

'It wasn't our fault we crashed,' she went on.

'I know,' he replied heavily. 'But that won't bring it back.'

He heard her gasp.

'*Look!*' she whispered.

Mika slowly turned and rose to his feet. A short distance away, between two ancient oak trees, stood a magnificent red deer stag. He was the colour of autumn, a rich russet, with a muscular neck, broad chest and thick ruff. He held his head proud and his antlers curved wide, like the branches of an elegant tree. Against the green of the oaks he was glorious; the King of the Wood; the most magnificent beast that had ever lived. But despite his strength and rugged beauty, his eyes were tranquil, like pools of liquid conker, and they gazed at the children with all the wisdom of the moon in their silence.

Everything waited. Everything shone with a soft golden haze, and in the stillness, they noticed for the first time that the light was flowing from one living thing to another, as if they were all connected: the trees, the birds, the soft mounds of moss, the majestic stag and themselves; the light ran in a stream through them all.

The stag's nostrils quivered as he took in the smell of burned Pod Fighter, oak and mutant children. But instead of walking away from them, he stepped forwards to follow his original path. They held their breath, praying they wouldn't break the spell, as he walked right past them with hinds and dappled fawns trotting in his wake.

'Even the real animals like us,' Audrey whispered in astonishment, as the deer melted into the forest.

'They know we won't hurt them,' Mika replied quietly.

'The light moves through us,' Audrey whispered. She put her hand on the trunk of the burned oak tree and watched it flow from her skin into the bark. 'I wonder why I didn't notice before.'

'On our side of The Wall,' Mika said, 'people don't touch very often and we're surrounded by concrete and metal, not trees and animals.'

Audrey touched his cheek and smiled as the light flowed from her fingertips into his face.

'It's made me realize something,' she said, thoughtfully.

'What?' Mika asked.

'How important we are to each other,' she replied simply. 'And what we've been missing. I feel so happy here, Mika. So happy.'

Mika touched her face and watched the light pass between them but he didn't smile; instead his eyes darkened with sadness.

'What's wrong?' she asked.

'The war will kill it all,' he replied quietly. 'It will all die. When everyone finds out how they've been lied to, they'll want the war. They'll send us over here to fight the giant borgs and the forests will burn, the animals will be killed and then the nightmare *will* be true; there won't be anything left but concrete and floodwater.'

'Then we have to stop it,' Audrey replied. 'We *can't* let that happen!'

'How are we going to stop a war?' Mika said, burning with frustration. 'I hate adults! All they know how to do is lie and destroy things!'

'I don't know,' Audrey replied. 'But we have to try. Because if the trees and animals are killed, then everyone will always be sad. I want my mum and my aunty to see this. I want them to feel like I do now. I want everyone to feel it, and then maybe they'll realize how important it is.'

'So do I,' Mika replied bitterly. 'But the adults control everything. They won't listen to us.'

'But we won't be alone,' Audrey pointed out. 'The rest of the children will help. Imagine how happy they'll be when they find out all the trees and animals are still alive. They won't want to kill them in a war, because when we grow up, this will be our world. This is our world, Mika. This is *our chance*. I want to grow up feeling like this. We thought we were supposed to be doing something. Maybe this is it.'

'Maybe,' Mika replied.

'We have to try,' she said urgently.

She stood before him, her green eyes shining with hope and urgency, surrounded by living forest, and suddenly anything seemed possible, even stopping a war. Mika took a deep breath and his lungs filled up with clean forest air.

'You know, your eyes are the colour of leaves,' he said softly. 'And your hair is the colour of deer. You look like a scruffy forest fairy.'

'Is that a compliment?' Audrey asked, looking down at her muddy, ripped clothes.

'Yeah,' Mika replied, with the trace of a smile. 'So . . . we're going to stop a war.'

'Yes,' she said firmly. 'But first, we're going to find your sister.'

52
YOU HAVE TO BREAK A
FEW EGGS

Mika stood in the doorway of Mal Gorman's office, stinking of wood smoke, with mud on his sneakers, feeling surprised by what he saw, which was remarkable considering what else he had seen during the past twenty-four hours. Gorman was sitting behind his desk in a hospital hover chair, which had this strange frame thing around it, attached to him by tubes and wires that punctured the papery skin on his arms and chest. Machines beeped quietly and his heart rate limped across a small screen that he turned to glance at now and then for reassurance that he was still alive. There was an echo of fear in his eyes that made Mika wonder what had happened to him since they last met. It was as if the old man had encountered a monster more frightening than himself, though Mika couldn't imagine one.

Gorman's office was within his private apartment, and it was decorated in the same antique style, with wood panelling and old landscape paintings and a large mahogany desk. Behind him, the sea heaved up the black cliffs of Cape Wrath as if it was trying to grab the old man through the window and it seemed a fitting backdrop for the monster who'd stolen Mika's sister and told him she was dead; the person who'd tricked thousands of poor children into believing they were playing a game.

'You came back,' Gorman said quietly.

'Yes,' Mika replied. 'I promised I would.'

'I'm sorry I tried to kill you,' Gorman continued, as if he was talking about something completely ordinary like forgetting to put sugar sub in Mika's tea. 'I thought you'd run away.'

'I know,' Mika replied, steadily. 'But that doesn't matter now. I'm back, like I promised.'

'Yes,' Gorman remarked. 'And that is quite astonishing.'

Gorman looked at the boy in the doorway and marvelled. This twelve-year-old mutant from a refugee town had survived a riot, been chased by squadrons of Pod Fighters, outwitted the Ghengis Borgs guarding The Wall, then been shot down over a forest that must have looked as alien to him as the planet Mars. Then, he'd survived the wolf borgs, who'd ripped Mal Gorman's men to pieces, and returned to Cape Wrath before eleven o'clock the next morning, looking calmer and more sensible than ever. Mika Smith was more than astonishing, and by returning from the other side of The Wall, he had proved his trustworthiness beyond any doubt.

Gorman looked at Mika and felt proud that he had found such a child. Despite the fact he'd cut himself to ribbons, only the night before, he felt nicely in control again, and that horrible feeling he'd had, that he was mixed up in something strange with this boy and his sister, was gratefully buried in the darkest corner of his mind. Mika had come back and everything was as it should be.

'Who are the people living in those mansions?' Mika asked.

'Come in and sit down,' Gorman said, waving him towards

the chair in front of his desk. 'We have a lot to talk about. Do you want anything? Would you like a drink, or some breakfast?'

'No, thank you,' Mika replied. It wasn't food he hungered for at that moment, it was Ellie. The hook dragging him towards her now felt as if it was ripping his heart, and he was fighting to keep the pain of it from showing on his face. Ralph appeared with a small dish of Everlife pills on a tray. Mika sat down in front of Gorman's desk and waited for him to begin.

'The people living in those mansions,' Gorman said, 'were the richest and most powerful people in the world before the plague. They owned the business corporations, and their businesses created all the things we needed for survival, like medicines and food, technology and power. And now of course they're even richer and more powerful, because they own the best part of the world. It's all like that, Mika, from France to Argentina: trees, animals, rivers, lakes, as pretty as an old-fashioned picture postcard.'

'What about the towns and cities?' Mika asked.

'All gone,' Gorman replied. 'All tidied up and cleared away. The southern hemisphere now looks like it did three thousand years ago. Difficult to imagine, isn't it?'

'Yes,' Mika replied.

Gorman took an Everlife pill from the dish and Mika watched him eat it, feeling hopeful. The old man seemed happy, despite the weird frame thing around him, and Ellie felt within his grasp again.

'They started planning the plague fifty years ago,' Gorman continued. 'But I didn't know then, of course. I'd just bought a log cabin in Canada. What a waste of money that turned out to be. The business corporation leaders formed a secret society called the World Conservation Club and their mission was to save the planet. Because at the time, if we weren't chopping up nature and burning it or eating it, we were covering it in concrete or blowing it up with bombs. Every month, more forests disappeared and more species of animals became extinct. Every year, we used up more things and the wars got worse and so did the floods caused by global warming. Everyone complained, but they didn't do enough to make a difference. A few people started riding bicycles and others reused their plastic bags and meanwhile Earth was gasping its last, desperate breath.

'So of course it was a good idea to stop people destroying the planet, but unfortunately, the World Conservation Club didn't want to save it for everyone, they just wanted to save it for themselves. When something you take for granted is nearly gone, Mika, it becomes precious. Do you understand? Animals and trees became the new diamonds and pearls. Suddenly the rich didn't want designer shoes and handbags any more, they wanted birds and trees and forests for their gardens. But unfortunately, the poor people who'd made them rich and powerful were in the way. We were living on the land they wanted. So they decided to get rid of us. And the best way of doing that was to make us scared of the thing they wanted; so they made us scared of nature.

When people saw the Animal Plague on television, they were petrified. Within a year, the whole population of Earth had moved to live behind The Wall, whilst on the other side, the rich were cleaning up and building their new mansions.'

'Why didn't you join the World Conservation Club?' Mika asked, thinking Mal Gorman was an ideal candidate for such treachery.

'I tried,' Gorman said bitterly. 'So did lots of people when they heard about it. It was a difficult secret to keep. But you could only join if you were invited, and to be invited you had to be famous, rich, beautiful or useful and I was none of these things. However, if you *found out about the club*, but they didn't want you, they offered you a good job on the horrible side of The Wall so you'd keep your mouth shut.'

'So you got your job in the Northern Government because you found out?'

'Yes.'

'Does that mean lots of people on this side of The Wall know the plague didn't happen?'

'Quite a few,' Gorman replied. 'All members of the government know. The Minister for Defence used to be a hairdresser; he was cutting a famous actress's hair when he found out. Unfortunately he messed it up, so they didn't let him join. The Chief of Military Intelligence was a pool cleaner and overheard a couple of politicians talking. It wasn't so bad to begin with, living behind The Wall, but now it's getting impossible; there are too many people and not enough space. We can't live like this any more, Mika. The World Conservation Club stole two-thirds of the planet from us and now we want it back.'

A nurse came in to check all the tubes and wires going in and out of Gorman, and Mika, sensing this was a private moment, stood up and walked to the window to look at the sea. He felt confused. His mind was now filled with opposing ideas and feelings, and the decision he and Audrey had made while they were in the forest, to stop the war, now felt naïve and hasty. It was all so complicated; a part of him was glad the World Conservation Club had tricked everyone to save the trees and animals, because people weren't looking after them and they nearly became extinct. But at the same time the Club had caused desperate suffering for billions of people; for forty-three years they had lived on food made of mould and died in The Shadows because there wasn't enough space for them, while these rich people had been living in mansions surrounded by forest. It seemed as if people and nature weren't able to live together and that a choice had to made between one or the other. But even more confusing were his feelings about Mal Gorman. Now the old man had explained everything so reasonably, he didn't seem such a monster after all, he seemed like a man trying to make a better world for everyone, humans and nature alike. Perhaps they didn't have to make a choice. Having lived behind The Wall for so long, maybe people would be sorry that they had abused the natural world, and if the government won the war, they could all have a second chance to live together; humans and nature in harmony.

Although Mika's heart and all his instincts screamed against it, he began to wonder if the war might indeed be necessary. But not for long.

The nurse left and Gorman asked for another blanket, which Ralph tucked carefully over his knees. Gorman dismissed him with a flick of his fingers and fixed Mika with a soulless smile, then he began to paint *his* vision of the war and its outcome.

'The enemy's technology is much more advanced than ours,' Gorman told him, 'because they kept all the best scientists and engineers. They have a brutal army of animal borgs. You've seen the hawks and the wolves, but they've got lots of others: even sharks guarding the seas. But we have our army of children and new bombs,' he said proudly. 'Bombs powerful enough to blow the borgs apart and leave a crater the size of a football pitch. We're going to obliterate every single one of them and win this war within a few months.'

Bombs, Mika thought, that make craters the size of a football pitch.

He tried to calculate how many giant borgs they would have to destroy, and all of a sudden, he saw forests burning and animals lying dead, everywhere.

'And after we win the war,' Gorman continued, with a greedy glint in his eyes, 'we will be the ones living in mansions. Your family will be one of the lucky few to come with us to live on the other side of The Wall.'

'What about everyone else?' Mika asked, before he could stop himself. 'What about the people in The Shadows?'

'You don't think everyone will be able to go back?' Gorman scoffed, with a cruel smile. 'Do you?'

Mika flinched as he realised the Northern Government wasn't trying to win back the world for the people who were suffering, they just wanted it for themselves! It was even worse than he and Audrey had thought! The forests would burn and children and animals would die so a handful of greedy politicians could move from the Golden Turrets into mansions! What about everyone in The Shadows? What about the parents of the children who would die? What about the trees and the animals?

Mika felt a torrent of anger well up inside him and he dropped his eyes so Gorman wouldn't see it. But it was too late, Gorman had noticed him flinch and knew exactly what he was thinking. The beeping of his heart speeded up and an amber light appeared on the screen and there was a horrible moment during which Mika felt Ellie slipping away again.

'You promised me you'd come back and do whatever I wanted,' Gorman snarled, with his eyes protruding from their bony sockets. 'Have you changed your mind?'

'No,' Mika lied, quickly. 'I'll do whatever you want!'

'Are you sure?' Gorman snarled. 'You're not going to get all sentimental about a few poor people, trees and animals, are you?'

'No!' Mika insisted. 'I promised to help you!'

'Good,' Gorman replied, relaxing a little. He took a deep breath and the amber light on the screen disappeared. 'You'll understand when you get older. War is a messy business, but you have to break a few eggs to make an omelette. If we let everyone move to the other side of The Wall after we won, it would be a horrible mess again; it wouldn't be worth the effort. They don't deserve it, Mika. They had their chance and they blew it.'

Mika's heart filled with darkness. He could see the bird's egg lying amongst the leaves, hear the roar of the people from The Shadows, and sensed the Telly Heads standing around him, licking their wrinkly lips. He felt desperate; he wanted the nightmare to stop.

He looked at Mal Gorman and considered killing him. *Kill* the monster who'd stolen his sister! Make *him* feel the pain of the people in The Shadows! Make *this monster* suffer the way the animals would when the bombs fell on their homes! The roar grew in his mind until it was pushing behind his eyes like a horned demon, wanting to cause Gorman pain, wanting to kill him ... But suddenly Mika felt Awen leaning against his legs, and this time he had brought reinforcements; Mika sensed he was surrounded by thousands of invisible friends.

Anger destroys, something whispered, *anger makes sadness. Find Ellie. Deal with the nightmare together. All of us. Together.*

'Do you want to know why I chose you?' Gorman asked, unaware how close he had come to death.

'Yes,' Mika replied.

'The giant borgs think you're animals,' Gorman explained. 'You and the other mutant children are the only ones who can cross The Wall and survive.'

'Animals?' Mika repeated incredulously.

'Yes,' Gorman said. 'We used to believe your mutations were caused by pollution and that you were simply humans gone wrong, but now we suspect you are a new type of human, a hybrid. But we don't know everything yet, we're still doing tests.'

Mika said nothing, shocked by this information. But when the shock faded, he felt pleased that he was a different type of human to this awful man.

'Because the animal borgs won't kill you, you'll be an ideal spy during the war,' Gorman continued. 'Your task will be to go over The Wall and bring back information. Will you do that for me?'

'Yes,' Mika lied, feeling the warmth of his invisible friends pressing against his body.

'Good,' Gorman said.

'When are you going to tell everyone The Secret?' Mika asked. 'Our parents want to know who we're fighting.'

'We can't tell them yet,' Gorman said. 'Imagine what would happen if everyone found out tomorrow what's on the other side of The Wall.'

Mika imagined it and reluctantly agreed: if The Secret got out now, the consequences were too horrible to imagine. When everyone realized how beautiful it was on the other side of The Wall, they'd want to go back to homes that no longer existed. They'd try to climb over The Wall, and if they were lucky enough to get past the Ghengis Borgs, which was doubtful, Mika dreaded to think what would happen when the animal borgs found them. He remembered the bloodied fangs of the giant wolves and shuddered. They'd be ripped to pieces. It was better they didn't know.

'So what *are* you going to tell them?' Mika asked. 'They want to know who the enemy is.'

'We're going to tell them we're being invaded by aliens,' Gorman said.

'Aliens?' Mika repeated. 'They'll never believe that!'

'You want to bet?' Gorman replied, raising his eyebrows. 'They'll see it on television . . .'

'Will they?' Mika said, with a resigned sigh. 'Of course. They'll believe anything they see on television.'

More lies, he thought disdainfully. All they do is lie and destroy.

He got up from the chair and gazed through the window at the sea.

Gorman watched him contentedly, thinking how perfect he was, and something made of forest air and silence filled the room. He had no idea Mika had just played him at his own game.

'Can I see Ellie?' Mika asked, quietly.

'Yes, you can,' Gorman replied. 'In fact, I'm so very pleased with you, I've decided you can take her home to see your parents. Just for one night.'

'Thank you,' Mika said, with tears pressing in his eyes.

53
A GHOST COME BACK
TO LIFE

Mika waited for Ellie in the room at the top of the fortress, where he and the other finalists had watched the aurora borealis. It was only days before that he'd stood in that space with the silks wafting in the sky over the North Sea but it felt like a lifetime, even another lifetime. Everything had changed: the world he lived in, his future, but most of all him. He had touched earth, he had breathed forest air, he had discovered he was part of a beautiful world he'd thought was gone for ever, and he'd found Ellie. He paced and watched the sea and for a while he felt like a firework with its fuse lit, a bit dangerous – as if when she walked through the door he would erupt and fly around the room breaking the lights, setting fire to things and taking lumps out of the ceiling. Then he felt all soft and gooey, as if when she walked in he would melt and she would find nothing more than a puddle of love in the middle of the floor. Then he felt both of these things, that he was a firework about to explode, but instead of sparks, he was full of love and it was all going to be a bit messy.

Awen appeared and stood by the door with his nose sniffing the gap. Suddenly his muscles tensed and the end of his tail began to flick.

'Is she coming?' Mika asked, and Awen looked over his shoulder with his mouth wide as if he was smiling. Then Mika heard her: she was running towards him. A man's voice shouted, 'Ellie! I said WALK!' Mika's heart began to bounce like a rubber ball. Awen took a step back and Ellie exploded through the door like a gust of golden wind with her black eyes burning and her hair and her clothes blown around in her storm. Then her light surged forward, reaching out for him.

Touching her felt like a deep sigh. As if at that moment of contact, the hook was removed from his heart, so that ache inside him, that throbbing wound that had brought tears to his eyes every time he thought of her, began to heal.

And Ellie; with one great sob of relief, she achieved the impossible, she was a ghost come back to life. With Mika's arms around her and their lights coursing like two-way traffic, she was flesh and blood again.

Awen wedged himself between their legs and the man with the gun watched nervously. The room seemed brighter all of a sudden and it wasn't because the sun had come out, it was because the children seemed to be . . . glowing. He didn't like it and he wondered what to do. He sensed something had happened when Ellie and Mika touched. Something Mal Gorman wouldn't like.

The twins pulled apart and looked at each other with tears of happiness in their eyes. There were so many important things they wanted to say to each other, but with a gun pointed at their heads, it wasn't the right time.

'I like your hair,' Mika said, flicking it with his hand. 'It suits you.'

'You've grown,' Ellie said, with a wobbly smile.

'Yeah, so Mum keeps telling me,' he said, grinning. 'I've got Mal Gorman to thank for that. All that lovely Fit Mix.'

'How are Mum and Dad?' she asked, her eyes full of pain. 'I miss them so much! They think I'm dead, don't they?'

Mika nodded sadly. 'But I knew you weren't,' he said. 'And now I've found you, I'm taking you home.'

54

BORN IN THE DARK

The man with the gun was right to feel nervous while he was watching Ellie and Mika, because they *were* glowing, something *did* happen when they touched, and Mal Gorman was *not* going to like it. As the twins came together, a quiet shift occurred, as if a mechanism that had jammed on the day they were parted was free to move again. Initially, the signs of this change were subtle; as Ellie and Mika rose out of Cape Wrath in their chauffeured pod, Puck began to leap around his plastic tree leaving a cat's cradle of golden light in his wake.

A few minutes later, something interesting happened on the other side of The Wall. Helen was escaping from her son's house, where she'd been locked up like a prisoner for weeks. She climbed out through a window into a rose garden in her night-dress and yellow wellies, and just as her feet touched the lawn, she was astonished to see every bud on the rose bush next to her burst into bloom as if she'd just flicked the switch that turned them on. Then, as she hobbled into the shrubbery, hundreds of birds began to sing as if they were celebrating her escape.

'Nice to see you too,' she muttered. 'But I can't stop and chat; I have a friend to find who needs my help.'

Far away, in the Golden Turrets, Asha and David were cuddling on the balcony of their new apartment. Behind them teams of glaziers and carpenters were fixing all the things that had been broken during the riot. Asha's eyes were red from crying; they didn't know yet that their children were coming home, but suddenly she smiled. 'Flowers,' she said, looking towards the distant horizon. 'I can smell flowers.'

Even in The Shadows, which was now blocked off from the level above, signs of the change could be seen. Kobi Nenko and his father were wading quietly through the dark water in the streets of old Soho. Nevermore, the raven, peered out of Kobi's rucksack, and the kittens he'd made for Audrey wriggled in his pockets. Suddenly, he stopped and looked down to see a ripple in the water around his legs.

'What is it?' his father whispered.

'Something's happened,' Kobi said. He looked up at the metal ceiling above their heads. 'I wonder what's going on up there.'

Ellie and Mika were quiet as they flew towards London. They slouched, exhausted, across the curved seat of their chauffeured pod, with Awen sleeping on the floor in front of them and the man with the gun watching vigilantly, as if he was expecting daffodils to sprout out of their ears at any moment. He had a horrible feeling something was about to happen. And he was right.

'Do you think Mum and Dad will recognize me?' Ellie whispered.

'Of course they will!' Mika laughed. 'I can't wait to see their faces when *you* walk in the door. They're going to be so happy, Ellie. They've kept all your things. Don't worry, it's going to be fine.'

Ellie bit back tears of relief and put her head on Mika's shoulder, able to relax for the first time in over a year. They gazed out of the window, waiting for the first glimpse of the golden city, and Mika remembered how Audrey had described it, with its third, invisible level, where even richer people lived, and felt a fresh wave of astonishment, that they had never realized it was there. Then he remembered the children in Cape Wrath and wondered how they were feeling, so far from home with their dreams shattered. He heard Ellie speak to him, silently, as she shared his thoughts. *'They'll want to help us,'* she said.

'I know,' he thought. *'But will they be able to?'*

'I hope so,' she replied. *'We need them.'*

He remembered flying over The Wall and how he'd felt when he saw trees on the other side and wished his friends knew that their world was still beautiful. He wanted them to know where the real treasure lay and not to give up hope, because they still had a prize worth playing for, and without realizing he was doing it, he told them.

Far away in the fortresses, the children were sleeping, laid out on rows of hard white beds in identical long white gowns. They had been told to sleep until they were needed and so they did, trapped in the moment the implants had been fitted to their heads while the Telly Heads stood around them, licking their wrinkly lips.

But as Mika remembered flying over The Wall, wanting them to know what was on the other side, it was as if a door opened between his mind and theirs. A soft light grew in their dreams and the Telly Heads faded away and suddenly *they* could see the dark trees below them and *they* were discovering the astonishing truth about their world. They ran through the dark forest and felt the cold nose of a wolf borg pressed against their hands. They watched dawn light pour through the trees, dappling the carpet of bluebells and they stood by the burned oak looking into the eyes of a deer while everything around them glowed with a soft golden haze.

The dimly lit dormitories in which the children lay were as quiet as tombs. The only movement came from the nurses who walked through the rows of beds checking the wounds around the new implants for signs of infection. In a dormitory in Cape Wrath, a familiar form appeared; a woman in a white dress with a blue belt and smart black shoes. From behind she looked like Mary Poppins, but when she turned, she looked like a corpse: her eyes faded by Everlife pills as if she took them out at night and soaked them in bleach, her skin stretched tight like tea-stained tissue paper and her lips bony and hard. It was Briony Slater, the Fit For Life nurse, who had come to Mika's classroom all those weeks ago. And she was the first person to notice the change in the way the children were breathing.

'There's something wrong with them,' she said, watching a boy gasp in his sleep.

'Perhaps they're dreaming,' another nurse suggested.

'All at the same time?' Slater replied. 'I doubt it.' She adjusted the blanket over the boy with claw-like hands, but immediately he wriggled, messing it up again. 'Damn you,' she cursed. 'Stay still.'

She watched him frown in his sleep, but he seemed to obey her and settle.

'Good boy,' she said firmly. She stood by his bedside and began to make a note, but before she finished it, she was distracted by a girl whispering behind her.

'What's she saying?' the other nurse asked, looking towards her bed.

'Wake up?' Slater replied. 'I think ...'

The girl pushed her blanket back as if she was hot, and moved her head from side to side on the hard pillow.

'Wake up,' she whispered feverishly. 'We've got to ... wake.'

'Can they wake up?' the other nurse asked, watching the girl nervously.

'Of course not,' Slater scoffed. 'They're not allowed to do anything unless we tell them. Be quiet!' she shouted. 'Lie still!'

She glared at the girl until she obeyed.

The nurses continued to walk between the beds, inspecting the wounds around the implants, but after a while, it became impossible to concentrate. All around them, children were moving restlessly and whispering in their sleep.

'They're scaring me,' the other nurse said. 'I want them to stop. What if they *do* wake up?'

She jumped nervously as a child whispered behind her.

'I've already told you,' Slater snapped impatiently. 'They can't.'

The reluctant nurse approached the girl in the next bed and the whispering suddenly intensified so it sounded like the wind rushing through a copse of trees.

'Wake up!'

'Wake up!'

'I think they *are* waking!' she said anxiously. 'Look!'

Slater walked impatiently across the dormitory to where the other nurse was standing and leaned over to look closely. The girl's eyelids were flickering.

'See,' the nurse cried. 'She's trying to open her eyes! There must be something wrong with the implants.'

'Maybe,' Slater said uneasily. 'Perhaps I'd better tell someone. I'll get one of the engineers down here to take a look at them.'

She began to walk quickly towards the door at the end of the long dormitory, and the other nurse, not wanting to be left behind, hurried after her. Meanwhile, the children began to gasp and thrash as if they were fighting with their covers and before the nurses were halfway down the dormitory, the first child opened her eyes and sat up in bed. She put her hand to her forehead and winced with pain as she felt the implant buried in her skull. The last thing she could remember was walking into the arcade with her friends. 'Where am I?' she asked frantically, looking around the dimly lit dormitory.

Slater walked to the end of her bed and fixed her with an icy glare. 'Go back to sleep,' she demanded. 'It's not time to get up yet.'

'No!' the girl cried. 'What have you done to me? Tell me where I am!'

Slater ignored the girl's questions and turned her back. She was scared now; all around her the implanted children were waking up and she wanted to get away from them. She moved towards the door again, but before she could reach it, several children managed to stagger out of bed to block her path. One of them was Tom, Mika's friend from Barford North.

'Go back to your beds!' Slater shouted, trying not to sound as frightened as she felt. 'All of you! At once!'

'No!' Tom cried, finding his voice. 'Tell us what you've done to us.'

The throbbing pain in his face made it difficult to think and he felt rushes of panic and confusion as he tried to figure out how he had come to be in such a horrible place. He thought of his mother, sick and alone at home. He looked at the foreheads of the children around him, with their implants and fresh swollen wounds, and realized he had one too. He saw a girl he knew from their arcade, Ana. She climbed out of bed and ran to him sobbing and he put his arm around her. Gradually, the children began to remember the dream that had woken them. Then their panic and confusion turned to outrage.

'Go back to your beds!' Slater shouted, now surrounded by hundreds of children.

'No!' Ana cried. 'There are *trees and animals* on the other side of The Wall!'

'GO BACK TO YOUR BEDS!' Slater bellowed again. 'How DARE you disobey me!'

'You lied to us!' Tom said furiously. 'You told us we were playing a game!'

'You're sending us to war!'

'We won't do it!'

'We won't fight!'

'Yes, you will!' Slater shouted. 'How can *you* understand

about *war*? You don't know anything! You're just children and you'll do what you're told!'

'We have to get out of here,' Ana cried. 'We have to stop it!'

'Lock them in there,' Tom said, pointing towards a storage cupboard. 'Quickly, before anyone comes.'

The children closed in on the nurses and began to push them towards the cupboard.

'Don't be silly,' Slater said, her heart beating wildly with fear. 'Stop this at once. Get in your beds and go back to sleep and we'll forget this ever happened.'

'No,' Tom said, firmly. 'We will *never* forget this happened.'

Frantic with fear, the nurses lashed out, but the gentle force moving against them was too powerful and they couldn't escape. They fell through the door on to piles of laundered gowns and it closed with a click, sealing them in darkness.

Then the dormitory was quiet again, but this time, it wasn't because the children were sleeping, it was because they had gone.

* * *

The bark of the elder makes whistles for the children
To call to the deer as they rove over the snow;
'I was born in the dark,' says the Green Man,
'I was born in the dark,' says he.

Anon

In loving memory of Rosa
Thank you for the pasta.

THE THRILLING SEQUEL
TO THE ROAR . . .

THE
WHISPER
EMMA CLAYTON

OUT OF THE SHADOWS

"exciting" Eoin Colfer

COMING SOON

ISBN: 978-1-905294-89-3, £6.99